D0769024

Caribbee

Kydd Sea Adventures by Julian Stockwin

KYDD

ARTEMIS

SEAFLOWER

MUTINY

QUARTERDECK

TENACIOUS

COMMAND

THE ADMIRAL'S DAUGHTER

THE PRIVATEER'S REVENGE*

INVASION

VICTORY

CONQUEST

BETRAYAL

**Published in the U.K. as* TREACHERY

Julian Stockwin

Caribbee

A **Kydd** Sea Adventure

McBooks Press, Inc.
www.mcbooks.com
Ithaca, New York

Published by McBooks Press 2013
Simultaneously published in Great Britain by Hodder & Stoughton,
a Hachette UK company

Cover art used under license from Larry Rostant © 2013.
Maps drawn by Sandra Oakins.
Interior design by Panda Musgrove.

Library of Congress Cataloging-in-Publication Data

Stockwin, Julian.
Caribbee : a Kydd Sea Zadventure / Julian Stockwin.
pages cm. -- (Kydd Sea Adventures ; Book 14)
ISBN 978-1-59013-668-3 (hardback) -- ISBN 978-1-59013-672-0 (paperback) -- ISBN 978-1-59013-669-0 (mobipocket ebook)
1. Kydd, Thomas (Fictitious character)--Fiction. 2. Seafaring life--Fiction. 3. Great Britain--History, Naval--18th century--Fiction. I. Title.
PR6119.T66C37 2013
823'.92--dc23

2013017720

Visit the McBooks Press website at www.mcbooks.com.

Printed in the United States of America
9 8 7 6 5 4 3 2 1

To all my shipmates, old and new

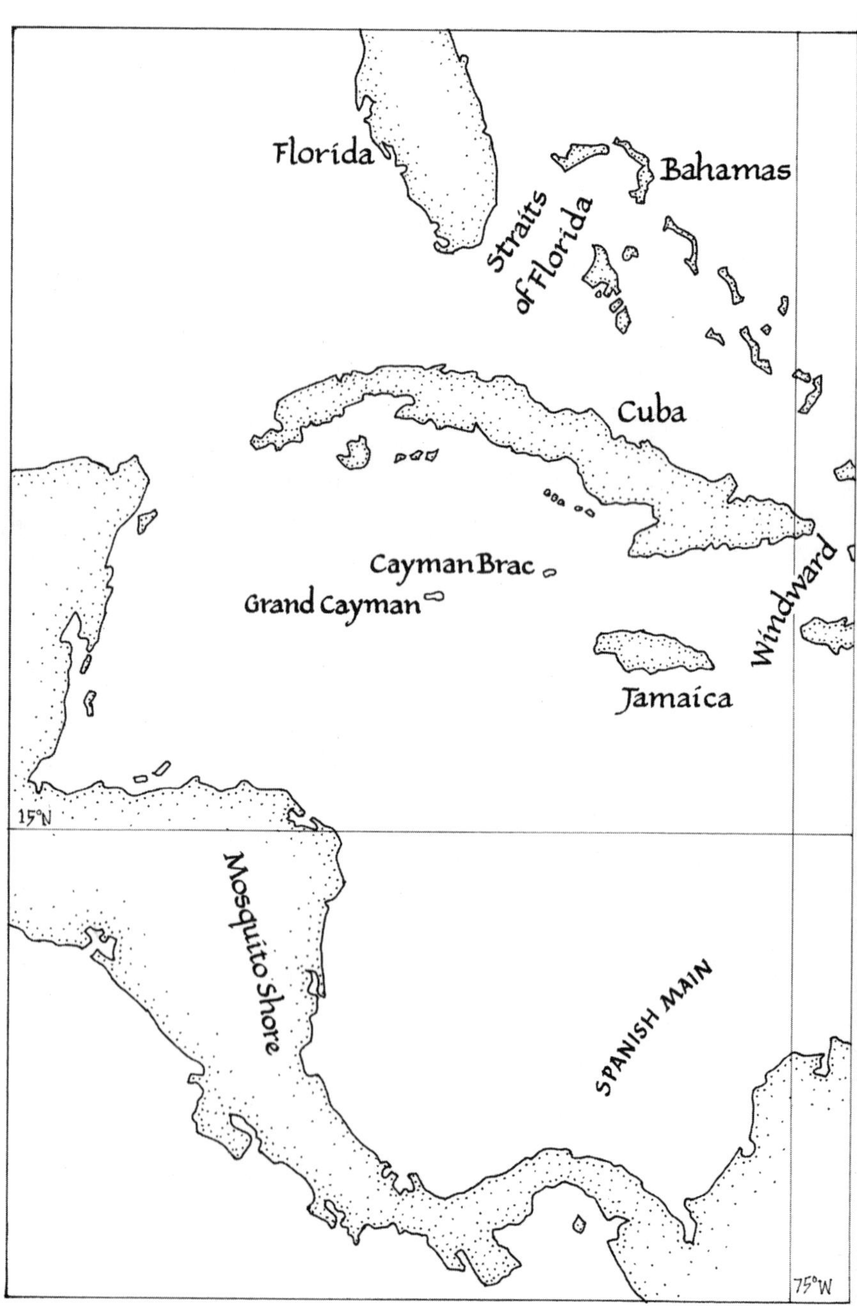
Florida
Bahamas
Straits of Florida
Cuba
Cayman Brac
Grand Cayman
Windward
Jamaica
15°N
Mosquito Shore
SPANISH MAIN
75°W

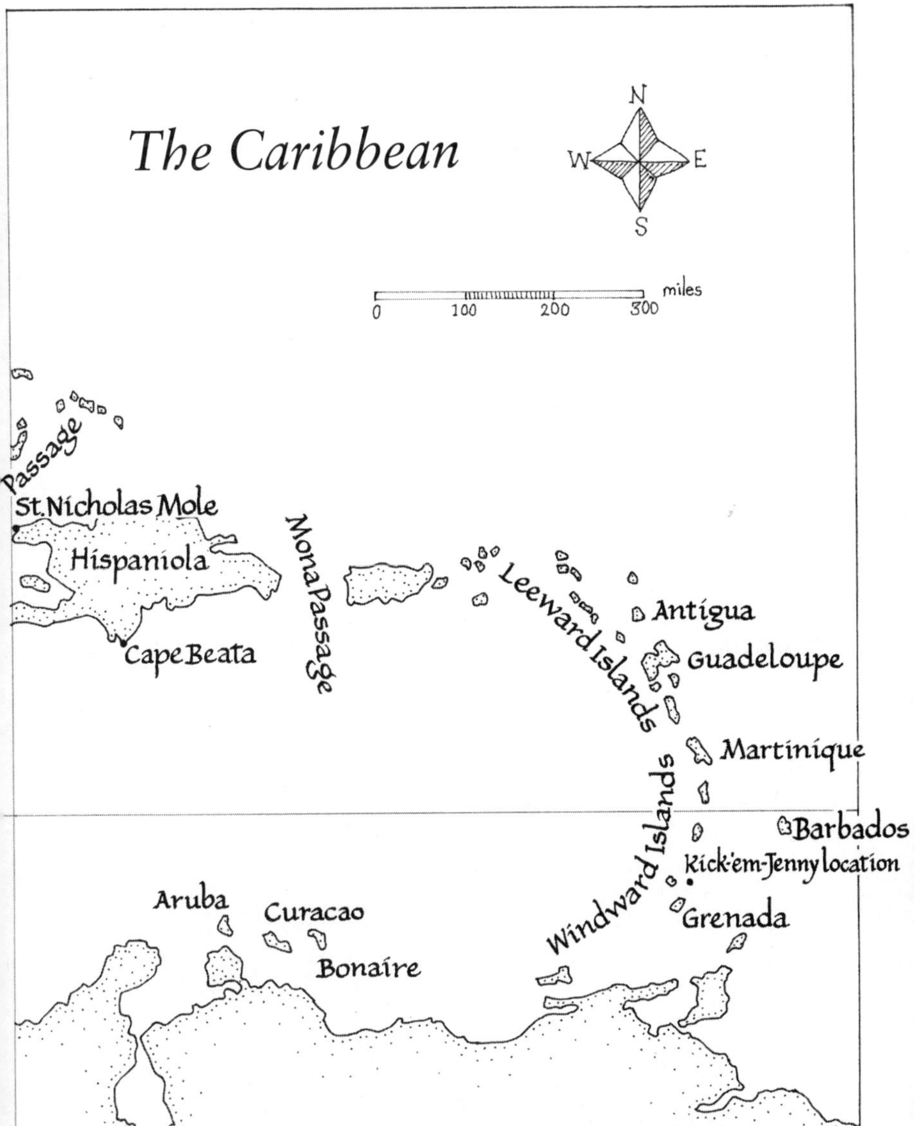

The Caribbean

N
W E
S

0 100 200 300 miles

Passage
St. Nicholas Mole
Hispaniola
Cape Beata
Mona Passage
Leeward Islands
Antigua
Guadeloupe
Martinique
Windward Islands
Barbados
Kick-em-Jenny location
Grenada
Aruba
Curacao
Bonaire
Vice-Royalty of New Grenada

Jamaica

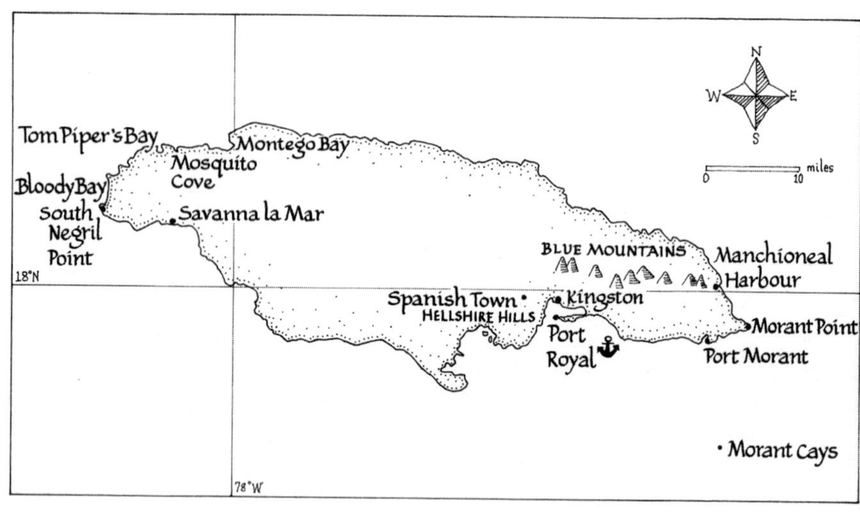

Curacao

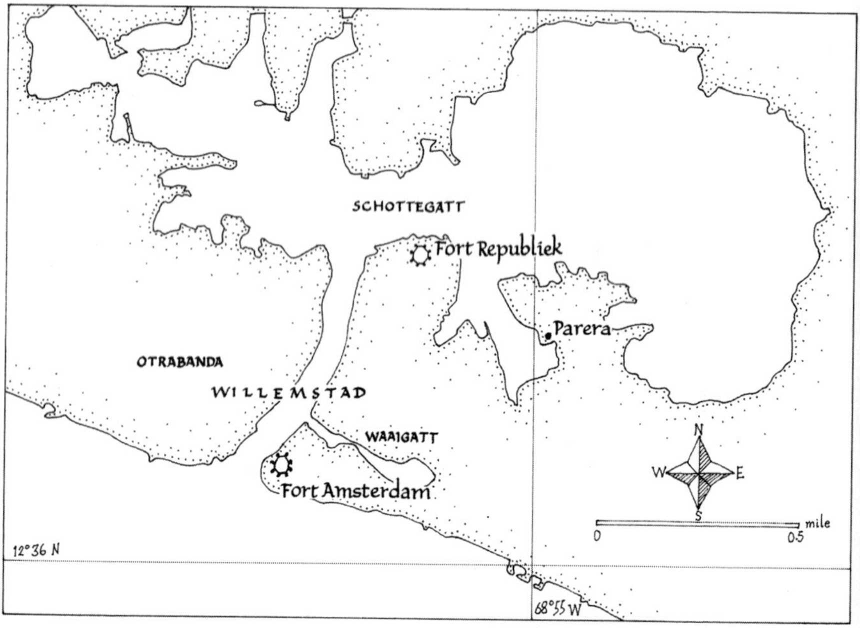

SCHOTTEGATT
Fort Republiek
Parera
OTRABANDA
WILLEMSTAD
WAAIGATT
Fort Amsterdam
N
W
E
S
mile
0
0.5
12°36 N
68°55 W

DRAMATIS PERSONAE

Thomas Kydd, captain of *L'Aurore*
Nicholas Renzi, his friend and confidential secretary

SHIP'S COMPANY, *L'Aurore*—Gilbey, first lieutenant; Curzon, second lieutenant; Bowden, third lieutenant; Clinton, lieutenant of marines; Dodd, marine sergeant; Oakley, boatswain; Poulden, captain's coxswain; Stirk, gunner's mate; Kendall, sailing master; Saxton, master's mate; Calloway, master's mate; Searle, midshipman; Doud, seaman; Wong, seaman; Tysoe, Kydd's valet

OFFICERS, OTHER SHIPS—*Admiral Cochrane, Leeward Islands Squadron; *Admiral Dacres, Jamaica Squadron; *Captain Brisbane, *Arethusa*; *Captain Pym, *Atlas*; *Captain Dunn, *Acasta*; *Captain Lydiard, *Anson*; *Captain Bolton, *Fisgard;* Captain Tyrell, *Hannibal;* Lieutenant Beale, *Hannibal;* Lieutenant Buckle, *Hannibal;* Lieutenant Briggs, *Hannibal;* Lieutenant Griffith, *Hannibal*; Lieutenant Hubbard, *Hannibal;* Lieutenant Mason, *Hannibal*; Midshipman Jowett, *Hannibal*; Midshipman Joyce, *Hannibal;* Maitland, sailing master, *Hannibal*

ARMY—Captain Hinckley; Major Wyvill

OTHERS—Hayward, seaman; Richard Laughton, Renzi's brother; *Francis Mackenzie, governor of Barbados; Jonathan Miller, American businessman; Daniel Thistlewood, plantation owner; Louise Vernou, French royalist; Wilikins, confidential secretary to Dacres; Miss Amelia Wrexham, society belle; Charles Wrexham, chairman of planters' association

**Indicates historical character*

Chapter 1

"S-SIR! Mr Curzon's compliments, an' we've raised Barbados!" came the wide-eyed report.

The frigate *L'Aurore* had been at sea for long weeks, beating up the coast of South America in frantic haste on a mission that might well see the catastrophic situation of the British in Buenos Aires reversed. It had been a voyage of daring speed and increasing privation as provisions and water ran low under the pressing need for hurry. Reduced to short allowance, the griping of hunger was constantly with them.

Captain Thomas Kydd looked up from his desk. "Thank you, Mr Searle."

The ship's youngest midshipman hesitated, unsure whether to wait for a response for the second lieutenant.

Kydd laid down his pen. "Tell Mr Curzon I'll be on deck presently."

Apprehension stole over Kydd as he contemplated his task: to persuade a senior commander-in-chief to detach part of his fleet to go south in rescue of an unauthorised expedition that had sought to liberate South America from the Spanish.

It had all started brilliantly. Their tiny force had quickly captured the seat of the viceroyalty of the River Plate, Buenos Aires, but then the population had turned on their liberators and forced the surrender of their land forces. Commodore Popham, still at anchor off the port there, was desperately seeking support to retake the city.

From the quarterdeck Kydd gazed across an exuberant expanse of white-flecked blue sea to a distant light grey smudge, Barbados—where was to be found the Leeward Islands Squadron. There were just hours left to ensure that his arguments to its admiral for weakening the defences of the vital sugar islands by parting with his valuable assets were sound and convincing.

"A noble achievement, our voyage, sir, I'm persuaded," Curzon offered, as they neared.

"A damned challenging one," agreed Kydd, absently. There was murmuring that he didn't catch from the group around the wheel behind him but it wasn't hard to guess its drift. These were men who had left shipmates as prisoners to the Spaniards and they were expecting to see them freed soon by bold naval action.

Barbados was at its shimmering tropical best. After the intense blue of the deep sea, with its gaily tumbling white combers, and shoals of bonito and flying fish pursued by dolphins, there was now calm and beguiling transparent jade water above the corals. Along the shore coconut palms fringed dazzling white beaches. Neat houses on stilts with distinctive green jalousies perched above the tide line.

It was an impossibly lovely prospect for those who had voyaged so long and endured so much but, mission accomplished, they must leave and return to that grey southern madness.

By the time they had made the bluffs of South Point and left the brown and regular green of sugar fields safely to starboard, anxiety returned to steal in on Kydd. There was the possibility that the Leeward Islands Squadron was at sea, in which case it could be anywhere and would have to be found. However, his real concern was that, as a junior frigate captain, he was going to debate high strategy with a senior admiral. But there was no alternative: too many brave men depended on what he was about to say.

He was in full dress uniform well before they opened Carlisle Bay. It was soon established that the fleet was in, an imposing sight—three ships-of-the-line, escorting frigates and many others. But Kydd's eyes were on just one, the largest, which bore the flag of the commander-in-chief, Leeward Islands Squadron.

He knew little of the man: that he was a Cochrane unrelated to the one Napoleon called "the wolf of the seas," that by reputation he was cautious and punctilious but had nevertheless distinguished himself in battle, and that he was yet another Scot who had reached flag rank in the Royal Navy. None of this was going to help.

An officious brig-sloop rounded to under their lee and, after a brief exchange of hails, *L'Aurore* was shepherded into the anchorage to take up moorings with three other frigates. It felt odd after so long under a press of canvas to be at rest with naked masts.

In his mind Kydd went over yet again the burden of what he would argue. If successful they could be returning south within days with reinforcements and if not . . . Well, would he have to go back empty-handed?

An expressionless Coxswain Poulden kept tight discipline in the boat's crew as they approached the flagship. *Northumberland* was in immaculate order, the welcoming captain in white gloves as Kydd stepped aboard, carefully lifting his hat to the quarterdeck and waiting while the boatswain's call died away. Then he was escorted to the grand cabin of the commander-in-chief.

"Captain Kydd, is it not?" Cochrane said, in a dry Scots burr, rising from his desk.

"*L'Aurore* frigate, thirty-two guns, sir."

"As I can see. Her reputation for speed on a bowline is known even here, Captain."

"Sir, I've news of great importance, a matter that sorely presses, bearing as it does on our situation in the south."

"Oh? Do carry on then, sir."

"I'm directed by Commodore Popham, my commander, to make my number with you in respect of an urgent operational request he has to make."

"I see." Cochrane's manner became unexpectedly mild, almost whimsical, as if restraining a humorous confidence. "And you are his emissary. Then do tell what this might be at all."

"I'm not sure how much you know, sir, of our descent on Buenos Aires, which—"

"You'll take a sherry, Kydd? I favour a light manzanilla in this climate. Will you?"

"Thank you, sir. We met with some success initially, seizing the city and quantities of silver, but—"

"Do sit, Captain. I'm sure it's been something of a trial, your long voyage."

"—but he now stands embarrassed for want of reinforcement," Kydd went on doggedly.

"Which he begs I might furnish."

"Sir, the matter is pressing, I believe, and—"

"And I'm therefore grieved to tell you that your mission is in vain."

Was this a direct refusal before he'd even mentioned the details? "Sir, I have a letter for you from the commodore that establishes the strategics at back of his request."

Cochrane laid it on the desk, unopened. "That won't be necessary."

Kydd felt a flush rising. "Sir, I do feel—"

"Captain, two weeks ago your reinforcements touched here on their way to the River Plate."

"Why, that's—"

"Together with your commodore's replacement. He is under recall to England to answer for his conduct."

Kydd was thunderstruck.

"So that disposes of the matter as far as you are concerned, wouldn't you say?" the admiral said, toying with his quill.

"Um, yes, it does seem, sir, that—"

"Quite. Then I suppose it would appear that you and your valiant frigate are now without purpose."

Keyed up for a protracted confrontation, Kydd could think of nothing with which to meet this.

Cochrane leaned forward and said, with a frown, "I presume you realise how vital—how *crucial*—these islands are to Great Britain? You do? Then you'll be as distracted as I am, not to say dismayed, when you learn that this humble fleet is all that is left to me in the great purpose of defending the same. After Trafalgar we were stripped—I say *stripped,* sir—of ships of force and value. Should the French make a descent with serious intent, I have the gravest reservations whether I'm in any kind of a position to deter them."

"Er, I see, sir."

"So I have it in mind that, following the stranding of *Félicité* frigate, I shall be attaching you to my station pending Admiralty approval."

Kydd caught his breath. As a commander-in-chief, Cochrane was entitled to avail himself of the services of passing vessels, and there was little doubt that the Admiralty would be reluctant to go to the trouble of sending out a replacement when one had so fortuitously presented itself.

"A light frigate, of little consequence to operations in the south, while here I'm in great want of frigates both for the fleet and to go against French cruisers and privateers. Yes, my dear Kydd, consider yourself as of this moment under my command. Flags will find you a copy of my orders and see you entered into the fleet's signal card and so forth, and I've no doubt you'll wish to water and store while you can. We're shortly to sail on fleet manoeuvres, which will serve as a capital introduction to our ways."

There was nothing for it: Kydd had to accept that he and *L'Aurore* were now taken up and Popham's brave little expedition was replaced by a full-scale enterprise from England that didn't need them. Their being was now to be found in the Caribbean.

Cochrane mused for a moment, then rose and extended his hand. "Therefore I do welcome you to the Leeward Islands Squadron, Kydd—you'll find me strict, but fair." He rang a silver handbell.

A wary lieutenant entered. "Sir?"

"Flags, this is Captain Kydd of *L'Aurore* frigate. He's to join our little band and I leave him in your capable hands to perform the consequentials. Oh, and the residence will need to know that they'll be having another guest at the levee."

"Aye aye, sir. Er, it does cross the mind that Captain Kydd's presence might be considered fortunate at this time . . . ?"

"What's that, Flags?"

"The court-martial, sir. You now have your five captains."

"Ah, yes. Like to get this disagreeable business over with before we sail. Er, set it in train, will you? There's a good fellow."

Legal proceedings could not begin in a court-martial unless five post captains could be found to sit in judgment and cases had sometimes dragged on for months while waiting for the requisite number.

It was not the most auspicious beginning to his service here.

Back aboard his ship, Kydd cleared lower deck and told her company of developments, mentioning that with powerful reinforcements on their way their shipmates would soon be set at liberty, and announcing the agreeable news that they would be exchanging the winter shoals and lowering darkness of defeat in Buenos Aires for the delights of the Caribbean. It more than made up for the trials of the voyage.

In the time-honoured way, boats had already put off from the shore to the newly arrived ship, laden to the gunwales with tempting delights for sailors long at sea—hands of bananas, moist soursops, grapefruit-tasting shaddock, fried milk, not to mention bammy bread and live chickens, all dispensed with noisy gusto by laughing black faces.

Even Gilbey, the dour first lieutenant, was borne along on the tide of excitement and, wrinkling his nose at the mauby beer, insisted on picking out half a dozen fresh coconuts for the gunroom.

"That no good for youse, de fine buckra officer!" a stout lady said, snatching them back. "I got toppest kind, verra tender an' young. You leave others t' the kooner-men!" She triumphantly produced some smaller ones, still enshrouded with fine coir hair.

Kydd kept a blank expression. He knew very well what was going on from those long-ago times in the Caribbean as a "kooner-man" himself. Deciding not to interfere, he let Gilbey conclude the deal and stood back as seamen quickly moved in to relieve her of the store of bigger, older nuts. Quite soon there would be merriment of a different kind below decks: the L'Aurores would have wasted no time in "sucking the monkey"—quaffing the powerful rum that had taken the place of milk inside their purchases.

Curzon was compounding with Bowden, the third lieutenant, in the subscribing of a sea-turtle—calipash and calipee—and Kydd graciously acceded to joining them, looking forward to the warmth of a dinner with his officers.

Liberty ashore was promised as soon as storing was complete, but for Kydd there was first a stern duty. At the summons of the single court-martial gun booming over the anchorage, he boarded his gig for *Northumberland*. He noted others making their way over the glittering sea but he had been occupied with the rendering of myriad accounts, reports and the like to his new commander, and a probing survey of fitness of his ship. Today, therefore, was their first face-to-face meeting, and he was looking forward to making the acquaintance of those with whom he would serve in the future.

This time Kydd was gravely welcomed at the side by the admiral, then went over to join the group of captains standing together on the other side of the deck.

He lifted his cocked hat in greeting. "Kydd, *L'Aurore* frigate, new joined."

"New snaffled, I'd wager," one hard-faced captain retorted. "Always was tight with his ships, our Sir Alex. Oh—Sam Pym o' *Atlas* 74. We'll know more of you shortly, I'd hazard. Your first time in the Caribbee?" he asked.

Kydd caught himself. It was not, for he had been here as a young seaman—it seemed so very long ago. "Er, in the last war, as a younker only," he admitted, then went on, "Do we know who's to be tried at all?"

"Won't take long, if that's your meaning. Some foremast jack out o' *Hannibal* thought to offer his lieutenant violence on being given an order or some such. His Nibs can be relied upon to come down hard on any who—"

A sour-faced captain leaned forward and hissed, "Sssh, gentlemen. There's to be no discussing the case before it's heard."

The court met in the admiral's spacious day cabin, set out in its full panoply—dark polished mahogany on all sides, flag-draped side tables and the scarlet of marine sentries rigidly to attention. A long table set athwart dominated the scene.

In dignified silence, the captains filed in one by one and sat in order of seniority, the president of the court occupying the largest chair in the centre. On either side were tables for the prosecution and the defence, the clerkly judge-advocate decorously apart from both. The massed dark blue and gold of full dress uniforms filled the space with a powerful impression of the awful majesty of naval discipline.

"Are we settled, then, gentlemen?" Cochrane asked politely,

looking right and left. "I'm sure you know the rules. We'll take dinner at two but I'm not expecting a protracted session."

There were nods and murmurs. Kydd eased his neck-cloth, stealing glances at his neighbours, who, he could see, were adopting suitably grave expressions.

Properly sworn, the court was now in session.

"Then we shall begin. Bring in the accused."

There was a shuffling outside and the prisoner appeared, the clink of manacles loud in the silence.

"Your name and rate?"

"Dan'l Smythe, able seaman, sir."

Kydd took in the man: his expression was wary and his eyes darted about the cabin. Wiry and well tanned, he must be in his forties; this was no cringing youngster regretting an impulse. The voice was grog-roughened but steady. If the act had been committed while drunk, it would make no difference to the sentence.

"Daniel Smythe, you are charged that on the seventeenth day of September last you did . . ."

Kydd listened grimly. It was much as Pym had said but the twenty-second Article of War was being invoked, a capital charge—and he was sitting in judgment on the man.

"Do you plead guilty, or not guilty?"

"Not guilty."

There was a pathetic nobility in his manner. He had been brought from days' confinement below in irons to an abrupt appearance before so many senior naval officers, yet he was clearly going to play it through to the end.

The young officer who had been appointed to act in his defence looked nervous. He dropped his pen and, red-faced, fumbled to pick it up.

Opposite, the prosecuting officer waited with a heavy patience, then rose. "Sir, this is as clear-cut a case as any I have seen and I do not propose to try the patience of the court with a lengthy submission. I shall be calling but two witnesses, Lieutenant Beale, against whom the offence occurred, and *Hannibal*'s captain."

A ripple went about the court: if the captain himself was coming forward as a prosecution witness there could be little hope for the defence.

"Thank you, Mr Biggs. Lieutenant Hubbard?"

The officer got to his feet and addressed the court. "Sir, Able Seaman Smythe denies the charge, saying his actions have been grievously mistaken and—"

"Just so. Your witnesses?"

Hubbard hesitated. "Er, Able Seaman Hogg and Sailmaker's Mate Martin who were both—"

"Yes. Are they present?" Cochrane enquired.

Kydd frowned. If the only testimony Smythe could muster were fore-mast hands, things were looking bleak for him.

"They are, sir."

"Then we'll proceed. Mr Biggs?"

The essence of the case was laid out in dry, neutral tones. The captain had singled out a man in the crew about the main top bowline bitts as laggardly in his duties and had sent for Lieutenant Beale to hale him aft. There had been sharp words, a scuffle and a belaying pin had been drawn. Smythe had been restrained from actual violence by others in the crew. While being escorted to the quarterdeck, the prisoner had continued to struggle and utter threats until taken below and confined in irons. During this time a sizeable number of *Hannibal*'s company had shown common cause with Smythe and had assembled in a mutinous manner. The marines were turned out and the men dispersed.

"Call Lieutenant Beale."

"You were the officer on duty at the fore-mast?" Biggs opened.

"I was," Beale said, with a prim, disapproving air.

"Tell the court in your own words the events leading up to this unfortunate incident."

"Sir. On being desired by the captain to deal with the prisoner, I went to him and remonstrated with him for his conduct, he hanging back when ordered to sweat off on the slablines. He did then swear in a manner derogatory to the name of the Lord at which I said I would inform the captain of this. In reply he damned myself, the captain, and the ship all to Hell, at which I ordered him seized. He drew a pin from the bitts and would have had at me, were he not restrained."

"Can you in any way account for this behaviour?"

"Er, I believe the man was fuddled in liquor at the time, sir."

Kydd looked down. It was all playing out like some tragic play that could have only one ending, and he was powerless to intervene.

"Your witness, Lieutenant Hubbard."

Throwing a nervous glance at the stern features of the admiral, the young man addressed the witness, who lifted his chin disdainfully. "Lieutenant, this man is in your division?"

"He is."

"Then you'll know the prisoner is—how must we say?—famously short-fused. If provoked he may well act in a manner he might later regret."

"This is no excuse in a man-o'-war, sir."

"And you will also be aware that, two days before, this man had suffered a dozen lashes for insubordination?"

"Which rather proves the point, wouldn't you say?"

"That was not my intent," Hubbard said, with a growing intensity. "Rather, it is to give reason to the act. Smythe was doing his duty as best he could—with savage wounds healing on his back he was being asked to perform strenuous acts occasioning extreme pain. Is it any cause for wonder that he should react with such feeling to being told he was remiss in his duty?"

"This is not for me to say," Beale said woodenly.

"No further questions, sir."

It was as clear to Kydd as if he had seen it happening before him. The proud seaman, wanting to take his stripes like a man, had not reported sick and had done his best—until the prissy Beale had intervened. That his messmates had seen to it that he had rum to ease his suffering had only aggravated the situation and he had gone over the edge. What kind of ship was it that did not have the humanity to make allowances?

"Mr Biggs?"

"Call Captain Tyrell!"

At first the name meant nothing. Then into the court came a figure from Kydd's past. Short but powerfully built, thick eyebrows above deep-set eyes and a restless, dangerous air. Kydd was seeing again the first lieutenant of the ship into which he had been press-ganged so many years before, now post captain of a ship-of-the-line.

He would never forget those eyes, that pugnacious, challenging bearing—and as well how he had single-handedly faced down a gathering mutiny, the lion-like courage he had shown in the hopeless royalist uprising. And the pitiless discipline that had made him an object of hatred.

"You are captain of HMS *Hannibal,* sir."

"I am." That harsh, flat voice from those days before the mast.

"Can you tell the court what you witnessed on the day in question, sir?"

"I saw the prisoner at the slablines with the others and the villain was slacking. Idling, I say. While his party were hauling hearty he was shirking. Not standing for it, I sent L'tenant Beale for'ard to take him in charge and saw there was an argument. I stepped up to see what it was and with my own eyes saw Smythe draw a pin and take a murderous swing at Mr Beale. Then I—"

Hubbard held up a hand tentatively. "A—a point of order, Mr President?"

Cochrane frowned. "What is it, Mr Hubbard?"

"Simply a matter of clarification, if you please, sir. We have Mr Beale's testimony that the prisoner was restrained from making any blow, yet Captain Tyrell here has stated that an attack was made. May we . . . ?"

"Interrupting a witness is most irregular, sir. Yet I'll answer you on that—it doesn't signify one whit. The twenty-second Article of War, of which the prisoner stands charged, specifies clearly—and I quote, '. . . who shall strike, or draw or offer to draw, or lift up any weapon against him . . .' by which we may understand that the simple act of taking up the belaying pin with the object of injuring this officer in the execution of his duty is sufficient to condemn.

"Carry on, Captain Tyrell."

"Then I had the rogue taken up. This stirred up his accomplices who made motions to deny me. I must turn out the marines before I could restore order on my own decks, the mutinous rabble! I'm sorry to say that this ship's company is a scurvy crew, the worst scum it's been my misfortune to command, and I demand an example be made."

"Ah, just so, Captain Tyrell. Have you any further questions, Lieutenant?"

"Er, yes. Sir, have you had cause to punish Smythe on any previous occasions?"

"I have! Above half a dozen times, the vile shab!"

Cochrane stirred impatiently. "Captain, I'll not have such language in my court. Kindly confine yourself to the facts, if you please."

More mildly, he addressed Hubbard. "I think you can take it that the prisoner has a record of ill behaving. What in my day we called a 'King's hard bargain,' if memory serves."

There were dutiful smiles but the young officer was not to be deflected. "Sir, I have on hand *Hannibal*'s punishment book. I beg permission to read from it."

"What the devil—?"

Tyrell's objection was cut short by a look from the president of the court, who then replied, "If it's pertinent to the case, sir."

Hubbard took the book and began reading. "Twelve lashes for wry talk . . . half a dozen for being slow in stays and another dozen for silent contempt . . . mastheaded for six hours . . ." It went on and on, a revealing litany of suffering that told of a ship in the hellish thrall of a tyrant.

"This is for the last two months. And, additionally, may I be allowed to point out that I find in the eight months of this commission, at least sixty of the ship's company have been punished beyond that of Smythe and—"

"Hah! All that shows, damn it, is what I said—I've a mutinous crew of rascals that need discipline."

"Captain, you should answer questions as they are put to you, not offer general observations."

Tyrell smouldered. "Sir, I've the strongest objection to being told how to keep discipline in my ship by this—"

"Sir, my intent in this is to show that, far from being a persistent offender and a blaggard, the prisoner is of a one with the majority of the ship's company, the victim of the most heinous regime that—"

Cochrane slapped the table sharply. "We are here to try the prisoner, Lieutenant, not Captain Tyrell. We have indulged you this far—if you have other evidence, do produce it at the right time."

Kydd threw a glance of sympathy at Hubbard as the witness was stood down.

Biggs drew himself up importantly. "There really is no point in prolonging the business. You have heard two unimpeachable witnesses swear to this unforgivable act of defiance and I dare to say the matter is proved. However, if the court wishes I could summon a further fifty."

"Thank you, no, Mr Biggs." The admiral took a sip of water and dabbed at his mouth with a lace handkerchief. "Lieutenant Hubbard?"

Laying out the case for the defence was the work of small minutes, a man driven by despair to his own destruction, one to be pitied rather than condemned.

Hubbard then summoned his first witness. "Call Able Seaman Hogg."

The prosecuting officer was on his feet in an instant. "Objection!"

"Mr Biggs?"

"Those same ship's books," he said, with a tinge of sarcasm, "reveal that Hogg is not only in the same watch as Smythe but messes with him. I hardly think his testimony can be considered at all impartial, not to say disinterested. I ask that it be disallowed."

Cochrane nodded gravely. "This must be so—you can see that, can you not, Mr Hubbard? The word of a gentleman is one thing, that of the lesser sort quite another matter. This witness is excused."

"Then I call Sailmaker's Mate Martin," Hubbard said defiantly, "who does not mess with the prisoner."

Biggs rose wearily. "But is his tie-mate. Same objection."

It was the custom for those sailors with pig-tails to choose a trusted friend to plait it for a return of the favour. Biggs had been clever to discover this information, which had essentially completed the destruction of the case for the defence.

"Ah. Then I must disallow this witness too," Cochrane said uncomfortably.

"Have you any others you may call upon in their stead, Mr Hubbard?" he prompted.

The young officer's face burned. "None, it seems, that can stand before gentlemen," he said tightly.

"For God's sake!" Kydd blurted. "Can't we just hear what he's got to say?"

Cochrane looked sideways in astonishment. "Mr Kydd! I find your outburst both ill-timed and impertinent. Your duty is to sit in judgment after hearing the evidence. In silence, sir, not to intervene as you see fit."

Kydd dropped his gaze. It was not worth creating a scene—in any case, it was unlikely that the sailmaker's mate could achieve much for his friend now.

To his surprise, Cochrane harrumphed. "On reflection I have decided to allow this witness to speak."

After a small delay a stooped, apprehensive little man was ushered in. He stood blinking, in his nervousness passing his hat from one hand to the other.

"You are John Martin, sailmaker's mate?"

He gulped, then whispered, "Aye."

"And you know the accused, Daniel Smythe?"

Darting a quick look at the prisoner, he nodded hastily, then looked down.

"Come now, Martin, there's no need to be afraid. Simply answer the questions the way we agreed," Hubbard said kindly.

Biggs swooped: "Sir, this is insupportable. The witness has been coached in his answer by the defence!"

Cochrane leaned back heavily and sighed. "Mr Hubbard. I've given you every possible indulgence but this is—"

"Sir!" the lieutenant came back. "Martin is unused to appearing in public and I sought only to ease his fears in the manner of his speaking."

"Nevertheless, Mr Biggs's contention cannot easily be dismissed. I rule that this evidence is tainted. Stand down the witness. I rather think you must look to concluding your case, sir."

The prosecution's summing up was brisk, simple and short. The prisoner had committed the act before witnesses and no extenuating circumstances had been found. There could be no finding other than guilty.

Kydd looked across at Smythe. There was no change in his expression as he heard the damning words—he must have known there was no hope from the outset but he was not giving his accusers the satisfaction of showing fear.

Hubbard performed nobly. Allowed full scope for his speech, he spoke eloquently of the lot of the common seaman, of the harshness of his daily life at sea. He touched on Smythe's "very good" for conduct when discharged from other ships but when he appeared to veer towards a criticism of the regime of discipline in *Hannibal* he was stopped and cautioned.

"Thank you, Lieutenant. The court will now consider its verdict."

The cabin was cleared of all but the president and members of the court.

"A straightforward enough case, I would have thought," Cochrane said. "Does anyone have any strong views at all?"

This was Kydd's chance—but what could he do? The man had raised a weapon at a superior officer, an unforgivable crime in the Navy, and before his shipmates. If he were not punished accordingly they themselves would be in breach of the same Articles of War.

"He's culpable, of course," he found himself saying, "but in respect to the wounds of his flogging, should we not consider a mort o' leniency at all?"

"Impossible," Cochrane snapped. "The relevant article leaves us no leeway. If I have to remind you, the previous article allows '. . . upon pain of such punishment as a court-martial shall think fit to inflict, according to the degree of the offence . . .' but no backing and filling in this one: '. . . every such person being convicted of any such offence, by the sentence of a court-martial shall suffer death.' You see?"

He went around the table, brusquely asking for a verdict from each captain.

"Guilty," Kydd said dully at his turn.

"So, we are agreed. The court will give its judgment. Bring in the prisoner."

The man stood tense but with a glassy stare.

"Daniel Smythe. This court finds you guilty as charged of an offence contrary to Article Twenty-Two of the Articles of War. Have you anything to say before sentence is passed upon you?"

He lifted his manacles, then let them drop in a gesture of despair, but no word escaped him.

Even when the dire sentence of execution was pronounced he held his head high, his gaze on an unknowable infinity.

But Cochrane had not finished. "Your offence I note was made before others who seem inclined to sympathise with your act. I can see no alternative other than to follow the example of that great admiral the Earl of St Vincent. Therefore, as a warning to each and every one, in two days hence you shall be hanged at the fore-yard of your ship—by your own shipmates.

"Take him away."

After the verdict and sentence were recorded and signed by each member of the court, Cochrane declared it dissolved and leaned back, his face looking lined and old.

"A distasteful business to be sure," he muttered.

On the appointed day, at precisely eleven in the forenoon, a yellow flag mounted the main-masthead of *Hannibal.* From every ship in the squadron a boat left to take position off the vessel, spectators at the last act in the drama. Other ships warped about to allow their companies, turned up on deck in solemn ranks, to gaze on the scene and learn the fate of those who dared lift a hand against authority.

Kydd, with other captains, stood witness on the ship's quarterdeck, aware of his role as a symbol of the authority and majesty of law that was extinguishing the life of a fellow sailor.

"Had to end this way, o' course." Pym stood beside him, with a face of stone.

"How's that?" Kydd asked quietly, grateful for the human contact, his heart full of pity for the man whose life span was now being measured in minutes.

"You don't know Tyrell. Man's a martyr to discipline since 'ninety-seven, when he lost his first command to mutineers at Spithead."

So that was what was riding him, had intensified the driving obsession with rule and punishment.

"That's not to say he's shy in battle—he's the heart of a tiger and shows it. Just been unlucky, never in any fleet engagement worth the name and fears he's to be overlooked. Like in San Domingo here not six months back. A foul bottom and last into action when it was all but over."

"Still and all," Kydd said, in a low voice, "to have the men follow out of fear will never be my way."

A sharp slap and crash of muskets caused them to wheel round. It was the Royal Marines guard acknowledging the captain emerging from his cabin spaces. With a suspicious look that turned into one of controlled ferocity, Tyrell stumped to the quarterdeck.

"Bring up the prisoner!" he roared.

Hannibal's ship's company was assembled aft, massing in a silent press of barely concealed hostility. Their captain mounted the poop ladder and advanced to the rail, standing aloof in a belligerent quarterdeck brace and looking down on the hundreds of men.

No one moved. Tyrell continued to survey them grimly, saying not a word, letting the tension build.

There was a stir at the hatchway and the prisoner came slowly on deck, blinking in the bright sunlight, ahead of him the chaplain in black, behind him the master-at-arms and two corporals. He was halted at the break of the poop, then turned to face his shipmates.

It was the duty of the captain to muster the hands and pronounce before them why the prisoner's life was forfeit, all part of the ceremony of death that was intended as a dread spectacle of deterrence. Tyrell read out the relevant Article of War in savage, ringing tones before the ship's company standing, heads bared. In sharp, harsh sentences he set out why the man must die: the stern code of the sea had been breached and he must be made to pay.

He concluded and descended from the poop, nodding to the Royal Marines officer. A single drum, muffled by black crêpe, sounded a roll, then a measured beat as Smythe began the last journey, forward to the yardarm.

Kydd joined the line of officers who followed, just behind Cochrane's flag-captain, who was representing him. They assembled at the foredeck, and the grim ritual was ready to be enacted.

"Prepare the prisoner!"

The chaplain moved to Smythe and they knelt together. Kydd could hardly conceive of the despair and anguish that must be rushing through the man's mind—the boatswain mere paces away waiting with the end of the yardarm whip worked into a halter, on the other side the six-pounder gun-crew with their piece ready charged to signal the moment the prisoner was launched into eternity. And, all around, ships with their silent lines of men looking on.

The seaman rose, deathly pale, a studied blankness his only expression as he moved to the appointed place of execution. The halter was brought and put in place around his neck, followed by a black hood. Smythe had only to step on to the cathead and, at the signal, it would be over.

"Sir," the boatswain's voice croaked.

Tyrell took his time, looking up and then along to where the prisoner's shipmates waited, the long line of the hangman's rope in their hands.

"Carry on!"

But a loud cry broke into the awful stillness: "Hold!"

Tyrell wheeled about in astonishment. The flag-lieutenant hurried up and held out a paper, sealed and beribboned.

"What's this, sir?" he snapped.

"Admiral Cochrane desires you should read this publicly at this time, sir."

Kydd's heart leaped. Could it be . . . ?

His voice savage, Tyrell was obliged to announce to all the world that, of the commander-in-chief's mercy, the said prisoner was reprieved at the scaffold's foot.

"Take him down!" he snarled.

The hood was lifted, the rope removed from his neck—and, with a muffled groan, Smythe crumpled senseless to the deck.

Chapter 2

"I HEAR THE MAN WAS PARDONED," Renzi said, as Kydd entered. "As is the right of a commander on his station," he continued. "It does have its curiosities, however."

"Not now, Nicholas, I'm not in the mood."

"You see, in law he is a dead man at the moment sentence is pronounced—a reprieve therefore means he is a new man, debts dissolved but property disowned. I wonder if this extends to the state of marriage. His wife is a widow. Must she marry him again or is she free to seek another?"

Kydd shuddered, as if to shake off the stark memory of the rope. "Leave it be, old fellow."

He accepted some wine from his confidential secretary and friend of many years, then added, "And who do you think was his captain, as near drove the man to it?"

"I've no idea, but I wager you're going to tell me."

"Tyrell."

At first it didn't sink in. Then Renzi sat back with a tight smile. "*Duke William*—first lieutenant."

"The same."

"Well, well. Fearless as a lion but cold as a hanging judge." The smile disappeared. "Did he recognise you at all?"

"Sitting in judgment as his equal on a court-martial? Never a chance," Kydd answered, with a dry chuckle. "He's now captain of *Hannibal* 74, and thinks his crew the worst kind o' scum. I do pity 'em with all my heart."

"A noble sight," Kydd said, to the well-turned-out captain of foot next to him. The proud reply was nearly carried away by the gust of sound as the military band reached the raised dais. It stamped about with a showy twirl of drumsticks and tossing plumes, then retreated, to split neatly about columns of advancing redcoats marching to the oblique before forming line in review order, all in scrupulous time.

In Highland regalia, the governor of Barbados stood at attention, Kydd and lesser dignitaries respectfully at his side. The levee was drawing to a close in the warm evening and there was to be a grand dinner in the old St Anne's Fort.

The parade ground, the Savannah, was overlooked by the Main Guard, an imposing dusky red building with the white blaze of King George's cipher prominent and substantial stone barracks beyond.

The ordered scene lifted Kydd's spirits after the chaos and ragged misery of the south. The fact that they lay under the threat of a vengeful Napoleon striking at the vitals of Britain's wealth began to recede into the realm of fantasy at this stirring display of military pomp.

The proceedings came to a climax with the entire parade marching forward, six sergeant-majors screaming hoarsely to bring them to a simultaneous halt and ceremonial salute.

Honours of the day complete, the parade moved off, and Kydd and the others followed the governor through the tropical dusk past the drill hall and barracks to the Long Room, fronted by massive square columns.

Inside, it was a blaze of light, the massed brilliance of hundreds of candles in candelabra glittering on gold appointments. The illumination played, too, on the lustrous mahogany about the room and the polished silver set out on the U-shaped table formation. A small military orchestra struck up as the governor took position at the centre.

"Captain Kydd? Over here, sir, if you would." Grudgingly, Kydd allowed that the young subaltern in his elaborate epaulettes over the scarlet and gold of his uniform was a splendid vision. It had always been a source of resentment to the Navy with their austere dark blue and sparse gold lace; a naval officer needed to be at least a ship's captain before he was allowed even a modest epaulette, never the frogging and other ornamentation of even the lowliest army officer.

Kydd found himself on one wing seated beside an amiable officer, who introduced himself as Richard Wyvill, major in the First West Indian Regiment of Foot. "You're new out from England?" he enquired politely.

"No, from Buenos Aires," Kydd said, "as first came from the Cape of Good Hope."

At Wyvill's puzzled look, Kydd told of how the one had been taken, the other lost, in the daring recent feats at the fringe of empire.

Over a capital dish of okra and flying fish, Kydd learned more about the Leeward Islands and their place in the scheme of things, how the untold wealth generated by King Sugar was streaming to England to finance the war and on no account might be jeopardised. And how every effort was being made to deprive the French of the same, and the very real danger of their determined retaliation.

"Might the station still be called, as who's to say, a sickly one?" Kydd asked. In earlier times, a murderous toll in disease had been inflicted on the white soldiers and he had only narrowly survived yellow fever himself.

"It still vexes, but now we've whole regiments of blacks who are not troubled by such concerns." That left the white officers, but they would take their chances in the hope that those surviving would be in position for a speed of promotion that could never be matched at home. "And, of course, you sailors have only to keep the seas to find yourselves well clear of the marsh airs that bring fever."

"The governor—he looks a right sort of cove. Another of your Scotsmen, then?"

"Indeed. Francis Mackenzie, First Baron Seaforth, chieftain of the Clan Mackenzie, no less." When Kydd nodded amiably, he added, "As takes no mind of the curse of the Brahan Seer!"

"Ah, yes," Kydd answered blankly, to be enlightened that this was the dire prediction of the eventual downfall of the Seaforth Mackenzies by a shadowy figure more than two centuries back.

Lifting his glass, he saw Tyrell, four places up, forcefully making a point to a hapless colonel who sat back wincing under the tirade.

Kydd glanced across the table to Pym, who raised his glass and offered, "If you're looking for a cruise to line the pockets, m' friend, then you've come to the wrong place for that."

"How so?" Wyvill came in.

"Our Sir Alexander, he's not your prize-capturing sort. Takes it to heart since San Domingo that the Frenchies might desire to return and claim what they lost. You frigates'll be out keeping station on the rest o' the fleet all hours that God gives, sweeping up 'n' down to wind'd atwixt here and Bermuda. You'll see."

"He was at San Domingo?" Taking place earlier in the year, off the not-so-far-distant Hispaniola, it was said to have been the greatest fleet action since Trafalgar.

"He was—and for his pains had his hat blown from his head by a great shot on his own quarterdeck in *Northumberland*. Never forgave 'em."

There were appreciative chuckles while they did their duty on the spicy pepperpot.

By the time the cloth was finally drawn and the brandy had appeared, Kydd had mellowed considerably, the memories of the south continent now in full retreat. Cigars from Spanish Cuba were brandished, and in the blue haze he listened lazily to the ebb and flow of conversation. They were all post captains and senior field officers at this august gathering, he reflected with pride, and he was here by right, damn it.

He pondered yet again on the turn of fortune that had taken him back to the Caribbean as a frigate captain. It seemed so distant, his time as a young seaman, almost like another life. Only in the Royal Navy was it possible to break through in society as he had done, from the common sort to gentleman with all that it meant in terms of respect, politeness and comforts. In fact, if he did well . . .

"Dear fellow—do I see you content with life at all? That your elevated situation here at the centre of empire is not altogether a burden?"

"Just so, Nicholas," Kydd said, in satisfaction, then hurried to add, "Yet never so good as if my particular friend was present. How are you?"

Renzi did not reply. A strange expression crossed his face, and he rose and paced about the great cabin restlessly. "There's quite a different matter that concerns me."

"Oh? Please to tell your friend, old trout."

"It touches on your professional duty, which I've sworn never to trespass upon."

There was something in Renzi's tone that sounded a note of warning, but Kydd replied warmly, "Fire away, Nicholas. I'm sure I'll appreciate your words."

Renzi breathed deeply. "I've a nightmare that will not leave my mind."

"I'd have thought a rational sort o' fellow like you shouldn't have trouble dealing with such."

"You say that we're to be concerned chiefly with keeping the sea lanes free of vermin. Not to be scouted, true, but in my bones I feel that we'll soon be faced with much worse than that."

"That the French will make an attack? We all know they'd go on the offensive if they could, but we're ready for 'em! Or is it something else ails you, m' friend?"

"It is. Napoleon Bonaparte. I keep seeing him sitting there in the Tuileries brooding over Trafalgar and what it means to his imperial ambitions, witnessing our empire growing and *his* fading away. He knows that this is, for the most part, funded by the produce of our Caribbean islands and he would stop at nothing to put an end to it. If it's within his power to strike a devastating blow directly at them, as will deprive us of their substance, then at one stroke he reduces his most implacable foe to penury. No more subsidies to stir up the continental powers against him, no means to sustain the great Navy that protects them—in that event he's well aware that the only course left us is to sue for peace."

"You're rattled by the bugaboo Boney!"

"No!" Renzi drew up his chair quickly and, leaning forward, spoke as gravely as Kydd had ever heard him.

"Listen to me! The Emperor of France is a ferocious conqueror with a brilliant mind. We should never, *ever* underestimate him, particularly when crossed. Since Trafalgar he's all the time he needs to plot and plan a deadly thrust at our vitals, a terrible revenge. I feel it in my bowels that he's contemplating a master-stroke. It's a logical move for him—and so like the man."

He paused to draw breath. "Let me mention just two that come to mind.

"Properly planned this time, a battle group assembles needing merely a single sail-of-the-line from each of the Atlantic ports, but this easily outnumbers our Leeward Islands Squadron. It concentrates on one major island, say Jamaica, sweeping contemptuously aside any resistance we can put up, and lands a strong military force. They need only take Kingston and Spanish Town and they have the island.

"Moving quickly they retrieve their soldiers, leaving a garrison to tie down the troops we have rushed there. This time Barbados is invested—there are at least six landing places, which cannot all be defended. Bridgetown falls and with it the island.

"In one move the tables are turned. They are in possession of our largest sources of production—and with it most of our ports and dockyards. From these as their base, they may descend on our possessions one by one at their leisure, all before word reaches England and reinforcements are sent."

Kydd had seen for himself what Bonaparte could achieve; if it were not for Nelson's triumph at the Nile, history would be telling a much different story of his adventures in the Orient. And it would not be unreasonable to conceive that, secure on land after Austerlitz, Napoleon might personally lead the assault, if only for the glory that would be the lot of the victor.

Yet the French Atlantic ports were well blockaded and there were cruisers and sloops by the dozen keeping a weather eye for such—and they had only to alert the North American Squadron, which was wintering in Bermuda, to find ready assistance in a fleet action.

He nodded to Renzi to continue. "You mentioned two?"

"The other? Much cheaper and more easily achieved. A slave revolt! With just a couple of frigates he lands arms by night on every larger island into the hands of agents, who have promised freedom to the slaves for the price of rising up against their masters. If they were timed to move simultaneously, we would inevitably be overwhelmed."

Kydd tried to think of a reason why it couldn't happen but failed.

"The man has the cunning of a wild animal and is twice as ruthless. He *will* move against us—he has to. Depend upon it."

Struck by Renzi's passion, Kydd said weakly, "We've always known he's like to raise mischief in the Caribbean but so far . . ."

"Tom—I've never had such before but I do now confess to a dreadful foreboding. I feel it in my bones—there's to be a reckoning from Napoleon Bonaparte himself and it's to be aimed squarely at these islands. While in blithe ignorance we sport and play there's gathering a storm of retribution—and when it breaks, we will most assuredly be made to suffer."

"Nicholas, what are you asking me to do? This is a matter of high strategy and I'm certain it's been thought on by our lords and masters."

"Do? Well, I don't suppose there's anything you *can* do—except perhaps indulge me in my imaginings." He gave a half-smile. "Meanwhile, carry on, take each day as it comes and glory in your eminence in this veritable paradise."

True to his word, the commander-in-chief's orders went out shortly afterwards. They were precise and to the point. The frigates would sail at dawn and establish a secure perimeter for the fleet's assembly. When satisfied with his dispositions, the commander-in-chief would signal to make good a course to the north-northwest to pass along the entire island chain until 19 degrees north latitude was reached. In this way every entrance to the Caribbean from the open ocean to the east would come under eye. At this point the squadron would bear away to the northwest and do the same off the great Atlantic inward passages in the north, the Mona and Windward, then up to the Bahamas off Spanish Florida.

On their way north the squadron would stand seaward and conduct evolutions; on the return they would show themselves off the French-held islands of Guadeloupe and Martinique.

The evolutions would not affect *L'Aurore* for the four frigates would be out ahead in a broad line of search, kept in touch with the commander-in-chief by the sloops. In case of foul weather, rendezvous lines were established, as usual coded by number, their actual location kept separately.

In the event they fell in with a French battle-squadron, an

engagement was expected in which the Fighting Instructions and Admiralty signal code of 1799 were to be strictly observed. Positioned outside the line of battle, *Acasta* and *L'Aurore* were designated repeating frigates, another two to take station ahead and astern of the line. Kydd recalled that this was precisely what he had done at Trafalgar, and with the same signal code.

It was straightforward and he expected no difficulties. *L'Aurore*, however, was showing signs of wear after a winter in the south. There was a small but persistent leak, probably through timbers strained by taking the mud so often in Buenos Aires. As well, a fore topmast bore evidence of being sprung, and the carpenter was shaking his head over a strake repaired as best he could without a dockyard after taking a ball between wind and water. And, of course, as always, there was cordage that, after ceaseless operations aloft, was beginning to fray.

Nothing that a spell in a dockyard wouldn't mend, though.

Next day, in beautiful weather set fair to melt the hardest heart, the frigates put to sea. After a rapid reconnoitre they took up positions off the north of Barbados at the corners of a five-mile square and lay to.

Then the Leeward Islands Squadron weighed and proceeded to sea.

Kydd took his fill. It was always a grand sight, a battle-fleet moving out to take possession of the sea by right, a line of mighty sail-of-the-line in warlike arrogance and symmetry throwing down a challenge to whomsoever might dispute it.

They formed up: the flagship *Northumberland* in the centre, *Atlas* in the van and *Hannibal* in the rear. Kydd knew from his memories of *Tenacious* off Toulon that it was now the stuff of nightmares on the quarterdeck of every ship, to stay not only in the line of sight astern from the flagship but, as well, at the stipulated distance apart. This would be achieved only by judicious and delicate sail-trimming: more showing of a headsail, a quick clewing up of a topsail corner, spilling wind to bring down speed. All in a frenzied reaction to deal with chance wind-flaws, drifting with the current and the sheer sliding inertia of thousands of tons of battleship.

At last satisfied, Cochrane signalled the "Proceed." Ponderously, the line began to lengthen, the ships picking up speed and settling on course to the north-northwest, each vessel nobly moving out one after another over the sparkling, gem-like sea. And on each an officer-of-the-watch sighing with relief that the task was now resolved to keeping pace and distance with the next ahead.

Kydd reflected that the ignorant might scorn the entire exercise as futile and pretentious, but to know one's ship in manoeuvre down to mere feet was a priceless asset in battle and tight navigation—and it was precisely why Cornwallis off Brest exercised his blockading fleet into miracles of precision with none but the seagulls to admire the display.

Another hoist went up: frigates to deploy as instructed. *Acasta,* as senior, sent up her pennant, Captain Dunn now in command of the four. He lost no time in ranging out ahead. As the distant topgallants of the fleet sank below the horizon astern, he flew his signal for taking station, *L'Aurore,* the lightest but fastest, dispatched furthest to seaward of the four. They settled to their task—a sweep in advance of the fleet on a broad front all of sixty nautical miles across.

Within hours the frigates were a long way apart, a tiny patch of white on the horizon to larboard the only evidence of *Magicienne,* their next abreast, but still in signalling reach with the oversize flags each carried. And, far to the south, the topgallants of *Atlas* led the line.

Masthead lookouts were relieved of their important duty every glass—even half an hour so high aloft was a trial of the best of seamen, an Atlantic sea abeam causing a roll that ceaselessly swept and jerked them to and fro through a seventy-foot arc. One misplaced hand-hold and the impetus would tear them from their perch to pitch into the sea or end a broken corpse on deck.

Kydd remained on the quarterdeck, staying to see the sea-watch hanking and tying off after the sail-trimming, which kept them at a pace that would allow them to stay within signalling distance.

He was reluctant to go below for there could be no finer prospect than this: a lovely frigate at her best, in seas that lifted the heart with their beauty—and his to command, to direct and to cherish.

The twist of fortune that saw him and his ship now in the Caribbean had indeed snatched him from Hell to Paradise. But close on its heels another thought came: if Renzi was right, was it a fool's Paradise he was in?

The voyage north was uneventful, the island passages clear of enemy battle-fleets, the broad ocean innocent of threat. Under boundless blue skies and hurrying white combers they ranged on to the northwest until they stood in with the Straits of Florida and lay to, awaiting the fleet to come up with them.

The L'Aurores were getting tanned and fit after their ordeal. Kydd had not seen a man before him for punishment since they had arrived, and the roars of mealtime jollity on the mess-deck told of contentment and fulfilment. In their off-watch leisure, they congregated in companionable groups on the foredeck in traditional yarning over a clay pipe, some working at needlepoint and scrimshaw—the age-old arts of the deep-sea mariner.

One by one the line of ships hove up over the horizon, the original single line transformed by a previous evolution into two columns. In faultless precision, they wore in succession to bear away back to the southeast. The frigates then passed down the noble lines of battleships to resume their watch and ward ahead.

Days later, the long island of La Désirade was raised, a verdant outlier that pointed like a finger at Guadeloupe. The frigates were recalled to attend on the fleet and together, in a display of insolence, the Leeward Islands Squadron swept down on the capital, Pointe-à-Pitre, deep inside a bay.

Kydd stood watching the passing coast, richly green and so full of memories. It was here that he had nearly been made prisoner as the French had retaken the island a dozen years before. And as a young seaman he'd learned lessons of leadership and endurance that would stay with him for ever.

They closed to within a few miles of Pointe-à-Pitre, brazenly taking their fill of the scene—the little town with its neat houses, a large church and, in the small rock-studded harbour, dozens of small craft huddling in as close as they could, none that could be considered worth noticing by such a powerful squadron. For the citizens of Guadeloupe it must have been both terrifying and galling to see such might flaunted with impunity, even if a naval force alone could do little against them.

Having made their point, the squadron stood out to sea past the rumpled heights of the outlying island of Marie-Galante, with its cliffs and multitude of sugar-mills, then shaped course for Martinique, which they raised the following morning. This large island was the most important possession in the French Caribbean and Cochrane proceeded majestically on, in extended line ahead, past the volcanic peaks and crags of the west coast to the grand bay where lay the capital, Fort de France.

The port was well sheltered and spacious but Kydd had heard of the notorious banks and shoals that made it a hazard for any ship of size to enter, a problem to be faced if ever the British were to make an attempt on the island.

In light airs in the lee of the island, the battle-squadron passed by at a walking pace that a lone scouting frigate would never dare, giving plenty of time to contemplate the sights. There were ships by the score, some alongside at one of the three moles but most lay at anchor deep within the bay. Kydd lifted his glass: there inside were two small warships with no sail bent on.

Leaving, they passed close by the legendary Diamond Rock—silent now, but this impossibly steep conical monolith, only a mile or so off Martinique, had once been captured and fortified by the Royal Navy and commissioned as a sloop-of-war. They had caused havoc with shipping entering and leaving Fort de France until Villeneuve, with Nelson hot on his heels, had fatally delayed his battle-fleet to pound it into submission and then had fled back to Europe, his mission to bring destruction to the British Caribbean islands a total failure.

In shimmering seas they stretched southeast for another day and, late in the evening, made to an impeccable night moor and, duty done, the Leeward Islands Squadron went to its rest.

Chapter 3

"Only for a small visit, as it were, sir," Curzon, *L'Aurore*'s high-born second lieutenant, asked, in an uncharacteristically humble tone, "as will satisfy them on the particulars of our good ship."

Kydd saw no reason why not. Curzon had relatives in Barbados and, no doubt, had said warm things about *L'Aurore* that had aroused their curiosity. And his was a post of some significance in the ship; he was quite entitled to bring visitors on board.

Then Kydd had an idea, one that, now they were part of the defending force, would reinforce the ship's standing with the Barbadians.

"Certainly you may, Mr Curzon. But not for a short time, sir, I will not allow it."

"Sir?"

"If they cast about to muster a dozen others as well, then they shall all be our guests—at a quarterdeck ball."

It was generally accounted a princely idea, and the news went about the ship like wildfire. While officers could rejoice in the honours of the ball, the seamen would be treated to the edifying spectacle of their betters sporting a toe. And it went without saying that the ship would require prettifying to a degree: it would not do for *L'Aurore* to be paltry before the rest of the squadron.

"And I expect you to be forward in the matter of arrangements, if you please," Kydd told Curzon.

It was remarkable how the list grew. As a signals frigate, there was no shortage of gay bunting to drape about to soften warlike outlines—but how to indicate to the shore that flowers by the basket would be appreciated to place at the bitts and around the binnacle, and that a certain circumspection should be exercised in ballgowns in consideration of a frigate's modest space about decks?

Naturally, midshipmen would be in attendance on the guests—but could they be fully trusted in the article of politeness, manners . . . decorum?

And music: in *L'Aurore* the Royal Marines were stout hands with fife and drum but a society evening seemed to need a little more. The capstan fiddler, perhaps?

Boatswain Oakley could be relied on to see the lower rigging triced up out of the way, but what about the training-tackle ringbolts for the nine-pounders? Avoided without thought by any sailor, these iron rings, set in the deck inboard, would prove a sad hazard for a lady with eyes only for her partner.

Kydd left these questions to Curzon, while he bent his attention to whom else he should invite. The governor might well take offence were he not included. And this was a major naval station: the commander-in-chief must be on the list, but which others? By order of seniority, the captains of the ships-of-the-line must rate first—some had their wives and daughters but in all they would probably outnumber the Barbadians. The military? He had a hazy idea that there were three regiments garrisoned, implying three colonels of the same substantive rank as himself, who would frown at an all-naval gathering in an entertainment-starved island. And then there was . . .

It was getting out of hand—until a happy thought struck. "Oh, Renzi, dear fellow! I have a small task for you."

✦ ✦ ✦

Kydd rubbed his hands in glee. It was working out better than he had hoped. As they lay at anchor in the still, warm evening he reviewed arrangements. Guests would be arriving at dusk to a lanthorn-lit, gaily decorated quarterdeck, welcomed by the airs of a very creditable orchestra wheedled by Renzi from other ships. The deck was now clear of encumbrance: its guns had been trundled to the breast-rail at the forward end of the quarterdeck, then covered with deal planking and every tablecloth the gunroom possessed to form a creditable refreshments table. The ringbolts had been drawn by an obliging carpenter, which left the area abaft the mizzen-mast an enchanting ballroom.

Chairs were placed around the capstan-head for resting couples, and strung along the shrouds, a line of light cast a soft gold on the dance-floor, tended by a grinning ship's boy dressed as a page. A party of smartly dressed seamen waited expectantly at the ship's side, for ladies visiting *L'Aurore* would not be expected to scramble up: an ornamented boatswain's chair was waiting to sway them aboard.

"We have a 'regret unable' from the governor but the admiral and his lady will be attending," Renzi murmured, "for a short time only, he pleading advancing age. The garrison commander and wife accept with pleasure—I've allowed him two officers of local birth, and it would be churlish to refuse the colonel of the West Indian Regiment, they so ardent in their loyalty. As to our naval friends, I found it necessary to set the bar at post captain and that from only the larger sail-of-the-line. In all a very creditable response, I think you'll agree."

"Well done, Nicholas. Were there, as who should say, hearts repining for want of an invitation?"

"None," Renzi said smoothly. "Not when they learned that a second ball is projected, especially for officers of the middling sort and thereby promising to be of a livelier character."

"You wicked dog!" Kydd laughed with delight. "So I must throw the ship over to a jaunting on another occasion. A rattling good plan, brother."

He moved forward to greet the first guests, a puffing gentleman, who had insisted on taking the side-steps, while his wife alighted daintily to the deck from the boatswain's chair, apparently no stranger to the device. They were followed by Captain Pym of *Atlas* and his lady, piped aboard by a well-scrubbed boatswain, then a brace of young misses exclaiming with delight as their parents, too, made their way aboard.

"Punch, ladies and gentlemen?" Kydd offered after the introductions. He beckoned a hovering midshipman forward and turned to nod to the orchestra, which quickened its pace.

More guests arrived, and he found himself at the centre of a gaily chattering throng, his heart lifting at the happy scene.

"Upon my word, sir, but this is a pretty ship indeed!" The young lady curtsied as she came under notice from the great captain. "I've heard it's quite a flyer, sir."

"Why, so *she* is, my dear." Kydd tried frantically to remember her introduction at the levee, recalling in time that this was Amelia, the eldest of a substantial sugar factor. "As we sailors must call a ship 'she' for her flightsome ways, Miss Amelia."

She was in a filmy pale blue muslin gown, well suited to the warmth of the evening. It did nothing to hide her comeliness.

"I shall try to remember, sir," she said seriously, but dimpled prettily. "And you are her captain. How proud you must be!"

"She has her quips and quillets, as it must be said—especially in a lasking breeze—but, yes, I own myself much taken with her." Out of the corner of his eye Kydd caught an envious look from several nearby officers.

The boatswain's call sounded again and he raised his eyes to see which of the squadron captains would be next.

It was Tyrell. He stepped aboard, looking around suspiciously. Kydd excused himself to go to greet him. "Why, Rufus, we're pleased you're able to come. Will you—"

"May I present my wife, Kydd."

He had had no idea Tyrell was married or that his wife was on station with him. He gave a polite bow. "I hope you'll enjoy the evening, Mrs Tyrell."

"Oh, I'm sure I shall!" she exclaimed brightly. She was short and slender, her face lined but soft, almost wistful.

Tyrell took her arm firmly and snapped, "Come, m' dear—we have our duty to the others."

Kydd returned to his young lady. She had already attracted admirers: Lieutenant Bowden, handsome in his full dress uniform, and Lieutenant Clinton, of the Royal Marines, resplendent in his scarlet and gold. Both retreated in confusion at the arrival of their captain to snare their prize.

"Shall I be your escort while we take a turn about the decks?" Kydd said, offering his arm. A dazzling smile was his reward and they stepped off together. He was conscious that it had been too long since he had had female company of such quality, and he let her pleasant talk wash about him, contributing a little about this or that when it seemed appropriate.

The orchestra struck a chord and Curzon, as master of ceremonies, came forward to announce the first dance.

"Miss Amelia?" Kydd murmured, with an elegant bow.

"Why, of course, my captain!" she responded breathlessly, and they strolled back, past the motionless helm, its spokes intertwined with greenery and flowers, and on to the open area that extended to the curved taffrail over the stern.

There was immediate movement to the side and an outburst of clapping as it was assumed that Kydd had selected his partner to open the ball.

He beamed and bowed at Curzon, who took his cue and called the sets in foursomes. Amelia took her place at the head opposite and bobbed girlishly at Kydd's flourish.

In view of the warm evening the steps were measured but, even so, Kydd was grateful for a spell at the end of the dance and went to fetch a cool lime cordial for them both. As he returned, he noticed a bent figure out of the lanthorn light beyond the chattering groups. It was Tyrell, inspecting the fall of one of the lines from aloft. In *L'Aurore* the contented seamen took pride in their ship, spending the occasional dog-watch to point rope—adding a tapered finish to the end in a show of seaman-like skill.

Kydd guessed that in *Hannibal* this was something they would never feel inclined to do—and he reflected on how much Tyrell was losing to his ship by treating his men as he did.

He looked around for Mrs Tyrell and saw her in shy conversation with Curzon, doing his duty to leave no guest unattended. He turned back in time to see Amelia claimed by Bowden. She flashed him a smile before she was whisked away for a Tartan Pladdie.

Circulating, he made amiable conversation to Pym and his lady, politely remarking on her elaborate bead-embroidered evening dress, then partnered a Mrs Pulteney for the contre-danse.

Gilbey moved up to tell him that the commander-in-chief was approaching and Kydd took position to greet him. The calls pealed shrilly, and an agreeably surprised Cochrane came aboard for his promised visit, accompanied by his wife, a short but remarkably voluble lady in plain lemon who did not hold back her approval.

At refreshments Kydd artfully trapped Mrs Jobson, wife of the King's Harbour Master so that at the resumption of dancing he was well placed to lead her out for the Boulangère, a dance that involved facing first one partner and then another—which, by great coincidence, was Miss Amelia. At changes, it was the work of moments to transfer allegiance and, as smoothly as he had planned, they were together again.

"I do declare, sir, you cut a rare figure at dancing." Her eyes shone and Kydd glowed. "And in your own ship, as you were so good as to show me. You are too kind and I'm vexed as to how I might return the politeness."

She bit her lip prettily, then said brightly, "You must pay us a visit, sir. Do come and meet Papa—I'm sure he would be agreeable."

The dull thump sounded from some way off to the southwestward, its origin hidden by the hanging grey-white sheets of rain drifting in from the Atlantic but it was from the general direction of *Acasta,* which had been paired with *L'Aurore* for the routine sweep to the south of Barbados ordered by Cochrane.

Kydd wore *L'Aurore* around and headed into the murk to find his senior, who was summoning him by gun, flag communications being impossible in the conditions. The veil thinned and he caught sight of the sternwork of the big frigate and closed, passing around her lee and coming within hail.

Dunn was on her quarterdeck and raised his speaking trumpet. "I've just spoken to a Dansker who swears he spotted a heavy frigate in the squalls to the suth'ard," he blared, "standing to the sou'west."

Kydd waited. This would not be the first merchantman to report an innocent trader with painted gun-ports as a fearsome warship.

"He could be mistaken, but we can't take the chance on it being a scouting frigate for a Frenchy raiding fleet, thinking to enter the Caribbean not by the usual passages. I desire you'll sail south to eleven and thirty latitude, touch at Grenada for intelligence and return to Barbados. I'll be looking towards Trinidad. Clear?"

"Aye aye, sir."

"Should you fall in with the enemy you will waste not a moment in alerting Admiral Cochrane. This is your first and last duty."

"Understood, sir."

"Very well. Carry on, Captain."

The two ships parted and Kydd set to the mission. *L'Aurore,* with the northeasterlies right aft, risked stunsails to larboard for a fast run. The passage between Tobago and Grenada into the Caribbean from the Atlantic was not much more than thirty miles wide and, with luck and speed, he could be in its centre at dawn and in a prime position to spot any fleet.

L'Aurore did her best for him, eating up the distance into the evening and then the night. It was not comfortable going for it was one of her quirks that, with wind and sea aft, a deep rolling and twisting set in that had the boatswain looking anxiously up at the spars, and seamen passing hand to hand along the decks.

Casts of the log, adjusted for speed over the ground in a following sea, gave hope that they would meet their goal in good time. In the early hours they reached the 11 degrees 30 minutes track; Kydd bore up due west and shortened sail.

They were now astride the entry channel and at daybreak their crosstree lookout would be in a position to spy any sail on either side—if the weather held. If it was a questing frigate, the battle-fleet would not be far behind, and Kydd had his strategy ready for returning by the swiftest means: he would round Grenada and pass inside the Windward Islands until the wind was fair for Barbados, then raise it in a single board.

There were other factors in the equation but he had long ago concluded that worrying about potential problems was futile: they had to be met individually if and when they cropped up. He turned in and, after a sound sleep, was up with the others at quarters to meet the dawn.

The night changed by degrees into a new day, the tropical morning as usual arriving in minutes, the transformation from silent darkness to lively sunrise always a thing of rapture.

No sudden cry from the masthead shattered the calm, no menacing line of sail was seen widening across their path: the horizon was clear.

"Stand down, Mr Gilbey," Kydd ordered, and turned to go.

"Deck hooo!" The hail from the lookout was hesitant but insistent. "I *think* I see sail—broad on the larb'd bow."

"Get up there, m' lad," Kydd said to Searle, handing him his pocket telescope.

The youngster swung importantly into the shrouds and rapidly mounted to the tops and then the crosstrees where he joined the lookout. They spoke briefly and Searle held up the glass to where the lookout pointed.

After a few seconds he stiffened, slammed the glass shut and grabbed for a stay, riding it down to the deck. "Sir! It's a ship right enough, big 'un as I could see, but, er, it was setting sail as we looked at it." This accounted for the lookout's initial confusion.

"Courses or t'gallants?" Kydd demanded.

"Um, it seemed to be tops'ls only, sir."

It made no sense. Unless it was a scout in advance of the main fleet, which had kept on small sail only during the night so as not to range too far ahead. Or was it an innocent merchantman resuming full sail after a night under easy canvas?

If it was a frigate, then the fleet was close astern and he should heave to and stop his progress to leeward, needing as it did a beating back against the wind to make up distance lost. If not, then hanging back could result in missing an enemy further onward.

The deck fell silent, seamen and officers waiting patiently for his command.

Kydd decided: the only way to settle the question was to close with and identify the strange sail even at the cost of later clawing back his windward position. "We stand on. Hands to breakfast, if you please."

He stayed as the deck cleared. Then, as the sail was not yet visible, he went below himself.

He'd only just begun to eat when a messenger brought the news that the wind had fallen and the officer-of-the-watch feared the pursuit was in jeopardy. He swore under his breath, for his valet Tysoe had contrived jugged kippers and scrambled eggs, but when he reached the open deck, there was now no more than a playful zephyr.

"Masthead lookout!" he bellowed. "How's the chase?"

There was a pause, then a mournful "Standin' away. The bugger's fore-reachin' on us."

Kydd ignored Curzon's muttered profanity. With the wind coming in from astern, the conditions would reach out in their own good time and take the other too. And, conversely, any change for the brisker here would see them close on a chase helpless in the calms. There was nothing for it, however: all measures must be taken to come up with the fleeing ship before it vanished over the horizon completely.

All hands were turned up for the effort of clothing *L'Aurore* in as much sail as she could take. Stunsails to each yardarm, royals, bonnets, ringtails to the staysails and driver, watersails below the stunsails. Her slight motion increased, a cheerful bubbling at the forefoot, the creak of spars taking up wind pressure—but within two hours the lookout had lost the chase.

It was the worst outcome possible: they were no further forward in identification, while the chase now had freedom to break off to left or right—or to rendezvous with a fleet already within the Caribbean, which it would otherwise have led *L'Aurore* on to discover. The question for Kydd now was whether to press on along the same track.

A decision could not be delayed much longer: both ships were being carried into the Caribbean by a current as fast as a man briskly walking. They would be abreast of Grenada later in the day and he would be forced to either break off or go on.

He knew even as he thought about it what he would do. Keep on while the wind was still fair for Grenada, then tack about into St George's where there was a small British garrison and see if there was news, otherwise warn them. It helped that this was in fact more or less what he had been sent to do.

After midday the breeze freshened, the more extravagant sail was taken in, and by three they were bowling along. The chase was still not in sight. There was nothing for it—*L'Aurore* hauled her wind for the north, and before evening made landfall on Grand Bay, rounding Point Salines safely well to windward before opening up St George's Bay itself.

And almost immediately they saw, not more than a mile or two ahead, a terrified merchantman of precisely the same size and rig as their chase desperately making for the safety of the harbour.

It took a short visit only to establish that this was their quarry. The vessel had unusually shortened sail in the night to furled lower courses rather than topsails, the longer to remain out of sight at daybreak. And there was no immediate intelligence of an enemy in the vicinity. They had done what they could.

After spending the night at anchor in order to transit the coral banks to the north in daylight, *L'Aurore* proceeded back to sea.

There was no guarantee that the big merchantman was the ship seen through the rain squalls by the Danish but it seemed likely; in any event Kydd's orders were to return to Barbados and report. They slipped north past the steep, tropical slopes of Grenada, taking their leave of the area, and into the island-studded seas to the north.

"Lay Ronde well to starb'd," Kydd instructed, sniffing the breeze. He reluctantly left the sunlit brilliance of the morning and went below to prepare his day.

In the middle of the third paragraph of his report he froze, then jerked upright, listening.

Some preternatural sense had triggered an alarm—something so out of kilter with his ordered world that it made the hairs on his neck rise.

He waited, quill poised. It came again, more felt, than heard. The deep crump of an explosion—more; then sounds coming together.

He raced for the cabin door, nearly knocking down Gilbey, on his way to report, who blurted, "Gunfire! Heavy gunfire coming from out o' the north!"

A sudden chill stole over Kydd. It was inexplicable that somewhere ahead a fleet action was taking place among the maze of islands that made up the Grenadines. But, then, with St Lucia and Martinique not so far further on and Barbados itself to the east, was it impossible?

Napoleon's master-stroke.

Renzi was already on deck and pointed to a distant ragged smudge of smoke that spread as they watched. The rumbling became sharper, then tailed off and the smoke dissipated.

"All sail to bowlines," Kydd snapped, "then clear for battle." How he might join a major action with not the slightest knowledge of dispositions or foe was not clear, but his duty was: he must get his ship to the British commander on the scene as soon as he could.

Lookouts were tripled with orders to report the character and position of every ship they could see. If he could build a picture before he was engulfed in the madness of combat . . .

But they remained completely silent as the frigate made for the distant thinning band of smoke. Then, without warning, there was a sudden concussion and a colossal plume of flame and smoke shot up—some unfortunate vessel had blown up before their eyes. It explained why the firing had died away, just as it had those years ago at the Nile when there was utter silence for long minutes after the explosion of the French flagship *L'Orient*.

The racing wave kicked up by the blast reached them, still with enough energy to send *L'Aurore* into a fretful jibbing and tossing. Yet as they neared, there were no sightings. Not a sail, let alone a line-of-battle.

In an awed hush *L'Aurore* progressed on. Eerily, the entire battlefield was innocent of anything save the deep blue and emerald green of the sea. Not a single ship.

A cry from a seaman and an outstretched arm pointed to a dark speck in the water off the bow. Closer, it resolved into a body, clinging to a piece of wreckage.

"Bring it in," Kydd said tersely.

He was a black man, his body burned and bloody. As he was laid on deck there was movement, weak and spasmodic. Eyes half open, he rolled to his side to retch before flopping back with an agonised groan.

"What ship?" Kydd demanded bending over him. Then, when there was no response: "*Quel navire?*"

Someone brought a roll of canvas and packed it under his head. The surgeon arrived and inspected the man.

"Are we going to get anything from him, do you think?" Kydd asked.

Before the answer came, the man moaned hoarsely, then spoke inaudibly and closed his eyes in pain.

"Er, what was that?"

"Man, Kick 'em Jenny!" the man croaked with effort.

Kydd looked up, baffled.

"Sounded like, 'Kickum cherry,'" Gilbey offered.

A startled cry from forward took their attention. A seaman was urgently gesturing to a sight that clutched at every shellback's heart, out off the bow. From the Stygian gloom of the deep, an intense, spreading luminescence was rising, moving slowly, with infinite menace. Was a sea-monster of unimaginable size about to appear and devour them?

Petrified seamen watched as it took shape, rising, growing. With it came a foul smell that . . .

Renzi turned on Kydd in sudden understanding. *"Naples!"*

Kydd reacted instantly. "Hard down y'r helm! Get us away, for God's sake!"

L'Aurore heeled and ran from the hideous apparition but when they were not one mile off, with a cataclysmic spasm, an underwater volcano vented. Bursting skyward with a deafening blast, a towering plume of grey, shot with flame and lazily arcing black fragments, climbed and then subsided into lesser paroxysms, a fearful and stupefying drama of nature.

When the heavy rumbling had died away the man opened his eyes again and whispered, "Dere—she wake up. Dat Kick 'em Jenny!"

An invitation arrived from the commander-in-chief, Leeward Islands station to a formal dinner marking the first anniversary of the battle of Trafalgar and the loss of Lord Nelson. It was extended to every naval officer in Cochrane's command, and the guest of honour was to be the only one of Nelson's captains on that dread day who was serving on the station: Thomas Kydd.

The very highest in civil society would be invited to attend too, and in view of the unprecedented numbers, the governor had graciously extended the use of the state banqueting hall, the Long Room.

It would be, without question, the occasion of the year.

Kydd felt both humbled and elated. Guest of honour—that meant not only a faultless appearance but a speech, delivered before several hundred sea officers and important guests.

Renzi could be relied on to confect a splendid talk, replete with apt quotations from the classics and full of elegant, rolling phrases that would be commented on for months—but this time Kydd knew he had to make it his own: set down what it had been to be part of the exalted realm of Nelson's band of brothers; open to his listeners just what the brutal pressures had been on the little admiral, how he'd triumphed over every one to lead his devoted men to victory in the greatest sea battle of all time.

And perhaps share something of the humanity and warmth in the man, those details of administration and concern for the fleet, which showed he understood that the men in the ships won his battles for him and . . .

He reached for a pen and began to write.

The evening passed in a haze of exhilaration, splendour and moment. The glitter and array of so much gold lace on dark blue, medals, honours—and the sea of faces looking politely up at him when he got to his feet for the crowning occasion of his speech.

The room settled into a respectful silence while Kydd composed himself.

"Your Excellency, Sir Alexander, distinguished guests, fellow officers . . ."

The governor and Cochrane were seated to either side of him at the high table but he could see *L'Aurore*'s officers together on the right and, close by, Tyrell. Renzi was well down the room; as a retired naval officer he had been accorded the honour of attending.

"It's difficult for me to conceive that it's been but a single year since that day off Cape Trafalgar when . . ."

He told the tale simply but powerfully, giving fervent credit to the man who had himself raised Kydd to the eminence of post captain. He tried to give a feeling for the events his audience had only read about in the newspapers and chronicles, a sense of the unbearable tension of the great chase and its resolution in the final cataclysm of the coming together of two vast fleets.

He paused. The room was in utter stillness. "Gentlemen, before we toast the immortal memory of Lord Horatio Nelson, let me read to you words he wrote that, to me, are at the heart of his humanity and greatness as a leader."

Reaching down, he found a slim book and opened it.

"This is just a single quotation taken from his 'Memoir of My Life' written in 1799."

There was a rustle of appreciation. Anything the legendary admiral had said concerning his naval life should be worth hearing.

Kydd had no need to read, for he would never forget. Lowering the book, he let the resounding words echo out into the vast hall. "Gentlemen, Admiral Lord Nelson wrote, of the officers aft on the quarterdeck and the seamen of the fo'c'sle: 'Aft the most honour—forward the better man!'"

The room exploded with applause from all except Tyrell, whose face simply reddened.

Kydd took his seat, receiving congratulations from right and left and raising his glass in response to them all.

The evening was enlivened. Many brought chairs to sit by him and hear more of that momentous day; others passed by to touch his shoulder and murmur words of appreciation.

Then it was time to withdraw for brandy and cigars, an appropriate moment for the more staid to make their excuses and the others to form a companionable group close together.

"Can't top a Trafalgar yarn," Pym chortled, "but did I ever recount what happened when we raised the Spanish treasure fleet in 'ninety-seven?"

"Yes!" came from half a dozen throats.

"Then I'll tell you about it . . ."

The warmth and intimacy of a shared professional world reached out and enveloped Kydd, leaving him in a daze of contentment.

Then he noticed Tyrell on the fringe of the happy crowd, looking on expressionless, his glass near empty. Kydd realised what was going on: the others were ignoring him—his own fault, true, but sad for all that.

Dunn of *Acasta* followed Pym's dit with an interesting tale of bluff and chicanery among the Malays and the Dutch in the East Indies. Then a young officer shyly came in with a simple but harrowing account of an Arctic traverse the previous year.

The numbers thinned as the night wore on but Kydd was reluctant to leave and break the spell. He valued Renzi's companionship dearly but in any ship her captain had no professional equal with whom to make frank conversation, to offer advice, to exchange banter and risqué humour—to unbend and be at ease in like company. It was a precious occasion.

Finally Pym stood up and yawned elaborately. "I'm for the cot, I believe."

"I also," another added, but cocked his head meaningfully to one side. In one corner Tyrell sat, quite alone. There were two bottles on a side-table and he appeared to be talking to himself.

With a cynical smile, Pym looked at Kydd. "Well, m' lad. You're junior captain—the duty's yours."

It took him a moment to understand: Tyrell was in his cups and, for the sake of decency, had to be hustled out and sent safely home.

"Lives ashore. The carriage knows where," Pym murmured and, with another yawn, left with the others.

Reluctantly, Kydd went across to *Hannibal*'s captain to see what he could do—and stopped short.

Tyrell wasn't talking to himself, he was singing. In a tuneless, broken bass he was giving out the mournful "Valiant Sailor" of Anson's time, a century before.

It took Kydd aback—this was no hearty patriotic tune or lyrical trifle. It was a fore-bitter, one that seamen sang to each other and certainly not for the ears of the quarterdeck.

"Come all ye wi-ild young men,
A warning do take it by me,

And see you no more, my boys,
Sent off to a foreign countree . . ."

Hesitantly he moved into Tyrell's field of vision. "Rufus? We're all away now. Are you ready to leave?"

There was no acknowledgement of his presence. Tyrell's eyes were unfocused, his body swaying with the song. An empty glass in his hand beat time.

"*. . . we sailed all that night and into the day*
And the first ship we spied was a Frog man-o'-war!
We bore her head upright, a bloody flag we did fly
Each man was prepared, the Lord says who dies . . ."

Kydd touched his arm. "Rufus! Time to be quit, now."

With a bleary effort Tyrell looked up, but didn't stop.

"Your carriage is waiting!" Kydd said, louder.

The singing went on, raucous and uncaring.

"*Our yards, masts and rigging were all shot away*
And begob our great guns did they roar!
Why can't I be there with my Polly on the shore?"

Kydd glanced around the near empty hall in despair. A couple of footmen were standing by the door in studied boredom. "Over here, you men. Bear a hand," he called to them.

They came unwillingly, but Kydd made them take one arm while he took the other and they lifted Tyrell bodily. He made to struggle but saw it was useless and allowed himself to be dragged away, raising his voice in rebellious conclusion:

"*The decks were aswim in blood dire and red,*
It's then that I'm wounded full sore;
Dear Polly my love, with her black rolling eye
Here I lie bleeding, it's for you I do die . . ."

There was no hiding it now, and as soon as they made the open air, Kydd roared, "Cap'n Tyrell's carriage, ahoy! Lay alongside now, you villains!"

A small conveyance with an expressionless driver stepped up. Tyrell was hoisted in by the footmen, his cloak and cocked hat tossed in beside him, leaving him to sprawl in confusion.

Kydd felt a stab of pity at the sight of such a man brought low. The least he could do was to see him safe home. He pushed Tyrell to the other side and clambered into the vehicle next to him, propping him upright in a semblance of dignity. As an afterthought he found the cocked hat and clapped it on; it seemed to steady him and the singing stopped.

"Cast off," Kydd snapped, and obediently they started away, clopping down the road.

By the time they had made Tyrell's residence, a modest house at the fringes of the smarter Georgetown, he seemed to be back in possession of his wits. The carriage ground to a stop and Kydd got out, ready to hand Tyrell down, but he was imperiously waved aside while the other alighted, staggering a little before holding himself erect with drunken dignity.

"Your house, Rufus," Kydd said neutrally. "I'll bid you good-night now."

"W-what? Never!" Tyrell spluttered. "An officer an' gentleman, you are, Kydd—you'll come aboard for a snifter, as is the least I can offer a fellow cap'n."

"Er, I really must—"

"Stuff 'n' nonsense! You'll come in an' take m' hospitality like the gennelman you are." A thought struck and he leered suspiciously at Kydd. "That is, if you're not one of the blaggards who can't stand the company of a fighting seaman."

The door opened and light spilled out. "Is that you, Rufus?" asked Mrs Tyrell, hesitantly. She was in a mob cap and held a gown tightly around her, clearly called from her bed.

"Damn sure it is, Hester," Tyrell roared, "wi' a guest who's dry, for God's sake!"

There was nothing for it but to humour him. Kydd hoped it would not be long.

"Oh, it's you, Mr Kydd," she said faintly. "Er, do come in, pray. I must apologise for the, er . . ."

"Not at all, Mrs Tyrell," Kydd said warmly, removing his hat. "I'm sorry to inconvenience."

A disgruntled servant, still in his nightcap, stumbled up but was told firmly by Mrs Tyrell that the gentlemen would be supping alone in the front room and she herself would look after them.

They were settled into chairs and a single candle lit; what Kydd could see of the room seemed wan and eerily lifeless.

Mrs Tyrell brought a brandy decanter and glasses and left them.

"Here's t' honour an' distinction!" Tyrell said, gesturing grandly, then downing his drink in one.

"As is the right of every true sea officer," Kydd replied, conscious that he had been so blessed but his host had not.

The decanter splashed out more brandy and Tyrell waited meaningfully.

"Oh—er, to the saucy *Arethusa,*" Kydd said hastily, bringing to mind the most iconic ship of the age and impatient to be away.

"Aye! To the—" Tyrell stopped. A look of puzzlement, then deep suspicion crossed his face. "Why do you . . . Wha' do you know about what happened? I demand t' know!"

Confused, Kydd tried to think. Then he had it. Years ago, part of the blockading fleet off Toulon, as master's mate he'd been sent, without reason given, as independent witness to *Arethusa* frigate while the boatswain mustered his stores, returning none the wiser. Then, months later in Gibraltar, he had been sworn to secrecy by her gunner's mate, a friend, who needed to get it off his chest.

A simple, tawdry tale: the boatswain had conspired with the captain to sell stores and had been found out. Of noble birth, the captain had not been court-martialled and the pair had been quietly removed.

"Yes, I know about it, Rufus, but that was a damn long time ago." What was riding the man? Of a certainty he was not in the fleet at the time.

"Y-you know, then! I thought, after all these years . . . Who was it blabbed his mouth?"

To his horror, Kydd could see he was near to tears so answered softly, "The gunner's mate—as swore me to secrecy, Rufus."

"Ah. It had t' be, o' course." He stared away. Kydd was about to take his leave, but then Tyrell downed his brandy in a savage gulp and slopped in more.

"You wan' t' know why I did it," he challenged.

"Why, er—"

"Wouldn't unnerstan' anyway, you swell coves born wi' a silver spoon in your mouth. Get your place through family, y'r step through interest! Never know what it's like to be a common jack looking aft, clemmed in a fo'c'sle with wharf rats 'n' priggers, no hope for it ever." He drank again, heavily, then swayed, his head drooping.

Appalled but fascinated, Kydd had to find out what was driving him. "So tell me why, Rufus," he urged.

"Wha'? Oh, nothing t' tell, really. Always wanted to go t' sea, call o' the deep wha'ever. M' father was a doctor, didn't want me to waste m' life on the briny, so I up an' ran away to sea. Fetched up in a three-decker as landman, then t' *Medusa* as ordinary seaman."

So that was what it was! Tyrell had misheard *Arethusa* as *Medusa* and thought Kydd was bringing up his guilty secret, whatever it was. And, ironically, it seemed that not only was he from before the mast, as Kydd was, but thought that Kydd was not.

"And then?"

"Ah. That was our Cap'n Belkin." His thoughts wandered again but when they returned it was with a cruel smile. "A depraved brute an' no one knew it."

"I beg your pardon?"

"See, I knew what was going on, couldn't fool me."

"Er, what—"

"He shipped his fancy boy as a volunteer, the villain, an' I hatched a plan. I broke in on them while he's a-tupping. Ha! Should've seen 'em!"

He cackled, then went on, "So in course he has a choice. Public court-martial—or he sets me on his quarterdeck as midshipman."

The carriage returned through deserted late-night streets, giving Kydd time to come to terms with what had happened. He'd left Tyrell when he'd passed out, going out of his way to reassure his flustered wife.

It was all so plain now: the doctor's son of some education and standing had been smitten by the sea and had answered the call. He'd found life as a fore-mast jack a hard one and probably made it no easier by putting on airs, antagonising his shipmates. Then a chance had come to claw his way above them. In his later career as an officer, having claim to being a midshipman, he would not need to admit to earlier service before the mast any more than others would, including Nelson himself.

Kydd's thoughts raced. Did he sympathise? If not, who was he to judge? And how far did what he had learned explain Tyrell's brutal attitude to the common seamen, his prickly relations with fellow officers and misanthropic social behaviour? Guilt must play a part in his character, as would the need to prove himself, but Kydd could not see how such things could poison a soul so absolutely. Was there something else?

One thing he was sure of: Tyrell was an incomparable fighting seaman and for that, at least, he would give the man the benefit of the doubt.

Chapter 4

Their orders were delayed; in their place Kydd received a summons to a distracted Cochrane, who wasted no time in informing him of *L'Aurore*'s fate.

"You'll victual and store immediately. *L'Aurore* is to be attached to the Jamaica Squadron in exchange for *Nereide*. Clear?"

Kydd felt a pang of disappointment: he was doing well on the station—but the needs of the service . . .

"Aye aye, sir."

"You'll convey my dispatches to Admiral Dacres and I expect you to sail without delay."

"Sir."

"Oh, and I'll relieve you of your junior lieutenant. I have a vacancy through sickness I must fill."

Bowden.

It would be a wrench, for he'd known the young man since he'd come aboard the old *Tenacious* as a stuttering midshipman. They'd seen a lot together and he'd become a fine lieutenant who would be a credit to any ship. Now was not the time to object, though.

"I've appointed another, whom you may have as he recovers, fit to serve."

"Then he's in hospital, sir?"

"Yes. I haven't spare officers in my pocket, damn it!"

"Very well, sir."

"Then I'll not trouble you further. Good day to you, sir." Cochrane returned to his papers.

"Sorry, sir, he's already gone, like," the quartermaster said, as Kydd returned aboard, his regret clearly sincere. Bowden was well liked by the hands.

"Thank you," Kydd said heavily, but it was the way of the sea service. "Any word from the shore, let me know directly."

They were to sail within the hour but without a third lieutenant, and all that that implied for redistribution of men at quarters and divisions, as well as the obligation now of the first lieutenant to stand watches. Their replacement was still apparently in hospital, and when they reached Jamaica it was most unlikely that a spare lieutenant could be found.

"Hands to unmoor ship, if you please," Kydd ordered.

The move to Jamaica would be welcomed by the seamen: the rambunctious buccaneering reputation of the last century's Port Royal had not entirely disappeared, and Kydd brought to mind some famous times in the past had by seamen flush in the fob with prize-money.

"Fo'c'slemen mustered correct, sir." They were last to report—with the capstan manned they were ready to depart.

Kydd looked at his watch. "No sense in delaying. Weigh anchor, if you please. Cast to starb'd, Mr Kendall?"

"Aye, sir."

Topmen swarmed aloft to stand by to loose sail to take the wind on the starboard side when the anchor had been won, and the age-old quickening of the heart of an outward-bound ship touched them all.

"Thick an' dry!" came the yell from forward. The cable was taut up and down and with the "heavy heave" that broke the anchor's grip on the seabed they would be free of the land, their voyage begun.

"Gunfire, sir!"

Kydd had heard it as well, the distinct crack of a small gun. Someone pointed: a low-built cutter of the kind that swarmed by the score in Carlisle Bay was crowding on sail directly towards them, the smoke of the shot dissipating as they watched.

It was inconceivable that they were under attack but unauthorised gunfire in a naval anchorage was forbidden. A civil advice-boat with news or dispatches?

"Avast at the capstan!" Kydd snapped, but he was too late: a shout from the fo'c'sle and a simultaneous sliding of the bows downwind showed they were under way.

He thought furiously. "Belay the last—get that anchor in!"

It could not have come at a worse moment. With the unusual onshore southwesterly there was no time to take the turns of cable off the capstan, releasing the anchor to plunge down again, and therefore their only course was to get sufficient way on the ship to claw off.

"Make sail!"

Canvas dropped and the topmen raced in as the yards were braced around to catch the wind, but instead of an orderly and relaxed departure *L'Aurore* was sent close-hauled across the busy roadstead to clear anchored ships.

Another shot came from the cutter.

"See if we can heave to, Mr Kendall," Kydd said tightly, eyeing the shore. There was less than a mile of usable water for any kind of manoeuvre—there had better be a very good reason for the boat's antics.

L'Aurore passed through the cutter's wind, obliging the little craft to tack about, making a sad showing that left Kydd fuming. He was on the point of ordering the frigate to bear away and make for the open sea when it finally closed with them. A figure in flamboyant dress on its foredeck shouted up indistinctly.

Gilbey made impatient signs to come alongside and hailed irritably: "What's your business?" With its small local crew and shabby look, it was obviously not a government vessel.

"L'tenant Buckle, y'r third, come to join."

Kydd swore. "Get him on board," he snarled to Gilbey. "As quick as you may." As he stumped back to the wheel he could hear some sort of altercation concerning baggage and ground his teeth.

They were perilously close to drifting down on a brig-sloop at anchor—he had to take action. But as he was about to give orders to bear away, an inbound merchantman altered course to pass them to seaward, cutting off their track out.

"Get that looby inboard this instant!" Kydd bellowed furiously.

It was going to be tricky indeed: how could he—

"Flat out the headsails, douse the driver!" he roared. With sternway beginning to make itself felt, they had to move now. He swivelled to glare at the quartermaster. If he forgot to reverse all helm orders—

"Um, L'tenant Buckle, sir?"

Kydd ignored him. "Stand by at the braces!" he bawled down the deck. It would need faultless timing if they were not to be caught aback.

"Come aboard t' join, sir." The man seemed to have no idea of the situation and was dressed in a green morning coat and pantaloons tucked into tasselled boots.

Kydd turned to stare at him. "Get out of my way, you infernal lubber! Can't you see—"

Kendall broke in: "We has a chance, sir. See the sugar barge, done loading, and she'll clear the merchant jack in a brace o' shakes."

He was right—as long as they had sufficient way on to ensure tight steering. But it would mean committing to the single course of action and if that failed . . .

"We'll do it," Kydd responded decisively. Thank the Lord he had a tried and trusty crew. "Brace around!"

L'Aurore was no longer clean-bottomed. Her last careening had been in far-away Cape Town, and it showed in her sluggish responses. Her bowsprit nevertheless swung obediently to aim like a rapier at the merchantman.

"Er, what d'you want me to do, sir?" Buckle said eagerly. A generous-sized portmanteau lay at his feet.

They picked up speed, the coral bottom flicking past in the crystal clear waters. "Mr Oakley, double up the fo'c'sle hands. I want 'em to sweat when the time comes," Kydd threw at the boatswain.

"Can I help at all?" Buckle persisted.

Kydd saw red. "Get off the deck, blast y'r eyes. I'll wait on your explanation later!" he ground out, trying to see past him to the rapidly growing bulk of the merchant ship. Buckle stood irresolute and Kydd thrust him aside savagely.

"Stand by, for'ard!" he roared. But, as he had fervently hoped, close to the merchant ship the wind veered and eased.

"Helm up!"

As they rounded the ship's stern there were frightened faces at the rail on one side, and on the other the men at the sweeps in the barge simply gazed up in shock as the frigate swashed heavily past.

"Wh-where shall I put my baggage, then, sir?"

Not trusting himself to speak, Kydd waited until *L'Aurore* emerged on the seaward side to take the breeze happily, leaning into it with a will as they made for the blessed expanse of the open sea.

"Get below to the gunroom and wait until I send for you. Give him a hand, Mr Searle."

They had done it, but the situation should not have arisen in the first place.

Course set westward and order restored, Kydd went to his cabin and summoned Buckle.

Leaning back at his desk he took in his new lieutenant. An agreeable-looking young man in his twenties, with an anxious-to-please expression, he was still in his wildly out-of-place shore clothing.

"This is damned irregular, joining ship out of rig, Mr Buckle," rasped Kydd.

"Oh, that's because m' friends insisted on a righteous send-off, is all." The accent was peculiar, touched with a slight Caribbean lilt.

"And?"

"Why, nobody thinks to see you put to sea so quick, an' when they spy you ready to go, I threw m' gear together an' here I am."

"Was it you fired those shots?"

"I did! Always take m' duck gun everywheres and it surely came in handy this time."

Incredulous, Kydd began, "You thought to fire away in a naval anchorage . . ." He let it go rather than endure another explanation. "Be so good as to show me your orders, Mr Buckle."

They were correct, the commission dated only the day before and with Cochrane's signature. "Weren't you in a sickly way betimes?"

"Er, I took the fever an' was landed from m' last ship, but I know my duty when I sees it. When the call came, how could I not arise an' answer?"

"Quite. We'd better ask the doctor for a survey, just in case."

"Oh—that won't be necessary," Buckle said hastily. "I'm feeling prime."

Kydd frowned. There was something odd about the whole business. And the commission referred to Acting Lieutenant Buckle.

"Do tell me something about your sea time, Mr Buckle—and I'm bound to tell you that in *L'Aurore* it's customary to throw out a 'sir' every so often."

"Aye aye, *sir!* Well, I starts in *Mediator* as a volunteer o' thirteen years and—"

"No, your last few commissions."

It came out. From a prominent Barbados planter family, he had made midshipman at fifteen, managing to serve his entire career in the Caribbean, but had been unfortunate in the matter of promotion. His first service as lieutenant was in his previous ship and had been brief, terminated by a near-mortal but mysterious fever.

"What, then, was your last ship?"

"That would be fourth o' *Hannibal* 74, Captain Tyrell. A hard man, sir, cruel hard!"

A midshipman with no shortage of interest, yet well past the usual age for a lieutenancy, was questionable, but what raised Kydd's hackles was the suspicion that he had shammed illness in order to be quit of a lawful appointment—at Bowden's expense. No wonder he had "recovered" so quickly, the thought of shipping out in a frigate too good to miss.

"I'll be honest with you, Mr Buckle. I mislike the cut o' your jib. You're not my idea of a naval officer and I doubt others on board *L'Aurore* will disagree. We're at sea now and I don't have a choice, but mark my words, sir, there's no passengers on a frigate. If you're not in the trim of a sea officer by Jamaica I'm having you landed as useless. Understand?"

"You can count on me." Seeing Kydd's expression, he squeaked hastily, "Um, *sir!*"

"Go! And get in sea rig!"

With a sketchy salute, Buckle left hurriedly.

Sighing deeply, Kydd knew he had problems. He couldn't let the ninny take a watch on his own. His first lieutenant Gilbey would have to stand his share, which would not please him. And what the hardened man-o'-war's men aboard would think of Buckle to serve under . . .

"Sir?" It was the boatswain, knocking softly. He had an odd smile playing on his lips.

"Yes?"

"Bit of a predicament is all, sir."

"Oh?" Mr Oakley didn't often come across problems he needed to take to his captain.

"Like, it's the new lootenant. His dunnage don't fit in his cabin. Three chests an' other gear he has, sir."

"Has he, now. Then he's to take what he wants as will stow, the rest to go over the side. Clear?"

Grinning openly, the boatswain turned to leave.

"Oh, and ask Mr Curzon to attend me," Kydd added. Buckle would be second officer-of-the-watch to Curzon and Kydd decided to make him responsible so that there was no opportunity for his junior to create a disaster in the taut machine that was a thoroughbred frigate.

It was a fair wind for Jamaica, the reliable northeasterly trades nearly abeam with never a tacking to contemplate, the easiest blue-water sailing possible. Curzon had the deck. Hesitantly his second came up the hatchway and self-consciously fell in behind him.

The watch stared at him in wonder: not only was his uniform stiff new but he wore highly polished hessian boots, a cocked hat a shade too big and a marvellously ruffled shirt peeping out from under his coat.

"Good God," Curzon spluttered, his own plain sea uniform green-tarnished and well-worn.

"Hello," Buckle said brightly. "What do you want me to do at all?"

"We're on watch. I'm your senior—you call me 'sir.'"

"Oh, right, um, sir."

"You should have been here for the handover," Curzon said testily. "How else can you think to know your course and sail set?"

"Well, I had s' much trouble with that odious neck-cloth and things, I can't think how—"

"Course west-nor'west, all sail to royals, nothing in sight," Curzon said impatiently.

"That's, er, all sail—"

"If you don't know, why not take a look at the quartermaster's slate?" Curzon's words were heavy with sarcasm, for it was the officer-of-the-watch himself who chalked in the orders.

"Aye aye, *sir!*" Buckle went to the binnacle. "Er, do you mind if I take a look at your slate at all?" he asked an astonished quartermaster, who handed it over without a word.

He returned to stand companionably next to Curzon. "I do want t' get it straight, you see."

Curzon rolled his eyes heavenward, then told him, "Those men forrard at the fore topmast staysail. They're slacking—I want that tack hardened in properly. Go and stir them along."

Buckle strode forward importantly and stopped at the group swigging off. "I say, you men! Come along, now—work harder!"

Returning, he was met with a stony-faced Curzon, who curtly ordered him to keep close behind for the remainder of the watch to mark and learn—and woe betide if he once opened his mouth.

Days passed and *L'Aurore* pressed deeper into the Caribbean. It was now well into the hurricane season and Kydd, who had reason to fear them from his experience of these waters in the past, took to tapping the barometer every time he went below. But the airs remained fine and settled.

In flying-fish weather the boatswain took the opportunity of doing what he could to fettle the rigging—turning worn ropes end for end so wear took place at another spot, re-reeving same-sized lines to different tasks and taking up stretched ropes where they had slackened. The sailmaker sat on deck in the sun, patching and seaming, helped by his mates and skilled able seamen. By the main-mast midshipmen took their instruction in sea skills from the older men.

The gunroom gathered for supper. With Curzon and Buckle in charge of the deck, Gilbey, now off-watch, was idly reading an old newspaper.

The boatswain came in, found his place and sat, tucking a napkin around his neck.

"Are we a-taunt yet, Ben?" rumbled the gunner, Redmond.

"Not as would satisfy any blue-water sailor I knows." Oakley reached for the cold meats.

The master polished his spectacles. "Still an' all, eleven knots on a bowline satisfies me."

Gilbey lowered his paper and glanced around for pickles to add to his cheese as Curzon came in, shaking water off his hat. "You've left the deck to that damn looby?" he asked sourly.

"That, or be driven out of my wits before my time." He slumped into a chair and picked at the offerings. "The man shows willing, but . . ." He gave a theatrical sigh.

"We has to do something," Gilbey snapped. "I don't fancy standing watch an' watch for ever—which is what'll happen if'n he's landed in Jamaica. We'll never find another l'tenant there."

The warrant officers held silent: it was not their place to criticise an officer, but the gunner found a way. "Then there's no word yet about a l'tenant at quarters, then, Mr Gilbey?" he asked innocently.

That was the nub: this was a fighting frigate, and if their third lieutenant couldn't be trusted to lead his men at quarters or to take charge of a division, what use was he?

There was only an unintelligible growl in response.

Clinton said mildly, "He's a decent sort of chap, I find. Get him going about the Caribbean and he's an entertainment well enough."

"As we need in a ship o' war," snarled Gilbey, throwing down his paper. "How the fool got his step I've no clue."

Renzi, as always in a corner chair, set down his drink carefully. "It might be profitable for us to consider his origins before going to judgement on the fellow."

"His origins?" Curzon said warily. Renzi, with his learning, was accorded respect in their little world and all quietened to hear what he had to say.

"Indeed. He's born and bred a Barbadian, of a respectable family. So we must ask why, then, should he seek a life at sea?"

"And?"

"I believe he wishes to be at a distance from the life he was born into, even as he has a taking for his Caribbean world."

"A pity he thinks to be a sea officer."

"Er, I believe this, too, deserves our attention. Consider—his is not the life of ambition and ardour so warmly displayed in this gunroom. He harbours no desire to return, well promoted, to cold and unwelcoming England, to him a foreign shore. Therefore he contrives to see service in smaller, unnoticed vessels—your gun-brigs, cutters and similar, all of which carry little danger of unwelcome promotion."

There were smiles of understanding around the table. "He's badgered by his father for the sake of outward show to make something of this naval exile and passes as lieutenant. At this point the only way he can achieve his swab is to be appointed into a ship of size, which, unfortunately for him, is *Hannibal,* Captain Tyrell. I can only begin to imagine what he suffered before he thought to be taken by the fever."

He ignored Gilbey's ill-natured grunts, and continued, "Therefore we have before us an oddity, not to say curiosity, a naval officer whose entire existence has been within the confines of the very smallest of King George's sail. Now I ask you to conceive of duty in such for a youngster forming habits of sea service. No big-ship ways to encourage him to a respectful understanding of our traditions, no ocean-going routines to fall in with, no taste of the puissance of the great guns. In short, he's nearly as much a stranger to our life as the merest landman."

"If you saw him handle the men," Curzon drawled. "Good God! Even a—"

"He was perhaps the only midshipman aboard," Renzi went on, with quiet conviction. "He must command hard men, some twice his age. With none to stand at his back, he finds a reasoned, mild approach more to his liking than hard-horse discipline, and I dare to say he's well practised in the art. That our own tars do expect a more, er, hearty manner is not altogether his fault."

The master coughed quietly. "It's not unkind to say that he's a little rum in his nauticals, as we might say. I saw him brace around wi' men still on the yard and—"

"It would be strange indeed if, after such an apprenticeship in coastal fore 'n' aft rig, he's as well practised in ocean square-rig, wouldn't you say, Mr Kendall?"

"You're just takin' the bonehead's part!" accused Gilbey.

"Not at all," Renzi replied coolly. "I'm only pointing out that should you not recognise his limitations then you stand to be watch-keeping for months or years to come. The choice is yours, of course."

"Be damned to that jackass!" Gilbey burst out. "If he don't come it the sea officer soon, I'll—"

"Mr Curzon, sir," the mate-of-the-watch interrupted from the door, perfectly blank-faced.

"What is it?"

"Mr Buckle's compliments, and . . . and could you come on deck instanter . . ."

Kydd had made up his mind about his third lieutenant well before raising Jamaica. They had neither the time nor the facilities to nurse a lame duck to something like effectiveness. If only he'd stayed in a ship-of-the-line where it was easier to absorb such a greenhorn . . . To be fair he'd recommend that he put in service with a bigger ship first but still discharge him in Kingston. Better to have no third lieutenant at all than a morale-sapping passenger taking up space.

He brightened. Jamaica: memories came warmly to mind of those times at the beginning of the war when he was there in the old *Seaflower*. There was no question but that this part of the world with its exotics and matchless beauty would be a splendid place for his lovely frigate to serve.

This time, though, he was an officer of distinction and quality, captain of his own ship, and he would not want for comforts. He would be revisiting with a very different pair of eyes.

A first spatter of rain brought him to reality: they were being pursued by the lofty white curtain of a line-squall advancing with the breeze, and its outliers were just reaching them. It took him back to hot afternoons in the boat-shed where he had worked, waiting for the deluge to pass, the red rivulets appearing as if by magic, staining the green transparency of Antigua harbour, and that distinctive warm, earthy smell.

It would be good to return.

Ahead, the horizon was obscured by another squall, the white drifting veil lazily moving across their vision.

"Shorten sail, sir?"

"No, I think not." He didn't need to look at the chart: the only hazards between them and Jamaica were the Morant Cays, tiny islets with reefs over which the seas continually broke in a smother of white. In daylight, even through the rain, lookouts would spot these well in time.

The squalls thinned and lifted slowly to reveal the two-mile-long line of breakers over to starboard and well ahead.

"Take 'em south about, a mile clear." As they had been so many times before, the cays were a reassuring token of where they were, a mere half-day's brisk sail from Kingston, to the northwest.

Unexpectedly, over on the far side, the flutter of raised sail appeared. Two masts—and not square-rigged. The hull was hidden by the line of surf but it was obvious that the unknown craft had been anchored in the lee of the cays and on seeing them had cut his cable to run. Was this sudden flight the result of a guilty conscience?

"Helm down!" Kydd snapped. "Get after him!"

They were far upwind of the stranger and here the big square driving sails of the frigate would be decisive.

Interest quickened around the ship as word spread. Kydd's swift action had placed the chase squarely ahead of them and even before they reached the islets it was clear that in the fresh conditions they could look to overhaul the vessel before dark.

It couldn't be better: they would arrive in Kingston with a prize at their heel!

Speculation went back and forth. It was a schooner, raked masts and a black hull, no trader he—almost a caricature of a privateer and almost certainly lying in wait for inbound Jamaican traffic. It was their bad luck that the rain squall had hidden *L'Aurore*'s approach until it was almost too late.

Within a short time the schooner sheeted in for a dash to the north. Instantly Kydd had *L'Aurore* on a parallel course to keep upwind and closing slowly.

By rounding Morant Point at the eastern tip of Jamaica and staying ahead until darkness fell, it would be in a position where Kydd would be forced to guess whether it had decided to go to Hispaniola,

Cuba or even out into the open sea to the west.

The move closer to the wind was not to *L'Aurore*'s advantage. With the fresh breeze now forward of the beam the schooner was more than holding its own and the two ships raced ahead, every line taut and straining. Soon after midday the flat, palm-studded Morant Point was in sight but now the schooner was well in the lead and before *L'Aurore* could come up with the low sprawl, its distinctive pink earth, the schooner had vanished behind it.

"Sir, charts are talking of reefs offshore a mile, two?"

Kydd tried to recall when he had been last this way—but the small cutter that *Seaflower* was drew far less than a frigate. "Keep her away, then, Mr Kendall."

It was giving the chase a further advantage but it couldn't be helped. Mentally he decided on another hour or so beyond the point, and if they weren't within striking distance, he'd drop it.

The rain squall caught up with them just before they rounded the point, the energetic downpour now an irritating inundation that dampened the spirit and hid their quarry. They pressed on resolutely through the rain-slashed sea until, after one more spiteful flurry, the air cleared.

The grandeur of the sapphire-misted Blue Mountains inland was little consolation for the fact that the schooner was nowhere to be seen. It must be ahead somewhere—or had it tacked about in the murk and even now was stretching away to Hispaniola? Very unlikely—the risk of the rain clearing to reveal them crossing ahead before the frigate's guns was too much.

Then it must be beyond the next headland—Booby Point, according to the chart.

There was little to be gained in going to quarters—their size alone could be relied on to subdue any thought of resistance—but pulses quickened as they rounded it. Nothing.

Kydd felt a surge of irritation. "Clap on more sail," he told the master. "We'll go direct and catch him before Northeast Point, only another hour or two." If not, he would have to accept they had made their escape.

In and out of the rain squalls *L'Aurore* sailed, but when they reached the northeast tip of Jamaica, there was still no sign.

"Wear ship, if you please, we return," Kydd said heavily.

He watched Buckle fumble his duties at the main, saved only by Curzon's bellowed intervention, and his growing annoyance that his triumphant return was spoiled took focus.

"Mr Buckle to lay aft," he roared, and waited while the hapless lieutenant dithered over whether to abandon his men.

"Sir, I'm to tell you that you'll be landed at Kingston. You've no place in this ship."

"Sir?"

The crestfallen look that replaced his willing air nearly made Kydd weaken. "You've to learn your profession in a bigger ship first, I believe."

"I can get the knack, if you'll—"

"No. Get your gear together, Mr Buckle."

His shoulders drooped as he turned to go. Then he stopped and said humbly, "Oh, could I tell you something?"

Kydd frowned.

"It's that I've heard of your reputation as a fighting captain and, er, I thought . . ."

If this was going to be an emotional confession . . .

"Well?"

"I, um, you see, I was worried you'd think it an almighty cheek should I tell you . . ."

"What, pray?" Kydd said, dangerously.

". . . where t' go to hunt the chase."

"Oh? Where should I go, then?"

Taking a deep breath, Buckle began, "Y' see, when I was a boy, we came to Jamaica and I went playing in the John Crow Mountains."

"And?" said Kydd, heavily.

"Going by raft all the way down the river. Rare fun!" At Kydd's look he caught himself and hurried on: "Right to the sea, we ends in a little harbour, not big at all—but snug in any nor'easter."

Buckle waited for a response, and when there wasn't one he went on lamely, "When I was mid in the little *Ibis* I told Captain Hardison about it, and we always used it in place o' Port Morant, and never the need to haul back after."

"And you think the schooner is there?" Kydd snorted. "We've been close in with the land all the way up the coast and saw nothing."

"Ah, you wouldn't. The spit o' land we shelter behind is thick wi' trees and you can see naught from seaward."

Kydd grimaced, but decided it was worth a look. "Show me. You can read a chart?"

"I can, in course," Buckle said, with a wounded expression. "I passed l'tenant! But I doubts we'll see it there, it's so small. Manchioneal Harbour, Mr Hardison calls it."

"It's here," Kendall conceded. "No mention of holding ground, though."

"We'll give it a call. What depth o' water can we expect?"

"Oh, not as would float a frigate," Buckle admitted. "I just thought, well, the schooner might be lying inside, like."

Manchioneal Harbour was as he had said: from seaward it looked like an insignificant indentation in the coast, not worth the investigating.

Kydd gave orders that had *L'Aurore* heaving to well clear of the breakers driving inshore. "Take away a boat, Mr Gilbey, land on this side and peek through the trees. Mind you're not seen, and return immediately with your report."

The first lieutenant was soon back—the picture of satisfaction. "He's there, sure enough," he called up, from the approaching boat.

"Bung up an' bilge free."

"Well done, Mr Buckle," Kydd conceded. "We have him now."

The little harbour was as much a trap as a hideaway and they were the stopper in the bottle.

Yet one thing could bring everything to a halt. Although it was acting suspiciously, there would be no question of prize-taking if the vessel could prove it was neutral. Kydd decided that, as the officer most experienced at boarding, he would take the pinnace in himself. "Four marines and boat's crew," he ordered. "And Mr Saxton," he added. A master's mate rather than midshipman to take the tiller and add gravitas to the proceedings.

The boat surged in, sped on by the white combers, going beyond the spit and turning right into the harbour opening up inside.

And there was their quarry, sleek and low and lying to single anchor.

There was no identification but her lines seemed familiar to Kydd—was this a New England schooner, the like of which he had come across in his brief time in the United States as a lieutenant? As they approached, men appeared on deck, then the American flag jerked hastily up the main-mast.

This was going to be tricky, Kydd allowed: he'd had time to read only once his captain's appreciation of the current legal situation between Britain and the United States in the West Indies. In essence, the Americans were strict neutrals by international law, allowing them to trade freely with both sides, but there had been developments that he'd not yet been able to study for their implications. If he was wrong in the details, there would not only be an international incident but he himself would be cast into ruinous damages.

As they came alongside he stood in the boat and hailed: "In the King's name, I direct you to allow me aboard."

An older man with seamed features pushed to the side and broke into a smile. "Ye're English, thank the Lord! O' course y' may."

A small Jacob's ladder was flipped down and Kydd pulled himself up, Saxton following.

"We thought you was Frenchies, you crackin' on so serious as y' were." The man extended his hand. "Elias Dale, master o' the *Orleans Maid.*"

"Captain Thomas Kydd, His Majesty's Ship *L'Aurore.* You're American registry, then, Mr Dale."

He gestured up. "That's the Stars 'n' Stripes sayin' we are."

"Then you won't object were we to take a sight of your papers."

The smile eased a fraction. "Why, no, o' course not. I'll go fetch 'em."

While he was away Kydd took in the scene on deck. If it was a trading vessel he was a Chinaman. Fine-lined, there would be no capacious hold to cram full to increase profits, and the four six-pounders appeared altogether too well looked after. And, as well, the silent men crowding the deck in no way had the look of common merchant seamen.

Dale returned quickly. "There you is, Cap'n."

He thrust across a bunch of papers.

Well used to the ploy, Kydd passed them to Saxton to hold then selected them one by one to give each his full and individual attention.

Registered in New Orleans the previous year, the owners American, the port bound to was Charleston. So far, all seemed in order.

Kydd glanced up, sensing tension in the watching seamen. One tossed a marline spike from hand to hand—he fumbled and it fell on his toe. *"Merde! J'ai envie de chier!"* he swore, hopping about.

Saxton caught Kydd's eye, but Dale came in quickly. "A Frenchy from Dominica. I guess I c'n ship who I like, don't you?"

Kydd scrutinised the manifest. Aloes from Curaçao, indigo from Bonaire. And no bond listed to cover a valuable cargo?

"I request that you'll open your hold for inspection, Captain," he snapped.

"You'll rummage m' ship?" Dale said incredulously.

"That's what I said. If the goods in the hold match what's listed in the manifest, you're free to go."

The man didn't move. His face was tight.

"Now, if you please."

Kydd became conscious that there were even more men on deck, some advancing with violence in their eyes.

Dale held up his hand to them. "Now, I don't reckon on the ruckus you're causin', Mr damn Kydd. You see, m' men don't take kindly to it and there's one helluva lot more o' them than you've got."

"You'd take on a frigate?"

"Don't have to, friend. There ain't nothin' above a brig can enter here, an' you knows it. You're on your own, and while you thinks on it, I can wait here as long as I likes."

Kydd knew *L'Aurore* couldn't stay indefinitely: a cutting out would be expensive in casualties against a well-manned and alert privateer, and if he sailed away to get more appropriate support it would release them to leave.

But he had something up his sleeve. He folded his arms and gave a tantalising smile. "I think you may be wrong about that," he said coolly.

"Why, damn it?"

"My ship carries twelve-pounders, Mr Dale."

"Ha! What's that to me?"

"At this moment I have one landed on the spit, and when it's through to this side at, say, one or two hundred yards range, I doubt it'll take much more than ten minutes to smash you all to flinders, sir."

For a long moment the man stared at him, then sagged. "Then I guess you've got all the cards. What do we do?"

"The hold, Mr Dale."

His instincts had been right: what the *Maid* was carrying was most certainly not in accordance with the manifest. In fact, the rich assortment suggested quite another explanation.

Kydd gestured to the marines to come aboard. "Mr Dale. You fly the American flag yet you have plunder aboard that proves you to have been a-caper. Without a letter of marque and reprisal, my conclusion can only be that you are pirates, your hand set against each and any."

"Wha'—"

"As pirates, therefore, no civilised nation will dispute that you're beyond the law of man and deserving of extermination. I'm bound to hang each and every one of you on the spot. What do you say to that?"

It had the desired effect. Dale turned to look despairingly at a dark-featured seaman behind.

The man pushed him aside and, with a sullen bow, said, *"Je suis le capitaine de la* Pucelle d'Orléans, *le corsaire."* He drew out a document. *"Mon lettre de marque."*

Trying not to let his satisfaction show, Kydd took it. He'd forced their hand: this was the true captain of the privateer, the American a convincing act.

"Mr Saxton, strike that flag!"

His heart full, Kydd stood astride the quarterdeck with Renzi at his side as they approached Kingston harbour. He knew his friend must be aware of what he was feeling at the prospect of arriving back at the scenes of his youth. So much had passed. Would it be the same?

As they were a ship of significance a pilot was taken aboard at Port Morant, and Kydd was free to enjoy a sight he had last seen from the tiller of a tiny cutter putting to sea on that fateful voyage when they had been overwhelmed by the raw forces of Nature.

And today there was to be no slipping in between Drunkenman's Cay and the Turtle Head for a King's frigate: it was the direct route between Lime Cay and Gun Cay, and close about Port Royal Point, the years melting away as well-known seamarks passed.

Rounding the low, sandy point they opened the harbour, and there at anchor was the Jamaica Squadron. They were relatively few, however: a single ship-of-the-line, two frigates and a number of sloops. The rest must be at sea, Kydd reasoned. At the masthead of the largest there was no admiral's flag to salute but he recollected there was a fine admiral's residence ashore.

L'Aurore glided into the anchorage, secured a place among the frigates, slipped her bower and found her rest.

"I think I must make my number with the admiral, Nicholas. Should you wish to come ashore?" Kydd asked politely, as he completed his full dress uniform.

"In course, dear fellow. I am, like you, curious indeed to see if it's the locus that has changed or myself."

They made landing at the little pier at the end of one of Kingston's streets. In the naval way of things, Poulden, as Kydd's coxswain afloat, would do like service ashore and he was sent to engage transport.

The hot and dusty streets were as busy and colourful as ever, with the white-and-green-painted houses and tiny gardens with their profusion of tropical plants, the noise and babble of Jamaica on all sides.

Poulden returned with a ketureen, a light gig with a decorated sun-roof. Standing aside as the two boarded, he swung up next to the driver and ordered, "The Admiral's Pen, y' villain."

There was a show of whip-cracking, and soon they were bowling along for the cooler hills above Kingston, the breeze of motion welcome.

The residence, with a large blue ensign lazily floating at the mast, came into view and they drew up at the door. "I doubt I'll be long delayed, Nicholas. Do amuse yourself as you will, old fellow."

Renzi was content to close his eyes and breathe in the fragrance of frangipani.

Kydd was greeted by the flag-lieutenant and conducted into the cool inner office of James Richard Dacres, vice admiral of the Blue. Kydd had heard that he had been on station since the beginning of Napoleon's war, and his near fifty years of sea service had been steady and not undistinguished.

"Captain Kydd, *L'Aurore* frigate new-arrived, sir," he reported.

"Welcome, Mr Kydd. From the Leeward Islands Squadron, I believe, come to join our little band. And with a prize at your tail, I notice—you've a good notion of your duty, I see."

There was a shrewd intelligence behind his genial manner, and Kydd answered with a guarded "I have indeed sir, being recently come from Buenos Aires."

"Ah. One of Mr Popham's restless spirits. You'll be able to tell me more of your southern adventuring on some other occasion."

He paused for a moment, considering. "Now, sir. I can't pretend that your presence is anything other than opportune, not to say pleasing. You've been in these waters before?"

"Er, only as a youngster, sir."

"Yes, a midshipman's view of things can never be accounted reliable. Well, I will tell you myself what will be your chief concerns on this station. The Leeward Islands Squadron is rightly preparing for a descent by a battle-squadron from the Atlantic, presumably commanded by one bolder than Villeneuve. Ours, however, is a very different war, Mr Kydd. I don't have to tell you that these sugar islands are a fountain of revenue for the government, providing for all from coalition subsidies to the meanest fore-mast jack's shilling.

"But what we are seeing here, sir, is the imperilling of it not by fleets of men-o'-war but a piecemeal destruction by privateers. At Barbados the West Indies convoy assembles from all over the Caribbean for its voyage across the ocean and will be well escorted, but they must sail as independents from each sugar island before they reach there. I'm not able to provide escorts for all of them, so the others are ready prey for the corsairs that do infest these coasts.

"Understand this is your prime task, Kydd. Exterminate the creatures where you can, deter and dismay by your presence otherwise. No privateer born can stand against a frigate and they know it."

"Yes, sir."

"Good. This leads me to the next. While we bend our every effort to ensure our sugar cargoes reach England, we're duty-bound to prevent the French from delivering theirs. Thus their ships are fair game to us but they've been shamelessly making use of neutrals, particularly the Americans who see no sin in playing both sides. The law is clear, however: both the French and our own Navigation Act forbid them to carry cargoes between colonies and the motherland. At the same time, though, it allows them to trade freely with the same colonies on their own account."

"I'd heard there've been legal developments."

"Ha! Yes, you're right. Our American friends are found out. Their practice has been to take up French sugar on the pretence that this is their importing, but when they arrive in a United States port they turn their ship around and head for France with new papers that show it as goods produced at home for export."

"How then do we—"

"This is what they term a 'broken voyage,' and until a legal ruling recently, we've had to accept it. Now we look to see if Customs duty has been properly paid, cargo landed in bond and so forth as evidence that it's not a continuous voyage. Take no rubbish of words—we have it from the highest Admiralty court that the onus is now on the neutral to *prove* it's not carrying contraband."

"I see, sir."

"I'll find a lawyer fellow to cover the detail for you—Rule of 1756, Orders in Council of May this year you won't have seen, that kind of thing."

"I'd be grateful for a steer, sir, I will admit."

"Good. Don't want you hoist by some pettifogging legal snag."

He beamed. "A light frigate! Just the medicine to rid me of the vermin. And in so doing . . ."

"Sir?"

"Well, do I need to spell it out to you, Mr Kydd? Prizes! Our rightful recompense for service on this fever-ridden station. Have you objection to being enriched at the enemy's expense?"

"Why, no, sir!"

"Then I expect you to be forward in your efforts to land a few more, for both our sakes. I'll give you five days at Port Royal dockyard and then it's out in all weathers, m' boy."

"Five days, Nicholas. What we would have done with that before—raise a Bob's-a-dying as would have 'em know our ship's in port!"

"While your silver lasts, as you'll recall."

"Ah, here we have the Billy Roarers in port with a prize already in tow. The vice-admiralty court will condemn the *Maid* without too much ceremony, I believe, and then there'll be cobbs for every man to celebrate it."

He smothered a sigh, staring out of the stern windows at the glittering expanse of sea to the palm-fringed shore. "What I would have given for a fistful of prize money before . . ."

"I do seem to recollect that you seemed to have done quite well without, as saw you in a mort of pother."

With a lazy smile Kydd was obliged to agree, then went on, "But I own that being a frigate captain has its compensations, the doors to society among them. Speaking of which, I do look forward to seeing Richard again."

Chapter 5

Renzi's message to his brother was returned with a delighted note insisting he visit immediately, a gig being provided for his conveyance. Leaving behind the noise and smell of Kingston, Renzi and Kydd clopped along the dusty road inland, through the endless green sameness of the cane-fields, past grinding ox-wagons teetering under their load of crude sugar and plodding lines of slaves with their field tools and piccaninny followers.

Kydd found himself reflecting that Renzi's younger brother was so different from his friend. He'd been set up as a planter by their father and had done well for himself, was established and settled with an estate and lady. And now Renzi was returning to him, after all these years, with little to show for himself.

He sympathised. The age-old conundrum: was this the price of adventure, the wider world, excitements that others could only dream about? If so, it didn't explain Kydd, a young sailor when first in Jamaica, now returning in glory as captain of his own ship while, in the eyes of the world, his gifted friend had hardly progressed.

Kydd gazed out as they passed through a village, the gaily dressed people contrasting with their drab dwellings, but the enigma that was his closest friend wouldn't leave him—and then a darker thought stole in.

Kydd knew that for many years Renzi had loved his sister Cecilia but felt he did not have the means to be worthy of becoming her husband. Frustrated with his long dallying, Kydd had extracted a promise from him to seek his sister's hand the very day they arrived back in England. But as her brother, he had certain responsibilities: was he being fair to *her*, giving his support to her marriage to someone with no visible prospects whatsoever?

He tried to shake off the thoughts and was glad when they topped a rise and saw the Great House at the end of a winding drive, edged with the flower-entwined penguin hedge that he remembered from his earlier visit.

Richard Laughton was waiting on the veranda, thicker-set and with a harder look about him. He was wearing a broad smile, however, as he strode up to greet them.

"Well met, brother! So very pleased you're come. Your last letter was more'n a year ago and I'm much exercised to discover your news." He shook Renzi's hand with obvious delight, then turned politely to Kydd.

"I don't think I've had the pleasure, sir. You . . ."

"Ah, but you have, Richard," Renzi said. "Mr Kydd, as came with me when—"

Laughton's eyes widened in recognition. "No, it can't be!"

"It is, and now you must call him Captain Kydd, of the jolly frigate *L'Aurore,* or he'll have you keelhauled, brother."

They sat together on the veranda in cane easy-chairs. The houseboy produced sangaree and explanations were made, Laughton in frank admiration at the tale of Kydd's rise in the world.

Renzi fiddled with his glass. "You do seem content with your lot, Richard. Fortune's tide in your favour, it seems."

"Why, we do have our odd vexations but that should not concern you."

"The Trelawney Maroons?" The last time they'd visited bands

of escaped slaves living in the hills had descended to terrorise the plantations.

"Put down, and the rascals sent to Canada long since. No, this is an agreeable existence for a gentleman, it must be said."

He glanced up amiably at Renzi. "And for yourself? Is—"

"Richard," he said, "might I ask a service of you?"

"Of course! Say away, old man."

"It is that Thomas being now at an eminence, perhaps an introduction to those he will be among during his commission in the Caribbean . . ."

Laughton grinned. "I've no doubt that something suitable can be arranged for a handsome frigate captain, Nicholas."

"Thank you."

He went on delicately, "And as you will, of course, attend, brother, would you be so good as to let me know your wishes regarding your, er, name? That is to say, may I now introduce you truly as my brother?" The last time they had visited, Renzi, in the middle of his morally dictated self-sentence of five years on the lower deck, had asked to be known only by his name-in-exile.

"It would oblige should you continue to address me in the same way."

"As you wish," Richard replied. "I know you are not reconciled to Father, Nicholas, yet it pains me not to acknowledge you as kin. Can we not—"

"If you must, perhaps as cousin."

"Very well. You always were a character of some complication, Nicholas." He looked at him steadily for a moment, then went on, "Mother is well but cast down by your absence. Since I'm the only one graced with the receiving of your letters I've seen fit to keep her in the knowledge that at least you're still alive. Our father is in rude good health but refuses utterly to allow your name to be spoken in his presence."

When Renzi didn't respond, he added, "You're not one for letters, Nicholas, and I'm sanguine there's much you haven't told us. That last, you spoke of submarine boats and a Mr Smith going on a journey, and you said I'd learn all about it in due course. Can you—"

"Yes. Later, perhaps."

"Well, er, what are you doing with yourself at the moment, you and our doughty captain?"

"I . . . I'm a scholar of a detached character, well advanced in an ethnical theory that requires I gather data at the first hand in different parts of the world. For this, Mr Kydd is affording me accommodation in his ship in return for my acting as his confidential secretary."

Laughton politely heard him out then spoke flatly: "Nicholas. I speak to you as family. Whether you wish it or no, you are eldest and will later go on to inherit—"

"I think not. Father has taken steps to prevent that."

"But—"

Renzi interrupted him, "I am happy with my lot."

Laughton hesitated. "There are other concerns, brother."

"Which are?"

"May I know if there might be, as who should say, a lady in your life?"

"There is."

"Ah. Do I know the family? The north, possibly—or is it to be your London beauty?"

Renzi shot a warning glance at Kydd. "Neither," he said curtly.

"Come, come, sir, it is of some interest to us all, a good marriage bringing families of lineage together. Have you reached a settlement with the father?"

"I take that as impertinence, sir. This is entirely a personal matter."

"Nicholas, if you marry beneath yourself it's most certainly a matter for me."

Kydd bristled, but managed to say politely, "Richard, I happen to know your brother hasn't even *asked* the lady."

"Is this so?"

"My heart is entirely taken by the woman. I will marry no other."

"Then?"

"Then . . . it were better we changed the subject." Renzi took up his glass and looked stubbornly away.

Kydd glanced at him in concern, then turned to his brother. "You mentioned you had your vexations, Richard. How can that be in such a fine country?"

Laughton eased into a reluctant smile. "Since you ask it, Mr Sailorman, it's surely our losses to privateers. Let me tell you that a ship making for the Barbados convoy carries in her hold much of the season's hard-won yield. What you probably don't know is that we're financed in our operation by advances on London against that crop. If this is taken it's a calamity impossible to contemplate, so we must insure with Lloyd's. As the losses go up, so does the insurance premium—which, believe it or no, now stands above six per centum."

Kydd made a sympathetic murmur.

"And I'll remind you that's a cost in wartime always to be added to our operating expenses, or a sum to be subtracted from our profits, each and every time."

Acknowledging this with a nod, Kydd interjected drily, "I'm no man of business, m' friend, but even I can see that if the French are driven from the seas then they'll not get their own crop to market, and the sugar price must surely rise handsomely. I dare to say this goes some way towards compensating for the inconvenience."

"You're in the right of it, Thomas," chuckled Laughton. "But spare a thought for our other worries. For instance, here on a tropical isle we find the soil's quickly wearied, exhausted. Without notice a field will throw up stunted, pitiable growths no good to man or beast."

"Is there no help for it?"

"Yes, for those whose study it is to 'ware the signs. Guinea grass answers, sown promiscuous, on which we raise useful numbers of cattle and sheep, their manure a sovereign cure. And our new Bourbon cane strain, which—"

"So sugar might be accounted a profitable and reliable business for you, brother?"

Renzi's question made Laughton pause before he answered. "Shall we say I lose no sleep b' nights in torment that my produce will not find a market?"

He waited while their glasses were refilled, then continued, "As some facts of a domestic nature will best illuminate. Take your Hannah Glasse, much cried up for her family cookery. Her receipt for seed-cake in the Spanish way demands an entire three pounds of moist sugar, while for your common marmalade it's at the rate of one pound on every four oranges. And when the modern taste in tea scorns anything less than fourteen pounds of best refined for each pound of leaves, and with a population to be reckoned in millions, you'll see why I rest easy."

"Some might say it's all on the backs of your slaves."

Laughton's smile disappeared. "Pray what is your meaning, Nicholas? Are you to be numbered with the Abolitionists?"

"Do not be concerned, Richard. I merely point out what I'm told is to be heard on all sides these days in London Town."

"Then to them I'd say the same thing. These creatures are brought from the most savage and benighted region on the planet. Here they're exposed to a mode of living, three full meals a day and accommodation that they in their rude huts and ignorance couldn't even dream of. They are like children and require firm structure in handling, and even educating in the notion of work in return for the necessities of life."

"Under the threat of the whip?"

"Does not your child respond to a flogging if driven to it by necessity? Nicholas, I'm an enlightened owner. I rule with justice and mercy, not to say kindness. Not only do I clothe and feed them but have given over my own land to them for their growing of greenstuffs for the market—but I'd never be fool enough to believe they're anything but savages at heart."

"It seems a pity that—"

Laughton's face hardened. "If by this you're saying I should free all my slaves then, by the same business logic, I face an impossible situation."

"Impossible?"

"Quite. For by this action I would be utterly unable to compete with the produce of other nations that do retain labour without cost. And that applies to all of us—and then where is your government revenue stream? No, brother, accept if you please that slavery is a regrettable necessity in these modern times."

At Renzi's look he added, "Was it not your sainted William Cowper who said it best—

'I pity them greatly, but I must be mum,
For how could we do without sugar and rum?'"

"Ha! There's no arguing with that, Nicholas." Kydd laughed. "Let me tell you, Richard, your brother's an odd fish at times. I do remember when—"

"Yes. Well, no offence taken, old fellow. Now, I've been giving some thought to your social event . . ."

"Well, gentlemen, time to earn our salt." Kydd looked encouragingly at his officers. "And in what our brothers in a sail-of-the-line would die for, an independent cruise, and should we fall in with a prize on the way, then Admiral Dacres declares he would not take it amiss."

He was met with expressions ranging from the naked cupidity of Gilbey to the guarded interest of Curzon and the near hero-worship of Buckle, now no longer under threat of removal.

"Our orders are plain and direct: to rid the seas of any who would prey on our trade."

They all knew that. It was how he proposed to go about it that had their attention. *L'Aurore* was in prime condition now. Port Royal had gone to work on her defects so frayed lines, stretched canvas and strained timbers were things of the past. Whatever her captain decided, she would be ready.

Kydd carried on, "Any old Caribbee hands will know that for a frigate the regular way is to keep deep-water guard over the main passages into the Caribbean, they being choke-points for sea traffic of all nations, rather than aimless wandering about the seas, looking for distraction.

"I've a different notion. If I were a privateer . . ." in this company he could never admit that once he had been one ". . . I'd be looking to skulk somewhere close to a shipping lane to dart out and snap up, then make away briskly."

He flipped open the main chart of the Caribbean and found Jamaica. "Here are we, and there is Hispaniola," he said, indicating the large island to the east. "Windward Passage to its west, the Mona Passage to the east. Ocean traders, of course, do use these, but as a privateer I've another prospect in mind. Sugar vessels on their way to Barbados to join the England convoy."

"Ah—because they're sailing alone, we not having the escorts," Curzon grunted.

"An' their track always to be south o' Hispaniola," added Gilbey, thoughtfully. "Staying north to pick up the current. In which case . . ."

"Yes?" Kydd said.

Gilbey leaned over and studied the chart. "Why, here's a possibility," he murmured, "as is right handy for such." He indicated a large triangle of land that jutted out from the even east west line of the south of Hispaniola.

"How so?"

"It puts 'em closer to the shipping track, as well provides a lee either side should the weather turn bad."

"My thinking too, Mr Gilbey," Kydd said, gratified. "Now, here's the lay."

Underneath was a larger scale chart. He pointed to the tip of the triangle. "Cape Beata—and mark the island offshore. He has his lee and his anchorage both. I'd wager if there's any of the brethren lurking, it'll be there we'll flush 'em out."

"Supposing there's none found?" Curzon said lightly.

"Then we continue on to the east and Mona Passage, as if that is what we intended all along," grinned Kydd.

"Purely out of interest only, and being a mort hazy about this part of the world, just what forces do the Spanish have in the island these days?"

"Well, er, it's a tricky business to say, Mr Clinton," he told his lieutenant of marines, "as Hispaniola is in the character of two countries—St Domingue to the west under the French and Santo Domingo to the east under the Spanish. But there's been a slave revolt and—well, I believe we'll beg Mr Renzi to tell us the rest."

After politely summoning him, Kydd asked formally, "Mr Renzi, would you be so good as to tell us your appreciation of the situation obtaining in Hispaniola at present?"

His friend paused, marshalling his thoughts. "Not an easy task, sir, and one only explicable with a little history. The French colonised the western third of the island a century or more ago, the eastern two-thirds being Spanish since the days of Columbus. In 1795 the Spanish, at war with ourselves, saw it as impossible to continue to govern and yielded up the whole island to the French."

"So it's French."

"Not so easily answered. The slaves of the French heard of their revolution with *liberté, égalité, fraternité* for all, assumed it applied to them and, duly disappointed, rose in rebellion. They had a masterly general, one Toussaint L'Ouverture, who remarkably prevailed and made treaty with the authorities to abolish slavery in return for the former slaves remaining loyal to France. This was granted. When Napoleon Bonaparte came to power he first agreed to this, but then changed his mind and sent General Leclerc to restore slavery. Not Boney's most intelligent plan, I'm persuaded. L'Ouverture fought Leclerc to a standstill, even with France free to pour in reinforcements while we were at peace between the wars. So the French turned to treachery, offering to parlay, then kidnapped L'Ouverture and took him to France where he died in chains. With their great enemy removed, did they then triumph? Not at all. This betrayal inflamed the slaves beyond reason and under a singularly brutal leader, Dessalines, they flung themselves into as savage a war as any to be seen in Christendom. The burning alive of prisoners in village squares was the least of it, bestial conduct on both sides the rule.

"The result—stark catastrophe for the French, who in their efforts to bring back slavery lost fifty thousand soldiers and no less than eighteen generals, a far worse beating than ever we've been able to achieve over them."

"That's all very well, Renzi," Gilbey said, with irritation. "We've heard most of that. What we want t' know is who rules now?"

"I don't know."

"Then—"

"The French were ejected from the whole of Hispaniola. Dessalines has proclaimed himself Emperor Jacques the First, over a new-conjured nation he calls Haiti, and inaugurated his rule with a general slaughter of all white settlers. Bonaparte has vowed not to rest until it's recovered for his empire while Spain makes no secret of its desire to take back their eastern realm. Gentlemen, given this clash of claims, I would declare that the sovereignty of this island remains . . . unclear."

"Excepting they're each and all our enemy," Curzon came in smugly, "Therefore we can feel free to act as we will."

"Not so," Renzi replied, "as we have since made common cause with Dessalines, whom it would be folly to antagonise."

Holding up his hand at Gilbey's exasperated outburst, Kydd asked, "Then what should we conclude at all? What are the practicals in the matter?"

Renzi gave a brief smile and replied simply, "There is a species of mob rule and most grievous corruption abroad in this benighted island. There will be no Spanish garrison, still less French, for our good emperor detests any and all foreigners, including our own selves. Therefore we may fear no impregnable castle, frigates in harbour, or any sudden threat. I leave the rest to you."

Kydd nodded. "Thank you, Mr Renzi. Well put and clear. We sail tomorrow with confidence!"

Heeling to the fine northeasterly trades, *L'Aurore* made good time to Cape Beata; every man who could be there was on deck, eagerly scanning for prey. It was rumoured that their captain had second sight as regards privateers, and all expectation was that their arrow-straight passage was for a purpose.

"Get up there, Mr Buckle," Kydd said, handing over his own pocket telescope. "I want you to report from the masthead any vessels—at anchor or under way. If they flee, don't you dare lose 'em—keep them under eye. Clear?"

"Right, sir!" The enthusiasm of the reply brought a smothered cheer from nearby seamen but the third lieutenant had already swung nimbly into the shrouds.

A morning haze, however, lay along the coast and in its delicate pearl mistiness it was impossible to make out detail, but as they neared it began to lift.

Almost immediately there was a cry from the masthead. Buckle was peering with fierce concentration towards the firming sight of an offshore island, the mainland still lost in mist.

"What is it?" Kydd called up, in an impatient bellow.

"Er, sail, I think, sir. No—I'm sure!"

"Explain yourself, damn it!"

"Well, I saw him at first but I can't now." He craned forward, searching frantically in all directions with the telescope.

With a splutter of rage, Kydd hauled himself into the shrouds and mounted up to join him with a speed that had even the topmen looking thoughtful. "Now, Mr Buckle, what the devil are you trying to say?"

"Over there, sir. Next to the big island—he's gone now."

Kydd snatched the glass and scanned the coast carefully.

The emerging headland itself was unimpressive, leading down in a tame finish for a forty-odd-mile cape to end in flat, pinkish rocks. Offshore there were two islands. The nearest to the cape, Isla Beata, was a five-mile triangle and was separated from it by a channel. The other, much smaller, was further out still, a single island less than a mile across.

And not a sail in sight.

"You're sure you saw something, Mr Buckle?"

"I did, sir!"

"Did *you?*" Kydd snapped at the posted lookout.

"No, sir, can't say as I did."

Kydd twisted about and shouted to the other mast, "Main top lookout, ahoy! Did you sight sail?"

"None!"

Kydd swung out and down the shrouds. Before he made the deck, his mood had calmed: given the conditions, any sail could well have vanished into the mists closer inshore. "He's between the large island and the cape. Take us in, Mr Kendall."

They came more by the wind as they changed course and began

to open up the channel between. The master pursed his lips—the tell-tale white of sub-sea reefs was becoming visible in the two-mile gap. "It's shoal water in there, an' a strong current hereabouts, Mr Kydd. I don't reckon—"

"I've seen enough. Take us south-about then." He'd had an unobstructed view of the channel and there was nothing in it. They'd pass by the island to its other side, and if it was innocent of vessels, he'd have to admit he'd been wrong in his intuition.

Renzi stood by him silently as *L'Aurore* quickly passed the tip of the island.

"Nothing but empty sea," Kydd said woodenly.

"Still one place you haven't looked, dear fellow."

"Oh?"

"The outer island. Small, but enough to conceal. Should we put up our helm now we might profitably circle the island by wearing about it."

"We've seen three sides of it, no sign of anything." Alto Velo was only seven or eight hundred yards long, with a lofty conical peak.

"What have we to lose?"

"Very well, Nicholas. To please you. Mr Kendall, we wear about Alto Velo."

They fell off downwind but the fourth side was as bare as all else.

"Resume course, Mr Kendall."

"To?"

"It's the Mona Passage for us, I'm sorry to say."

The frigate paid off to return on its eastward course, the expectant groups of men breaking up and going crestfallen about their business.

"Um, I could swear . . ."

"What's that, Nicholas?"

"Nothing, really. Just that I thought I saw a fleck of white and now it's red, is all."

"On the island?"

"Well, at the end, near the waterline, as it were."

"Now, don't *you* start seeing things—I've enough with Mr Buckle."

But a thought, a long-ago memory, gradually took form and coalesced into a single idea. A sailor's yarn during some long-forgotten watch in the Pacific. Something about . . .

"Heave to! This instant, if you please." The differing motion on the ship brought the curious back on deck.

"Get a boat in the water, Mr Curzon—and from the opposite ship's side to the island."

Curiosity turned to astonishment.

"Er, and hail aft Mr Saxton."

The master's mate arrived, wide-eyed and expectant. When Kydd explained to him what he wanted, he broke into a wide grin and went away immediately to find a boat's crew.

L'Aurore got under way again, shaking out sail as though she meant to circle the island once more. But she had left her gig behind—the smallest boat on board, which, with bows towards land and its crew hunkered down out of sight below the gunwale, was near invisible from the shore.

For long minutes it lay bobbing to the waves until a hoarse cry came from forward. "She's away." *L'Aurore* had disappeared behind the green slopes of the island.

"Out oars," Saxton ordered crisply.

They were only five: himself, gunner's mate Stirk, and the seamen Doud, Wong and Pinto.

"Give way together," Saxton rapped. "Silence in the boat, fore 'n' aft!"

He was concentrating on the landing: there was a fringing beach with few rocks and the greenery was resolving into palm trees and the deep green verdure of a Caribbean island. He picked out the likeliest spot and conned the little boat in.

It hissed to a stop at the water's edge, the rich odour of the land welcoming them in a wall of warmth.

"Doud 'n' Pinto, away to the right. Stirk 'n' Wong, to the left," he ordered.

Doud eased the pistol in his belt and headed out with Pinto to follow the water's edge around.

Saxton went off along the beach behind Stirk and Wong. Then he realised that if *L'Aurore* was in that direction their quarry would be at the other end of the island—in fact, close by.

"Stirk!" he called urgently. "Go ahead and spy out the lay."

The big man loped quickly out of sight. Shortly afterwards his head bobbed above the bushes and he beckoned.

Heart in his mouth, Saxton joined him. Stirk pointed. No more than fifty yards away a black man sat on the beach, staring intently at *L'Aurore* far off to the right. Beside him were two large flags on sticks, one red, one white.

Stirk tapped Saxton on the arm and pointed again. Nearly out of view in the opposite direction around the point was a low-lined schooner, her sails loose in their gear.

That old yarn that Kydd had recalled had saved the day: in the American war the South Sea whaler *Amelia* had avoided capture by a privateer by the simple ruse of dodging about an island, a man ashore signalling to it the whereabouts of the other so that it could keep to the opposite side, always out of sight. It had been in effect the childhood game of chase in which a frustrated pursuer could never catch any quarry who made it to the fat trunk of a tree.

The watcher did not hear their tiptoe approach along the soft sand. They loomed up beside him and the man jerked around in fright. Then, from the other direction, Doud and Pinto appeared.

"So what do we do wi' the bastard?" Stirk asked mildly, fingering his weapon. "I can give him the frights, should ye need to ask him his code."

"No need," said Saxton, smugly. "I've got it figured!"

"Oh?" said Stirk.

"Simple. He stays in sight o' both, and signals where *L'Aurore* is by saying she is to my left or right, larboard or starboard. That's red or green at sea—he can use red but green won't be seen, so he uses white. See?"

"I reckon," Stirk said, in admiration.

The rest was easy. Leaving Wong to keep the man company, they took the flags and went to a point of rock. *L'Aurore* was approaching from the right—so Saxton took the red flag and furiously waved it to and fro as if in the utmost urgency.

There was an immediate response: the schooner hauled in on her tacks and sheets and got under way as soon as she could, rounding the point under a press of sail—directly into the open arms of the frigate.

"A splendid catch," Gilbey said, admiring the fine lines of their prize. An island schooner of about eighty tons, low and with a roguishly raked mast, she was built for speed over cargo capacity, as might be expected of a privateer.

Her crew, disconsolate on the main deck of *L'Aurore,* were not many, which implied men away in prizes. The captain, a bitter young man of South American origin, demanded to know who had betrayed them.

"His papers, if he has any. If none, I'm desolated to have to inform him that he and his crew shall swing as pirates," Kydd told Renzi, whose Spanish, since their actions at Buenos Aires, was now more than adequate.

"He shall fetch them, if he is at liberty to do so."

Returning with Curzon, the captain stiffly presented a folded parchment. It was a Spanish letter of marque for the schooner *Infanta* on a privateering voyage in the north Caribbean and appeared to have been issued under the hand of the viceroy of New Grenada in Venezuela.

"Very well, they're spared the rope. Get them below," Kydd grunted.

Curzon waited until they had been escorted away, then said, in an undertone, "I suspect you'd be interested in other articles I relieved them of."

Kydd called Renzi and, in the privacy of his cabin, they went through the haul. Innocent papers, such as would be found on any working ship: invoices for stores received, goods landed, repairs completed. Nothing to raise suspicion—except that the sea-port common to all was Puerto de Barahona, some fifty-odd miles further to the north.

"Aha! We have his bolt-hole, the devil," Kydd declared, with satisfaction. Any privateer needed a repair base, supplies to stay at sea and, even more importantly, a safe haven to which it would send back its prizes.

"You're not thinking . . ."

"I am."

"Then I'm obliged to remind you that this port lies in Santo Domingo—or should I say Haiti?—and by this we should be violating its sovereign neutrality."

Kydd hesitated. "Good point, Nicholas, but there's another side to it. I know privateering, and to put a private cruiser to sea needs funds and backing. I'll wager it's a joint venture of the port, and if this is so, then Haiti won't want to know of it or they'd be obliged to admit they're allowing military operations by a foreign power on their soil."

"Possibly. But even the sight of a frigate heading into the coast will—"

"She won't. They're expecting this *Infanta* to return after a cruise, and she will—bearing a surprise below decks."

Kydd grinned. Even more effective a blow than capturing one was the elimination of a privateer nest. Energised, he summoned Gilbey immediately and outlined the situation. "First, we get rid of the prisoners."

"Sir?" the first lieutenant spluttered.

"Yes. We land them on Alto Velo, pick 'em up later."

"Oh, I see, sir."

"Then I'm calling for volunteers for a species of cutting out in the *Infanta*."

"Aye aye, sir," Gilbey said, brightening. "May I know who's to command?"

"I'm thinking on it," Kydd said, but he'd already made up his mind.

A little later Lieutenant Buckle hesitantly appeared. "You sent for me?"

"I did. To say I'm sorry for doubting your sighting earlier."

"Oh, er, thank you, sir, that's good of you."

"And by way of amends—to offer you a chance."

"Sir?" he said warily.

"Your first command."

When a disgruntled Gilbey reported the lower deck cleared, Kydd appeared on the quarterdeck before his men.

He was satisfied by what he saw. Deeply tanned, fit and as individual as any long-service ship's company, they returned his gaze with confidence and trust.

"Mr Gilbey, take the names of the first fifty. Volunteers for a cutting out—step forward!"

To his astonishment there was only an embarrassed shuffling. "Volunteers! Step up to Mr Gilbey, lively now!"

After a space there was an apologetic call from the mass of men. "Who's t' be in command?"

"Why, Mr Buckle as made the sighting," Kydd said sharply.

Something like a sigh went through the crowded deck. The seamen looked down at their feet awkwardly.

Kydd was furious but there was nothing he could do about it: he had called for volunteers and there had been none. He could order Curzon in Buckle's place but that would destroy what authority the man still had.

Thinking quickly, he folded his arms and said casually, "Oh, and I perhaps omitted to say, *Infanta* being quite another vessel to *L'Aurore,* any prize recovered will naturally be to the account of *her* crew only."

"You can't say that!" Renzi hissed at him.

"Oh?" Kydd said quietly. "What else can I do?" He lifted his chin. "In any case, I'm sure you'll not fail to correct me in proper form—after it's over?"

The first to step forward was a defiant Doud, quickly followed by his long-time messmate Pinto.

Then boatswain's mate Cumby mumbled, "I'll go if'n Poulden does."

He was duly joined by the coxswain, who clapped him on the shoulder. "I'm not leaving th' cobbs all to you, mate." He sniffed.

Others moved forward. Then Clinton took off his hat in a mock bow and declared, "Should there be a confrontation ashore it would be singular indeed if the Royal Marines are to be excluded. Would a file of lobsterbacks be welcome?"

Kydd had his fifty.

"Shove off!" came Buckle's somewhat un-naval command.

Stirk held his tongue. He had his misgivings and they were growing; his coming forward had given his shipmates heart to do likewise. He glanced back at *L'Aurore,* seeing Captain Kydd looking down as they cast off. Why weren't all naval officers like him?

Square and true, worth any man's following.

The schooner swung away from *L'Aurore* and both ships took up close-hauled out to the east, to make an offing before going about and raising Puerto de Barahona, *Infanta* tucking in astern of her senior.

Stirk watched Buckle hovering around the wheel, nervously checking their heading. Nearby was Luke Calloway, master's mate and second in command, barely in his twenties.

Now, there was one of the right sort. He'd started out as an illiterate ship's boy and had pulled himself up by his own efforts. Stirk gave a wry grin: that both he and the captain had been old shipmates didn't trouble him—he was an old sea-dog and knew he could never hoist in all the book learning necessary to go further. Just as long as those like Kydd and Calloway earned respect by their actions he would take their orders happily.

This junior lieutenant was of another stamp. Like a young pup, he was trying too hard to please—and seemed to have had a very patchy naval background. Word had it he had no experience of square-rig worth a spit, and all of it within the Caribbean, hardly the nursery for young officers that the blockading squadrons offered.

Stirk took some comfort in that, as boatswain of the craft, he oversaw all manoeuvres and was in a position to intervene if things got into a tangle. Once action started it could be different . . . and then it might be another story.

The two ships put about at midday, allowing an easy sail while they closed the coast. The intention was to make landfall as dusk was clamping in, allowing enough light for recognising, but hopefully not so much that anything out of place would be spotted. Buckle seemed quite at home with schooner rig, not often to be seen in naval service, and sensibly turned in after they settled on their final board.

At daybreak, some twenty miles off the coast, *L'Aurore* heaved to and called *Infanta* alongside to take aboard the volunteers held back from the small passage. They crowded into the little schooner but it would get worse for them in their final approach when they would be crammed out of sight below.

"Mr Buckle! Is there anything more you need?" To Stirk, Kydd's voice from the quarterdeck sounded tinged with anxiety, which did little to settle his own unease.

"Er, I can't think of anything," Buckle called back.

"Then I'll wish you and *Infanta* good fortune."

The schooner got under way and passed *L'Aurore* to take position ahead. Any watcher on land would now see a plucky little craft crowding on sail in a desperate attempt to escape capture by making the safety of the harbour.

Stirk made the most of the fading light and went around the decks, checking. In the circumstances, the plan had to be simple. Enter Puerto de Barahona past any fortifications by bluff, and when within, spy out any vessel worth the cutting out. If there were anything to be gained by raiding ashore, then any general mayhem would be acceptable—a blue rocket would signal *L'Aurore* they were landing, a red that the defences were too strong.

The coast loomed, thickly verdant and rumpled; the port was neither enemy nor friend at first appearance, an unsettling lack of certainty.

Buckle stood stiffly by the wheel, clearly conscious of his role, pale-faced in his cocked hat and sword. "Right—everyone below, we're nearly there," he ordered.

"Sir," Stirk said heavily, "wouldn't ye like to be in somethin' more comfortable t' wear, like?" It was not up to him to point out the obvious: that an officer in the King's uniform was an unusual sight in a privateer.

Their run in was straightforward enough: chalk cliffs stood out stark in the fading light, angling down as if pointing to a cluster of buildings. Closer in, the harbour could be made out—a gap in two white-fringed reefs, then a low hook of land enfolding from the right. Small, but ideal for a privateer hideaway—no frigate was ever going to close with those reefs.

The schooner, with the last of the sea breeze behind her, surged inside them. Balked of her prey, *L'Aurore* gave up and headed back out to sea. All eyes in *Infanta* were on the low spit of land to the right. What would be revealed when they were inside it?

Long minutes later they had their answer: a near half-mile length of calm water with a sizeable brig at anchor and, at the far end, signs of a shipbuilding slip.

The helm went over and they sheeted in for the run-up.

"We go for the brig, do you think?" Buckle asked.

"Sir," Stirk said stolidly. Asking him what to do? At least he could see no signs of fear or panic in the man.

"What—" Calloway was looking astern in consternation. Not more than twenty yards behind was another, larger, schooner—in their eagerness they had not checked the other arm of the harbour to the left and they were now cut off. Trapped.

From its rakish lines and the number of men, it was definitely another privateer and it was after them, coming up fast. A swarthy figure stood on the bowsprit holding on to a stay and bellowing something aggressively. Other men began bunching behind him.

Stirk felt his gut knotting as he saw that Buckle's choices had narrowed to two: fight or surrender. But then he did an utterly unexpected thing: he waved and yelled back a lengthy reply in the same heathen tongue.

"Stirk—go below and, on your life, keep those men out of sight!" he hissed urgently.

"Sir!" He wasted no time in obeying, then returned, expecting anything.

But Buckle was hailing again. This time it produced a flurry of shouting and activity and then the schooner sheered widely around, and made off at speed for the reef gap.

"Wha'?" Stirk said in amazement, "Sir, can y' tell me, what was all that?"

"Why, nothing much. It was a Captain Romana, he was asking in Creole how we fared on our cruise. I told him we had all our men away in prizes, but if he was quick there's still a couple for him to take."

In frank admiration, Stirk touched his forelock to the man. Quick thinking like that made up for a lot in his estimation.

It had been close, but they were now free to move on the brig, and all attention turned forward.

"Stand by, below!"

The evening was drawing in with its usual velvet feel—but an edge of tension grew as the brig drew near.

There was a lanthorn in the rigging aft, but apart from that, it lay in peaceful stillness, lapped by tiny waves in a picture of tranquillity. Stirk noted in satisfaction that Buckle ordered sail reduced as they approached: they would have aroused suspicion had they careered into the anchorage.

The schooner eased its progress, ghosting the last few hundred yards as if to pass the anchored vessel. At the last minute course was altered to come alongside—still nobody was visible on deck, the glimmer of light through a side-scuttle aft the only sign of habitation.

"Now, sir?" Stirk wanted to know. If they were to storm the brig they needed men up on deck ready, sufficient to overwhelm any the other could muster.

"No!" Buckle said firmly. "We'll do it quietly. Take only three and go below to persuade 'em that resistance is folly. Understand?"

The two vessels nudged together and Stirk stepped across, cutlass drawn. With a fierce grin he led his men down the after hatch.

The only crew aboard were playing cards at a table in the diminutive saloon. They looked up in astonishment at the invasion.

It was short work to secure the ship. No shots fired, no sudden assault to waken the little town, and now they had a prize: it was a master-stroke. How it would be got to sea was another matter, of course.

When *Infanta* poled off to return to *L'Aurore* there were still no signs of alarm along the dusky shore and Buckle paused. "Do you think we should stir them up a bit? Let them know the L'Aurores have visited?"

Poulden looked at Stirk in mock resignation. "Aye, a good idea, sir."

The far end of the harbour was the loading wharf; it had a sugar lighter tied up to it. "That's depth o' water enough for us!" crowed Doud.

The schooner got under way and as they crossed the last hundred yards people began crowding along the shore.

"Come to see what we've got for 'em after our cruise." Poulden chuckled.

Infanta doused sail and glided in under the gaze of the curious spectators. Buckle hailed the crowd—one bent to take the line thrown ashore and others helped to haul in the schooner. In the twilight they had not seen anything amiss.

Suddenly a blue rocket whooshed up from the schooner, soaring high across the sky. *L'Aurore* now knew they were storming ashore and would have boats in the water to take them off if things went against them.

The people fell back in dismay—then a crowd of English seamen boiled up from the hatch brandishing cutlasses and shrieking war cries.

Most onlookers broke and ran; others hid as two armed parties made for their objectives.

One, under Calloway, raced for the shipyard, the marines beside them, with muskets a-port. The yard had closed for the day but the lock at the gates was no match for Wong's crowbar. Inside were two ships building on slips—nearby, pitch pots and teased oakum for caulking, perfect fire starters. Soon flames leaped and flared dramatically in the darkness.

The other party under Buckle made for the town, hurrying through the few mean streets and searching for opportunities for mayhem. Townsfolk scattered, screaming.

At the end of the road they were surprised to be met by shouts and desperate yelling. It was coming from men inside a stockade, English sailors held prisoners. "Turn 'em loose," Buckle said. "They're crew of the brig as will take it to sea for us."

One wild-eyed seaman held back. "I wants t' get evens on the Spanish. If ye'll follow me, I'll show y' where Don Espada lives, the bastard."

It was a mansion set out from the hill on the slope. As they approached there was the flash of muskets from the mock turrets, but in the bad light the shots went wide, and soon the men were crashing through the ornamental garden and battering down the door.

Muffled shouts came from within and Buckle ordered them all to fall back while he negotiated. The door was opened by a haughty Spaniard, who stood sullenly.

"Secure him and we'd better be on our way back," Buckle ordered briefly.

From the waterfront, they heard scattered musket fire. If they were prevented from getting back aboard, there could be only one ending to their adventure. A ball zinged from the road and another slapped through a marine's jacket.

"Take cover!" Buckle yelled. It was only another intersection before they arrived at the wharf—but they were under fire from an unknown direction.

"A flying column to secure the wharf?" Clinton suggested. Casualties would be severe, and worse, if they then held their positions until inevitably enemy reinforcements arrived.

"Waste of men. No, I'll—"

Suddenly, like a thunderclap in the still night air, a carronade smashed out. It could mean only one thing—*L'Aurore*'s boats come in support. The launch and cutter, under oars and stretching out fiercely, had opened fire when well out of range but it was effective: the unknown snipers had run for their lives.

"Go!" yelled Buckle, and pelted towards the seafront.

Calloway and his party were waiting for them in *Infanta* and they lost no time in putting out to join the L'Aurores, the schooner abuzz with jubilation.

"A right good mill!" Doud cackled, looking back at the leaping flames.

"You really think so?" Buckle replied, with obvious pleasure.

"Sir, I protest! It should've been my landing," Gilbey said, aggrieved, as the victors boarded *L'Aurore*.

"And lose my first lieutenant?" Kydd said mildly, looking down benignly on his capering men. "I'll have you know it was a close-run thing and events could have turned out in quite another way."

Gilbey did not appear mollified, but for Kydd it had been a resounding success: a prize won even if its cargo had been brought ashore. As a prize recovered it would count as salvage only but then again, with the release of the brig's men, there had been no need to provide crew.

The shipyard set afire would render the port useless as a privateer base and, in any case, the townsfolk would know that, its secret out, it would be under eye from the British fleet now on. And to cap it all, they had in custody one Don Espada, a Spaniard who'd been secretly running things there, to prove the situation.

That night while the seamen were enjoying an extended suppertime with a double tot, Kydd invited his officers to dinner, braving Tysoe's frowns to broach his private cabin stores. The wine was the best he possessed and the officers' cook excelled himself. This was going to be a night to remember.

"Wine with you, sir!" said Curzon to Gilbey, who was rapidly thawing in the happy atmosphere. Further down, Buckle was glowing in new-found respect.

"To Lady Fortune, who's done so handsomely for the Billy Roarers," Gilbey returned. He was never going to allow that Buckle was anything but the child of luck for his achievement. He then turned to Kydd. "In course, what you said about prize accounts is so much catblash?"

Kydd smiled thinly. "I've asked Mr Renzi to look into the matter and his appreciation is that if we grant that it is another vessel entirely, then those who were aboard her must be in the nature of deserters, they still being on the muster-roll of *L'Aurore*. Unhappily, therefore, it would seem that each must choose between a flogging or allowing their shipmates to share in the prize."

Renzi blinked, then offered with solemnity, "Or *L'Aurore*'s captain is court-martialled for misappropration of a prize before it be condemned."

It was a good point: prize rules were strict, and a charge of piracy could be brought against the captain of any King's ship who took possession of a vessel before it had been examined in a vice-admiralty court and declared subject to forfeiture, and therefore made good prize, no matter what the circumstances.

It stilled conversation about the table until Kydd said lightly, "Save only where the ship is a man-o'-war under the flag of an enemy power. And I take *Infanta* to be so, even if in a private line of business."

There was a relieved murmuring about the table but then Owen, the dry Welshman and purser, spoke: "Then it were better our books of account were put in order before our return."

"Books?" Kydd said, puzzled.

"Yes, Captain. Should you have taken up this vessel into your service, then there must be a line of disbursement for stores and equipment. Neither I nor the gunner nor boatswain can be expected to write off items consumed without a proper ticket."

"Oh. Well, what do you recommend, Mr Owen?"

"Why, there's naught to say. The deed is done."

Kydd sighed. The last thing he needed was the prospect of having to explain himself later to a clerk of the cheque concerning the expenditure of funds intended for *L'Aurore* upon another vessel.

"There's nothing I can do?"

"As I said, the books must be squared."

Kydd was irritated by this intrusion into the warmth of the evening. "How will we do that?"

"I can do this, but I must have your predated certificate that *Infanta* is taken up as tender to HMS *L'Aurore*."

A tender. A minor craft set in menial attendance on a much larger, usually a ship-of-the-line when in port, to convey passengers, supplies and generally be at beck and call. Then it dawned: a tender was borne on the books of its mother ship for stores and victualling, but much more important was what it implied.

"You shall have your certificate, Mr Owen."

Kydd grinned as the idea grew to full flower. "And thank you for the steer. Gentlemen, our sainted purser has solved our accounting problems and given us a splendid opportunity at one and the same time."

Kydd raised his glass to the mystified purser. "Do I explain, sir, or will you? No? Then it shall be me."

He had their full attention. "Mr Owen is pointing out that we now have a regular-going tender, just like a battleship. And what do tenders do? They go where they're bid, no questions asked. So if, while we're on patrol in the Mona Passage, it is sent on a whim to, say, twenty degrees north, there's none to gainsay us."

Enjoying the baffled looks around the table, he continued, "It being a rascally part of the world it is naturally armed. Which would be fortunate, should it fall in with an enemy. That is, any enemy."

Smiles began to appear as his drift became apparent. "Which is to say, even hostile merchant vessels who choose to cross its bows, which can never be suffered by any under the King's colours, even if only a paltry tender."

There was open laughter now. "So I must find an officer well acquainted with these coasts who I may trust with the charge of *L'Aurore*'s tender," Kydd concluded. "One not to be daunted by service in a small ship and one of undoubted sagacity in tight circumstances."

He looked about, then allowed his gaze to settle on the hero of the hour. "Mr Buckle, I give you joy of your command. Gentlemen, do raise your glasses to . . . His Majesty's jolly Privateer *Infanta!*"

Chapter 6

It was showy, but Kydd couldn't resist His Majesty's Frigate *L'Aurore* returning to her harbour home of Port Royal proudly at the head of a procession. Not one or two but four prizes followed in her wake at regularly spaced intervals, each with the ensign of the Royal Navy above that of the vanquished. They weren't the largest or most spectacular ever seen, and one in the amount of salvage only, but Kydd was confident it would put the admiral in the right frame of mind when he explained about the tender.

"North settin' current," the master warned, eyeing the less-than-hundred-yard gap between Gun Cay and tiny Rackham Cay. It was a tricky passage, but Kydd knew the current's effect would be offset by the balmy northeasterly. Kendall was right to bring it to his notice but this more direct course had the advantage that their approach would lead them close by the land for all to admire his little show.

They proceeded around Port Royal Point and into Kingston Harbour, punctilious in their salutes. Kydd allowed a smile at the thought of the words of jealousy aboard *Northumberland* at the sight of the pretty frigate arriving with prizes at her tail.

The admiral's flag was at the main, so he could pay his call immediately instead of taking carriage to the residence on the hill. He went below to change, reflecting that he would remember this time in his naval service as one of contentment, the larger war somewhere on the other side of the Atlantic and Bonaparte caged in Europe, powerless to affect this agreeable existence.

His gig put off for the flagship. Kydd had laid out his own money to revarnish the boat and then embellish it with Lincoln green inside, scarlet fittings and a peep of gold-leaf about the carvings of the stern-sheets. If *L'Aurore* was going to be a long-term feature of the Caribbean scene he wanted her to look the part. He mused idly that he should probably give thought to a residence ashore, a place to spend time out of the ship, acquire curios, perhaps, and to throw open for occasions of a social nature.

The boat had nearly reached the flagship and, as he looked about the familiar harbour, he wondered why there seemed to be so many ships. The small naval squadron was the same. It was the merchant shipping that was more numerous, some rafted together at anchor. Were they reluctant to put to sea for some reason? That didn't make sense, for if that was the case the naval ships would be out dealing with whatever the threat was.

He shrugged, and they hooked on at the main-chains. His action had resulted in prizes and he passed over the bulwarks to the keening of the boatswain's call with a light heart.

"Captain." The first lieutenant greeted him, but his features were tense and lined. "I'll see if the admiral is able to see you, sir." He hurried off, leaving Kydd on the quarterdeck.

Something was wrong but he couldn't put his finger on it.

A couple of lieutenants stood together to one side, talking in low tones.

"Boney's master-stroke, I believe," said one, his face grave. "As not to say, a war-winner."

"It's got Dacres in a whirl, right enough," the other agreed. "Helpless, can't do a thing to stop it."

Kydd went over to them. "I've been at sea—what's this about

Bonaparte striking back?" he demanded. He couldn't help recalling Renzi's foreboding that there would be some form of malevolent avenging of Trafalgar—was it now to be revealed?

"Ah, I do think the admiral should give you the news himself, sir."

Before Kydd could press the matter, the first lieutenant returned. "He'll see you now, Captain—if you'll be quick," he added, with embarrassment.

Dacres was at his desk, his flag-lieutenant by his side and two clerks at work nearby. He looked up, distracted. "Kydd. Um, a fine sight, your prizes. Well done. Anything to report?"

"Sir," Kydd began guardedly, "I saw fit to employ my first prize as a tender in the getting of more and—"

"Yes, quite, but we have more pressing concerns at the present time. You've been at sea and won't have heard. Napoleon Bonaparte has made his move, and I cannot deny that it's a great blow to this nation. The man's a devil and a genius."

"But, sir, what is it that—"

"You wouldn't credit it! Conceives of a way to reach out and destroy us here in the Caribbean where all the time we've been living in a fool's Paradise thinking he could not."

"Sir, if you'd—"

"No time to explain it now. Here—take this. It'll tell you everything. We'll be having a council-of-war shortly to see if we can do anything at all to head off the worst, and until then I'll bid you good-day, sir."

Kydd tucked the single sheet he'd been passed into his waistcoat and left. Outside, the first lieutenant was apologetic. "It's not a good time for him right at present. There is a meeting tonight at Spanish Town. Every planter and bigwig in these islands will be there baying for blood—anyone's!"

Consumed by curiosity, it was all Kydd could do to wait until he was seated in his gig on the way back before he drew out the paper.

It was ill-printed on cheap stock and in French, manifestly produced in mass for wide circulation. "From the Imperial Camp at Berlin. Napoleon, Emperor of the French and King of Italy . . ."

It was a decree. He scanned it quickly. To begin with there were nine clauses: aggrieved reasons why his enemy was in breach of international law and usage:

". . . that England does not admit to the right of nations as universally acknowledged by all civilised people . . ." Kydd snorted. The hypocrisy of Bonaparte, whose armies on the march routinely robbed and plundered rather than trouble with a supply train.

And ". . . this conduct in England is worthy of the first ages of barbarism, to benefit her to the detriment of other nations . . ." This was only the usual diatribe fawningly reported by the *Moniteur*—or was it?

The second part was a series of eleven articles to constitute henceforth "the law of empire" for France and her dominions in retaliation.

Riffled by the wind and with the motion of the boat it was difficult to take in all the details from the sheet—maritime law, blockade, prizes and neutral trade. What was it that had caused such consternation? This would need more careful attention than he could give here and he put it away, aware of curious eyes on him.

As soon as he was in his cabin he sent for Renzi.

"Flag's in an uproar, Nicholas." He slapped down the paper.

Renzi scanned it once, then reread it carefully. "A blockade of all of Great Britain? This is unprecedented in history, of course. Blockade is for the purposes of investing a port or ports for a military purpose, not for the strangling of a whole nation."

Kydd got up abruptly. "I'm calling a meeting of all officers. This has to be known. I'd like you to stay."

They appeared suspiciously promptly, and the paper was passed around.

"Barbaric," Curzon said, with studied cynicism. "Here it says every subject of England found anywhere, whatever their rank or condition, is hereby made prisoner of war. So Boney is making war on women and children, then?"

"Yes, but to the main points," Kydd said brusquely. "For the benefit of those without French, could I ask Mr Renzi to summarise?"

"Well, to begin with, the British Isles are declared to be in a state of blockade."

"And?"

"Consequently, all commerce with such in the wider sense is prohibited. This to include such things as correspondence—Bonaparte here is even going to the length of condemning any letter or packet addressed in the English language itself."

"Thank you, Nicholas. The main points?" Kydd prompted.

"All trade or merchandise exchange with England or its possessions is forbidden. This is defined as any property that is in any way to the interest of a subject of the Crown, anywhere in the world, and is subject to confiscation on the spot. Any vessel on the high seas that contains the property of an Englishman is an accomplice to our iniquity and is therefore declared good prize."

Renzi gave a dry smile, adding, "And half the proceeds of such confiscation go to merchants who have suffered at the hands of our evil frigates and privateers."

It didn't get a response.

"And, finally, it seems that a vessel of any flag touching first at an English or colonial port is to be treated as if it flew the British flag and is condemned."

There was silence as the implications became clear. "This is nothing less than a complete lock-down of England," Curzon said in awe. "Nothing can move."

"The admiral is in a taking, I'll confide," Kydd said. "There's really nothing he can do. We're stretched thin and he can't possibly provide more escorts. I'd think Barbados is in the same way. Weaken the squadron by taking escorts and we lie open to being crushed by a raiding battle-fleet."

"In this station we'd be in a similar moil, I'd think," Curzon came in, "should we be asked to provide escorts. We've nowhere near enough, and if that's what they have to do all the time, then the privateers will take their chance to return in strength, the vermin!"

There was little point in going further in a formal way so Kydd extended an invitation to supper that night where discussion over wine would allow feelings to be expressed.

He turned to Renzi. "Nicholas, there's to be some kind of meeting in Spanish Town, the chief people of the island to muster together to contemplate developments. I dare to say the Navy will not be invited in particular. I'm wondering if you can perhaps lay alongside your brother and let me know which way the wind blows?"

"It's ruination! We're to be pauperised!" The anguished voice rang out clear above the bedlam in Merchant's Hall.

"Sit down, you ninny!" Renzi's brother shouted in exasperation. "We'll work something out—but only if we keep our heads.

"I do apologise, Nicholas. They're rare exercised and can't see that this is a time for cool thinking if ever there was."

Fuming, the chairman threw down his gavel and folded his arms while he waited for order as other despairing shouts echoed about.

"What about demurrage?" a hoarse voice near them boomed. "Costing me guineas an hour, stap me."

"I'll have y' know I'm out for two hundred thousands if I can't get away this season's yield."

It was becoming impossible.

The one point of agreement had been that the decree struck at the very heart of their enterprise—and at the moment they could see not a thing they could do about it. Angry and frightened, they were lashing out at anything.

A neatly dressed planter with a spade beard twisted round in his seat and said soberly, "You'll be selling up by year's end, Richard, mark my words."

"Damn Bonaparte's hide!" Laughton ground out. "Just past a difficult year and now we're to lose everything. It's insupportable."

He stood up suddenly. "No point in staying here just to hear all this wailing. Let's go, Nicholas."

They shuffled down the row to leave; the bearded planter got up and left with them.

Outside Laughton drew a deep breath. "There's no denying it. We're in a funk. I can't see a way out of this."

He paced ahead in a frenzy of bitterness and frustration. "With no warning—out of the blue so we couldn't prepare. I rather fear . . ."

Renzi tried to sound encouraging. "The Navy can find you escorts, brother. And none can stand against our frigates."

Laughton turned back abruptly. "Spare me your nostrums, Nicholas. It's far too serious for that. Convoys only start at Barbados. How do you suppose that, with several hundred individual sailings a month from all over the Caribbean, they're going to find ships enough to stay by each one? It's nonsense and you know it."

"I only wanted to—"

"I'm sorry I spoke hastily, Nicholas." He managed a grin. "You've a fine mind and deserve to know why it's so monstrously difficult for us."

He paced on for a few more steps, then said, "You're concerned for your naval situation, and rightly so. We're on quite another plane and our worries more direct. Have you seen in Kingston Harbour, brother, the quantities of ships lying in idleness? You put it down to our fear of what Boney has waiting out there on the high seas. For us this is the least of our concerns, believe me, the very least."

"I don't understand, Richard. I take it they have full cargoes, ready to sail—then what other reason can there be to keep them back?"

"Dear fellow, you cannot see it, and can't be expected to. The sting in Napoleon's decree lies not in the threat to destroy our ships, which I doubt he can achieve, but in its very different and brutally effective result. Nicholas, he's closed the continent to us, destroyed our market. Those ships are laden with our sugar well enough but cannot sail—they have no destination. The commercial paper written against their safe arrival is worthless on both sides—we cannot deliver, therefore to sail is useless."

"How is it closed, exactly?"

"Article four: all property of an English subject is declared lawful prize, of any origin and wherever found. What this means is that no neutral will touch an English cargo or be deemed an accomplice, especially since the decree additionally states that any neutral touching at a port of England or its colonies is deemed to be in collusion for the purposes of trade and will automatically be seized."

"Do pardon my ignorance on the matter, Richard, but the continent has been for some time under the heel of Napoleon. How, then, until now was it possible for an Englishman to sustain trading links with it?"

"In course by the usual business practices. We have our own commercial agents in ports all over Europe, issuing notes against banks in England for our cargoes. These were carried in neutral bottoms and, while attracting the usual Customs exactions, were otherwise left alone. It may surprise you to learn that by this means it's been possible for me to trade with France itself."

"It does indeed, dear fellow. Especially so since Mr Pitt's Traitorous Correspondence Act treats trading with the enemy as a crime of high treason."

"As with all things in business, brother, do read the small type with diligence. The Act does not forbid the trading, rather its nature. Matériel of use to the military is of course prohibited but nowhere do I see sugar so proscribed. A little thought will reveal that the draining of French gold to pay for English produce has much to commend it, and there are Midland manufactories who are getting rich supplying to France and its subjects what they crave."

Renzi came back, "It did cross my mind that, in your own case, our assault and taking of the French islands here, together with our diligent hunting down of their shipping, does favour you with a receptive market and high prices."

"True, we've done well—but now that's a thing of the past. All British subjects in French territory are made prisoners of war. There go our commercial agents, leaving none to negotiate business. No neutrals will carry our goods—and that includes cargo from other sugar-producing countries around the Caribbean, for if we buy an interest in their crop it renders the whole subject to confiscation and they won't allow it."

Renzi gave a grim half-smile. The intricate web of international commercial relations was now shattered, the delicate threads of trust and faith at the core of international trading, which allowed the continuation of life-giving commerce in the midst of global war. It wouldn't be the sugar industry only, even if it was the biggest wealth producer, but also the goods pouring out of the factories as a result of the revolution of industry in which Britain was leading the world.

"Then there's insurance," Laughton went on bitterly. "When premiums go much above ten per centum, profit on the voyage dwindles to nothing and at present, for fear of what Boney will do next, the rates are beyond reason."

"So you are at a stand, Richard."

His brother gave a bleak smile. "Except that it is not to be borne. While our ships lie idle we must pay a *per diem* demurrage to allow our sugar to rot in the hold, an expense we cannot carry indefinitely. Yet we cannot sail for lack of market and increasing insurance rates. To sail—or not to sail. Nicholas, this is a dilemma for us. It makes trivial a decision such as to go with sugar or is it to be coffee, and is for myself the hardest I've ever faced."

Aboard *L'Aurore* Kydd listened soberly to Renzi's account of the meeting in Spanish Town. It seemed his friend's sense of foreboding had been fulfilled. Napoleon had delivered his devilish counter-stroke and, because it was in the realm of commerce and economics, the Navy were helpless to do anything about it.

"I can find no comfort to offer Richard other than that we carry on to do our duty," he told Renzi. It was a strange and disturbing feeling, being under threat of an enemy that could not be settled by sailing out to meet him in battle.

"Meanwhile our orders are the same. Keep the seas to put down any privateers or such as show their faces—although with none of our shipping abroad I can't see how they'll bother."

Then he handed a letter across. "This morning's mail. From our late and much lamented third lieutenant. As my confidential secretary I think you're entitled to see it, old chap."

It was in Bowden's strong, neat writing but on the front and reverse it had "in confidence" written in capitals across the top.

"To you. And asking for advice."

"Yes—read on."

> *. . . and so I suppose I'm asking you for counsel. I know my duty, that is clear, but the situation aboard has worsened to an alarming degree and I'm vexed to know what is the best course to take in the circumstances for the sake of all concerned . . .*

"Tyrell. Coming it the tyrant still."

> *. . . the topman came down from aloft as bid, but before he could be seized by the master-at-arms*

he cast himself into the sea and was lost. The four men on deck who called out in horror were taken and are to be flogged for contumacy. Moreover the entire starboard watch are under stoppage of grog for a week, occasioned by his hearing wry talk at their supper and none to own to it, and are as a consequence mutinous and intractable.

What is most disturbing is what is happening in the wardroom. They are a sullen, moody crew, for all believe the other is carrying stories to Captain Tyrell, for he knows what each is doing and saying and they durst not venture an honest opinion. I keep my counsel if asked, for if pressed it would be difficult not to betray what I think to be the true reason, that is, the captain is constantly prowling and spying on us privily . . .

Troubled, Renzi looked up from the letter. "These are not the actions of a balanced individual, dear fellow. Has he—"

"Go on."

. . . while ashore he drinks himself to oblivion, but at sea he never touches a drop that ever I've seen. But for all that, the night watches are much put out of countenance because it is his practice to roam the decks under cover of dark—but curiously, if he encounters any man, he does not notice, looking by him and pacing on. Mr Kydd, I'm concerned that should we fall in with the enemy we shall not make a good accounting . . .

"You'll find some position he should take, will you not?"

"How can I? Tyrell is captain under God and has done no wrong by the Articles of War. It's the sea service and he wouldn't be the first hard-horse captain hated by those under him. And on deck at night—does every mortal always command a good sleep?"

"Still, I take pity on poor Bowden."

"If Tyrell had friends by him they'd ease his course but he has none."

"Of his own doing," Renzi said drily.

"He has an unfortunate manner, true, but does it make him a lesser commander? As a King's officer Bowden has a loyalty to his captain that must prevail over all. There is no other course."

"So. We sail this afternoon," Kydd said, helping himself to another warm roll. "I'm to circumnavigate this island of Jamaica, our presence a deterrent and comfort, I'm told. I rather fancy it will be a leisurely voyage, time for once not being of the essence."

Tysoe noiselessly cleared away the breakfast things and went for more coffee.

"The only question to be faced is whether this is to be conducted clockwise or the other. What do you think, old trout?"

"We've seen much of the east, would not a west-about route now be in order?"

The coffee arrived and Kydd had an idea. "Tysoe—you hail from hereabouts, don't you?"

"From this island, yes, sir," he said quietly.

"Which part, if you don't mind my asking?"

"I was born at Breadnut Island Pen, which is in Westmoreland County, sir," he answered softly.

"Um, and where's that?"

"Out to the west, as far as you may go."

"Tysoe, how would you like to visit your mother and father? If they should be in good health, that is."

He held still and then whispered, "That would be good, sir, very good."

"How long has it been since last you saw them?"

"Sir, I was eight years old when taken from them."

"Eight! How so?"

"A captain in the Navy thought to take home to England a little black page-boy. It was the fashion then, sir."

"But your parents—"

"Were slaves, sir."

"Oh, I see. Er, what happened to you after then, Tysoe?" Kydd asked. He had acquired him years ago in Canada as a junior lieutenant, when no other would have him as servant, and realised now that he knew little of his previous history.

"I was in service with the Duke of Rutland until I . . ."

Became too big to be a pretty page-boy, thought Kydd. But then how would it have been to grow up the only black boy below stairs with the servants, and no one to look out for him? There must be depths to Tysoe's character that he'd never suspected.

"Then I was seen and taken up by a sea officer who was of a noble family and wished to have about him one of polite accomplishments, if you'll pardon the expression, sir."

"Captain Codrington?"

"No, sir. That was later, when I came under his notice and he arranged to have me as his personal chamberlain in *Tremendous* 74, in the Mediterranean," he said, with quiet pride.

It must have been a bitter blow when the aristocratic Codrington had died of a stroke in his own great cabin, leaving Tysoe in Halifax without employment to fend for himself. He must have felt he'd come down in the world when the raw Lieutenant Kydd had asked for him.

"And now you're here in *L'Aurore,* and with more sea service than myself, I'd wager."

"Oh, no, sir, that cannot be," Tysoe said shyly.

"Well, we're off to west Jamaica this afternoon. Have you a thought for what you'll give them both?"

Leaving the feverish atmosphere of Kingston, *L'Aurore* spread her wings for the open sea. As always, Kydd felt a lift of the heart at the first rise and fall of a live deck responding to a grand seascape—sparkling, clear and limitless. Orders were essentially simple: to show themselves, to be seen for what she was—a powerful agent of the Crown, able to express the resolve of Britain to defend what was hers wherever it might be.

The muted talk of Curzon and Gilbey on the other side of the quarterdeck, however, was of Napoleon Bonaparte and his war-winning strategy.

Away from the Hellshire hills and past Portland Point, they went looking into the wide reaches of Long Bay, with the prospect of a night at anchor off the steep sides of the Santa Cruz Mountains.

The wind dropped and they were left to enjoy the warmth and splendour of a Caribbean evening, gazing directly into the vast broadness of a spectacular tawny orange sunset. It was difficult to conceive of a wider world locked in war while sitting in wardroom chairs on the quarterdeck, watching the majestic sight with a glass of punch in hand and exotic scents wafting out from the land on the soft breeze.

The next day saw a leisurely sail past marshes and mountains until they reached the tiny old sugar port of Savanna La Mar. Keeping well off the reef-strewn approaches, Kydd sent in a boat, which returned with no news of strange sail and they sailed on.

Tysoe maintained a dignified manner but it was surprising how often he needed to adjust the stern windows, be on deck to check the direction of the wind and linger as they rounded South Negril Point and glided past the lonely wilderness of the Great Morass towards the north.

Long before their anchor plunged into the impossibly lovely sea-green transparency of Bloody Bay, Tysoe was ready on deck. He was dressed plainly but that did nothing to conceal his patrician bearing and gentle manner. The bundle by his side was not large but well tied, his face unreadable as he surveyed the unexceptional seashore.

"It's been a long time . . ." Kydd said, unsure how to bridge the distance between the captain of a King's ship and his valet—and also how to reach out to someone whose parents might still be slaves.

"Yes."

"Um, your parents . . . are they still, er, slaves?"

Tysoe tore his gaze away and said softly, "No, sir. The older Mr Thistlewood in his kindness manumitted them. They have a small patch to grow and sell foodstuffs and they are content."

Relieved, Kydd said more briskly, "Well, I find that the boatswain requires time to, er, rattle down the larboard main-shrouds, which will mean we must delay sailing a further day. Be sure to be back aboard by the daybreak after next. Will that be enough?" he added, in a softer tone.

"It will, I'm sure. And I'm beholden to you for your thoughtfulness, sir."

"Well, here's something I want you to give them from me," he said, handing over a small package. "Off you go—you know the way?"

There was a gentle smile. "I do."

He boarded the boat, and as the crew bent to their oars, he looked back once. Kydd was startled to see the glint of tears in the eyes of the man he had known for so long, and at the same time had never known.

"A fine thing you did today, dear fellow," Renzi murmured.

"A good man, it was nothing, really."

Collecting himself, Kydd said, "On another matter entirely, it seems to me a damned waste of splendid scenery were we not to do something about it. I have it in mind to call a Ropeyarn Sunday for the hands tomorrow, and shall we step ashore? I've a yen for a spell on land."

Was it the wafting breeze carrying the warm scent of sun-touched flowers or was it the sight of the lazy sweep of pristine beach beyond the crystal depths? Kydd was gripped by the sudden feeling that he and his ship were under notice—that these days of idyll and beauty couldn't possibly last and were about to be cut short by the brutality of war. It brought to his mind the ironic name of this place of tranquillity and allure: Bloody Bay.

"Nicholas, I've a sense we're not long to enjoy this paradise and I mean to make the most of our situation."

"Odd. I have the same sentiment," Renzi murmured. "And the same hankering."

Kydd smiled. "Ask the boatswain to lay aft, if you please. I have plans."

At dawn the first boats headed inshore, over the pellucid water, to hiss to a stop in the bright sand. Laughing delightedly, barefoot sailors splashed ashore with gear and, under directions from a jovial Oakley, began setting up for the day.

First there was the pavilion: a masterly contrivance that saw a topsail spread to vertical oars and robustly stayed, with, inside, tables of barrels and planks. Then, in deference to the officers, another was constructed at a suitable distance with the softer cotton of boat sails, and well equipped with chairs, a table and items of civilised ornamentation suspended decorously from the leech cringles of the sail.

It was time: the signal went up and the remaining L'Aurores swarmed ashore. Wearing togs of every description, they were ferried to the beach where they broke loose, like children, running up and down, splashing each other and behaving as utterly unlike man-o'-war's men as was possible. Some had brought their hammocks, which they tied between palm trees, while others lay in the shade, smoking their clay pipes and yarning.

The inevitable cricket pitch was laid out and a noisy game of larboard watch against starboard began, while still others simply wandered along the near-mile-length of the beach, revelling in the break with discipline.

When Kydd arrived, Rundle the cook was in despair at the arrangements. "How's I going to bring the scran alongside without I have m' coppers?" He groaned.

Trooping back aboard to be fed was not to be contemplated by free spirits. "Toss the salt pork on a fire," one sailor offered.

"Burgoo an' bananas," came in another.

"Well, what do the folks around here do for a bite, then?" a third said in exasperation.

Nobody seemed to have an answer—but Kydd knew someone who would. "Where's Mr Buckle?"

"Why, he's officer-of-the-watch in *L'Aurore,* sir!" As junior that was of course where he was, lord of a near-deserted vessel.

"He's to step ashore and report."

Buckle soon saw what was needed. "It's a barbacoa as is used, sir. May I . . . ?"

"Certainly—you're in charge."

In the centre of the beach seamen were set to excavate a pit and light a fire to which was added a number of large stones to get white hot. Others trotted respectfully behind Buckle as he approached the curious villagers, who had collected to take in the diverting sight of "kooner-men" rollicking ashore. In fluent native Creole, he negotiated the purchase of a pig and had it slaughtered, dressed and wrapped in banana leaves.

It was placed in the pit and thick maguey leaves were piled on top. By the time the morning had developed into a beautiful day, mouthwatering aromas were already drifting about the beach.

That wasn't the end of Mr Buckle's talents. He endeared himself to the seamen when he fashioned a strop around his girth and used it to shin up a palm tree to cut down coconuts for all hands.

After that it seemed churlish to Kydd to send him back to exile in the frigate so Buckle took delight in instructing the stewards on the most delectable ingredients for a punch and how the old-time pirates had made a buccan, the wooden frame on which meats were smoked to preserve them.

As Kydd lazed in his chair he felt that life needed little more to achieve perfection. The enveloping warmth of the sun, tempered by the breeze over the sea, worked on his body and he eased into a delightful torpor. He had only to open his eyes and there was his trim frigate no more than a couple of hundred yards before him; the thought that he was actually being paid and honoured to take the lovely vessel across the ocean, away from the rain and cold of England to this Elysium, tugged his lips into a smile.

Renzi had a book, which he was reading with a smile of contentment, and on the table was their punch and exotic tropical fruits.

Left alone with his thoughts Kydd drifted off to sleep as the heat increased to midday and the noisy rollicking on the beach subsided.

As the afternoon sea breeze began gently to blow, the pig was at last declared well and truly cooked. It was quickly surrounded by ravenous sailors, but Buckle had it well organised: following Kydd's lead, the wardroom nobly declined their droits of the joint and took equal shares with the men. The pig's left side was declared for the larboard watch, the right for the starboard. Further, in accordance with parts-of-ship, the fo'c'sle hands took the forward portion, the waisters the midships and the afterguard the rump end. To even things out, choicer cuts were smaller in size but could be bartered for larger but less favoured pieces.

The entertainment this provided lasted for some time, helped by a ceremonial issue of two-water grog from a tub decorated with exotic blossoms. The beach, facing directly into the setting sun, was then treated to the majesty of another Caribbean sunset. The evening drew quickly in, a warm and sensuous tropical dusk tinged with violet. All too soon shadows deepened and it was time to return to the ship before it became too dark to see.

As Kydd had intended, it had been a time to remember, to be put away tenderly for future times when their mortal existence itself would be under threat.

The following morning *L'Aurore* readied for sea.

Kydd was prepared to be generous in the interpretation of "day-break" but when the sun was well up, the ship gone to sea-watches and the first lieutenant pointedly checking his fob watch, it was time to take action.

It was unlike Tysoe to be late—he, who would berate the steward for bringing up the breakfast a minute past six bells: it was incomprehensible that he would be adrift from leave.

"I'll not sail without the villain," Kydd swore. A quick note was written, politely requesting the plantation owner of Breadnut Island Pen to remind Tysoe of his duty to be back aboard and this was given to a midshipman to deliver.

Hours later he had not returned. "This is insupportable, sir," Gilbey complained. "A King's ship held on account of a laggardly servant and dawdling reefer! We have to get about our business—leave 'em both to cool their heels until we're next this way."

"You're forgetting yourself, Mr Gilbey," Kydd retorted. "Mr Tysoe is ashore on a mission."

"Indeed, sir?" There was disbelief in his tone that rankled with Kydd.

"Yes, he is! If there's to be a slave revolt, who better to send in to discover it?" This was at least half true; Kydd had conjured up the excuse for later, if any at the admiral's office queried his resting at anchor in this distant quarter.

Nevertheless there had to be a limit. Mentally resolved to weigh anchor at midday he was relieved to see the boat return shortly before, but it held only the dusty figure of young Searle.

"I'm to give you this," the lad said, handing over a note.

It was short, but to the point.

> *On the matter of this Tysoe, I thank you, Captain, for your politeness in returning my property, one Quamino. Yr obedt etc. Daniel Thistlewood, owner.*

"What does he mean by this?" Kydd said in astonishment. "Did you see Tysoe, at all?"

"I did, sir. In the house only for a moment, then he was sent away, sharp like."

For some reason Tysoe had been mistaken for a runaway slave and had been taken up. Time was short and this needed settling quickly at the highest level. Kydd saw there was only one way to get it done: to go himself.

"How far is it?" he demanded.

"Oh, at the foot o' the mountains, 'bout four miles, sir. I had to walk," Searle said apologetically. "I didn't have the coin to hire a horse 'n' trap."

Swearing to himself, Kydd told Gilbey, "Stand down sea-watches. I'm going to fetch the rascal. Mr Searle will accompany me. Do you wish to come, Mr Renzi?"

As always, even a hundred yards into the land the air changed—from the sea where at least a zephyr could nearly always be relied on to a still, enclosing heat, wreathed with the odour of dust and animal droppings. Kydd was thankful when the hired cart got under way and there was a breeze.

He waved away the inevitable flies, reflecting sourly that making even a single mile out to the open sea they would all vanish, defeated by the cleanliness of a ship.

But he was here because of Tysoe. It was not only the recollection of years of faithful service, but also the intolerable thought of his noble self spending the rest of his days as a plantation slave.

Beside him, Renzi said nothing, calmly observing the scrubby landscape. Kydd was darkly amused to see Searle sitting bolt upright, keeping "eyes in the boat," as if with the captain in his gig.

The cart ground on until at last there was a hedge of sorts each side of the road, leading to the plantation Great House, a sprawling white edifice with a dark-varnished veranda and set about with blossoms.

They descended at the entrance and a white-clad houseboy appeared. "Captain Kydd to see Mr Thistlewood," Kydd told him, but a figure emerged from the house and pushed him aside.

"I'm Thistlewood," snapped the thick-set man in leather boots and wide hat, his face hard and deeply tanned. "What's your business?"

Kydd removed his hat politely. "I'm here to set right a little matter, if I may. I gave leave for my manservant to visit his parents and he's failed to return. I wonder if you could—"

"That's this Tysoe, then. Surprises me it needs a Navy captain to come looking."

"Yes, that's the fellow. Do tell him that we're about to sail and—"

"He's not going back."

"I beg your pardon?"

"He's not about to leave here, cully. He's my property and he stays." The man's eyes narrowed and he folded his arms.

"I think you may have mistaken his identity. He is—"

"I know who he is—there's no confusion. He found his parents. Then they all fell about weeping and the like. He's their son, without any kind o' doubt."

Kydd shook his head in bewilderment. "Then if you know who he is, why can't he return with us?"

Thistlewood gave a hard smile. "Seems to me you have a strange notion of slave law, Mr Sailor. That there is known as Quamino, a piccaninny born of slaves, right here in my father's pen. The law says therefore he's a slave himself, property of his master. There's no going up against the law now, is there?"

Renzi spoke: "We happen to know they were manumitted years ago."

"You're right."

"So he's a free man."

"We're talking his folks, not him. They're free right enough."

"If—"

"The deed of manumission. You want to see it? There's Phibbah and Cuffee, no mention of Quamino. He were illegally borne off to be a page-boy well before they were freed, so by any law o' the land he's still a bound slave."

It was all too clear. The casual handing over of one of the many plantation children those years ago had come back full circle to trap Tysoe. Thistlewood had seen his chance to acquire an accomplished houseboy to flaunt in planter society, and the law was on his side.

Frustration boiled up in Kydd. "I've a King's ship wants to sail. You're delaying me by this tomfoolery! I demand that—"

"Nothing stopping you. Sail away."

"I won't let it rest, sir! This is nonsense and you know it!"

"I think not! Why, I see I've a case for damages. Yes—loss of earnings in a slave unlawfully detained for . . . let me see . . . thirty years? Your admiral is going to be pleased with you, he gets a lawsuit against the Navy that carried him off . . ."

It was getting nowhere. Despairing, Kydd said, "Well, er, I'll buy him back."

"He's not for sale. Now, I'm sure you're busy chasing pirates or such, so I won't detain you any longer."

Kydd threw a beseeching look at Renzi.

"Ah, then we'll make our farewells." Renzi said smoothly, "with our earnest apologies for taking up your time. Come, gentlemen."

Aghast, Kydd hesitated but Renzi was walking to the cart. Then he stopped and turned, with a disarming smile. "Oh, I'd forgotten. Just one small detail we'll have to trouble you with. It shouldn't take long."

"What detail? I haven't got all day."

"Why, as secretary to the ship, I can't have loose ends to disturb my captain later, can I?"

"Get on with it."

"It's the little matter of Tysoe's oath."

"Oath?"

"Yes," Renzi said, brow creased in a clerkly furrow. "You see, on enlisting in any ship of the Royal Navy a man has to swear to serve the King. Now, all I need is an affidavit signed by Tysoe that he no longer wishes to bear allegiance to His Majesty, this being countersigned in a release by his captain, and he will be free to take up duties with you immediately."

"He's a slave, damn it. Has no right to go swearing oaths! He's still my property and—"

"Unfortunately, the oath was sworn, whether in error or no. And the one to King George may not be put aside. It has prior standing over any other in the kingdom. Why do you think deserters are hanged at the yardarm? It is because they have violated their oath to the sovereign. We don't want that happening to your slave now, do we?"

"God rot me! If every slave was allowed to enlist we'd be—"

"They are not, Mr Thistlewood," said Renzi, clearly pained by his language. "This is why the law does disallow it."

"So—"

"It is clearly stated that should a slave or apprentice, or any bound by law to a master, attempt to decamp by enlisting, then the master may on representing the case claim him back, with costs against the captain."

"Then—"

"Providing he does so within the span of thirty days. Our muster-roll has no evidence that any such claim was made against the person of Tysoe. Therefore he was entered in full as a bona-fide member of the ship's company."

"So you're saying—"

"Do present this man that we may hear the revoking of his oath. Then I'm sure Captain Kydd will be happy to initial his release—won't you, sir?"

Thistlewood saw his answer on Kydd's face. "I'm not letting him go—get off my property now or I'll set the dogs loose," he snarled.

"Oh dear." Kydd grinned. "It seems we have here an attempt to conceal a deserter. I do believe I'm quite within my rights to use lawful force to recover same. Mr Searle, go to the first lieutenant and ask him to land five hundred men—armed. I mean to arrest this villain."

"Aye aye, sir!"

"Wait! I'll get him—but I'm after compensation."

"For a piccaninny?" Renzi said disapprovingly. "A child under the age of ten is considered a liability, not an asset, Mr Thistlewood. Rather, the Crown should be seeking recompense from you in the article of his bringing up. Now, does this mean we have to . . . ?"

As *L'Aurore* heeled to a fine sea breeze Tysoe brought in their wine, as if nothing whatsoever had happened that day.

"Thank you, Tysoe," Kydd said courteously, as he always did, but he didn't fail to catch the glimmer of feeling that passed unacknowledged between them.

In fine good humour, he chuckled, and said to Renzi, "Topping it the lawyer, Nicholas. I didn't know you had it in you."

"Ah, well, it was all I could think of at the time."

"Does it mean anything?"

"Not as far as I know. I made it up as I went along—it seemed to fadge."

It was raining. Not in the sense that an Englishman would recognise but a white mist drifting across the surface of the sea. It could be seen from the comfort of his cabin prettily stippling the water outside the sweep of his stern windows, while on the upper deck it would bring a pleasant cooling to the men on watch; the sun-warmed planking would be gently steaming and the lower edges of each water-darkened sail busily dripping along its length.

They were in no hurry. As visibility was obscured they had shortened to topsails while, in this northeaster, they made an offing away from the reef-strewn northern coast of Jamaica.

When the showers lifted to a thinning sprinkle they were quite unprepared for the sight of a ship some distance away in the eye of the wind.

Kydd, called on deck, snatched the telescope from the officer-of-the-watch and trained it carefully. With all friendly merchant shipping at a standstill in port, this could be only one of three: a French frigate, one of their own patrolling frigates or an enemy privateer.

For reasons of size this was not a privateer and for a certainty no other British frigate had reason to trespass on their patrol line. It had to be the enemy.

His heart beat faster. This was how it always began, out of the blue on a quiet day, a sudden sighting, a swift confrontation, then danger and death.

"We're to join action shortly, I believe, Mr Gilbey. Men to quarters as soon as you may, if you please."

The next few minutes would be revealing. Would their opponent fight or fly? *L'Aurore* was as close to the wind as she could lie—being directly upwind the situation depended greatly on whether the other decided to turn and bear down on them, in which case they could look to broadsides within no more than an hour, the enemy being in the position of choosing their course of attack. If that happened, there would be no reason to loose courses, the larger driving sails, for almost always combat took place under topsails. For now, they would keep them set as they were.

Then another curtain of misty rain spread across, and when it thinned and cleared they had their answer.

And it was a puzzler. The ship was now considerably to the right of where it had been, under full sail, its course directly for the land.

Kydd raised the telescope. Broadside on, every detail of the other became plain—and he had his explanation. This was no warship: it was a merchantman—a large one and making to flee inshore as fast as it could. A Frenchman desperate to break out to the Atlantic with a cargo of colonial sugar, so much needed in the motherland.

He rubbed his hands in glee as he announced the news to cheers from the quarterdeck.

"You may stand down the hands, Mr Gilbey." This was now merely a chase.

It was odd that the vessel had not tried to lose itself in the open expanse of the Cuba Passage but, then, it probably reasoned that it didn't stand a chance against a predatory frigate and was heading instinctively for the nearest land, hoping to shake them off in the shallows.

This was probably the better decision, for *L'Aurore* at that time was stretching out on the starboard tack. To close with their prey, not only had they to put about on the other tack, but as well set their big courses abroad on all masts first.

The ship made the coast and had just disappeared on the far side of Pedro Point by the time they had started closing with it, some hours behind. Impatiently, Kydd waited for the rocky bluffs to pass, opening up the long north coast of Jamaica—and their quarry. But it was nowhere to be seen.

Frustratingly, the twisting coastline was deeply indented, beaches and coves endlessly stretching into the distance. This was what the wily captain was counting on—with local knowledge, a hideaway in one, such that his pursuer would be delayed, looking into them all.

Then Kydd realised he had a trump card. "Mr Buckle!" he hailed down the deck forward.

The young man hurried back from his station at the fore-mast. "Sir?"

"Should you be fleeing a hunter, where would you head?"

"A'tween us and Montego Bay, why, there's only two places will take a full-rigged ship. Tom Piper's Bay the larger, Mosquito Cove the smaller. And my money's on the last."

When the frigate opened up the first bay they saw right into its mile or more depth but with no result. They sailed onwards, on Buckle's advice ignoring the many smaller ones until they came up with Mosquito Cove. It was narrower but just as deep and they could see into it completely—but when they looked, right to the end, there was nothing.

As they prepared to get under way again there was murmuring about the deck and Buckle looked crestfallen, but then he brightened. "I remember there's a small watering place inside past the narrows on the left. If he's there and warps close in we won't be able to see him from seaward. Sir—he's in there!"

It had to be—to go to ground so promptly when there was nowhere else.

Kydd thought quickly. If it was to be a cutting out it could be tricky in the narrow shallows, and if there was a better way . . .

"Launch and cutter in the water, both with carronades. Lively, now!"

While they were being hoisted out he had a quiet word with the boats' crews, who quickly caught on. When *L'Aurore* shook out sail, the two boats pulled strongly for their positions—out of sight, one either side of the entrance.

Any interested observer would notice that, after a while, *L'Aurore* had tired of the pursuit of her vanished prey and had put about, returning down the coast whence she'd come.

Two hours after the frigate had disappeared there was movement—and through the narrow entrance emerged a wary merchantman under full sail. Like a bolt slamming shut, the two boats tugged hard on their oars, coming to a stop in the middle of the entrance before slewing around—to face out, each with a loaded carronade and effectively barring the way back.

And *L'Aurore* had already wheeled about in anticipation and now came down to claim her prize.

Kydd could not resist the urge to board the vessel himself: he wanted to meet her captain, who had proved both cool and intelligent and, but for Buckle, would have been able to make good his escape.

As they approached the disconsolate vessel, Kydd felt the first stirrings of unease. Even from this distance, the ship didn't have the feel of a Frenchman or a Spanish. She had an indefinable alien air about her, the cut of the sails, the lead of the working rigging, and when they came alongside he was sure.

It was an English ship.

As he swung over the bulwarks, there was no mistaking the vessel's master, who was standing by the main-mast with an expression of disbelief.

"Captain Kydd, Royal Navy," he said, with just a trace of irritation. "It was a merry dance you led us, sir, my congratulations."

"As did you, old chap! 'Pon my word, a King's ship strange to these waters and with every appearance of a damned Frenchy!"

"Which was that, sir?"

"I thought all the world would have heard. *Étoile* 32, Captain

Sieyès out of La Rochelle, new sent to harass our Caribbean interests and already struck."

"No, I hadn't heard. Now, you'll oblige me with your papers, if you please . . ."

The rest of the boarding passed off without comment and ended with a shared Madeira in the saloon.

When Kydd returned to his ship he had much to think on and, first, the existence of a French commerce-raiding frigate in these waters, a serious development, which would be causing a deal of concern to Dacres. That it resembled his own French-built vessel was an inconvenience, frightening the innocent, but it couldn't be helped.

What was more troubling was that, from what he'd heard, the standing of the bottled-up British merchantmen had changed drastically.

Commercial pressures had risen above fear of the unknown. While the L'Aurores had been disporting at leisure, one ship had plucked up the courage to sail come what may. Others had realised that if it won through to any kind of market it could set its own prices, an intolerable position for those left. They had sailed together, some risking a voyage without insurance, putting out in the desperate hope they wouldn't be seen in the more than thousand-mile passage to the convoy rendezvous at Barbados.

As the word spread, from every sugar-producing port others would be joining the mass flight—an impossible number to protect. The French frigate and the ever-present privateers would, with great satisfaction, swoop to the kill.

All feelings of diversion and languor fell away. This was the new war and unquestionably *L'Aurore* was critical to it. It was probably the best course to return as soon as he could to Port Royal for orders—but they were on the north coast of Jamaica on the opposite side. There was little for it but to reach the eastern end by long, tedious boards in the Cuba Passage and call at Port Morant, the naval dispatch station, to see if anything had changed drastically in the meantime.

The atmosphere had altered in *L'Aurore:* the jollity of the past days had evaporated for it was plain to all that the balance had shifted to the defensive and they were in the front line. And if this French frigate was with another—they often hunted in pairs—they could at any moment be fighting for their lives.

In a near calm they reached Port Morant, at last to be met by an advice-boat with a general order that wherever *L'Aurore* was to be found she should be sent with all urgency back to Port Royal. The war had caught fire.

Chapter 7

No sooner had *L'Aurore* rounded Port Royal Point than her pennant number shot up on the flagship—captain to repair on board immediately. Kydd had expected this and, as *L'Aurore* glided to her anchorage, her gig was already lowering.

"Where the devil have you been, sir?" Dacres greeted him, and when he tried to answer brushed him off with, "Belay that, we've a pretty problem on our hands. Sit down."

As Kydd had already found out, after one or two had put to sea the rest of the merchantmen had scrambled to follow. "Never mind we can't protect 'em, they have to do it." Dacres glared at Kydd as though it was his fault, adding, "And now they're being taken."

"Enemy frigate?"

"You've heard? Yes, they've sent a pair of raiders—a 32 and a 28—under a dasher of a captain from La Rochelle, Sieyès. Damn desperate timing for us, I thought." His tone hardened. "They have to be stopped. Losses at this scale are not to be borne, sir."

But if the Navy was to be employed in escorting, it could not be on patrol—a dilemma for the admiral that could only be solved by the removal of the threat. Kill the enemy frigates and the Caribbean could revert back quickly to its previous relative peace.

Dacres continued, "I have every one of my cruisers out after them, save *Anson* and yourself. Now you'll have my orders before sundown to put yourself under Lydiard's command, and the pair of you will have the Windward Passage and north of Jamaica to yourselves. You're to store this hour and I'll expect you to keep the seas in all weathers until they're found and put down."

All weathers—this was the tail end of the hurricane season . . . What was very plain was that while their Caribbean trade was so vulnerable this pair had to be hunted down, whatever it took.

Kydd lost no time in setting *L'Aurore* to storing and took the opportunity of going to *Anson* to confer. She was of forty-four guns, one of the class of heavy frigates cut down from a ship-of-the-line to a single gun-deck. Pellew had gone on to glory in one, *Indefatigable,* and others had since distinguished themselves around the world. They had every chance of success—if they found their quarry.

"Kydd? Good to meet you at last." Lydiard had a jovial manner, his twinkling eyes hinting at a well-developed sense of fun.

"Er?"

"At Alexandria in the last war. Saw off Mongseer Crapaud in fine style, if you remember, you being ashore with your, um . . ."

"Plicatiles. And damnably unhandy beasts they were, too, those little boats."

"Just so. Well, we've quite another job to do now, one that'll stretch us beyond the ordinary, I fear."

"That's how to run 'em to ground first," Kydd replied.

"Indeed. I've done a study of the captures so far, trusting we can chase up a pattern of where the devils are operating. And it's the damnedest thing—some taken off the Leewards, others as far away as Honduras, then Santo Domingo. You'd swear they had wings."

"Privateers?" Kydd offered.

"Only if you grant they've more than doubled their numbers in a month. We've been getting the better of the beggars since the beginning of the year and we've kept good watch on Guadeloupe and their other nests. No sign of 'em breeding—and besides which, this big jump in numbers we've lost only happened since the frigate pair arrived in these waters."

"I'd like to know just how they're causing so much ruin."

"Stands to reason, they've got us on the run by flying from place to place and never tarrying long enough for us to catch 'em by the tail. Odd, though—for all their seizures, no one's ever come across a prize of theirs to recapture. Where are they sending 'em in, we ask?"

Kydd digested it all. "Taking the long way around to be sure?" he hazarded.

"Could be, but this is to say that on the main point we've no suspicion of where to look to ferret 'em out. That's why every sail o' war Dacres has is out in a different place. Spread thin, but it's the only way. We've got a plum spot, the Windward Passage, but who knows?"

"Um. So we're a scouting pair," Kydd reflected. "Stay in sight until one of us spies something and whistles up the other."

"Ah—I was thinking more a distant sweep. Lay away to each side, return to an agreed rendezvous each dawn. Any sighting, retire instantly towards the other."

"Nelson before the Nile."

"Aye, Nelson style."

The two frigates slipped to sea in a gathering dusk, their strategy decided; a fast run to the Windward Passage between Cuba to the north and Hispaniola to the south. Then put about for a more thorough search: *L'Aurore* to comb the waters along the coast of Cuba while *Anson* looked into the deep gulf in Hispaniola that led to the old French trading harbour of Port-au-Prince.

In the steady northeasterly they drove into the night and, at precisely midnight, went about on the other tack to lay north. Dawn found them flying onwards together, in the increasingly brisk conditions an exhilarating sail. This was a relatively rare experience, for generally there was always the nagging need to conserve canvas and cordage, spars and rigging.

They were therefore treated to the breath-catching sight close abeam of a fellow frigate stretching out under full sail, heaving majestically, every line and scrap of canvas taut and thrumming with a sea music that set the spirit soaring.

By the afternoon they neared the coast of Cuba and, in a neat evolution, both frigates tacked about simultaneously, now hard by the wind on course for their goal, which, given that the weather held, they would raise comfortably by daybreak the next day.

As it happened, the spanking breeze freshened and veered more easterly. As they took up on the new tack, it was with seas smacking hard against the bow, sending spray shooting up to curve and sheet aft, soaking the watch on deck, but at least there was no longer the jerking roll from before when the waves had marched in on their beam, now only a determined pitch and toss as *L'Aurore* butted into the weather.

"Not to worry overmuch, sir," Kendall said quietly, "but I times these waves at less'n eight seconds now."

It was the master's duty to bring sea signs to Kydd's attention, and this was one that could be of significance in the Caribbean in the hurricane season. "Oh? How's the glass?"

"Fluky—we're under twenty-nine an' a quarter, but hasn't dropped worth remarking these last four hours."

Kydd had been in hurricanes before and had no real wish to try his ship against one now; it was prudent to be wary. He glanced ahead: storms swept in from the east and all were individual in their characteristics but there were common portents. At the moment the horizon was clear and there was no high overcast. His concern diminished—it looked to be a regular blow coming in from the Atlantic, more boisterous than usual perhaps but—

"Sail! I see sail—no, two—up agin the coast!" The lookout's hail broke into his thoughts, but already the heavier frigate with her greater height of eye was preparing to go about and Kydd lost no time in conforming. Two sail together was unusual to the point of incredible—there was every possibility that their hunt was over.

After an hour only, the pair were visible from the deck: two pale blobs against the darker green-brown of the Cuban coast, quartering the wind and making remarkably good speed. There was movement out on the yard at *Anson*'s main-course—she was setting bridles to the forward leech of the sail, with bowlines stretching it out into the teeth of the wind to claw the last particle of drawing power. They must do the same, for any delay in closing with the fast-moving chase there across their bows would end with *L'Aurore* losing them into the distance.

They were steering an intercepting course, paying off downwind as the two passed ahead five miles distant, then angling in to a stern chase. By now it was certain: the two were French frigates and they were declining action, preserving their ships for their primary task of hunting helpless prey.

It settled quickly into a hard chase. The two ahead stayed tightly together and had every stitch of canvas they could abroad, barrelling into the gathering sunset. *L'Aurore* and *Anson* similarly stayed close and tried every trick they could to claw their way up on the pair, but as time passed it was clear they had little chance of hauling up on them before dark.

Dusk drew in, the waves in contrast as they became shadowed, the white of combers startling in the gloom.

Anson set lanthorns aglow in her mizzen-top and, without needing orders, Kydd fell in astern for the night, the weather showing no signs of easing.

There was a moon. It was clear and bright behind them, and with its light on their sails, the enemy frigates were pitilessly revealed.

It was an even match—the contest was anyone's to lose, and by any man aboard: a mistake in the deceptive light, a line let go too soon putting intolerable strain on a spar, and the ship would be out of the race. Worse—for the remaining frigate it would then be two against one and a different story entirely. Of course it applied to the French as well: if it happened to them, *L'Aurore* had to be ready to take on the wounded bird while *Anson* raced on after the other.

Nerves at concert pitch, the four ships stretched out over the sea—until everything changed. A veil of light cloud had spread up from the horizon behind them, high and innocent; now it was joined by denser, lower cloud, which crept out, hiding the stars one by one until it reached the moon. Obscured, its light dimmed, the gloom deepened, then assumed the blackness of night, and the frigates ahead were lost to sight.

It was decision time and Kydd did not envy Lydiard the task. Because their speeds were so even, it was probable that the French would still be in sight in the morning. But they had the opportunity to get away, to make off under cover of dark. They could not turn to starboard for there lay the Cuban coast, but they could to larboard.

The enemy commander would be weighing the advantages of a turn-away against the probability that his opponent would second guess that he would seize the chance to strike out from his course at some point in the night, in which case his best move would be to keep right on.

Which would Lydiard decide?

The seas were increasing: Kydd felt their savage urge under *L'Aurore*'s counter, heard the muffled swearing of the two helmsmen as they fought to keep her steady, and knew in his heart what it meant. Before midnight he had confirmation—the barometer was dropping. It was the rate of fall that was the most important, and since the afternoon, it had passed the twenty-nine-inch mark with no sign of slowing.

Somewhere out in the night bluster a storm was gathering, but whether or not it was a dreaded revolving tropical tempest—a hurricane—only time would tell.

The lights of *Anson* were still ahead. The decision had been made: it was to stay on their course. Kydd could only guess Lydiard had reasoned that, all other things being equal, the French had chosen to keep on the track their mission required, quite in keeping with the overriding need to fly at utmost speed from one place to another.

He slept fitfully in the jerking cot and woke in the crepuscular pre-dawn light, dressing hurriedly. The motion of the ship was the same but more exaggerated—could they fight a blazing action in this? He crushed the worries as they rose, for when day broke the French might well have gone, Lydiard's decision the wrong one.

Anson's bulk materialised ahead as the dawn asserted itself, grey and sombre. She was plunging on regardless, a comforting sight, but all eyes were on the steadily widening circle of visibility—and then suddenly, gloriously, there were the French.

Some way to starboard but still ahead, and appreciably closer.

But that made for difficulties. Normally the chase would continue until either the quarry got away or were overhauled. Then it would be battle—but the conditions overnight had worsened, the winds veering even further aft. Waves were leaving long streaks as they were tumbled on before the relentless pummelling, which now had real force behind its steady streaming from the northeast, and the low cloud was starting to drive before it.

Everything now pointed to the near certainty that a hurricane was out there and all prudent mariners would be taking steps to get out of its way. But in the fast deteriorating conditions all four still plunged on before the storm.

"Mr Kendall," Kydd called across, to the grave-faced master, "shall we talk?"

"Aye, sir."

They stood together, each with a firm grip on a rope, eyeing the white-streaked seascape with concern.

"Glass is at twenty-eight an' three-fourths last time I looked, sir."

Kydd glanced up to the fast-moving clouds overhead. "Yes, it looks like a hurricanoe right enough," he said. "And we're driving before it."

There was a rule of thumb that said to face into the wind and the whirling chaos of the centre was somewhere off nine points on the right hand.

Kendall sniffed the wind. "And it veers," he muttered. "That means . . ."

He didn't have to explain it to Kydd. The winds feeding the massive gyre did so at an angle, coming in the same all around the rotating mass. Generations of mariners had learned, however, that all was not equal, finding out the hard way that while there were two directions to step out of the way of the onrushing storm only one was to be trusted.

Turning off to the north side would find the ship up against head winds, which by their angle would try their malignant best to suck the vessel into the centre. Not only that, as the hurricane track nearly always curved to the north, it would continue to bear down on the fleeing ship.

A turn to the south, though, would have the same winds impelling the ship under and behind the deadly system, much to be preferred. This side was called the navigable, the other the dangerous semicircle.

It was easy enough to find out their situation. By the same rule of thumb, it could be seen that if the direction of the wind as the storm approached continued to veer against the compass, to change clockwise, they could be sure they were in the north; if it backed, they were in the south.

". . . and so we're plumb within the dangerous semicircle," finished Kydd.

"Sir."

After his two experiences of a hurricane, years in the past, every instinct tore at him to put over the helm and flee before it was too late—but he could not. While the chase went on he was duty-bound to stay with it. And while the Frenchmen had their turn-aside threatened they were staying on course, and while they did so, *Anson* was never going to let up the chase and Kydd must stay with her as long as he could.

It was now a test of nerves: sooner or later they had to break and run. Who would be first?

Meanwhile, heavy-weather precautions had to be taken before conditions worsened further.

Royals and topgallants had long since been handed and, in conformity with *Anson,* a reef put in the topsails. Weather cloths were spread to give some relief to the helmsmen, and life-lines rigged fore and aft. Below decks it was vital to see to the securing of the guns, their breeching and tackles doubled and seized, while the spare tiller was laid along, and relieving tackles for its lines rigged. All that a prudent seaman should do aloft or alow was put in hand.

As the morning wore on, a gale developed, a hard, streaming pressure that had men staggering and all canvas hard as a board, a rising doleful drone among the lines from aloft shredding nerves. Spindrift was driven from seething crests to sting and blind, and *L'Aurore* began to stagger, an uncomfortable surge and jerking as the underlying swell grew.

By midday there was low racing scud above them, with an ominous thickening of the horizon to the east, an ugly darkness tinged with green edging that was the nightmare of a hurricane astern of them.

They were now down to close-reefed topsails on fore and main but with the mizzen staysail and storm mizzen in place of a topsail on the after mast, and still she laboured. Worry set in. Time was fast running out and with it their options.

It was crazy, but it was war. Through angry, foam-streaked seas in a hardening gale, four ships still clung to their duty, heaving and bucketing along in a chase to the death.

Kydd looked up for the thousandth time to the straining canvas and frantically thrumming lines and knew a decision could not long be delayed. He snatched a glance astern, then at the angle of the wind on their bow and finally at the tableau of fleeting ships—and made up his mind. The first ship to break away would be *L'Aurore*.

It was a giddy relief, and he could see the same in Kendall's face when he told him.

"We's going to have a hard time of it, I'm thinking," he shouted, in Kydd's ear. "Can't turn aside to the nor'ard—land's too close." Kydd was only too aware that the standard method of escaping the clutches of the dangerous semicircle, by taking the worst of the weather on the starboard bow and clawing out, was not possible.

The alternative was shocking. It required that they fall in with the wind and let it drive them across the very maw of the hurricane as fast as they dared in a bid to make the opposite side before they were overtaken by the ravening storm.

If that were not dangerous enough, there would be the fearful risk that conditions close in would be too much for their fine-lined ship and they would be forced to take in all canvas and lie a-try. When still within the dangerous semicircle, the end would be inevitable—with no ability to fight her way free, *L'Aurore* would be drawn unresisting into the very centre of the madness to her certain annihilation.

Kydd looked ahead for the final time, taking in the sight of *Anson,* the heavy frigate still smashing her way powerfully onwards after the distant pair, just visible huddling together in the rack of flying spray and mist, then ordered, "Up helm!"

Like a nervous colt, *L'Aurore* slewed around until the winds came in from astern and then began her mad run downwind across the path of the hurricane. Never at her best dead before the wind, she began an edgy, screwing roll that made moving about the bucking deck a trial, but she picked up speed like the thoroughbred she was. He knew that Lydiard would see them departing but he would understand what was going on. He comforted himself with the thought that, as the lightest of them all, it stood to reason that his ship would be first to break out.

The last he saw of *Anson,* she was still pressing on into the wind-torn seas after her now invisible foe until all were swallowed up in the ferocious weather.

Now it was a fight for survival, all thoughts of the chase gone. Inescapably every mile made took them closer to the heart of the storm but at the same time urged them nearer to the other side.

This was, quite simply, a race, and one determined by the skill and nerve of the captain in keeping sail on to the last moment to avoid the dreaded lying to. And hanging over it all was the unthinkable catastrophe of but a single spar carried away under the strain, in turn throwing intolerable stress on others until *L'Aurore* was nothing more than a drifting wreck, to be fallen upon by the triumphant hurricane.

The scene was grand—breathtaking and awful at the same time. Seas were lashed into a fury, their seething crests smoking white and leaving long, tiger-clawed lines of foam as they raggedly advanced in a heaving surge, seeming oddly bright under the dark, hellish sky. The heart of the hurricane was somewhere to larboard in the worst of the contrasting darkness and stinging white—it held a quality of supernatural dread, a terrible beast drumming towards them, its banshee howl making conversation impossible.

Calmly, the master was at the compass with a slate, squinting into the wind and taking regular bearings. It was a vital task, for after plotting they would know the path the hurricane was taking. When the bearing of the centre passed across the estimated track they would know they had at last passed out of the dangerous semicircle. Until then they could do nothing but run before the blast while rolling in mad, jerking swoops.

Then, without warning, catastrophe struck.

Above the quarterdeck a tremendous crack sounded clear over the storm's roar. Before anyone could react, a heavy spar swept down, with a terrifying rip and bang of straining canvas instantaneously giving way, with the tortured twanging of ropes tried beyond endurance. Skewed by the merciless blast on the ragged remnants of canvas, it crashed to the bulwark, pulping one man and sending two into the boiling sea.

Kydd, knocked to his knees, was disoriented at first but saw the quartermaster leap to the fire-axe on the mizzen-mast and begin a frenzied hacking at the tangled mass of rope and torn canvas. Coming to his senses, he threw a glance up. The driver gaff had given way at the jaws, the hinging point of the long spar that ran out from the mizzen-mast along the top of the big fore-and-aft sail, then had tumbled down, rending the sail and leaving severed lines streaming out to leeward.

Crushing from his mind the knowledge of the men in the sea gasping out the last of their lives, he tried to think.

The ship was now unbalanced, beginning a fishtail slewing with canvas on fore and main only—Gilbey at the main-mast and Curzon forward would know to douse sail instantly, but where did that leave them? As near as, damn it, helpless. As if to underscore his thoughts, *L'Aurore* sheered to take the wind broadside; she rolled deeply and uncontrollably for she had no canvas to steady her, locked now in a drifting curve that would end in her drawn to destruction in the hurricane's heart—the penalty for not yet having won clear of the dangerous semicircle.

In some way balancing canvas had to be bent to the mizzen-mast, but all spars and rigging had been snatched to ruin by the plunging spar and there was nothing left on which to set any kind of fore-and-aft sail of the kind needed. It was now desperate, and minutes counted before they were drawn too far in to set anything to claw their way out. The life of every soul aboard was in his hands. *What was he to do?*

Unaccountably a picture came to him of *L'Aurore* lying peacefully at anchor in Port Royal, the sun high and baking hot, but on the quarterdeck there was relief in the shadow cast by the tautly spread awning. At first he couldn't see it—then, marvellously, he understood. The awning was of the thickest grade of canvas and not too dissimilar in shape to the ruined driver, but more than that, its design incorporated a euphroe, a piece of shaped wood that allowed multiple lines to be secured to it.

He had his sail; with the euphroe, a single block could be used to haul it up in the hammering blast and its foot could be spread by the fallen boom.

"Mr Oakley!" he yelled at the boatswain, who was heaving frantically at the wreckage. "Take a crew and rouse out the quarterdeck awning."

The distracted man goggled at him in horror and Kydd realised he must have thought his captain had taken leave of his senses. He shouted a hurried explanation and the boatswain raced to obey. Messengers were sent to the two forward masts to prepare to get under way again while the remainder of the wreckage was cut away.

The block? Someone had to mount the shrouds to the mizzen-top to secure one tightly there or all would be in vain. Kydd gave another, searching, look up. There was the throat halliard that had previously held the jaw—it was a tackle of two blocks, now with the lower torn away, leaving the upper. It was in place. It would do.

But how? A line had to be reeved through and sent down again to the "sail" for hauling up but that line had to be strong, very strong—and therefore thick and heavy. Who could take such a weight up the shrouds one-handed? No one.

In despair Kydd saw his idea fading on the practicalities. Cudgelling his wits he came up with a solution: a pair of seamen with a light line mounting opposite shrouds. They would use this to haul up the tail of the heavy rope, reeve it through and send it down. That was it, blast it!

He glanced about to select those he would send. There was Poulden at his post by the wheel. It was insanely dangerous work, but the man was a natural seaman. Another? Then a mad thought entered. It was his idea: had he the right to order others into such peril? The answer, of course, was that he had the right and the duty, but a stubborn streak took possession of him.

"Poulden!" he bellowed, beckoning to him.

Catching something of the urgency, his coxswain hurried up. Kydd laid out his plan. Without any change of expression, Poulden crossed to the fallen gaff and reached out for the end, snagging the signal halliards. He cut off a length, coiling it around his body, leaped to the shrouds and started mounting them.

Kydd, taking the opposite side, launched himself up. Clear of the deck, the wind was frightful, bullying and wrenching as he climbed, doing all it could to tear him from his hold. He reached the futtock shrouds and discreetly took the lubber's hole route into the top to find Poulden grimly hanging on at each sickening roll, which, magnified by height, always ended in a brutal jerking.

The line went down to where, below, the boatswain was completing the euphroe double seizing. It was grabbed and the heavier rope bent on. Kydd grasped Poulden's belt as he used both hands to bring up the line, and then they had it.

Lying flat, they peered over the after side of the top down to where the remaining throat-halliard block swung crazily. Hooking his feet where he could, Kydd reached down for the block. At first it avoided him, painfully trapping his fingers against the mast. One-handed, he managed to seize it and manhandle it over to one side against its strop—and Poulden got the rope through in a single try.

Kydd held him again as he drew the rope through the big sheave with both hands until its hanging weight told—and they were done.

By the time they were back on the deck the makeshift driver was jerking up and on the other masts sail was being shown to the wind. To his immense relief Kydd saw that it was working.

Noticeably steadying under the high canvas, *L'Aurore* got under way again, slow but very sure.

The centre was so near now, rearing up in appalling dark majesty as if to fall on its prey—but they were winning through. As they crossed the hurricane's track it was now necessary to bring the wind by degrees on to the quarter to break out of the deathly grip of the revolving storm, by taking advantage of the rotation that was now thrusting towards the rear.

Point by point they edged outwards, the wind, which before was coming in from astern, now off the starboard bow. Then, as they won more sea-room, it was abeam until finally it was on the quarter and they were on their way out of the maelstrom.

Against all the odds they had won, but they were not yet out of danger. Their jury-rig driver sail had saved them but it would be useless in the vital manoeuvres of wearing and tacking about, and therefore they could take up on any course—so long as it was on the starboard tack. It was imperative to find somewhere to come to rest and repair.

And providentially they did, but not in the way Kydd would have wished. Some two hours later, with visibility in the still violent conditions down to a mile or two, across their path appeared the loom of an island.

Gradually it extended right across their field of vision, a dark, wooded land that seemed to hold such menace. It was downwind from them, therefore a lee shore. And without the ability to stay about on to the other tack to get around its unknown length, there was only one thing to do.

"Stand by to anchor—both bowers!" he roared. "And the last five fathoms with keckling," he added, with feeling. It had been many years ago but he would remember always the terrible effect of razor-sharp coral on anchor cable.

The men worked with furious intensity for they knew only too well that if their anchors were not ready for letting go by the time they came up with the land they would most surely drive to destruction on the lee shore. Heavy cable, many fathoms of it, had to be brought up from the cable tiers in the lowest part of the ship, hauled along the deck and finally bent on to the anchors on the outside of the bow. Back-breaking work, but with time slipping by, no relief could be had.

Under just enough sail to steady her, the sore-tested frigate closed with the island, which continued to stretch across the horizon. But which island was it? To the west of Jamaica where, without a doubt, they had been blown, there were none in the half-a-thousand miles right to the Yucatán peninsula—except the Caymans. Kydd racked his tired brain, trying to remember how they lay on the chart, then said, "Compliments to Mr Buckle and ask him to step aft."

Looking the worse for weather, his third lieutenant presented himself.

"Can you tell me the name of this island?"

"Why, yes, sir."

"Well?"

"That's Cayman Brac. You see the long bluff—"

In the wind's bluster Kydd had to lean forward to catch the words.

"Yes. Is that all?"

"There's two Caymans here, three, four miles apart. Not much in 'em, a handful o' settler families."

"I thought they had quite a few—Georgetown, is it?"

"Ah, no, sir. You're thinking on Grand Cayman."

So, a third island—with a dockyard for repairs? "How far is that?"

"Oh, seventy, eighty miles."

Out of the question—and time was getting short. "We're to anchor here while we repair. Is there anywhere in sight you recommend?"

Buckle gave it thought. "There is, more over to the north. As I remember there's a small landing place."

"A settlement?"

"Not really, sir. Just a fort on the heights above."

"Well done, Mr Buckle! It couldn't be better." That had dealt in one with his greatest anxiety: that an enemy might chance upon them while they were helpless at anchor. They'd safely moor under the watchful guns of the fort.

While the lieutenant conned them in, Kydd scanned the shore. The coast was relatively steep and a tiny plain fringed the shoreline all along the north. Close in, the island was beautiful—but would be *L'Aurore*'s grave if the anchors gave and she blew ashore in the still seething gale. At the right time both bower anchors were let go, the frigate continuing in to the full scope of the cable and then, under their restraint, was swung around to ride it out, facing into the wind and out to sea. It was masterly timing and a feat of seamanship that could only have come from a matchless ship's company.

Normally there would be gun salutes and the military flummery of one commander recognising the authority of another, but there was nothing from the low structure peeping above the trees atop the bluff. There was no flag but that was probably because in high winds any would have been torn to rags in minutes. Nevertheless, to set his mind at rest Kydd needed to be sure that the fort knew its business.

"I'm going to pay a call on the redcoats. You know what to do, Mr Gilbey."

He left the first lieutenant to start the unenviable task of clearing away the raffle of fraying rope, remnants of canvas and awkward spars on deck in order that the boatswain, carpenter and sailmaker could get to their work.

The boat, going with wind and waves, made good speed inshore in the still boisterous conditions. Kydd had known better than to go for full dress: one of the boat's crew was set to constantly bailing from seas over-topping the gunwale and by the time they had crossed the outer reef with its creaming seas he was soaked.

He grabbed the sea-slimed ladder on the little jetty and climbed up, his knees nearly buckling at the unforgiving solidity of the land.

There was no one about. All along the beach palm trees were in frenetic motion in the hard wind, and he slitted his eyes against the grains of sand that whipped about his face.

Having hauled the boat clear of the tide line, its crew stood by while he trudged up into a scrubby wooded area, following the rough track. Calloway was with him, respectfully behind. Then the track veered sharply to parallel the beach under the line of the bluff. This was not leading to the fort—Kydd stopped in vexation. Unless they found the right path it made no sense to go on.

They returned and cast about for any track that led up the face of the cliff and eventually spotted one. It was ill-used and overhung by sharp-leaved vegetation that was lashed by the wind, but eventually it emerged at the top, a hundred or more feet above the sea, in a bare and scrubby flat area.

"Where the devil . . . ?" Kydd glanced about but could not see a fort. "You go that way, I'll take this. Hail when you spy it."

He struck off to the left, irritably batting at waving fronds but stopped when he heard a hesitant call. Relieved, he turned and retraced his steps. Rounding an outcrop he saw Calloway pointing to a deserted ruin.

L'Aurore was facing out to sea, innocently snubbing to her anchors and wide open to devastating attack. An enemy had only to come in on her stationary bow to be free from defensive fire, then criss-cross with impunity while smashing in appalling destruction down *L'Aurore*'s length. It would take minutes only before his command was reduced to a blood-soaked wreck.

In a fever of anxiety he turned and ran down the track. "Get back! Boat in the water, damn you!" he roared at the stunned boat's crew. He had a short time only to come up with a solution—and racked his brain on the passage back.

It might work! He bounded up the side-steps and found Gilbey. "The launch to take away the kedge," he said briefly.

The half-ton anchor would be slung under the launch and carried well to seaward and to one side, there to be dropped. The cable in *L'Aurore* would come in through a stern port and then be heaved in on the capstan, thereby bringing the frigate around parallel to the shore.

Any enemy now would not meet a defenceless ship bow-on but instead a whole broadside, a wall of guns.

The weather was moderating, a brief glimpse of blue sky lifted spirits, and determined faces could be seen around the ship as they set to with the repairs. It was not easy work, for now the seas were coming in on the beam and, without the damping effect of sails, the rolling was tedious. With heavy spars on deck, it was a dangerous place to be.

They worked on without pause; only the tools and material they carried on board could be used and the stakes could not have been higher.

In the event they had barely two hours before sail was sighted.

Kydd realised the imperatives of weather applied just as much to Frenchmen as any other. This frigate's captain had no doubt seen *L'Aurore*'s departure and soon after had himself broken out of the dangerous semicircle in the same seaman-like way. It was no coincidence that they had ended up in the same place.

At this point it was likely that he would be looking to round the end of the island to seek shelter in its lee but would be surprised and puzzled to see the English frigate stolidly at anchor on the wrong, weather side.

What was very certain was that there must be a reckoning between them. One or the other would leave their bones in this place and for *L'Aurore,* without manoeuvrability, the odds were that it would be she.

Kydd felt frustration build. A fair fight in the open sea was one thing; tethered like a goat for the slaughter another. And there was nothing he could do to speed the repair. The carpenter and sailmaker, with their mates, the most vital men in the ship now, were not to be chivvied into hasty work or the consequences would show at the very worst time. They had to be left to get on with it; Kydd must hope they could finish before the weather moderated and the French emerged from their comfortable lee side to close with them.

But he would have to interrupt their labours: even in these conditions standard procedures required that in sight of the enemy he closed up his ship for action. Once around the headland, though, he could stand them down to resume their efforts.

All eyes were on the foe. Under comfortable sail it did not seem particularly interested in them; this was the thirty-two-gun frigate, the larger of the two, and therefore was probably Sieyès' command.

Kydd studied the ship carefully through his pocket telescope: every sail was trimmed to perfection and drawing well, and it was not evident that she had just come through a hurricane. The ship's lines showed it was of recent construction—that implied a fit of eighteen-pounders; thirty-two-gun twelve-pounder frigates, like the pre-war *L'Aurore,* were no longer being built.

The odds were lengthening.

Hull-up, it was apparent they were making to clear the point, passing slowly across their field of vision to the right. Kydd could not help a jet of envy at the sight of the powerful frigate—the French were certainly master ship-builders and it would be a close thing on the morrow when—

"He's not going to wait, the beggar!" yelled someone.

Kydd looked again. In a lazy curve, the frigate was altering course towards them.

He swallowed hard. This was a most unwelcome development and did not add up. Why was the Frenchman going in against an alerted and positioned ship with all her men ready at their guns? His duty was to avoid battle damage at all costs. Whatever the reason . . .

"Stand to your guns!" Kydd barked, then turned to Gilbey and told him to check that the decks were clear aft.

They were as ready as they could be.

But when the frigate had straightened and settled on course to engage, all became clear. There was to be no braving of *L'Aurore*'s broadside—instead Sieyès, in one audacious move, was going to end the battle before it started.

The big 32 was taking all the time it needed to sail past *L'Aurore*'s stern, delivering an overwhelming punishment as it did, raking down the length of the tethered vessel, bringing about the utter destruction Kydd had dreaded, and not taking a shot in reply.

This could only be contemplated by a consummate seaman, utterly sure of himself and his ship's company to consider such a manoeuvre—running close to deliver the blow but then wheeling about on a sixpence in the perilously short distance before the reef and shallows to reach out to sea again for another pass.

They were helpless to stop it—or were they?

"Chain shot! Every gun—load with chain!" Kydd bellowed urgently. He ignored the bewildered looks from the gun-deck. There was so little time.

"The carpenter—tell him to step up on deck this instant," he rapped.

What he had in mind was a once-only move. If it failed, they were most certainly finished.

The enemy frigate lined up for its run with deliberation, as deadly as a bullfighter bringing his sword up for the kill. Nearer and nearer, every detail of the ship showing clear and stark—from the men at the guns to those standing by the ropes for the whirlwind of action that must follow the crushing blast.

Kydd watched with an icy calm: timing alone would determine whether his men lived or died.

It was the forefoot of the oncoming warship that was his mark—the angle between that and—

"Now!" he roared.

In a blur of motion the carpenter swung his razor-sharp broad-axe. It thudded into the bar-taut cable of the kedge, near severing it in one. Under the strain the rest parted and fell away. Released from her position athwart the wind, *L'Aurore* immediately began swinging back to face into the gale streaming in, held as before by her bower anchors. And it brought her broadside around to bear—the tables had been turned.

So close, the enemy frigate was committed but had not reached the point where its own guns could bear—the timing had been perfect. With great satisfaction Kydd saw consternation on the opposing quarterdeck as he blared, "Fire!"

The guns thundered and blasted in a deliberate broadside—but upwards, producing instant and visible ruin in the Frenchman's rigging. Canvas ripped and tore as if by a magic hand, severed lines streamed away and the fore main-yard folded gracefully in two, bringing down with it the fore topsail above.

Sieyès had been over-confident: he had not reckoned on Kydd throwing away his only defensive posture and, more importantly, to abandon the British preference for hammering round-shot into the hull for the French practice of shots into the rigging. Now he was about to pay the price.

And it wasn't long coming. Fighting desperately to come around in time, with their damage and in the prevailing conditions, they didn't stand a chance and, slowly but surely, like the inevitable climax of a Greek tragedy, the frigate struck.

Immediately it slewed and heeled, the seas surging and smashing against the bare, glistening hull like a half-tide rock, beginning a merciless battering and assailing of the doomed ship. By morning there would be nothing but wreckage.

It had been only minutes from start to finish.

Chapter 8

At his book by the stern windows in the great cabin Renzi heard movement on the deck above, then stillness. A few minutes later the silvery shriek of the boatswain's call was on the air—the captain had returned from the admiral. Oakley liked to make a performance of it, ornamenting the upper notes with clever trills and tailing off in a perfectly contrived falling cadence.

Renzi knew Kydd set great store on the ceremony of piping aboard, not for the honour and personal satisfaction it gave but for it being a token of the discipline and order that arose naturally in the practice of the ancient customs of the Royal Navy.

A little time later his friend emerged into the cabin, Tysoe magically appearing to strip him of his finery.

"Not as if you seem gratified at your reception, brother." Kydd certainly did not much resemble a frigate captain returning after reporting the destruction of an enemy to his commander.

"Oh, he gives me joy of my victory, Nicholas, and mentioned that Lydiard went on to place a prize crew on the other Frenchy after he lost spars in the storm and hauled down his flag."

"Then?"

Kydd broke off to order sherry from Tysoe and continued, "As he's much vexed and distracted by dispatches from *Lapwing* sloop.

It turns out that while we were putting an end to the frigate pair, in quite another area we're taking losses still, proving it can't be them."

"So the conundrum remains," Renzi reflected. "Widely separated actions, which can't be by privateers because we have most under eye in Guadeloupe and Martinique, and there's no other port in the Caribbean that can sustain same."

"It's more puzzling even than that. What no one can reckon is where they're sending their captures to be condemned and sold—or any word at all about what happens to their crews. As if they've vanished entirely."

"So, an unknown enemy performing unknown evil acts, the result of which is not known."

"Don't jest, Nicholas. The planters are in a right taking, saying it's the work of the devil. Some believe this is Bonaparte with a secret weapon and you can be sure I'm not going to tell 'em of Mr Fulton's submarine boat." His brow suddenly furrowed. "You don't think . . ."

"Well, I did say there would be a serious retaliation by Mr Bonaparte, but I'm not sure it's to be that, not unless he's improved his torpedoes greatly."

Kydd settled into his chair. "Are we then to suppose that they're taking their captures somewhere right away, with a view to mounting a convoy to sail 'em to Europe all together?"

"We cannot dismiss the notion, dear fellow, but this does not address the first cause. How are they able to strike without our patrols see them? Where is their base that can sustain whatever they are at in so many different parts of the Caribbean? What is our defence against it? We beg to know."

"These are questions that we can't answer, not at anchor here in Port Royal. Dacres is insistent on it: we're driven to sea until we find the rogues and put a stop to it. *L'Aurore* sets out as soon as we've stored and fettled, but to where, no one has any notion."

Renzi murmured his sympathy, but could find little of value to contribute. It was a perplexity in the extreme, for if this was the grand revenge he had always feared Bonaparte would inflict, it was succeeding only too well.

While Kydd got on with his paperwork he bent his mind to the problem with all the logic he could muster. His instincts told him that it had to be accepted it must be a species of secret operation that was being conducted, since their regular naval forces had never encountered any of its participants at any time. And they were suspiciously successful, implying some form of intelligence being gained and exploited.

He himself was no stranger to clandestine activity, at one time having been at the centre of a plot to kidnap Napoleon, and he knew the excruciating level of detail required to carry it off. He sombrely recalled Commodore d'Auvergne and his crushing burden of control, the string of agents stretching from Normandy to Paris itself—and their useless bravery.

So what, then, if the French had set up such a network? The British could claim no monopoly on covert operations. What if there was a web of agents across the Caribbean, being controlled by a gifted French naval officer much like d'Auvergne? Someone with an equal grasp of detail, who was pulling the strings of a commerce-raiding operation quite unlike the usual.

Tightly integrated, centrally managed and intelligently deployed. In essence, a fleet. After Trafalgar, there being no foreseeable prospect of an invasion of Britain, the forces gathered for its execution had been idle. There would therefore be a large number available of those *chaloupes* or *prames*, escorts for the invasion barges, small but powerful enough to stand against anything less than a frigate. An "admiral" in command of a sizeable detachment could, with information supplied, send them dodging about the Caribbean, like assassins, quickly extracting them from the scene of the crime before detection and sending them on to the next. Yes. It made sense.

"My dear fellow, it does cross my mind that there is an explanation for what we are seeing. Consider this."

Kydd looked up from his writing and, point by point, Renzi laid out his reasoning.

"Why, that's not impossible, I'd say. We had a tidy fight of it against some off Calais in dear old *Teazer*, if you remember." Kydd looked thoughtful. "It would need an organising brain of the first rank, and reliable captains who know their duty and can navigate. But if your idea's right, there's one thing you need to show."

"Their central base."

"Just so. Your admiral needs somewhere to maintain his fleet, victual and water, all the usual, as well as have a port to hold all his captures. Which to be legal have to be condemned as good prize in a French court sitting wherever that may be. To be honest with you, I can't think of such a one."

It was the weakest part of the idea—but who was to say it was impossible, if no one had yet undertaken a search for such a secret base?

"Nicholas, you've a right noble headpiece and this is what I'm going to do. We're going to Dacres together and you shall put it to him yourself."

The commander-in-chief of the Jamaica Squadron heard him out politely and sat back to consider. "A pretty theory, Renzi. Much to commend it." He pondered further. "I like the bit about Bonaparte employing his surplus invasion escorts. And the French have some very able officers, very able. The whole thing's not impossible."

He fiddled with a paper knife, then carefully placed it down and said abruptly, "But I can't move on it."

"Sir?"

"No evidence. No evidence at all. Surely we'd have heard

something. A sighting of a *chaloupe* or similar. Very distinctive in the Caribbean, I'd have thought."

Renzi waited.

"And always we come back to this question of his base. He's not only to supply his ships but has to keep up communications. We'd certainly look to have intercepted at least one dispatch cutter but we haven't. We'd then find where it was headed and therefore the base."

"Sir, if we ferreted about in earnest, made good search of—" Kydd began.

"No. Not possible. Every ship we have must keep to the sea-lanes, if only to discourage the beggars."

With sudden weariness, he added, "I've no idea what's out there doing this damage to our interests but it's causing me much grief. If you come across the slightest piece of evidence in support, do let me know—or if you can construe where your secret base is, I'll get the nearest ship to look in on it. Otherwise there's not much more I can do."

"Sir," Renzi asked quietly, "with your permission, may I consult the patrol briefs and casualty reports? To see if there's some kind of pattern?"

"Very well. See Wilikins, my confidential clerk. He'll dig 'em out for you. Now, Mr Kydd, when did you say you'd be ready to sail?"

"Mr Renzi, is it? Then how can I be of service to you, sir?"

He was a dry individual but had a warmth and willingness that reached out to Renzi. "Why, Mr Wilikins, that's so kind in you. Would you be so good as to lay out for me the fleet's patrol reports of this last month and a Caribbean chart? I have a need to consult the one in relation to the other."

"Of course. Er, may I know what it is that you're investigating? I have knowledge of the archives we hold to some detail," he added modestly.

"Thank you, no. It's a conjecture only, not worthy of interrupting your day, sir."

"Why, that's no imposition, Mr Renzi. Just between you and me, in our usual round there's little to divert an active mind. I'd be glad to help."

It was tempting: this was a man who knew the station intimately and could no doubt contribute detail that would otherwise take him weeks to unearth. And as the admiral's confidential secretary he would surely be reliable.

"Then I accept, with thanks. Now, Mr Wilikins, what I'm about to tell you must be in the nature of a confidence. Pray do not speak of this to others." If rumours of a French fleet of predators got abroad, they would terrify Jamaica.

There was a pained look, but the man agreed.

"Very well. You're no doubt aware that we've suffered losses among our trade much above the usual."

"I am—Admiral Dacres speaks of little else," he said, with feeling.

"In this matter I have a notion, a possibility only, of how such might have been achieved."

"Therefore it must of a surety be pursued, sir."

"Then do hear what I say now, Mr Wilikins. Your views will be valued."

Renzi laid out his arguments for a secret fleet controlled by a master hand, an organisational genius able to provide supply and havens for his assets and a port of size able to contain his captures, until now undiscovered.

The clerk suddenly sat down, pale behind his neat spectacles. "Why, sir, that is quite an idea, some might say a flight of fancy."

"Nevertheless, it is one answer in logic to our dilemma."

"Yet a hard thing to prove, sir. What, may I ask, do you plan to do, should you take it further?"

"Which I shall certainly do, Mr Wilikins. The admiral does not intend to move on this without he has evidence. If I can deduce the whereabouts of this base and it is shown to him, the theory turns to fact. He will then be able to strike at the heart of the operation and bring it to a close."

"I see. This will take some pains, I'm sure. How will you proceed?"

"The time and place of each capture to be plotted, then related in terms of distance to each conceivable candidate locality in turn. You see, to achieve his successes he must have a network of information concerning the sailing of each victim. If we calculate the time necessary to alert and get response, and place it next to this, it will disqualify some and push others to prominence. We will find it on the basis of mathematical elimination, never fear."

"A daunting task," Wilikins murmured.

"The stakes are great, sir."

"Most certainly, Mr Renzi! The idea is novel but has its features. Let us begin."

"Very good. Now, where to start—Haiti?"

They began with St Nicholas Mole, an old French port going back to the 1600s and well known in the past as a nest of corsairs, but immediately ran into difficulties. The casualty reports they were working to had in nearly every instance the actual position of capture only loosely defined. That a ship had sailed on this date, bound for a given port, had simply not arrived on schedule, the bracket of dates producing an unworkable margin of error.

"Unfortunate. We shall have to think our way to another solution, Mr Wilikins," Renzi muttered.

A variation, perhaps, with the range of uncertainty represented by a line, a strip of paper, which could be overlaid one over the other for a visual match?

By evening they had gone over the permutations of only four of the possible harbours and there were many more to cover. The willing clerk offered to work on, but Renzi needed time to think and took his leave.

The next day he redoubled his efforts but, by the end of the afternoon, could see that he was not going to arrive at a computed solution. But what else was there?

With sympathy, Wilikins saw Renzi rub his eyes. "There's one thing we may try, my friend," he offered hesitantly. "But it's only my humble idea."

"Say on, my dear sir," Renzi said, eager for anything that could break through the morass facing him.

"I've heard it answered in the days of the great Admiral Rodney."

"Please go on."

"Well, there were bad losses from privateers in those days. So many that, faced with ruin, Lloyd's insurers sent an investigator from England to determine the facts. He came and immediately offered a great reward to any who could uncover their nest, their *locus domesticus*. In fact, one of their own came forward privily and informed, claiming the reward, which allowed the admiral to mount an operation to extirpate them."

"Umm. The power of venality to overcome loyalty is never to be scorned, sir."

"Unhappily I fear we have not the time to petition Lloyd's, Mr Renzi."

"Ah. You may leave that to me, Mr Wilikins. I do believe we shall pursue your idea, sir. And not a word to a soul, remember."

The clerk brightened. "Of course not. So gratified to be of assistance, Mr Renzi."

"An irregular proceeding, sir, most irregular!" Dacres sat back and frowned. "In the character of a Lloyd's man you'll be offering a reward for the uncovering of a nest of privateers? What has this to do with a naval fleet operation?"

"You'll grant appearances will be much the same, sir. Some curious soul will have seen such—a quantity of vessels issuing from and arriving at a place they have no right to be, large amounts of victuals being shipped in, numbers of country ships at anchor and—"

"Yes, yes. But where the devil am I going to find the cash for this reward, I'd like to know, sir?"

"Others may well point out that Admiral Rodney found his way to funding it and believed the happy outcome more than recompensed him."

"Humph. Well, now persuade me how you'll not be flammed by a rogue claiming to know and doesn't."

"Sir, I'm to tell you I'm not unacquainted with the arts of dissimulation. Were Commodore d'Auvergne to be present, he would speak warmly of my conduct on his behalf, er, at significant events for this country of a clandestine nature."

"You're admitting you've been acting as agent in some species of hugger-mugger operation."

Renzi winced. "Not as if I'd wished to have it known, sir."

"Of course not, no employment for a gentleman, I can understand that. Your secret's safe with me, Renzi."

"Thank you, sir."

"And I've a mind to see this through—anything that has any sort of chance of ridding us of the vermin. What do you propose?"

Several days later, *L'Aurore* was due to sail within forty-eight hours, and Renzi found himself making for the Shipp Inn on Queen's Street in Port Royal. Here, all those years ago, he had roistered with one Tom Kydd and his shipmates, who had found themselves unaccountably crew of *Seaflower* cutter—it was a warm thought. It would be awkward, of course, if he was recognised, but in an old-fashioned wig and spectacles he didn't think it likely.

It had changed little and he couldn't help but give a tiny smile as he took up solitary residence in the snug, which he had hired for the night. He sat, with an untouched pewter of stingo, and waited.

Reward posters had been pasted up all about the town, proclaiming the existence of a Mr Smith from Lloyd's of London come to investigate the recent losses. It seemed he was offering a large reward of an undisclosed sum for information leading to an uncovering of the privateers' nest. All dealings in the strictest confidence and prompt payment in bright silver dollars assured.

It was an outside chance. And if he came away empty-handed it would probably mean the end for his prospects of revealing the plot—if it existed. His logical mind, however, came back stoutly with the observation that, while there was at the moment no evidence in support, it did explain things better than any alternative.

At the front of the tavern sailors roared with laughter as they downed rum punch but this was to the good—he didn't want to be overheard in his dealings.

As the evening wore on, the happy noise began to get on his nerves. He saw off four hopefuls, transparently ignorant, then called for a pie and soup, as much for a change as to fend off hunger. The pot-boy brought in the food, curious about the strange gentleman sitting alone and sober in a haunt that in former days had seen many a pirate plotting a voyage of plunder.

It was soon approaching midnight; Renzi had to conclude that if there was a clandestine base apparently no one had seen it. The idea of a secret fleet, however attractive in logic, remained just that—an empty theory.

The tavern quietened as the revellers departed. Renzi decided he'd give it until twelve and then leave. At a few minutes to the hour the pot-boy entered hesitantly, wide-eyed and holding out a folded note. "I'm t' give you this'n."

Renzi found a coin and the lad disappeared quickly.

The note was roughly written and in block capitals: "I HAVE THE

GRIFF YOU WANTS. ITS BIGGER THAN YOU KNOW. I'LL HAVE ALL MY COBBS TONIGHT, OR NOTHING. IF YOU WANT TO PLAY, SHIFT INTO THE OTHER SEAT."

Instantly, Renzi came to full alert, his heart thudding. This was near professional—in some way he was being put under observation as he read. Carefully he rose and went around the table to the chair he had out for visitors. It had its back to the door.

He glanced again at the rest of the note. "THEN DONT LOOK ROUND OR YOUR A DEAD MAN."

He sat and waited for the blindfold. He heard the door open and soft paces, then dark cloth was fastened around his eyes. More paces around the table and the scraping of a chair.

"Right, cully. Now we talks."

The voice was low and had a West Country burr. The man had evidently waited until the tavern was nearly clear of customers before he had made his move.

"I'm Mr Smith of Lloyd's Insurance," Renzi said neutrally. "Do you have information on a privateers' nest as will interest me, Mr . . . er?"

"No names." He paused. "I've surely got something as will blow ye out of y'r seat, never doubt it. What I want t' see first is the colour o' your money."

"Very well." Renzi felt inside his waistcoat and brought out a soft hide purse, clinking it suggestively before pouring out the contents in a little stream, sliding the silver towards himself where he could see it through chinks directly down from under the blindfold.

"That?" the man said in disbelief. "Won't buy a monkey his mort o' joy-juice. Have to do better'n that."

"I can," Renzi said levelly. "Much more. I have it close by—no need to tempt a man to slit my throat and run with it. How much depends on what you can tell me."

"I've more t' tell ye right enough. But what's to stop ye runnin' off without payin' after I tells yez?"

"What's to stop you slitting my gizzard after I hand over the silver, just to keep your secret safe?"

The man chortled. "Seems we've come to a chock-a-block."

Renzi was quick to pick up that he was a seaman: his reference to the state of a tackle, when the lower block has run up against the upper, stopping the hoist, had given him away.

"Not necessarily," Renzi said carefully. "This you shall have when you've satisfied me with your information. The rest comes only after a runner takes a note containing the information to one of my colleagues, who will countersign it, and returns to me here with this evidence that the secret is secure in our hands."

"An' you'll be waitin' here, o' course."

"As will you, my friend, and the money."

There was a heavy silence while this was digested.

"No tricks!"

"You have my word."

Renzi got straight to the point: "So then, where is this privateers' nest, at all?"

"Ha! This is where you're on the wrong course entirely, Mr Smith. 'Cos they's not privateers, not at all. We're talkin' Navy, French Navy, as has a whole fleet as they're controlling from the one place."

Renzi felt a wash of relief mixed with elation but fought it down. He put out his hand for the coins, neatly divided them in two and pushed one pile across. "Which place?"

He felt the man reach across and draw the remainder to him but didn't try to stop it. He was in too much of a fever to hear the rest.

"Curaçao."

In a rush of insight, Renzi saw how this could be all too possible and cursed himself for not considering the island before.

It was small and lay on the other side of the Caribbean, not far off the continental land mass of South America and of trifling importance in trade. However, it was still a tiny remnant of the Dutch empire, and the Hollanders, under a puppet government of Napoleon, would certainly do as they were told. Renzi's pulse raced. "You've seen them yourself?"

"Last voyage we did. Sees 'em come an' go at a trot in the Schottegat, as is within Willemstad."

"You can't tell me anything else?"

"Well . . . the admiral cove is a right Tartar an' he's ashore in a big place at Parera, can't miss him. Heard his name was Duperré or such."

"Is the island fortified? Do they have ships-of-the-line there?"

"Why you askin' me this? I've told you all I saw. Now, let's see the rest o' the rhino!"

Mind racing, Renzi tried to think. With the location of the base now known, it was really up to Dacres how he acted. Further questions could wait. The main thing was, he had what he wanted.

"This does appear satisfactory information. You will have your reward once the runner returns. If you would be so good as to stand behind me as I remove my blindfold to write . . . there."

He scribbled the bare facts on the back of a poster. Curaçao—the French Navy, Duperré in command. Then a request to countersign.

Handing it over his shoulder and being careful not to turn, he said, "Do get a messenger to take this at once to a Mr Wilikins." He gave the address and added, "He is not expecting this. Nonetheless the messenger is to be insistent he be called to sight and sign it." He hoped the confidential clerk would forgive being roused from bed but he would quickly realise the import of the paper.

Time passed. Renzi, blindfolded again, sat uncomfortably. The man discouraged conversation, and when the pot-boy returned, he snatched the paper and slapped it on the table, resuming his position behind.

"Look at it!" he demanded, as the blindfold was again lifted.

It was duly signed.

"Where's these cobbs close by, then? I'll get 'em now."

"Do I get a name? In case I have more questions."

"No. Find them dollars."

Renzi felt inside his waistcoat on the other side. "I did say close by," he said lightly. Drawing out a similar hide bag he spilled out the coins in a noisy cascade. A hand immediately came out and swept them up, then roughly pulled down the blindfold again.

"Don't take it off for a count o' fifty, cuffin." There was a scraping of the chair and the door closed.

The admiral's eyes gleamed. "Curaçao! The devils—let's take a look."

He crossed to the table and spread out a chart of the Caribbean. "Ah! You see?"

The island was at the south point of an inverted triangle where the northern base was Jamaica to one side and the Leeward Islands to the other, each spaced equally apart—a near perfect sallying point.

"A rapid descent would—"

"Your success in the intelligence line is well remarked, Mr Renzi. Matters of naval strategy may be safely left to myself."

"Only that a delay would allow our losses—"

"This is out of your hands now, Renzi. There are higher matters to consider, touching as they do on strategicals of an international significance."

"Yes, sir."

"For instance—how do I act in this? We've not had the smallest difficulty from the Hollanders in this war but any move against the French there would be an intolerable provocation."

He frowned, steepling his fingers. "So this compels me to make a decision in which there can be no middle ground. To be obliged to leave them to their depredations—or mount a full-scale invasion with all the consequent expense and peril."

"Sir, they cannot be left to it."

"An invasion of any enemy territory, Renzi, is not to be contemplated lightly. We must be assured of success, else we shall be put to scorn by the world."

"Quite, sir." The words chosen were revealing: Dacres was seriously contemplating a direct assault in depth by himself and was not inclined to share the glory with the larger Leeward Islands command. If the latter were brought in they would necessarily take control and credit, but would therefore also take the odium in the event of failure.

For several moments Dacres remained wrapped in thought, then said sharply, "And we only have the word of this unknown common seaman as to what's afoot—and, come to think of it, providing me with the only evidence thus far that your theory is not some wild fantasy."

He glared at Renzi as if it were entirely his fault that his day had turned so complicated.

"Sir, I've no reason whatsoever to doubt the man. My experience tells me he's—"

"Your experience, sir? What is that to me?"

"I did mention before, sir, that I have in fact previously acted in the capacity of a—"

"You did, and I'll bear it in mind."

He brightened. "And, now I have done so, a solution to my dilemma now presents itself." A pleased smile dawned.

"Yes. This is what we'll do. While putting in train the preliminaries of planning and requisition for a descent on the island, there will be our man who goes to Curaçao itself in some cunning guise and sees for himself what's the truth of the matter. You'll see, of course, I can't allow an invasion unless it's absolutely necessary."

Renzi knew what was coming. "Our man?"

"Who better than yourself, Renzi? You say as how you have all this experience . . ."

Wilikins was delighted. "How exciting for you, Mr Renzi! To go into the midst of the enemy as it were and—"

"Pray contain yourself, Mr Wilikins," Renzi said huffily. "Quite apart from the fact that I'm to act the spy, a calling I do cordially detest, the danger to be apprehended is great indeed. And might I prevail upon you to employ the utmost discretion in this business? As of this moment the admiral and your own good self are the only ones to be aware of this affair, but if it should become known to a wider extent I would most assuredly pay for it with my life."

The clerk blinked, then regarded Renzi gravely. "That is something I would regret above all things. Nothing shall be spoken beyond these four walls."

"Thank you," he said, touched at the little man's sincerity. "And now, Mr Wilikins, have you any information at all concerning the island?"

"Ah, yes, we do. Your Captain Bligh had a confrontation with the Dutch there in the last war and did record much of his experiences. My predecessor, though, had a quaint notion of the art of filing and its recovery may take some little time."

Kydd sat down suddenly. "This is a hard thing to put on a man, Nicholas. You would not have been thought the less if you had refused—are there not, should we say, men of that profession Dacres could call upon?"

"There is little on this station that warrants the maintenance of such, therefore no. Time is very limited and any person entering in on Curaçao must have knowledge of military and naval affairs to be aware of the significance of what he observes."

Kydd looked at him with the tiniest touch of amusement. "And as it's your theory to be proved you won't leave it to another."

"Not at all," Renzi said, with dignity. "We are beset by the greatest threat yet launched by Bonaparte. If it succeeds in cutting off our Caribbean trade, he will take note and deploy it elsewhere. It has to be stopped—and I know my duty."

"Yes, Nicholas, you always did." Kydd pondered. "It'll be a tricky thing. We haven't any good charts of that side of the Caribbean and a night landing from *L'Aurore* will—"

"Rest your concerns, dear fellow. *L'Aurore* will not be needed."

The baffling light winds relented at last and, resolving out of the bright haze ahead, the island of Curaçao spread gradually across their field of view.

It had been only three days but the strain of maintaining his disguise was telling on Renzi. The amiable American master had gone out of his way to show an interest in his business prospects, this Herr Haugwitz coming all the way from the small Hanseatic town of Bremen. Just how did he think he was going to deal with the twin hazards of Napoleon's decree on the one hand and the iniquitous British on the other?

Renzi had countered the well-meaning interrogation in heavily accented English by saying that he was on an exploratory trip only, to gauge possibilities for a product that, for commercial reasons, he was not at liberty to reveal. It had satisfied and he had had then only to fend off the friendly prattle of a gregarious captain gratified that his modest vessel had been selected for the passage.

The pilot and Customs cutter appeared and, while the formalities were concluded, Renzi's pulse quickened.

It was the very height of impudence to think he could just come to the Dutch colony, spy out the operation and leave. But that was what was planned, and the longer he stayed the more dangerous his situation. The American had told him that he was calling to offload molasses and take aboard seventeen barrels of aloes and then would be off—say, two days in all. Renzi had every intention of leaving with him.

On its own a simple count of men-o'-war in harbour would be misleading for there would be far more out at sea on their predatory occasions, but it would be necessary only to sight two or three to confirm matters. And he knew where the controlling base was and the name of its principal. He had only to verify they existed and he would have all the proof Dacres needed that this was indeed the place.

The shoreline was beautiful: long beaches overhung with palms and studded with houses; judging by their spacing from each other, they must be well-appointed villas.

Renzi could not see the town of Willemstad and its harbour until they drew closer, then made out a channel. It was barely a couple of hundred yards across but they confidently entered it in the light but steady easterly trade wind.

So close, every detail was clear: dominating the entrance to the channel on one side was the angular pentagon of a stone fort; further in, the buildings of the town were charming reminders of Cape Town's Dutch-influenced architecture, almost in exaggeration with their exuberant colour and quaint grace. At the far end of the channel stood another impressive fort, atop the heights of a conical hill where it was able to menace the channel and the inner harbour that now opened up.

"The Schottegat," Renzi was informed. It was an impressive sight—two or three miles of open water snugly within the island, completely sheltered from the worst hurricanes. Eagerly his eyes darted about, taking in what he could of the harbour and its seafront.

There were sea-craft in abundance, from small native coastal smacks to respectable traders at the inner wharves, but safely out of the way at a trot, a row of mooring piles set out from the shore, five near-identical low-built schooners were roped together.

They were not in view for long as the ship rounded to and doused sail. Lines were sent ashore and they were hauled alongside.

"Well, Herr Haugwitz, we're here in Curaçao right enough. This'n is Willemstad—where you stayin', may I ask?"

Renzi indicated that he rather hoped to have the use of his cabin for the two days while he had his meetings. This was agreed on and Renzi was left to his own devices while the ship prepared to land its cargo.

It was baking hot—unlike the more northerly Jamaica, surrounded by sea, this was an island only thirty miles off the great mass of the South American continent and at only twelve degrees above the equator.

He looked about. It was not a large town, mainly located in a typical neat Dutch grid of streets, situated on both sides of the channel. Around the Schottegat were boat-builders, warehouses, wharves—all the usual sights of a sea-port, together with the odour of fish offal, sun-baked dust and an indefinable scent, which, Renzi guessed, was the blossom of some exotic fruit.

Around a little inlet, near the roped schooners, was Parera, where the mysterious Duperré was said to be. Renzi felt light-headed—it had all been too quick, too easy. Was it a trap? He couldn't see why—no one had known he was coming.

So, all it needed was for him to step out and uncover the secret—if, in fact, it existed.

He hefted his small case. It carried convincing documents copied from a genuine merchant, contrived by Wilikins to portray a cautious representative of a Bremen trading house out to gauge prospects away from the English Caribbean. They should pass muster . . . in any ordinary circumstance.

He also had a paper with the roughly written address of an apothecary on the opposite side of the channel, helpfully provided by the American captain. With poor English and no Dutch, of course he was lost, wasn't he? It sounded thin and he prayed his answers, if he was questioned as to why he was off the beaten track, would pass muster.

It was hot and dusty on the road that wound around the inlet. Ahead he saw a discreet cluster of old buildings overhung by greenery standing alone, perfect for the role of secret operations headquarters—but were they?

Cheerful local traders passed by, some of whom waved at him, a small flock of goats was being fussed up a hill and a pair of voluble washerwomen argued as they toiled along with their bundles. All so normal—and so out of kilter with what his intellect was saying, that this had to be Napoleon's greatest threat to the Caribbean yet.

He came nearer, trying not to be seen peering too closely. The buildings were not deserted—he could see activity inside. A horse whinnied out of sight, from behind the house, then someone rode out. Renzi dropped his gaze, trudging on, then sensed the animal turn and come towards him—but it broke into an easy canter and went by.

Letting out his breath, he raised his eyes. The intervening vegetation made it impossible to see much of the interior of the buildings. He dared not linger and ambled on, admiring the scenery until he saw how he could approach the schooners without being seen—go along the foreshore and peer around the point.

Out of sight from both the buildings and the trot, he stopped not fifty yards away from the vessels. In rising excitement he saw what he was looking for. Each was armed with guns far beyond those required for self-defence, including a pair in the bows—chase guns, never needed in an innocent trader. Swivels, others. They had to be armed French naval ships.

He had half of what he needed. Now for the rest.

His attention was taken by a chilling sight. A man-o'-war was gliding slowly into her moorings. A big one—a thirty-six-gun heavy frigate, by the look of her. With a closer look, he saw she was Dutch, no doubt tasked to guard the operation.

He retraced his steps—and from a safe distance took in the decayed grandeur of the old buildings, its overgrown garden. It was impossible to penetrate, short of a stealthy creeping-up, with all this implied in frightful danger. He could see no way to get close enough.

After all this, was he to return without the vital confirmation?

He felt for the piece of paper in his pocket and decided that boldness was the only way forward: he'd go up and knock on the door and ask the way to the apothecary.

Pausing to consult his fob watch, he shook his head and looked around in frustration. He noticed the most imposing of the buildings and, on impulse, opened the garden gate and walked towards the front door. Almost immediately, to his intense satisfaction, two men silently appeared and fell into step behind him.

There was movement and the hum of voices inside, but it quickly fell away at his hesitant knock. He turned to smile uncertainly at the two behind him. They remained expressionless and Renzi knew that he was irrevocably launched into an encounter that could have only one of two possible endings.

The door was snatched open by a powerfully built man, who deftly stepped aside while Renzi was hustled in by the pair to a small, bare room. It held a table and two chairs only.

"*Asseyez-vous,*" ordered one of his escorts, before taking up position implacably across the door.

Renzi blinked in confusion, not understanding the language.

"*À présent!*" snarled the man again, gesturing unmistakably at the chair.

A short time later a younger, more open-faced man entered with another, older, and sat opposite. "How can we be of service to you?" he asked mildly, in French.

"*Oh, ich verstehe nicht französisch,*" Renzi said weakly, clutching his case but inwardly exulting. If this was not a French naval officer, he stood well flammed. The only task now was to beat a hasty retreat with his precious information.

At his words the younger glanced at the other significantly. *"D'Allemand,"* he muttered.

The older nodded and replied in French, "He's a spy, of course."

"You think so, *mon amiral?* A spy who thinks to come right up and knock on the door? And doesn't know French? Even the English are not that stupid!"

So the older must be Duperré, he surmised, discreetly noting his features with interest.

The younger turned to Renzi and, with an encouraging smile, said kindly, "We know you're a spy, my friend. Now we're going to take you outside and execute you."

Renzi smiled back, but spread his hands sorrowfully in incomprehension. "Sorry, sorry. You spik Engleesh, I unnerstand."

As if he was to be fooled by that old trick.

"*Merde.* Go and find someone with German for this imbecile," the young man said, and, with another sharp look at Renzi, left.

The swirl of the day resumed: voices raised, orders loudly given amid much bustle. Renzi caught snatches of what was being said, every bit worth hearing.

". . . the admiral said . . . took a fat sugar scow off Morant . . . get this signal off . . . he must be at the rendezvous point as agreed by . . ."

It was conclusive. He had both heard and seen enough. This was indeed the tactile reality and proof of what he had logically foreseen. Sudden impatience seized him—but then he realised that the greatest danger was yet to come: if the German speaker was a native, could he keep up the pretence?

A cold wash of apprehension went over him. He was comfortable with the Hochdeutsch of Goethe but city slang was beyond him.

Footsteps approached and the young man brought in a nervous waiter, still in his apron.

"Guten Tag. Wie heißt du?" he asked, after prompting.

Renzi felt a flood of relief. The man was Alsatian with an atrocious accent.

He beamed. "My name is Haugwitz, a merchant of Bremen. Do tell these gentlemen that I have no wish to intrude, merely to ask the way to this address." He handed over the paper with a winning smile.

It was passed across for scrutiny. The young man looked up, then reached out for Renzi's case.

"Tell Monsieur Haugwitz that I am admiring his satchel. Where was it made at all?" He detached it from Renzi's grasp and rummaged inside while Renzi nervously allowed that it was a family heirloom, passed down from his father and therefore from Oldenburg.

The papers inside were riffled through, then replaced and the case handed back. "Tell him he's a fool to turn east, the apothecary is to the west—over the channel in Otrabanda. Show him out, and point him in the right direction."

It was translated and Renzi made much of thanking all in sight. Smothering a sigh of relief, he gave a friendly wave and set out once more.

Chapter 9

Mysterious land under their lee, the three frigates glided quietly inshore, a thickening in the gloom of a moonless night. As one, sail was struck and their anchors tumbled down—the Curaçao expedition came to its rest.

"Well, now, Nicholas. How do you feel that you've caused an armada such as this to stir?" Kydd said, in a tone that suggested he was only half in jest. They were together on deck, watching as the ship secured from sea.

"If truth be told, rather less than overjoyed, brother."

"Since your report I've never seen Dacres so far heated. Volleys orders in all directions like musket fire, rages at his flag-lieutenant for not performing miracles and conjures another frigate from somewhere for the final assault." Kydd shook his head in wonder. "What was it you told him?"

"Naught but what I witnessed. It was not a conversation I'd like to repeat and I'm glad to be out of it now, having done my duty."

"How so?" Kydd asked curiously.

"Well, if you must know, he made me swear on my honour to the truth of what I was telling him, high words about a gentleman's honour and so forth. An inquisition to which I'm unaccustomed, dear fellow."

"You can surely see that he's concerned he's not following some fantastical logical theory that will be laughed at later if—"

"I know what I saw and heard."

"Yes, but he's to mount an invasion of Curaçao as the only means he has to lay hands on the villains running your operation. The expense of such has to be justified to their lordships of the Admiralty later, of course, and to take up precious men-o'-war at this time is not a trivial matter, old trout."

Renzi smiled thinly. "Quite. I do observe, however, that he is letting it be generally known that this is a strike for empire against the Dutch, and keeping quiet about the other. I'd like to think it's a ploy to protect his intelligence source, but rather suspect it to be a way of keeping face should we fail in our larger object."

"You're being hard on the man, Nicholas. With no other in support o' your theory, can you blame him for steering small?"

"Umm. So we are three frigates only?"

"It will be four. *Fisgard* joins us here as soon as she can. While we could have ships-of-the-line, should we ask, we need frigates as can sail up the channel."

"Is that Aruba?" Renzi said, looking at the island that loomed in the blackness.

"A place of assembly only. One of your three Dutch islands with Bonaire. It's a night's sail from Curaçao—don't want 'em dismayed before time. If they tumble to what we're about, they won't know which island we're making motions towards."

"So, four frigates to set against an enemy who's ashore with, I'm obliged to remark, a plenitude of forts and guns? It will be a singular plan indeed that sets sail against soldiers."

"Well, we won't be long in the waiting. All captains will come together in an hour to hear of it."

"Aboard the saucy *Arethusa?*"

"The same. Charles Brisbane. Never met the fellow, but heard he was with Nelson at Bastia, and not so long before we arrived, with Lydiard in *Anson,* took the Spanish frigate *Pomona* from under the guns of Morro Castle at Havana, a fine piece of work. Well trusted by Dacres, which is why he has this command."

"So—*Arethusa, Anson, Fisgard* and ourselves, no soldiers, no artillery, no horses . . ."

"More than a match, don't you think?"

It was with a twinge of envy that Kydd came aboard *Arethusa.*

This famous ship, subject of ballad and many a fore-bitter sea-song, was a heavy frigate and it showed. Besides guns half the size again of *L'Aurore*'s, her every dimension was bigger—length, beam, spars, anchors and accommodation. The grandest, Captain Brisbane's own great cabin, was no exception and was furnished as to be expected of a successful senior captain with prize money to spare.

The man was tall and carried himself with a peculiar intensity, his eyes large and expressive. He was an impeccable host and quickly settled his guests to a small but well-planned supper.

Soon Kydd found himself reminiscing with the amiable Brisbane about Jervis, the irascible Lord St Vincent, while the older man brought to mind in an amusing way the Great Siege of Gibraltar so many years before.

He knew Lydiard of *Anson,* of course, and after giving a modest account of Trafalgar, he heard in return of him in an eighteen-gun sloop assisting a British warship in an epic battle against an enemy frigate that had ended when it finally struck. As luck would have it, it was recounted, when boats were lowered to take possession a damaged fore-mast fell and the French took the opportunity to re-hoist colours and make their escape.

"Right, gentlemen," Brisbane said, as supper things were cleared away and a light Madeira was produced. "I rather think it time to talk about the morrow. This is not by way of a council-of-war but your acquainting with my plan, which, should it fail, will be my responsibility entirely."

It needed saying: a council-of-war implied a shared liability. Brisbane was not a commodore and had no other authority than that of senior captain but was making it clear he was taking the burden for failure entirely on himself.

"The first matter that we must touch on is—"

A distant wail of boatswain's pipes sounded faint and clear. "Ah—that must be William now. Stout fellow, he must have cracked on sail quite unreasonably to be with us."

He waited until there was a polite knock at the door and a pleasant, much-weathered officer appeared.

"Ah, yes. Gentlemen—Captain Bolton of *Fisgard,* who cannot abide to be overlooked in the article of fighting."

After introductions were complete, Brisbane resumed:

"As I was about to say, I would have you under no misapprehension as to the main objective of this descent on Curaçao."

There were puzzled looks and he went on quickly, "Which is, you'll be surprised to learn, not to add further conquest to His Majesty's dominions but for quite another reason. I have confidential instructions from Admiral Dacres that direct me to turn my best endeavours to the locating and extirpation of a secret base from which the French are conducting a species of *guerre de course* by naval means against our sugar trade."

He cut short the general stir. "This is the reason why we have been so singularly unsuccessful in our protection, being unknowingly beset by a fleet operation under naval direction when we expected it to be privateers of the common sort. This must be stopped or we suffer ruinous loss to our commerce at great hazard to our conduct of the war as a whole."

"Charles, would it be impertinent to enquire as to how we've gained possession of this information?" Lydiard asked.

"I'm told it's from a source of intelligence that the admiral considers of the highest quality. I conceive it may be relied upon, old fellow."

"Then—"

"Then it does colour the nature of our assault. We have the location of the base and it is my intention that, once we have penetrated their defences, we hold while we send a flying column to surround and destroy the operation, after which time we withdraw."

He considered for a moment, then added, with a wolfish smile, "That is, unless we are sanguine that we have succeeded beyond the ordinary. In which case our assault might then be better termed an invasion."

Kydd warmed to the man. Here was a leader who was not going to let opportunities pass for want of enterprise.

"Let's talk now of what we face. The harbour of Willemstad is called the Schottegat and is in the nature of an inland water of considerable extent. The only entrance is a mile-long channel, a hundred yards or so wide at best. On the right side is the older main town, on the left extensive civil works. The town is protected by Fort Amsterdam, a large fort at the seaward entrance of the channel to the right. It rates two tiers of sixty guns in all. There's another, Fort Republiek, even bigger, at the other end of the channel, also on the right."

"So we land on the left?" Bolton said.

"Ah, no. With both forts on the right, the Hollanders will feel sure we'll land up the coast on the left, form up and advance on them. Without a doubt they've their soldiery there, waiting to welcome us. I've a notion we're to surprise 'em and take the direct route to the right."

"In the teeth of these forts? A brazen move, I believe," Lydiard drawled.

"You think so? But then our hand is forced—it's to the right a mile or so that the base is located."

"Er, we've heard nothing of their sea forces," Kydd interposed, remembering what Renzi had said about seeing a thirty-six-gun frigate in the harbour.

"Oh, yes," Brisbane replied airily. "A twenty-two-gun corvette and a thirty-six-gun frigate were mentioned. These may inconvenience and will have to be silenced, of course."

Kydd started. This was not a plan: it was a disaster in the making. Was he the death-or-glory type that every sailor feared?

Lydiard seemed uneasy, too, and said carefully, "An attack from the front against a prepared enemy is a perilous undertaking at any time, Charles. Could not the main objective be secured by other means—for instance, by the privy landing of a party at night to take the base and its people?"

"I rather fear the risk is too great."

"The risk?"

"That in failing it would alert the Dutch to what we're chiefly about. No, this cannot be allowed. We go forward as before."

"If the objective is so important," Kydd interjected, "might we not delay until we can rouse up some military reinforcement and be sure of it?"

"It is *because* it is so important that we cannot tolerate delay, dear chap."

He suddenly grinned. "To see you all so mumchance is diverting in the extreme. Let me ease your concerns a little. I have given this much thought and come to the conclusion that to do the opposite of what they expect is our best chance. In this case they will be reckoning that we stand off and salute them with a long cannonade, then send in troops to contest the field in the most obvious place—the clear flat ground to the left of the channel."

"And instead?"

"You will have noticed that the channel orients down to the sou'-sou'west. With the present easterly we may count on a fair wind to sail on directly inside at the first whisper of daylight. Now, if I were the Dutch commander I'd situate his thirty-six somewhere near the entrance, moored a-crossways to offer his broadside to any unwelcome guest, supported by the corvette in likewise pose."

"Sealing off the channel to us? A hard thing to face."

"No, for he can't impede access by his own shipping and must leave a space. Where they can go, so can we. Consider—without warning we appear out of the dawn and without a by-your-leave boldly continue on into the channel, past the fort, past the ships, all of which need time to close up for action. Too late! The town lies under our guns."

"And then?" Bolton said coolly. "We've marines, armed seamen—do we then at our leisure step ashore and take the capital?"

"I shall be clearer. The flying column lands and makes straight for the base. That is essential. The rest depends on planning and forethought, with the ability to change objectives at short notice. As I said, I've given it much consideration. Here are the details, gentlemen."

Brisbane produced a scheme from his desk that was a model of military planning. Each ship had its own task: *Arethusa* would lead and tackle the thirty-six. *L'Aurore,* the lightest, would follow with the vital task of landing the flying column when practicable. The heavyweight *Anson* would be next, anchoring mid-channel to menace the worst of the opposition, while *Fisgard* would take the rear and go to the support of any in difficulty.

At the individual level, each ship's company's Royal Marines and seamen would be divided between "boarders" and "stormers" and a skeleton working crew, enabling snap decisions to be made on the spot for their deployment depending on progress.

"And when the forts wake up?" Lydiard said, with a half-smile. "When we're at anchor at point-blank range? This is a target even a militiaman may not miss."

"An observation well made," Brisbane said smoothly. "This is why each ship will contribute to a party armed with crow-bars and axes who will force entrance into the sea-gate of Fort Amsterdam through the portcullis while the Fisgards storm the rear of the fortress with ladder and grapnel."

There were gasps but whether in shock or admiration it was difficult to tell.

"Recollecting that this fort is intended to defend to seaward—we shall be assaulting from landward."

"And the other?" persisted Lydiard.

"Fort Republiek will be helpless, as being unable to fire on account of ourselves being within the town limits."

In the cool of the night, there was a gentle, lulling heave to the sea and it seemed preposterous to believe that they had any kind of a chance—Kydd's experience at the assault and conquest of another Dutch outpost of empire, Cape Town, had shown him how only the professional military had what it took to conduct an advance on the enemy in their own territory. By comparison they were amateurs—courageous, spirited and intelligent, but amateurs for all that.

"Everything depends on our forcing entry past the fort," Bolton said slowly. "If we knew that was assured . . ."

"It'll be assured if we do it," Kydd snapped. "Clap on all sail and press on and we can't fail."

Unsaid was what would happen if they penetrated into the desperately restricted waters inside but then found it untenable to remain. To turn completely about by some means and effect a retreat under overwhelming fire . . .

As morning imperceptibly lightened the tropical seascape in a soft violet, the four frigates hove to ten miles off Curaçao, south of Willemstad and the channel, and safely out of sight.

There was that preternatural heightening of the senses as always felt before an action, but Kydd had much to occupy his mind.

Details: the division of seamen into boarders and stormers, the equipping of the boatswain's party with the right gear, the clearing away of an anchor for rapid letting go and more—down to the colour of the field sign that each man would wear.

Last, every single boat the ship possessed was put into the water for towing.

They were ready.

Brisbane was not one for ceremony, and it was his single flag "preparative" whipping down in *Arethusa* that set the little armada on its way.

By degrees the light strengthened, and when they made landfall, visibility in the mists of morning was enough. Formless as a dream, the rumpled coast gradually took on reality. The channel entrance was impossible to miss, the gentle fall each side in the even run of the shoreline unmistakable—as was the squat menace of Fort Amsterdam firming out of the haze.

They were committed.

Arethusa took the lead, *L'Aurore* fell in close astern and the others followed, arrowing on a line of bearing straight for the channel entrance. A quiet torpor seemed to lie on the day-fresh landscape—not a thing moved. They came closer; a Dutch flag drooped atop the fort. *Arethusa* and each ship following had battle-ensigns a-fly but hoisted at the main-masthead of each was a large white flag of truce, a legitimate move that Brisbane hoped would confuse and delay any response. But it was at the cost of preventing any British ship opening fire while such a flag flew.

Nearer still, and not a gun had fired. Ahead, however, by the seaward entrance, just as Brisbane had foreseen, the thirty-six was moored athwart, its broadside squarely across their track. Beyond, the spars of the corvette were in a similar position, and both had left a space clear for ships to pass.

It was astounding: arrow-straight for the enemy's vitals and still no gunfire, only the gentle whisper of wind in the sails, the familiar creaking and slatting to be heard in any ship under sail, and ahead the entrance broadening.

A sudden thud—the white of a discharge from the fort rose and swelled in the light airs. The ships stood on. Two more from the casemates. Did they not see the flags of truce? If so, they were ignoring them. Then an uneven firing came on, which hid the fort in roiling gunsmoke.

They had engaged too soon! In the time of reloading the four ships were up with the entrance and then inside, insanely close to the fort, with the town slipping by closer than Portsmouth Point.

Then the light morning breeze hesitated—and backed into the north. Instantly the moment became fraught with peril. Headed by a foul wind, the ships slowed and began to yaw. It was the worst of luck, and Kydd's mind raced as he tried to think how Brisbane could retrieve their predicament. No complex signals were possible in the rapidly changing circumstances and it was inconceivable that four ships in the tight space could back away now.

Then, as if relenting, the winds veered back to the east and they took up again on their perilous course.

There was a burst of musket fire from the left side as soldiers ran up, and then they were past, heading for the anchored thirty-six. Aboard there was frantic activity on her deck. Men boiled up from below but stopped, paralysed with fear at the sight of the heavy frigate about to pass by her stern to smash in a pulverising broadside. But she did not, for the flag of truce was still flying and not a single shot had been fired from any British ship.

Arethusa's helm went over and in the same instant her anchor plunged down and she slewed about, her bowsprit crazily jutting over the little seawall and path, pointing directly into the town. By now gunfire had broken out generally in a bewildering chaos of noise and powder-smoke.

L'Aurore followed and, passing *Arethusa,* did the same, clearing the way for *Anson* to take position mid-channel. Peering back through the rolling smoke it looked as if *Fisgard* had taken the ground with the foul wind and was swinging across the water but then she broke free and, as planned, heaved to ready.

Kydd saw that something was going on in *Arethusa.* A group of officers were clustered around the capstan as Brisbane conspicuously bent to a task: the air was filling with the whip and slam of shot, but he was writing. He finished, folded a note and handed it to a midshipman with a strip of white cloth pinned around his hat.

The brave lad tumbled into the gig and under a large white flag was pulled frantically to a landing place at the Waaigat, a side-water for small craft. Kydd gave a grim smile: Brisbane was giving them chance of surrender before broadsides at point-blank range devastated the town. It was a terrible risk, though, for at any time the Dutch artillery could arrive to smash the ships to ruin.

There was no slackening in the gunfire from the shore and first one then another man fell in *Arethusa,* and *L'Aurore* took her first casualty, a fo'c'sle hand, Timmins, who dropped into a motionless huddle.

Kydd felt anger rise. Then the midshipman came into view and scrambled up the side to report to Brisbane.

The white flag at the masthead soon whipped down and *Arethusa*'s boats were in the water, striking towards the stunned thirty-six, Brisbane waving his sword like a madman.

"Boarders, *awaaaay!*" Kydd roared, and stood aside as men raced to take up their weapons and man the boats. Gilbey seemed to have been infected with the same frenzy and, with drawn blade, bellowed warlike curses at them while they stretched out to take the enemy from the other side. The gloves were off now.

In minutes it was all over in the thirty-six, and Brisbane himself hauled down its colours.

With rising feeling Kydd looked around. *Anson* had sent boats, which were now alongside the corvette, and fighting was taking place on its upper deck. There could be only one outcome there.

"Stand to, the stormers!" he called. It had to be soon or not at all: the enemy could not be given time to bring up forces in mass.

Then he saw what he had been waiting for: Brisbane had taken boat and the men bent to their oars to head for the jetty followed by his other boats.

"Flying column, away!" he roared. "Mr Curzon, warp alongside the thirty-six and take possession. Stormers, away!"

Kydd took the tiller of his boat as it filled. This was the vital flying column that had to succeed. Beside him a set-faced Renzi sat. Kydd grinned at him and ordered the boat to bear away inshore, bellowing at them as he, too, was caught up in the excitement.

The zing and smack of musketry was all about them but Kydd, with a storm of emotion, had seen that every one of the frigate captains was now in a boat heading in. He waved his sword aloft in a crazy show and saw them all return the gesture.

The boat following each was packed with marines, and as the boats made to land at the jetty they stood off and kept up fire over the heads of those storming ashore. Quickly they assembled and trotted off to the south, in the direction of the ominous massive ramparts of Fort Amsterdam. Kydd motioned his stormers to join them.

The flying column was headed in another direction, to a little jetty on the opposite side of the Waaigat. "Go!" The men needed no encouragement—they formed up quickly. Ten in all: marines, seamen, Kydd and Renzi. Muskets and cutlasses. To take on an entire naval base.

As they made off, Kydd forced himself to an objective coolness. This was not to be a frontal assault on the base but, rather, a holding operation, keeping enemy heads down while a decision was made. Renzi's information was enough to indicate that the base was only lightly defended, if at all, due to its clandestine nature. Possibly it could be carried by the men he had, that was his decision, but made only after a reconnaissance.

This side of the Waaigat there were few buildings and the road was deserted. Their rapid progress had wrong-footed the Dutch—a furiously rising swell of firing to the south was probably the storming of Fort Amsterdam and their attention was no doubt all there.

"How far more, Nicholas?" Kydd panted. Renzi was by his side—it had been given out that he was aware that this was to be a glorious occasion and wished to be present to record the action but in reality his presence was crucial in identifying the location.

"Not far—under a mile in all. Round this hill and along the shoreline a space," he gasped. Sea life was not the best preparation for a fast march and Kydd noted Sergeant Dodd behind breathing deeply too.

The glittering expanse of the Schottegat came into view and with it their objective.

"Fall back!" Kydd ordered, bringing them all out of sight, remaining to peer past a thick bush.

"The old building with the garden near overgrown," Renzi pointed out.

It was quiet—too quiet. But then again a wise French commander of a secret base would lie low and keep watch until the purpose and gravity of the British assault became known, then make his move. Any forces he might have would therefore be held within the building—and ready for them.

They didn't have too much time, however, for at any moment the tide of war could turn against those storming the fort and a retreat would be forced on them. Kydd darted a glance around. "We've got an advantage. Sar'nt Dodd!" He had spotted one thing in their favour but wanted confirmation.

"Sah!"

"Am I right? The building yonder is more or less on a point of land sticking out into the Schottegat. Doesn't that mean we need only advance on this side to be sure we have 'em under eye all the time?"

"Er, yessir."

"Very well. Half o' your men to make a stand here in line, the rest with me."

They didn't have the luxury of time to take a cautious approach: they would have to show themselves and rely on those covering them to spot where musket fire was coming from and deal with it.

Kydd, with four men only, ran from bush to tree, dodging until they got close, then dropped to see what they could. There were no lights inside, understandable as such would be aiming points. But there was a menacing, absolute stillness that played on the nerves.

Did the French have an unpleasant surprise waiting? Were they even now squarely in the sights of hidden marksmen waiting for them to trespass before giving away the secret of their presence by opening fire?

Doubts tore at Kydd. The distant firing around Fort Amsterdam was slackening. Now individual shots were all that could be made out. Something had happened. One way or the other there had been a victory won—or lost. There was no more time.

"Watch out for me!" he said hoarsely. He got to his feet and sprinted for the door, falling to one side on the expectation of a sudden eruption of armed men.

Nerves keyed up to the limit he listened. Nothing—not even a creak or whisper.

There came the sound of running feet—but it was Dodd arriving to take position the other side of the door.

Kydd stood motionless, listening. Not the tiniest whisper—just the thudding of his heart.

He flashed a warning look at the sergeant. They had to move, and in a violent swing Kydd crashed against the door—and fell sprawling as it gave easily. Dodd stepped over him quickly and went in, bayonet at the ready. Scrambling to his feet, Kydd caught up and, every nerve taut, they moved forward.

There was a sudden crash from a side room. They wheeled to meet the threat. A cat miaowed its annoyance, ran out and was gone.

Cautiously they peered into the room. There was nobody. The other rooms were the same—just the sad debris of a deserted house, the smell of decay. Feverishly they cast this way and that.

At the rear of the house, French windows opened on to a pleasant but overgrown sitting-out area and an ornamental pond that stank with weed. Neglected and shrivelled fruit hung from a small orchard and grass was thick and rank.

And still there was not the slightest betraying creak or scrape.

Kydd blinked and tried to think, retracing their steps and looking about more carefully.

They searched the house room by room until at last he was forced to accept that there was absolutely nothing anywhere, not the tiniest scrap of evidence to show that this had once been a threatening secret naval base.

"Call 'em here, Sar'nt," he ordered.

The rest arrived, hesitantly looking about, Renzi's face set tight.

"Nicholas," Kydd asked in a low voice, "are you not mistaken in your locations? There's nothing here to—"

Renzi looked stunned, but managed, "It was here, I'll swear. Just that . . ."

He went quickly to a side room. "This is where . . ." He tailed off, staring at the few sticks of mildewed furniture, odorous rubbish in a corner, a broken child's toy and shook his head in disbelief.

"But I—I . . ."

"You men take the garden. Sar'nt Dodd, I want you to take a good look around outside. Anything—anything at all as will show us where the Frenchies went."

"Sah!"

"Now, Nicholas. I have to ask it of you—you're entirely sure this is where you were taken?"

With a worried, hunted look Renzi hurried from the house out to where bemused marines and seamen were poking about in the grounds and by the gate. He reached the road, then turned and looked back at the house. "It is! This *is* the place!"

Kydd joined him. "Then we've a pretty tale to take back to Brisbane, not to say Admiral Dacres. I do hope you have explanations, old fellow."

"Excellent, excellent!" Brisbane said, rubbing his hands with glee. "We reduced Fort Amsterdam in something like ten minutes. The citadel yielded without a fight and the town is ours. The last resistance remaining is Fort Republiek on the hill there. I'm shortly to warp up all four frigates and threaten a bombardment as will shake 'em out of their clogs, the villains, then all Curaçao will be ours."

He collected himself and asked solicitously, "And, it being the whole point of all these fireworks, you've laid hold on the secret Frenchy base, I take it?"

"Um, not as who's to say, Charles," Kydd answered awkwardly, "they being not at home to us."

He gave a quick account of their morning, finishing with a weak smile.

Brisbane said, "Why, it has to be they made for the hills when they heard our first shots. Won't help 'em, for the island will be ours before noon and we'll make search for wherever they went to ground. Don't worry, we'll find 'em."

Kydd looked up at Renzi. "Now, don't take this amiss, dear fellow, but if sworn to it, I'd be obliged to say there was nothing in any wise in that house that gives us reason to think anyone was there.

No scraps o' food, papers, odd military bits that show they left in a hurry. Nothing."

"I—I can't account for it, that I'm forced to admit . . ."

"An unkind cove would say further there's not even the slightest piece of evidence to show that would justify our invasion of Curaçao in any sense, none at all."

"It's impossible! I just can't understand it . . ."

"Sit down, Mr Renzi," Dacres said heavily, eyeing him with distaste. "You've heard that Captain Brisbane reports not a single sign whatsoever of a Frenchman or a base? None, sir!"

"This is quite unaccountable to me, sir," Renzi began, "being that we found the right house and—"

"There was no evidence at all that Frenchmen were ever there. This is insupportable, sir! You gave me your word of honour on what you say transpired there."

"Sir, I—"

"On your say-so I went ahead with a damn risky invasion of a whole island. What do you say to that, sir?"

"Why, there's no possible reply I can make, sir."

Dacres snorted. "Except the action was carried off with the greatest success, I'd be a laughing stock."

His expression eased fractionally at the reminder of military conquest in his name and he continued more equably, "As it is, you should be grateful there was such an outcome as none now will question its reason."

Renzi kept his silence, burning with embarrassment and anger.

"I don't quite know what Commodore D'Auvergne saw in you, Renzi, but as some species of spy you don't cut it with me, I have to say. Experienced, my left foot!"

Gathering his papers, he snapped, "I see no further need of your services, sir. You may indent for outstanding expenses to Mr

Wilikins and I shall bid you good-day."

Rising, Renzi blinked away his anger. As he left Dacres called after him, "And, for God's sake, let's hear no more of this tomfoolery about secret bases and phantom fleets."

Kydd tried to be sympathetic but was no hand at disguising his true feelings. "Bad luck, is all, m' friend. They're sure to be, er, somewhere. A rattling good theory—copper-bottomed logic and, um, well reckoned. Not your fault it didn't turn out right."

Renzi said nothing, glowering at his glass.

"Still, one good thing for you, Nicholas."

"Oh?"

"*Nereide* frigate returned from the dockyard while we were gone."

"So?"

"Cheer up, old trout. That means we're to return to Barbados. You won't have to look 'em in the eye any more."

"You don't believe I saw anything. You think it was all an opium dream."

"I didn't say that."

"Never mind. I'm doubting my own senses anyway."

Kydd tactfully steered the conversation away. "At the end of the hurricane season Barbados is a fine place. I've a mind to enjoy it, brother."

"With Miss Amelia?"

"Why, if she takes a fancy."

L'Aurore slipped out of Port Royal the next day in company with *Arethusa*.

It was a pleasant passage to Barbados, the two frigates conscious of making a fine sight as they stretched away through the very centre of the Caribbean.

As they neared the Leeward Islands, though, it became clear that the seas were deserted—swept clean. To fail to raise a single sail in all that distance was not natural. Whatever was feeding on the West Indian trade was abroad still, mysterious and malignant.

It was deeply unsettling.

Dispatches had gone ahead by cutter, and by the time they reached Barbados the whole of Bridgetown was out *en fête* to see and greet the victors of Curaçao. As they came to their moorings in Carlisle Bay boats streamed out, some with quantities of ladies intent on throwing flowers on to the quarterdeck; others stood screaming their adulation, and still more came out simply to circle the two frigates and gaze on the heroes of the hour.

But what brought the greatest flush of pride to Kydd's face was the Leeward Islands Squadron manning yards in their honour, lines of great ships acknowledging valour and achievement.

It had been a breathtaking adventure crowned with success, but deep within, it was disturbing. The main objective had been missed—was this, then, the people seizing on any good news to alleviate an impending apocalypse?

"Ship open to visitors until sunset, Mr Gilbey," Kydd told the first lieutenant, then went below to sort out his paperwork. Back under the command of Cochrane, there were so many matters to attend to, not the least of which was the rendering of his accounts to the satisfaction of the acidulous clerk of the cheque.

He worked at the pile and was pleased at progress when a messenger arrived. "An' Mr Curzon would be happy to see you on deck, sir."

This was unusual to the point of puzzling, for it was the general form for an officer-of-the-watch requesting his captain's presence on deck in filthy weather as a situation deteriorated.

Kydd tugged on his hat and emerged on the upper deck, ready for whatever had to be faced.

"Sir, she vows that no other will do to receive her expression of admiration for the action just passed."

"Why, Miss Amelia!"

The officers all about the banqueting hall roared with laughter. Brisbane was a fine speaker—modest, entertaining and with a good line in anecdotes that his all-naval audience were in a mood to appreciate.

The baffling losses had built a frustration that demanded release, and the evening was well on its way. It was a pity that Renzi could not attend—he was out of sorts after his humiliating experience and this warm gathering would have restored a measure of equanimity. Why he had claimed he had been taken into a secret base and concocted a story that had had Dacres mounting an expedition was an utter mystery. Kydd sincerely hoped it wasn't a delusion brought on by his conspicuous lack of literary success.

"Wine with you, sir!" The youthful sloop commander just along was looking at him with something uncomfortably like hero worship.

He graciously complied, realising a little self-consciously that there was every reason for the attitude. Not only with the legendary Nelson at Trafalgar, he had service going back as far as the beginning of the last war, during the dark days of the French Revolution. And now he was a proven frigate captain roaming the seas . . .

The feast had been cunningly prepared with old favourites but, in deference to the climate and setting, many a Caribbean delicacy as well. He tucked into more jerk pork and idly listened to Bolton, two down, weave a complicated yarn about *Fisgard* and the North Sea.

There was no doubt now, he was succeeding in life. The Curaçao action would be noticed in England and he had been a principal in the affair. And, of course, with the taking of two significant-sized warships with little damage and three minor there would be useful awards of prize money to look forward to.

And in society—there was no mistaking the gleam in Miss

Amelia's eye and the envious looks of her sister. There had been a casual invitation from her father for an at-home in the near future, whatever that meant . . .

Yes, things were looking rosy for him, he concluded. As long as this vexing threat hanging over them was dealt with.

The spirited hum of conversation slackened as the cloth was drawn, and blue smoke spiralled up as the brandy came out. Several officers left to "ease springs," leaving their places empty.

Kydd allowed his thoughts to wander agreeably as he relaxed back in his chair.

Suddenly aware that a figure had taken the vacant chair opposite, he refocused and prepared to engage in easy conversation.

It was Tyrell.

"You! Um, Kydd, isn't it?" The man's voice was thick with drink but it still held a steely hardness.

"It is." He was enjoying the evening too much to have it affected by a bitter and aggrieved sot. He would indulge the man for a few minutes, then make his excuses.

"Damn it, man! I've seen you afore, sir, and I'd like to know where."

Kydd's warm feelings drained away.

If this ghost from his past was intent on laying bare those raw memories of his brutish rite of passage into the Navy, he would resist. Yet the feral presence before him of the one whose terrifying figure had most haunted his existence then still had the power to unnerve.

"If you must, Rufus, it was I who saw you home the night of the levee if you'll recall."

"Not that, y' fool. Years past, some time in the last war. Long time back. Where did I see you? Answer me, sir!"

Kydd took a breath, then steadied. He replied coolly, "Why, the London season, perhaps. Vauxhall Gardens by night is not to be missed and—"

"Never trifle with such tommyrot! Popinjays prancing up and down like ninnies, gib-faced dandies with fusty tomrig in tow—I've forbidden my wife to attend ever, against her fool wishes I'm sorry to say, and I'm surprised you see fit to show your face at such—such folly!"

"Then I'm at a stand, sir," Kydd drawled carefully. Wanting to strike back at the apparition from his past, he forced himself to muse artlessly, "In the sea service—were you at the Nile at all? I was a lieutenant in *Tenacious,* as I recollect, and—"

"No!"

"At Trafalgar, then. I was at the time in my present command and had the honour—"

Tyrell's face reddened. "Neither!" he retorted. "I've always been disappointed in m' hopes for a fleet action of merit. No, sir, I've a notion it's to be years before . . . and somewhere . . ."

"Then at the theatre? Do you favour Miss Jordan at all? Much faded now but an actress of fine parts, I'm persuaded."

Tyrell thumped the table angrily. "I never forget a face, sir," he grated. "As many a deserter who thought to hide can testify. No, Kydd, I'll have your number and won't be denied."

Just south of the Garrison Savannah Renzi had found a small, perfectly formed beach, which, with its arc of offshore reefs, was not favoured by the fisher-folk or, it seemed, by others. His mood was black and he didn't want company.

He went to a gnarled tree overhanging the glistening white sand and sat in its shade, gazing out over the translucent green seas, waves lazily creaming in at regular intervals. The hot smell of sun on sand was soothing and he felt his mood gradually ease.

He had some thinking to do. It had been a humiliating and embarrassing experience, not only for his standing with the admiral, which was not so important to him, but more for his friendship with

Kydd. Did Kydd really believe that he had made up a story about stealing into a secret base to cover the failure of his logical theory? If so, it was difficult to blame him, for there was not a shred of independent evidence that such did in fact exist.

He realised he had now to face a disturbing, frightening possibility. Was it all a species of dream, of ardent wish-fulfilment, generated by a fevered brain to . . .

To what? As far as he was aware, there was no mental instability in his family, no incidents in his past to lead him to doubt his senses now. Even so, he was no medical man and it had to be considered.

Two possibilities. Either he was mad, deluded and not responsible—or he was not.

Take the first. There was nothing he could do about this and presumably he must wait for the inevitable spiral into madness. So, do nothing.

The other. If he was not, then . . . it had really happened. And therefore he must find an explanation consistent with the facts as reported by his own perceptions.

Fact: he had heard from the informant directly, one who had without prompting confirmed his theory and told him where to find the base.

Fact: he had acted on this and duly uncovered it. While there, the experience had been entirely what he would have expected, given the circumstances.

Fact: a short time later, at the taking of Curaçao, the self-same house had been utterly without any sign that it was his secret base, and the losses had continued. It was beyond reason to imagine that a complex operation conducted there and hastily vacated would have left no traces whatsoever.

He heaved a sigh. It would take a heroic effort of imagination to reconcile these.

After cudgelling his brain for as long as he could bear it, he lay back in the sand, looking up through the gently waving branches to the immense bowl of innocent blue sky, and let his mind wander.

So what would *he* do if he were the commander of a clandestine naval operation needing to keep its secret secure? Presumably anything: if it were knocked out, so would be the nerve-centre of the planned predation. How would he go about this? It would seem reasonable to take every care to seal tight the headquarters so none could possibly suspect its existence, the consequence of discovery being so catastrophic.

Yet that didn't fit with what he had seen. That was not how it had been in Curaçao: the building was not properly guarded and, in any case, while the Dutch were French allies and vassals, they were proud and independent, and it would be a questionable thing indeed to rely on them allowing a covert operation on their sovereign territory.

But he had overheard with his own ears naval talk, the name Duperré and so on. In complete agreement with what he had heard from his informant. It made no sense at all unless . . .

A new thought took shape, one that, wildly improbable as it was, brought together these mutually conflicting elements and went on to explain everything.

He sat up, energised. It would of course imply a brilliant mind, one with organisational skills well beyond the ordinary, whose grasp of the shadowy world of undercover operations was nothing short of masterly—for he was considering that the entire business with Curaçao had been nothing but a charade, aimed squarely at himself.

This great mind had heard of Renzi's theory of a fleet controlled and deployed centrally against Britain's Caribbean trade, probably from some public indiscretion by the dismissive Dacres. He had realised that someone had stumbled on the truth and needed to move instantly before any steps were taken to uncover and neutralise his base.

The move Duperré—if that was his name—had taken was breathtaking, a perfect solution. Comprehensively discredit Renzi and thereby his theory.

The result would be no more talk of searching for a mythical secret base: the Royal Navy would go on to become spread impossibly thin in endless vain patrols.

And, damn it, Duperré *had* succeeded: thanks to the clever failure at Curaçao, there was not the slightest chance of Renzi's theory ever being revisited or any other explanation listened to.

Masterly.

But Duperré had had necessarily to yield one vital point. As a result of his subterfuge, he could not help but provide Renzi with a priceless piece of knowledge: by going to such lengths he had confirmed that what Renzi had come up with was the reality. He had been right after all.

The realisation came in a releasing flood that begged for action. He scrambled to his feet and began pacing up and down, reviewing what had happened.

Orders must have gone out to send a clever agent whose task it would be to contact Renzi and give him information that bore out what he already believed, while at the same time dispatching men and orders to Curaçao to set up the dummy base in accordance. Really quite simple and, being prepared to accept anything that supported his theory, Renzi had fallen for it. A stickler for detail, this canny mastermind had been so thorough in his orders that not the tiniest scrap or indication would be found—the careful replacing of rubbish and other forlorn detritus of a long-deserted house was nothing short of artistic.

Then how would the fleet operation work? The crucial element was communications. To achieve such rapid response to both threat and promise there had to be an incredibly speedy method of passing on information and orders.

Renzi's pacing quickened. To get intelligence out implied a network of spies relaying news of planned trading-ship movements, however it was done. That would result in orders to the nearest predator, wherever concealed, to lie in wait for it.

Then there was intelligence of naval movements. Much more difficult but not impossible. Knowledge of patrol lines, the known habits of individual captains—an astute and imaginative mind could make much of this. Then the word would go out for redeployment and the other half of the equation was fulfilled.

Finally, a central headquarters was required from which this controlling genius could operate his chessboard.

That *had* to be how it was.

Renzi's first reaction was to tell Kydd—but he would then, very reasonably, demand proof. And there were so many unanswered questions. If the base was not at Curaçao, then where was it? As he'd reasoned before, there were very few places that met the conditions for a secret lair.

A network of spies spread throughout the islands was a cumbersome and expensive proposition—and, above all, why had the Navy not intercepted at least one of the fast advice-boats or whatever was used in the tight communications system with them? Equally, how was a naval fleet, even of smaller ships, able to stay so long at sea without returning to port?

He had to find an answer to each question before he broached the subject to anyone—but how?

Chapter 10

L'Aurore HAD HER ORDERS by the time he returned on board. They were to take passage for Antigua to the dockyard at English Harbour for a minor refit, then relieve one of the inshore frigates in blockade of Guadeloupe.

"It's been a long time, old friend," Kydd said softly.

Renzi gave a wry smile, bringing to mind adventures ashore and afloat there when they had been common seamen together. Kydd had been a healthy young man in a lusty environment and there were things that he would not necessarily wish to be reminded of. "Yes, indeed, dear fellow. Conceivably the master shipwright will never penetrate your disguise in your lofty elevation." He laid down his book and chuckled companionably.

In the event it was quite another who came aboard in Antigua with the survey party, a genial and competent officer who let slip that Caird and his daughter had returned to England years before. And there would be no nostalgic reunion with the copper and lumber house where Kydd had first met a dark temptress, Sukey, or the little house he had lived in as Master of the King's Negroes. Now that he was a post captain, this was far out of sight in his past.

The survey was quick but thorough. "Naught but what can't be put right in a brace o' shakes," was the pronouncement. The ship would stay at moorings with her crew quartered ashore.

For her captain, there was no question of remaining in the coarse surroundings of the dockyard. It was expected he would take residence in the north, at St John's, where the admiral's shore headquarters was situated.

"Shall we take carriage for the capital, Nicholas?" Kydd said lightly, as Tysoe laid out his best clothes. "I do believe the society there will be quite up to expectations."

Renzi hesitated. "Brother, if there's anything I crave more than peace and quiet at this time I'm at a loss to think it. I have for companionship my books and my thoughts and, while your doughty mariners are on shore, my solitude."

"Of course, old chap, I do understand," Kydd came back.

With captain and officers heading north and the crew streaming ashore, there were only the standing warrant officers and three hands left aboard with Renzi. The frigate seemed to have grown larger, the echoing spaces and stillness broken only by the chuckle of water and the odd creak.

But this was an unmissable chance to take up his studies again. A considered comparison of the new German school of ethnics with the French encyclopedists would be a refreshing start, and in his cabin he pulled down the requisite tomes.

Within the hour he found it impossible: his head was so full of recent events that he knew he would get no rest until they had been settled to his satisfaction.

But how could he pursue the threads until all had been exhausted? As a mental exercise it would lead only to frustration, for a logical syllogism without sure data was nothing but a futility. However, to get data he would need to venture out into the field and acquire it. Was he prepared to do this when he had always declared he scorned and detested the practice of spying?

He laid down his pen, resolved. *If* the goal was sufficiently worthy, he would do whatever it took . . . *Was* he mad? He would set out not as an agent of a nation's secret service but on his own account, a freelance amateur without direction, following his own instincts.

Yet it had powerful advantages: he could beg leave from *L'Aurore* and go anywhere he wished, do anything he wanted, for he owed nothing to any higher authority. He need tell no one so there would be none to criticise if he failed. And his fate if he was caught would be the same whether he had been an accredited spy or otherwise.

Excitement flooded Renzi. The overall objective was clear: to find the genuine base and bring back proof so persuasive it would be impossible to ignore. Then he would be vindicated. Triangulating from known positions of the losses to pinpoint it had proved inconclusive. But as he reflected on his earlier conclusion about the degree of risk and unreliability of setting up a covert naval base in a dominion out of their direct control, he realised that, if this was to be accepted, the converse must therefore be true: the only safe location was on French sovereign territory and, if that was so, the odds shortened considerably.

There were only two islands of significance still in French hands, Guadeloupe and Martinique. Putting aside all other concerns, it narrowed the search immensely—he had only to reconnoitre those.

He'd start with Guadeloupe, so conveniently close and— What was he thinking? He was known, a marked man. There was no way he could move about enemy territory even in some form of disguise: he'd likely be recognised on the spot.

His hopes died. If he could not get the proof there was no point in going on.

In despair he slumped back. But then . . .

The thought of Guadeloupe had triggered another memory

from the past, from even earlier in the war when Kydd and he had been part of the ill-fated assault that had been thrown back when revolutionaries had landed and wreaked a bloody revenge. They had escaped, along with any royalists who could. Among them had been the gentle and wistful Louise Vernou.

The last he had seen of her was here in Antigua, at St John's. Presuming she was still here, could she have kept up some form of connection with her family or friends in Guadeloupe? It was worth a try, at least to gather information or even clues. For all he knew, it might develop—a secret correspondence with those on the island in a position to know, trusted by reason of being her family?

Kydd accepted his arrival with well-concealed surprise. He was staying in a country villa within sight of the light-yellow-brick church and the well-remembered harbour. "Why, Nicholas, you're joining me for the season?"

"For some reason, dear fellow, I feel restless, not to say out of sorts. I'm persuaded a change of air from that to be found in the bowels of a frigate will answer." He had determined that he would tell Kydd nothing until he had his proof.

"Then do consider this your home while you're in the north, m' friend."

The next day, on the pretext of taking the air, Renzi set out. It could not have been easier. Recalling that Louise Vernou had taught French to English officers in the past, he enquired at the admiral's headquarters and found a list of teachers. Among them was her name.

Memories flooded back: he and Kydd had been billeted on the family and grown close. Then, when the revolutionaries had triumphed, he had escaped Guadeloupe in a merchant brig with her, leaving Kydd with the last defenders. On the way they had been mauled by a hurricane but had made St John's and then had parted.

He remembered her gentle smile, quiet dignity and old-fashioned politeness, which had stayed even as the insanity of revolution and bloodshed had reached out to engulf her world.

Her teaching rooms were near the waterfront, a small but tidy house with a neat garden, her sign discreetly in the front window. As he walked to the door he paused, hearing a sturdy masculine voice chanting irregular verbs, then soft encouragement from her.

For a long moment he remained standing there, unwilling to have the memory of years stripped away to a harder present.

The chanting stopped, there was a murmur of voices and the door opened to let out a young redcoat officer, who flashed an embarrassed smile at Renzi and left quickly.

"Is there anything I can do for you, M'sieur?" Louise Vernou asked softly.

She had hardly changed. She was wearing a modest but elegant blue dress, and the touch of grey in her hair he'd remembered had barely advanced. That direct, almost intimate gaze held his without recognition.

She waited politely.

"Madame Louise Vernou, I believe," he said gently, in French.

It came to her then. Her hand flew to her lips, and her eyes opened wide. "*Mon Dieu*—can it be . . . ? It is! M'sieur Renzi!"

She swayed for a moment before Renzi caught the glitter of tears. Then, with a sob, she flung herself at him.

He let the emotion spend itself, holding her slight body tenderly as she connected once again with the fearful events of years before.

She pulled away, dabbing her eyes. "I do apologise," she said in English. "I forget your country does not value the open expression of feeling as do we. Please to come in, M'sieur."

As soon as he entered Renzi caught the same subtle fragrance that he had first met when he and Kydd had shared a bedroom that had belonged to her. It touched him; the madness of war had spared this gentle soul.

"Tea?" she enquired, her voice tight with emotion.

They sat side by side in the drawing room while the maid brought refreshments.

Louise looked at him intently, then said quietly, "You never were the simple sailor, Mr Renzi, were you? What do you now?"

"Je vais vous expliquer à un autre moment," he answered. Her English was greatly improved but his French was better.

She hesitated. "I'm not sure if I want to know the answer, but could you tell me this? What became of the young sailor, Tom Kydd, your friend? He gave up his own place in the boat for me," she added, with a catch in her throat. "Such a fine man and true."

"You may not believe me if I told you, Madame."

"Do, please!"

"In English Harbour dockyard there lies a smart frigate, her name *L'Aurore*. Her commander is . . . Captain Thomas Kydd."

"Vraiment? Quelle merveille!" she squealed, her hands working together. "What happened? You must tell me."

"Dear Madame, I rather feel that it were better told within the civilities of a dinner perhaps. Do you—"

"This very evening. It shall be here, and I will prepare it myself. Do you object, sir, if it were we two alone?" she added, with a coy smile in her eyes.

The fish was exquisitely cooked in a delicate sauce and the little dining room touchingly feminine with its carefully chosen pieces and faultlessly draped hangings in the soft gold of the candlelight.

Their converse was intelligent and attentive; they relished the courtly exchanges, the courteous deferences and gallantries of the old order.

Renzi recounted the epic adventures that had led to Kydd's rise to eminence in his profession and his own calling of scholar, while Louise told a poignant tale of being wrenched from her homeland, her brother's suffering under the guillotine and her quiet waiting existence in exile.

It called for a *vin d'honneur* and a promise that she would be allowed to meet Kydd once again at the earliest opportunity—and then Renzi knew it could not be put off any further.

"Louise, *ma chère*, what do you know of the current perils that face us in the Caribbean as we dine together here so elegantly?"

She looked puzzled. "Surely the tyrant is now vanquished in these parts. He makes imperial decrees as he struts in the Tuileries, but they cannot affect us here, not with your great navy that prevails over all."

Renzi let his expression sadden. "Dear lady, there has recently arisen a threat that is even now wreaking ruin all over the Caribbean. I would not trouble to mention it, save it is causing the gravest anxiety to Captain Kydd and his fellow officers. It is such a scourge as bears on all our spirits."

"How can this be, Nicholas?"

It was easily told, the ruinous losses, all unexplained—then, after he had extracted a promise of secrecy, the probability that it was the result of a clandestine naval operation by numerous small craft, which had to be centred and directed from French territory.

"And you believe this to be in Guadeloupe?" she asked shrewdly.

"Just so."

"Then . . ." she began uncertainly.

"Louise, do you have family still in Pointe-à-Pitre? Or friends you may still talk with in other parts of the island?"

"You want to learn if anything is known of this *port de guerre* there," she replied quickly. "And I have to tell you that, no, to communicate with them, *ce n'est pas possible*."

"There is no way you can get word to them?"

"I know why you ask, and if it were possible I would try, but you must understand this war is like no other. Revolutionaries and islanders, both live together in suspicion and hatred, and if by any means I could get through to any in Guadeloupe they would pay for it with their lives."

There was no way forward—except one. Even before he spoke Renzi despised himself. "Louise . . . this leaves only one alternative. To land someone on the shores of Guadeloupe to see if such a base exists."

Her eyes on him were still and luminous.

"I wish with all my heart it could be me," he said, "but I am known to them and would not survive to bring back the information."

"And you want me to go there and be a spy. Now I know what it is you do. Is this why you came to me tonight, Mr Renzi?"

The sudden chill in her manner struck him to the heart.

"There is none other I could think to turn to. Please believe me."

She put down her napkin and spoke coldly: "Sir, I'm astonished—no, I confess amazed at what you've been saying. I thought you a gentleman of reputation, of learning and discernment, and I find you speaking of spying. And, what is more, to a lady!"

He couldn't meet her gaze.

"No, sir, I will not do it. I cannot abide dissimulation and deceit. You will find another."

There was one last throw—one that had been used successfully before. By spymaster d'Auvergne on himself.

"I'm grieved to hear it, Madame," he said softly. "Especially since it is impossible another will be found in time . . ."

She said nothing.

"And therefore I have to beg you will consider the future."

A candle guttered in the stillness.

"When you must be obliged to recall that a grave duty to your country was presented that only you may perform—and you chose to turn your back."

He raised his eyes to meet hers.

"These are not words to use to a woman, sir," she said levelly. "If by them you seek to shame me into complying with your scheme, you have failed."

"Then for me, for the sake of Tom Kydd, who saved you from the revolutionaries?"

"Not even for him—or you."

Nothing could be read from her expression. She sat rigid and unyielding.

"Then . . ."

Unexpectedly she smiled. "Nicholas, I have the strangest feeling."

He blinked.

"I cannot believe you are a spy at all. You are too gentle—you care about the old things. And . . . and you're an honourable man."

"In truth, I am not, *ma chère*."

"It must have cost you much to come to me with what was in your heart."

A lump rose in his throat.

"It will have been a great matter that weighs so much on you."

He nodded dumbly.

"Very well, I will save you. From yourself, that is to say."

"Er . . ."

"Yes. I will not do this thing for you—that you must accept."

"I do, Madame Louise."

Paradoxically he felt relief that now she would not know the terror and degradation that was the lot of the spy.

"Then you will understand when I say that it is for *la belle France* that I will do it."

Renzi realised she was sparing him the pain of having her on his conscience. He reached across, took both her hands and kissed them. "Madame," he said quietly, "do believe me when I say I am truly humbled."

The moment hung until she withdrew her fingers and rose,

turning away for a space before she came back brightly, "Then, *mon brave,* we should be started."

An Argand lamp was lit and brought to the table while the maid was summoned to remove the dishes and dismissed for the evening.

"No brandy until we have completed our business," Louise said firmly. "Now, what is it we have to do?"

The essentials were simple: to discover by any means if there was unusual activity inside blockaded Guadeloupe consistent with Renzi's theory.

He took pains to detail to her what might most betray its existence but emphasised it was only the vital secret of its being that was necessary; the rest was out of her hands.

That settled, there was the conceiving of a story to account for her presence there, one that could stand against any question and would be credible to all as she moved about, observed and listened.

It was all progressing much faster than Renzi had expected, and it was Louise who came up with her story.

"A sad tale. I ran from the war, fearful of my fate. I was taken to St John's by a kind naval officer"—Renzi bowed politely—"who took me into keeping. He tired of me and turned me out for a younger woman. Cast down and yearning for the sound of *le français* about me and craving food that was civilised, I paid a fisherman to return me to Guadeloupe, where all I care for now is a quiet life."

"Bravo!" Renzi exclaimed in admiration. "Worthy of Manon Lescaut!"

It was certainly credible and her dignity of bearing would deter all but the most determined enquiries.

She would take a bundle of what treasured possessions she could carry and, understandably, have her small means in English currency.

Now all that was needed was for the landing and rendezvous to be made.

"There's a quiet little village, Petit-Bourg, on the left of the bay before Pointe-à-Pitre. Leave me there, and I'll make my way into town."

"You must be so careful," Renzi implored.

"Why? I've nothing to hide. They may search me, question me—I'm a ruined woman and all I wish is to end my days on the soil of France, M'sieur."

There were other details. How long would she need? There would have to be devised a plan of signals for when she was ready to be picked up, a thorough understanding of the tides and moon by date . . .

And would *L'Aurore* be available to them for the vital landing?

Renzi explained what had happened leading up to Curaçao, his humiliation and the likelihood Kydd would refuse to be involved in yet another theory.

"I understand. Then we shall invite Captain Kydd to a cosy dinner, we three, *hein?*"

"The evening went well?" Renzi asked at breakfast.

"Why, yes. The admiral keeps a capital table and the Antigua people were most civil in their appreciation of our late action." He reached for the plate of salt fish and ackee. "Saving their anxiety about their shipping, which is serious and vexing to them. And yourself? Something of an old acquaintance you were dining with, you said."

"Um, yes. You may recall her—Madame Louise Vernou," Renzi said off-handedly, pouring more coffee.

It didn't register at first. Then Kydd dropped his bread roll and rounded on him. "You didn't say, you sly beggar! She's here—in Antigua still? I must see her, Nicholas!"

"Well, yes. She asked to be remembered to you, of course, but do recollect, old fellow, that she recalls you as a young and unlettered seaman of somewhat direct manners and speech. You will not alarm her at all?"

♦ ♦ ♦

The door was flung open. Louise ran to Kydd and hugged him tightly, then held her arms outstretched, her eyes sparkling. "My brave sailorman! To see you again—looking so handsome and commanding!"

Kydd blushed with pleasure, then performed an extravagant bow, protesting in his best French that not only was he enchanted to meet her once again but that the honour was to be accounted entirely his.

Her astonishment melted to delight and the evening promised to be a wonderful reunion.

"When I saw you on the land, those wicked people all around you, I cried so much to leave you. And now you tell me you were in no danger at all and went off to Jamaica."

"Er, that's true enough. But afterwards . . ."

"Have you found an *amoureuse* at all, Thomas? It's not seemly that a man of such distinction and *élégance* should toil alone."

"Er, not at this moment, Madame Louise. My sea duties do claim me, I find."

"I'm desolated to hear this. But you will have seen sights inconceivable to we land creatures."

The dinner passed off in great style. Then, as the armagnac was produced, Louise casually said, "Oh—before I forget this thing. I have it in mind to visit my cousin very soon. We were very close and I so worry about her in these . . . *douloureux* times."

"I honour you for it," Kydd said comfortably, cupping his drink; the armagnac was magnificent.

"She will be cast down, that poor one, and I wish to take her some comforts. You are a captain of the sea, M'sieur, who may advise me wisely how I might safely travel."

"Er, where will you visit, Madame?"

"Why, Guadeloupe, of course! Where she has been since—"

"What?" blurted Kydd. "No—this is not possible! Louise, the whole island is under the strictest blockade and . . . and . . ." He tailed off, at a loss to put into words the utter impossibility of what she was asking.

"There are no cartel ships?" Renzi asked innocently.

"None, and well you know it. Louise, you cannot do this. They've a villainous crew in power and you being a . . ."

"Nonsense. I'm merely returning to the place of my birth for a quick visit. Who can object to that? Besides, I shall keep quiet and no one will notice me."

Kydd fell back speechless, then returned strongly, "Well, it's just not thinkable. We have the island under the closest watch and not a sail moves in or out without we know it. Why, *L'Aurore* herself will sail in two days to be part of the blockade."

She brightened. "*Hourra!* Then you will stop and row me in a boat onto the land. I don't mind where."

"No!" Kydd spluttered. "This is war, Louise, have you forgotten? And on a King's ship!"

"A pity," she said sadly. "Then it must be that I ask a little fisherman to take me. They say they're most obliging for a silver dollar."

"A *fisherman?* Louise, do give up this mad idea, I beg."

"She does have a point, dear fellow. We've nothing to fear of what the French can bring against us, and simply to heave to, a quick landing—"

"Nicholas! This does not concern you, and I'll thank you to keep your suggestions to yourself. No, Madame, this I cannot do, and that is my final word."

"All quiet, sir," Curzon murmured. The night was inky black but the bay off Pointe-à-Pitre was well known to English ships, used to lying off the buoyed channel that led through the reefs, effectively sealing it off from all movements.

"Hmmph. Well, get it into the water—we haven't all night."

There was a muffled squeal of sheaves as the gig was lowered and voices aft as Madame Vernou was helped into the boatswain's chair to be swayed down into the boat. Renzi came to assure Kydd of her safe embarkation but thought better of it and returned to board himself.

"Push off, sir?" Poulden asked laconically.

"Er, yes, please do," Renzi said, distracted by the necessity of trying to read the boat compass in its awkward case. West-by-north would see them past the treacherous Cay Ronde and therefore the reciprocal course would be needed to take them back to *L'Aurore*.

The boat's crew bent stolidly to their oars and all too quickly the frigate was lost in the darkness.

Louise sat quiet, not inviting conversation. Renzi could only guess at what was going through her mind at this return to her home after all these years and shied from the thought of the danger he was thrusting her into.

The passage in was not a concern. Nothing would be about—the French had no reason to have patrols out—but once she was ashore . . .

He shifted uncomfortably.

Out of the blackness ahead several lights shimmered dimly. This would be Petit-Bourg—their destination.

"Not far, Madame."

She nodded slowly, her eyes fixed on the shore.

There was a sudden bump and the gig was displaced to one side by some underwater obstacle. Reefs?

"Easy, oars. Bowman, a pole in the water ahead."

"No matter," Louise said softly. "We're past. Go to the right of the lights."

They smelt the fish quay well before it loomed out of the darkness.

Louise went to rise, but Renzi pulled her down again. "Doud!" he hissed.

The lithe topman sprang for the rickety ladder and, after pausing for a moment to listen, pulled himself up and over. He was soon back. "Clear!" he whispered.

Her bundle was handed up first, then it was her turn. She did not hesitate and hauled herself up quickly. At the top, smoothing down her dress, she picked up her bundle and, without a single glance back, lifted her head and went off into the black of the night.

In the morning *L'Aurore* spread sail and continued on her patrol, a lazy circling of Guadeloupe, taking the inner passage between it and La Désidérade and the other islands, Marie-Galante and the legendary Saintes.

Four days later she hove to off Pointe-à-Pitre and that night prepared to pick up Louise.

Renzi insisted on going in the boat, and when they reached their position off Petit-Bourg, he tended the dark-lanthorn ready to signal the reply.

The men lay on their oars and waited. It was still and calm, the rippling of water along the boat the loudest sound, but the soft blackness remained inviolate.

The boat thwarts were hard and Renzi squirmed uncomfortably but never took his eyes off the shore.

An hour passed, another. The current was taking them gently away to the north and every so often the boat had to be brought back.

One by one the lights were disappearing on the land and by midnight they had all winked out.

And still nothing.

This was worrying: a moonrise was expected about two and they could not risk being seen so close inshore. What if . . . ?

Dark thoughts crowded in. Renzi forced them aside and tried to concentrate. The men were, in the age-old way, lying across the boat yarning quietly together, the drone of their voices and occasional snicker getting on his nerves.

If indeed Louise had been taken up, there would be questions under duress—it was too much to expect that she could hold out against torture, and if that was the case, there was every chance that an armed launch was now on its way out to intercept them.

The first sliver of moon appeared. They had to leave.

"Out oars, we're going back."

Kydd was waiting at the taffrail. "Where's Louise?" he demanded.

"Shall we go below?" Renzi answered wearily. "There's something I have to tell you."

In the cabin Kydd exploded: "You persuaded the poor innocent to go into Guadeloupe after your crack-brained secret base? Are you insane, Nicholas?"

"It has to be logical. I've—"

"Be damned to you! Have you any idea what you've done? She's all alone in there, for God's sake, probably at this minute in some stinking French prison waiting for . . . for . . ."

"She went of her own accord, brother. Her choice!"

"Of *course* she would! To please you, damn it! I can't believe it of you—taking advantage of a tender-hearted woman like that for your own ends."

Kydd's eyes narrowed. "I'd never have thought it, Nicholas. You of all people, full of your morals and logic, you've no idea of what it is to be in the real world. Not stopping to think what you've—"

"I'm going in to find out what happened to her," Renzi said quietly. "If you'll set me ashore tomorrow night, I'm determined to find her."

"And look for your lunatic base!"

Renzi's eyes glowed dangerously. "I said I'll go after Louise."

Kydd paused. "Two wrongs don't make a right. I'll not allow it."

"I'm going."

"No!"

"Then this minute I'll go overside and swim ashore, I swear it."

"You've no chance, Nicholas. You'll be taken as an Englishman the first person who sees you."

"That's my affair. I'd be obliged if you'd linger here for another day, then put me ashore."

"You're quite determined on it, aren't you?"

"I am."

Kydd drew a quick breath. "Very well, I won't stand in your way."

"Have a care, sir!" Doud hissed anxiously from the boat.

The top of the fish quay was deserted, a patchwork of shadows; beyond, lights of the village. Renzi cautiously edged to one side, tiptoed to a stack of lobster pots and peered over.

The road wound out of sight past a group of houses and in the other direction there were deserted pig-pens and a farmhouse with lights ablaze.

Cautiously he stepped out. He was dressed plainly, in dark clothing with a makeshift knapsack on his back. There was no point in disguise: he was a stranger and his accent marked him out as an Englishman so his only hope was a rapid entry and exit.

His plan was simple: to reach Pointe-à-Pitre in an hour or so and find Louise's well-remembered house near the waterfront. If there were any of the family Vernou left, that was where they would be. If not, he'd have to think again.

After he had passed the last house, he breathed a little easier. Lofty palm trees and thick bush lined the road; if he saw or heard anything he could be out of sight in a second. He moved quickly, wryly recalling that this was the self-same road that, years before, Kydd had taken with his party escaping from the capital when it was captured by the revolutionaries.

The night was cool and the thinning sky overhead allowed him a glimpse of the stars and the comfort of knowing his direction. He caught the glimmer of water to his right: the head of the bay, and it was therefore only about ten minutes to the bridge and the same to the other side to the capital.

Houses began again, some with lights. He hurried past them, his heart thumping when a dog began a sudden howling and someone came to the door. He froze and after a moment the door banged shut, the dog now barking maniacally.

It fell silent after he reached the road to the bridge. In French Europe, bridges were often guarded as a matter of course, and it was too dark to see if there was a *factionnaire* at this one. As quietly as he could he followed the road on to the bridge but his footsteps became a wooden thumping. He pressed on, trying to think of what he would say if stopped.

He was two-thirds over when he heard some way behind him the creak and grind of a cart. He hurried along, then saw the unmistakable outline of a sentry-box. He stopped in panic and glanced back: the cart had reached the bridge and was beginning to cross it.

A figure stepped into the road out of the sentry-box and his heart quailed. The man gestured irritably to him but, in a flood of relief, he saw he was motioning him out of the way. No doubt merely the bridge-keeper, making sure farmers paid their dues if they tried to cross at night.

Renzi mumbled something and pressed on to the streets beyond.

It had been many years and the darkness made it difficult to recognise where he was.

A couple passed on the opposite side, talking animatedly.

Were the Vernous on the north or the south side of the square? A man turned the corner and walked directly towards him. Renzi swayed a little, as though intoxicated, and the man passed wide in distaste.

Suddenly he recognised an odd wrought-iron pattern of a gate and recalled it was at the corner just up from the house.

He hurried on and there it was, with a light in the upper-floor bedroom where, long ago, he and Kydd had been quartered. His heart beat fast but he had to play it with the utmost care. He passed by without curious looks, trying to remember what was in the street behind, then recalled it was the grassy path that led to the waterfront, close to where he and Louise had got away in the brig, leaving Kydd alone.

He doubled back along the path—no one was following. As he drew abreast of the rear of the Vernou residence, he jumped over the low picket fence into the hibiscus bushes and was underneath the little balcony of the bedroom.

He'd brought to mind the noisy creaking of the rickety steps that led down from it that had made it impossible for himself and Kydd to slip out by themselves. With a last look around he leaped for the underside of the balcony. This was much quieter, but if he was seen, the game would be over.

He heaved and swung his legs up—they caught and he rolled over the rail, landing on the balcony with a light thump.

The curtains were drawn and he could not see who was inside. If it was Louise he was safe—if anyone else . . .

Taking a deep breath, he tapped lightly. There was no sound from inside so he tried again. Then he heard movement, someone coming to the window. If there was screaming . . .

The curtains were drawn back and it was Louise.

She stared at him, as if at a ghost, then recovered, her key rattling nervously as she unlocked the little door.

"Quickly—come in!" she hissed, pulling him in bodily. Before she closed the door she looked out carefully, then drew the curtains and turned on him.

"You fool! The Citizen Watch Committee don't trust me and are out."

"Louise, you're safe. I was so worried—"

"For now. I'm followed, watched—this is why I cannot go to your rendezvous."

"How will you—"

"You must get out—now! There is no secret base here, nothing I have heard or seen in Guadeloupe. You must go, M'sieur Renzi. Go back to your ship while you can."

HMS *Hannibal* did her best. An old lady of a previous war, she had neither the agility nor the deadly grace of the newer 74s and now, matched with them in line-of-battle, she was showing her age.

The flagship in the van braced up into the wind in breathless pursuit of the mock enemy, the other two astern sharpened in, but it was too much for the second in line. She tried but could not come up to the wind as close as the others and inexorably sagged away to leeward.

On the quarterdeck her captain turned red and roared murder at the sweating men set to bringing in every last inch on the sheets.

"She's as high as she'll go," her sailing master mumbled, looking up at the sails, straining hard as boards, the tiniest flutter threatening on every weather leech.

"If I want your opinion, Mr Maitland, I'll beg it of you," Tyrell snarled sarcastically. "Until then, hold your tongue, sir!"

The master retired, his face set.

"Hard in that fore topmast staysail, you vile set o' lubbers, or I'll see your backbones, every one, I swear!" Tyrell bellowed forward, eyeing the flagship, whose starboard side now stretched away in full view as they fell further away from the line.

On the foredeck the raw acting fifth lieutenant, Mason, tried manfully to obey, his high-pitched voice carrying aft to the sombre group watching on the quarterdeck as he urged on his men. As was the case in so many other stations in a notorious ship unable to attract volunteers, he was short-handed and three men were few enough to put on the soaring triangular staysail.

Without warning the sail broke free. Flogging out savagely, it sent men sprawling into the scuppers.

"God rot it!" roared Tyrell, "The bloody dogs—can you believe it? They let go the rope!" he spluttered, beside himself with rage. "Hale 'em all aft—every last man jack o' the lubbers!"

They shambled up, the white-faced Mason with them.

"It was an accident, sir," he began.

"Hold your peace, Mr Mason. I'll deal with you later."

Tyrell stared down at the three men, his face working. "I know what you're up to, you black-hearted rascals! Don't think I don't—I'm wise to you! Your little game is to make *Hannibal* look a shab before the admiral, isn't it?"

"Sir, it really was—"

"Well, it won't work, and now you're going to pay for it." The men stared back in bitter resentment, knowing better than to say anything.

"Sir, the sheet carried away. The line was rotten!" Mason burst in.

Like a snake, Tyrell rounded on him. "You're dismissed the deck, Mr Mason. Get to my cabin and wait for me there—this instant, sir!"

No one caught Mason's eye as he turned stiffly and went below but Bowden saw the glitter of tears of frustration as he went. It was a cruel and unnecessary thing to inflict on the earnest young man and his heart went out to him.

"You three, you're in irons until tomorrow forenoon and then you'll be up before me. Failing in your duty, which I daresay will earn you six at the gratings—and another half a dozen for the shame you brought on your ship."

Ahead, the flagship had noted *Hannibal*'s unweatherly clawing and had considerately paid off a little until the line was whole again but it didn't mollify Tyrell, who stumped about the deck, like a caged beast.

It was the same throughout the rest of the day, his brooding figure a malignant presence likely to appear silently from behind whenever officers or men were talking together. He did not go below until well into the evening.

The wardroom was in a black mood—there was little talk and few amused asides. Every officer was suffering: even the ponderous first lieutenant, Griffith, had been subject to a tirade in public for some petty shortcoming and he now kept to himself. Bowden occupied his time quietly, reading when he could, sometimes writing long letters home—careful not to express any criticism to his uncle and guardian, now a rear-admiral.

It was the unguessable arbitrary nature of their captain that sapped at morale, on one day demanding haste at all costs, then on another furious at the consequent compromises in quality, sometimes cruelly dismissing the efforts men were making for him, and at the next extravagantly rewarding mediocre performance. It made no sense.

The morning brought with it a heavy tropical downpour. The flagship ahead disappeared in grey-white curtains of solid water and the officer-of-the-watch grew lines of worry, which deepened as they plunged on, blind.

Tyrell paced up and down the quarterdeck, cocked hat jammed tight sending streams of water down his oilskin. Quite able to leave for a comfortable dry cabin, he remained morosely on deck, occasionally looking up at wet sails trailing sheets of water as they caught the rain.

Once, he flashed a gleeful grin at the officer-of-the-watch, who jerked with surprise and answered with a weak smile. "Get those good men below in the dry, Bowden, there's a good fellow," he ordered, pointing to four sailors forward.

"Aye aye, sir," Bowden replied, knowing it could well change the rare good mood to a raging tantrum if he objected and pointed out that they were posted in the eye of the ship for the express purpose of warning of collision with the invisible flagship ahead.

The rain stopped, the decks began steaming under a hot sun, and Tyrell finally went below to change. As soon as he had gone the atmosphere brightened.

Bowden caught movement out of the corner of his eye, Midshipman Joyce stealthily descending from aloft. He realised what was going on: the young rascal was engaged in the old game of baiting a marine.

The target was the poop-deck sentry, standing on duty with his musket, motionless and facing inboard. Joyce took out a piece of twine and secured it to the rigging and its other end he ever so carefully tied to the marine's queue. Mission accomplished, he retired to await results.

Shortly, from out of the cabin spaces, a genial Tyrell emerged, looking about him with satisfaction.

The marine on the deck above snapped to attention, keen to show his alertness on duty by the routine of pacing across the deck to take a new position the other side. He shouldered his musket smartly and stepped out.

The twine tautened—the hapless marine was jerked backwards and crashed down, musket clattering. Disoriented, and on hands and knees, he looked around bewildered for the source of the attack.

The quarterdeck roared with laughter, Tyrell joining in. Joyce, clearly apprehensive at the possible consequences, gave a relieved smile.

When order was restored Tyrell ordered crisply, "Sar'nt of the watch, lay aft."

The beefy soldier reported warily.

"We've a younker here doesn't show sufficient respect to your Royal Marines, Sar'nt. Give him a musket and set him to marching the length o' the ship, fore and aft, until I say stop."

Under the heavy musket the slight midshipman set out in good imitation of a Royal, stiffly swinging his arms and with a professional look of blankness just a trifle overdone. He was encouraged throatily by the sergeant, and shouts of support came as he passed by working seamen along the gangways to the foredeck and the root of the bowsprit, where he stamped around in a creditable "about turn" before marching down the other side.

Bowden watched with relief. Was their tyrant at last lightening up?

Time passed and, visibly tiring under the unfamiliar weight of the musket, Joyce was no longer playing to the gallery, now trudging on in a mindless tramp, eyes fixed to the deck in front of him.

"Er, sir," Bowden ventured, "stand down Mr Joyce? He's been going for an hour."

"No." There was no compassion of any kind to be seen in his face.

The spiritless plodding went on—and on. Now there was pity and rough sympathy in the looks from the seamen for it was obvious that Joyce was suffering. He stumbled on doggedly, determined not to give in.

"I'll be below," Tyrell told the officer-of-the-watch and abruptly left.

Joyce crumpled to the deck.

Instantly the skylight on the poop opened and Tyrell popped into view, bellowing, "The last order was 'march,' Mr Joyce! I have you under my eye, and if you stop again, I'll see you court-martialled for disobeying a direct order."

Shocked, the quarterdeck could only look on silently as the lad got to his feet and, with a superhuman effort, thudded the musket down on his shoulder and started off, a nightmarish shamble with staring eyes.

"Send for the doc," Bowden whispered to a messenger.

The surgeon came, a shrivelled individual. "That man's not fit to continue," Bowden said in hard tones. "Do you not agree, sir?"

Looking about him fearfully, the surgeon went to Joyce who, in his Calvary, didn't pause, slogging on endlessly, seemingly in a trance. "I, er, cannot see that—"

"What in Hades are you doing there, Surgeon?" thundered Tyrell, who had shot out on deck.

"Why, um, this man's—"

"Do you think to interfere with my authority, sir?"

"Er, not at all," quavered the man.

"Then get about your business, sir."

Bravely the sergeant came up and faced Tyrell. "He's had enough, sir. Can't you—"

"I'll not have my orders questioned!" he roared, to the deck in general. "The next man who interferes will be arrested on the spot."

The watch on deck lowered their eyes and returned to their motions while the pitiful figure staggered on.

It couldn't last: near the fore-mast and without a sound the lad collapsed, the musket skittering across the deck. With a piteous effort he tried to rise, swaying on his feet, then dropped, this time moving no more.

Deadly looks were shot aft as seamen ran to him but Tyrell seemed not to notice, gazing up lazily to take in the set of the topgallants, at the seas creaming in to windward.

Bowden felt anger rising. It threatened to overwhelm him. He stared obstinately out to sea until it passed, leaving him shaken.

That night he came off watch at midnight, thankful for the sanctity of his little cot where he could fight down the images of the day. He eventually drifted off into a restless sleep.

At some time in the early hours he was jerked into consciousness by the sudden pandemonium of cries and running feet above.

Heart thumping, he dropped to the deck and, pulling on a coat, headed for the after hatchway as fast as he could.

"What's happening?" he asked hurrying figures in the darkness.

"Don't know," one man said hoarsely. "I'm getting topside, whatever!"

As he fought his way up, Bowden's mind tried to grapple with sensations. The ship was still under way, for a live deck was under his feet with none of the deadly stillness to betray a grounding on a reef. There were no shots or firing, no stentorian orders or thundering drums in urgent summons to action—just men spilling up on deck from below in a bewildered throng.

He hurried to the wheel. The quartermaster was standing stolidly next to the helmsman.

"What's the alarm, man?" Bowden demanded.

"As we split the fore course, sir," he said calmly. "Captain wants we should shift to a new 'un and won't wait for day."

Bowden couldn't believe his ears.

"So he clears lower deck o' both watches an' we do it now."

It took his breath away. The fore course was the main sail on the fore-mast. To replace it with another was a major task: not only had it to be handed, secured and sent down, but the replacement had to be roused out from decks below, lashed together in a long sausage and sent up, tons' weight of canvas on bending strops into the tops, the work of hours.

In the darkness it was unthinkable—but it was happening. Bowden went forward in the gloom: sullen men were being mustered for the job. He peered up at the sail. It was indeed split, from top to bottom along a seam but apart from spilling its wind it did not seem a danger to the ship.

It could have waited until morning, but by his action Tyrell was condemning the entire ship to loss of precious sleep to which they were entitled. The watch below would have had barely an hour of rest since their last duty, and while seamen would willingly go aloft to save the ship this was no man's idea of a life-or-death situation.

There were growls and snarls under cover of darkness, but the work went on. Lines stretched along for hoisting, buntlines overhauled and above, almost invisible in the darkness, topmen manning the yards and fisting the canvas as the sail was brought in.

It was madness. Tyrell stood to one side, watching, his arms folded truculently as the sail was made up for unbending. Then, out in the night, there was a despairing shriek, cut short by a sickening thud as a man out on the yard scrabbled, lost his hold in the blackness and plummeted to his death.

All work ceased. A venomous muttering began but Tyrell stalked immediately to the centre of the deck. "Get those men back to work, damn your blood!" he roared up to the tops. "Now!"

It was a turning moment. Bowden sensed the resentment turn to a visceral hatred, the sullen obedience now a feral wariness.

Hannibal was headed into the unknown.

It was an hour after dawn when the last line was belayed and the sail trimmed to the wind. The men went below without a word but the glances flashed aft could not be mistaken in their meaning.

As the day went on there was a rising feeling of menace, as if a fuse had been lit. Bowden had the last dog-watch and watched apprehensively as the bright day changed by degrees into a creeping darkness. At three bells a figure detached from the cabin spaces and shuffled towards him. It was Joyce.

"Sir, I'd be obliged for a piece of your time," he said, in a low voice.

"Of course," Bowden said, and moved up the deck out of hearing of the group at the conn.

Joyce seemed to have difficulty bringing out the words, then blurted, "I was asked by the men where I stood an' all."

Bowden went cold. There was no doubting the meaning. The ship was a powder keg.

"In the event of . . ."

"Aye, sir."

There was only one answer. "On your honour, you must stand true to the ship."

"I knew you'd say that, sir." He hesitated, then added, "An' I thank you for it, Mr Bowden." He moved painfully away.

Bowden paced forward. His duty now was clear and there was no putting it aside. He must formally tell the captain what he had heard.

Or should he stand back and let the man take what was coming to him for his inhuman treatment of his men?

The moral case for allowing things to take their course was strong, especially as by disclosing what Joyce had told him he was condemning the boy to a court-martial at the least for breach of the Articles of War in not having immediately informed the captain himself.

On the other hand if he didn't and it turned into a bloody mutiny there would be lives lost and a vengeful Admiralty would be pitiless. By forewarning it could be prevented—and his oath to the Crown would remain untarnished.

By the end of the watch he had decided.

"Come!" Tyrell sounded irritable.

Bowden entered the great cabin, its spare and bleak appearance so different from that in any other ship-of-the-line he had seen.

Tyrell was standing by the stern windows, his hands clasped behind his back. "Yes?" he said, without looking round.

"Sir, I wish to report—"

"Ah, Bowden," Tyrell said, swinging round to face him. "Always pleased to see a loyal and upright officer. What is it I can do for you?"

Taken aback by his welcome, Bowden hesitated.

"You want to report . . . ?"

"Ah, sir. A grave matter." Whatever it took, he would not involve Joyce by name.

"Oh?" The amiable expression remained unaffected.

"Sir, I was approached by a member of the ship's company who saw fit to inform me that certain unnamed individuals were disaffected and no longer reliable. Sir, in my opinion the people are in a state of incipient mutiny."

It was said.

"Why, you came down to tell me this? God bless you, Mr Bowden, for your concern on my behalf. Is there anything else?"

"Er, this is to say, I've no reason to doubt that the men could rise at any time, sir, and—"

"Calm yourself, Mr Bowden, it's not as you fear. When you've been in the Service as long as I, you'll realise that the scum are always in a state of mutiny, the dogs. Only hard discipline keeps 'em tranquil."

"Sir, I—"

"For you, for the sake of your fears, I'll take steps. You'll learn that swift and decisive measures are an infallible remedy for these vile creatures."

"Er, thank you, sir."

"Captain of Marines this instant!" he called loudly, to the sentry outside his door, who hurried to obey.

The officer arrived, breathless and confused.

"Ah, Captain. I'll have every marine sentry throughout the ship on duty with their bayonets ready fixed. Fixed, you understand?"

"Um, yes, I'll do it now." His eyes darted from Bowden to Tyrell with incomprehension but he left quickly.

"There. The sight of naked steel will always steady the wayward, don't you think?" Tyrell said pleasantly.

Bowden could think of nothing to say. For any marine between decks the bayonet would be an intolerable impediment and impossible to wield, and what the seamen would think of this passed belief.

"If you suffer any further disquiet, please feel you can approach me at any time. This is the duty any captain must owe his officers."

"Er, thank you, sir, I will."

The wardroom at supper was tense. There was little conversation and each officer avoided any other's eye.

The table was cleared and the president called for port. With deliberate emphasis he invited Mr Vice to make the loyal toast, which was given in guarded tones.

Afterwards, when normally the wardroom would relax into comfortable reminiscence, there was only an awkward silence. There were wary looks about the table, one or two comments on the dishes and then nothing.

"Damn it!" Griffith burst out. "Is no one going to speak?"

Eyes turned to him.

"Clear the cabin o' the serving staff!" he snapped. "And send away the sentry."

This was unprecedented. In effect the first lieutenant was reducing those present to the wardroom officers of *Hannibal* only.

"No one to leave! Who's the officer-of-the-watch?"

"Mason," someone said nervously.

"Right, we'll do without him. So we're all in this together—agreed?" he snapped.

"What can you mean by that, sir?" gasped Jowett, the second lieutenant.

"What I say, sir," Griffith ground out, his voice dropping to a conspiratorial quiet, "is this. It can't go on and, whether we like it or no, we're the ones to suffer in the end."

The third, Briggs, had no qualms about an opinion. "He's mad, of course. Anyone who's passed by the Bedlam hospital knows what to look for."

"And what's that?" growled Maitland, the sailing master.

"Does it matter?" said the Captain of Marines. "We all know he's beyond reaching."

If the Royal Marines were no longer prepared to stand with their captain, it was a matter of desperate gravity.

"Here's my view, and it's one that I sorrow to hold." Griffith regarded them gravely. "We have to declare him mad, unfit to command."

"And then?" Jowett gave a dry laugh. "I'd not like to be the one who tells him. I have it from my man that Tyrell carries a pair of pocket pistols on him wherever he goes."

Bowden spoke up quietly: "It's a nice point, though. If we do nothing and there's a meeting with the enemy, I have m' doubts the men will fight for him, and we're a liability in the line-of-battle. If we *do* take steps we could be each and every one damned for the rest of our careers . . ."

"I don't know why you're all so gib-faced," Griffith said bitterly. "It's down to my account who's the 'leader' in this . . . rising."

"Talking of rising," Briggs said strongly, "we should bear it in mind that if we do indeed make such a move, the ship's company will see it in their best interest to drop any ideas they may have for a mutiny, or similar."

"That's a good point. We're only a couple of dozen against six hundred," muttered Maitland, staring into his glass.

"Against?" Bowden asked, with irony.

"We've only to hang out a signal to the fleet and—"

"Don't be a looby," Jowett sneered. "They'll never let us, and they'd have to wait only for nightfall to be off to wherever they're carrying the ship. Anyone watching won't have a clue what's happening, and if it's night, well . . ."

"That's as may be," Griffith said, with finality. "I'm to demand that before we leave this cabin we've decided on our course."

"To take *Hannibal* from Captain Tyrell or no," Bowden said levelly.

"To prevent a rising of the hands and carrying of the ship over to the enemy."

"I say we take it to a vote!" Briggs put in.

"Now hold on, young 'un," Maitland said in alarm. "We're not ready f'r that, like!"

Bowden tapped twice on the table with a spoon. "Let's not lose sight of our options," he said, flashing an apologetic smile at the first lieutenant for his interruption. "First we have to be sure things can only be resolved by the captain's, er, removal. This is a step with no going back. And if we do, then is it to be by main force or another way?"

"Another way," Jowett said forcefully. "Simple—the doctor declares the man insane, we put him to bed and all is sweet for us."

"It does have the merit of being quick and sure," agreed Griffith. "Doctor, you'll do this for us?"

The surgeon shrank from him in fear. "I c-can't!"

"Why not, pray?"

"It's that . . . Well, I'm not qualified, am I?"

"Damn it!" exploded Griffith. "If you're not, who is?"

"I know why he won't," Jowett said with venom. "He's worried that if he certifies Tyrell mad and Surgeons' Hall won't have it, he fears he's to be cast in damages."

"Let's keep our tempers, gentlemen," Bowden said, then asked, "Doctor, we have to take some kind of action. Is there a middle course, one that recommends he be retired immediately on grounds of ill-health, or some such?"

The surgeon shook his head mutely.

"You'll get no sense out of that lubber," Jowett growled. "We'll have to do the business ourselves. Anyone knows the symptoms of mad?"

"Hold hard, Mr Jowett," interposed Maitland. "You're not reckoning on the consequences."

"What fucking consequences?"

"If we declare him mad but the ship's doctor declines, it'll be taken as an act of open mutiny."

The table fell into an appalled silence.

"So we just carry on as before? I don't think so," Griffith said slowly. "He's getting worse, thinks there's plots against him—he'll one day likely up and skewer some poor wight he thinks is after his blood."

"Or worse," Briggs said morosely. "I've heard of things happening in Bedlam that would—"

"Where did you . . . ?"

"When I was young, my aunt was taken to the asylum with the night terrors and shakes. We had to visit her as she got worse."

His face fell sombre in recollection. "To see how she changed, why, it was—"

"Yes, well. So, then, you're the one to tell us the symptoms," Jowett said firmly. "What do we look for? What things say you're a mad cove?"

"Umm. Well, she used to write long letters to all us younkers and in the end the writing was so bad we couldn't understand it."

"Bad writing!" sniffed the purser, in an offended tone. "And that's a thing. These days I send him papers, and get back scrawls I can't figure and dursn't ask."

"For Christ's sake!" snarled Griffith. "This has gone on long enough."

He looked about the table significantly. "Whether we like it or no, whatever happens in the near future will be on all our heads, no escape for any. I've a notion to act now, do something before it all comes down on us in a way we won't like."

Encouraged by one or two nods, he went on, "So this is what I'm proposing. We draw up a list of all the crazy, strut-noddy things he's done and said."

His head whipped around to the terrified surgeon, as he snarled, "Then get our doctor to sign that he's seen all this and thinks it the behaving of a cheerful, well-living cove. Or *not*—as the case may be," he concluded grimly.

"I—that is to say, I, er—" the surgeon stammered.

Griffith turned on him with savage intensity. "You'll sign, Doctor. I take my oath on it."

He went on more quietly, "In this way we can say that, while we're no taut hands in the matter o' lunacy, we're standing down our captain for the good of the Service as being our judgement of his condition."

"Good idea," Briggs agreed enthusiastically. "And then—"

But the first lieutenant hadn't finished. "Now, for this to save our skins it has to be all of us or none. Nobody to hang back. If it isn't, we're done."

It didn't have to be spelled out: in going behind Tyrell's back to the admiral with their demand, they were in breach of every moral rule of conduct of a naval officer, and even if there were no legal consequences they would be tainted by the action for the rest of their careers.

Bowden froze. Everything in his being screamed at him to shy away from the awful chasm they were approaching, but if he did, this would be betraying not only his fellow officers but as well the countless seamen who had suffered.

"So. How about it, gentlemen? Do we take a vote on it?" Griffith's eyes went about the table, to each man in turn. There was no escaping it—they were all in or . . .

"Then here it is. Officers of *Hannibal* now assembled. Do you now accept and determine that Captain Tyrell is, um, not of sound mind as can continue in his position and must be declared unfit?"

No one dared speak. The moment hung interminably.

"I'll take a show of hands. Raise 'em if you're in. Gentlemen?"

Bowden, his mind now resolved to an icy coolness, joined the rest as every hand was raised.

Griffith smiled in grim satisfaction. "Then we're in agreement. We're a day only out of Antigua. When we're hook down, I'm going ashore with you at my back and we brace the admiral!"

Chapter 11

"You're sure there's nothing?" Renzi asked, with a sinking heart. If the secret base was not here then it must be in Martinique, a much larger island, and there he would be without the advantage of a pair of eyes on the inside.

"Guadeloupe is not such a big place. Any strange thing would be much talked about."

"Yes, that must be so," Renzi said, with a dogged expression. "We must get back to the ship for the rendezvous soon."

"Then we leave without your questions answered, I fear."

Renzi nodded: the sooner they left before her presence was compromised, the better. "But I do thank you for your bravery, which I will never forget."

Louise bit her lip. "There is one little mystery, but it does not concern Guadeloupe."

"Oh?"

"Well, my *épicier*—my grocer, I think he has a *tendre* for me—he let slip he's been doing very well lately. I ask him why his profits are so good. He says to me that if I promise not to tell anyone, he will let me know. I agree so hc confides. It's only that the Villa Tartu on Marie-Galante has been re-established by the old general and they're asking him to supply so many foodstuffs he stands amazed." She paused. "Perhaps now he regrets talking to me. He may become suspicious and go to the authorities."

Renzi snapped alert. "The island opposite?"

"Yes, you can see it from here, but it's only small," she said doubtfully.

Renzi's mind raced. Such would be ideal for quarantining the existence of an operational base. But how was he to check it out? There was one thing that would impel it to a first-rank priority in his investigation—if he saw any of those who'd so comprehensively fooled him in Curaçao heading out to Marie-Galante.

"Er, where do you catch a boat to the island at all?"

The morning sun woke him. Out of sight, high in the crook of branches in a tree overlooking the Porte de la Marina, he nearly tumbled out. He pulled himself back gingerly and took stock. In the night he had chosen well: the tall tree was quite close to the jetty and well within range of Louise's opera glasses, safely folded in his waistcoat pocket.

He would have to remain in his hideaway until dark but *L'Aurore* would not be returning from her circumnavigation for some days yet. He had time.

At nine the first boat left, with the grocer's produce heaped in the bottom. There were five passengers and Renzi could see them clearly as they waited by the jetty and boarded—but he recognised none.

The next boat did not depart until a little before noon, and again there were none boarding he knew. This was not good: it implied that there would be only one or two more crossings that day.

Dusk was drawing in when the last boat came into view. None of the three waiting was of interest, and Renzi looked about in vain for a figure hurrying up at the last minute. Then he saw that the approaching boat had passengers in it—obviously it was coming back from the island.

And there in the bow was Duperré.

He was unmistakable, with his dark features and heavy build, and behind him were two more he recognised. Renzi watched them step on to the jetty and stride away in the direction of Pointe-à-Pitre.

Impatience surged. But if he were seen by any of them or others somewhere in the town there could be only one fate for him.

He waited for dark before noiselessly dropping to the ground and making his way to the Vernous.' Louise was waiting with a candle in nightcap and gown, her eyes wide. "Well?"

"It is here. On Marie-Galante."

She hugged him impulsively. "I knew you'd find it! So, now you can go back and—"

"No."

Uncertain, she waited for him to finish.

"I know it's here but no one will believe me unless I find proof—something they can hold in their hands, trust in."

After Curaçao it could be nothing less . . . and that meant only one thing.

"You will have to go to Marie-Galante?" she whispered in awe.

Renzi gave a wry nod, the evidence, whatever that could possibly be, was there. All up to this point was wasted unless he could lay hands on something that in itself would convince. If he left now he had nothing. There was no other course left to him. He had to go.

"Um, yes," he agreed heavily. "But how?"

There was only one available method to get there: the passenger boat. And what were his chances of slipping through in daylight?

But could he ask Louise to go? She would, he knew, but he had already put her in much danger . . .

"It is impossible, it would seem," he said, "with no—"

She stopped him with a hand on his arm. "There may be a way," she said shyly, "if it be we two together."

"We two?"

Lightly withdrawing the hand, she explained, "The grocer provides them with their daily victuals. I will supply them with the *gourmandises* every Frenchman desires. You will be my porter."

It might work. Certainly it was in keeping with a widow trying to supplement her means with a little business, and even if turned back, they had a way to get to the island.

"Well done! We shall do it. Er, how?"

"Don't stand there, *mon brave*—we've much to accomplish before morning."

It was the early boat. Louise stood primly in her best rig, her porter in ragged work clothes and a broad, drooping straw hat squatting behind her, zealously guarding four trays of sweetmeats draped with muslin and a bag for returning empty dishes. Renzi kept his eyes cast down, his skin uncomfortably prickling where it had been rubbed and stained to a convincing dark hue.

"Quickly, Madame," the boatman urged, and was awarded an icy glare as Louise stepped delicately aboard. Renzi scuttled on behind her, clearly overawed by the well-dressed passengers.

"*Larguer!*" The bowman poled off and the land-lubber porter was fetched a smack on the head from the swinging boom, which brought a laugh and sent him into a defensive crouch in the bottom boards.

The boat caught the wind expertly and hissed through the blue sea, in any other circumstance a sensual pleasure with the breeze caressing the cheeks under the enveloping warmth of the morning sun. The islands were at their best, the green of their vegetation the deepest Renzi could remember and the fringing white beaches a languid temptation.

Grand-Bourg was the capital of Marie-Galante. It was a modest town with a single pier and scattered buildings nearly hidden by lush vegetation. On a slight rise there was the dull red stone of the top of a fort, its embrasures set to command the small harbour, but what Renzi noticed most was a reef nearly a mile long offshore that the boat had to manoeuvre around—the fort and this barrier would make any direct British assault on Grand-Bourg a costly affair.

Bumping up to the low landing stage, the boat emptied while Renzi bent to fiddle with the trays.

"Come along, Toto!" Louise ordered imperiously, nodding to a passer-by, who had removed his hat in respect.

It was not far: the Villa Tartu was pointed out a little way inland, at the end of a neat avenue of palm trees.

They walked on without speaking, Renzi taking an obsequious position close behind as they approached the old general's grand residence. As they got nearer his pulse quickened. Not only was there a pair of sentries at the doorway and a tricolour on a mast but definite activity inside.

He was beginning to have second thoughts about involving Louise but forced himself to focus. Evidence: he had to get unassailable proof. But this was a reconnaissance only, a spying out for what must come later. An observation—then a burglary?

"Halt!" The sentries moved forward suspiciously. "Who are you, Madame, that you come here?"

"Madame Vernou, imbecile!" Louise snapped. "Weren't you told to expect me?"

"We've no word of a Vernou. Have you papers?"

"Papers? You fool! I've been asked by your *commandant,* M'sieur."

"To what purpose, Madame?"

"He requests me to come with some of my legendary Vernou *sucreries* for your officers with a view to regular supply," she replied scornfully.

"Ah. Are those . . . ?"

"These are my rosewater jellies and those are my bonbons." A hand went out, which Louise slapped firmly. "They are not for your sort. Where is your officer?"

"Well, I can't really—"

"*Mon Dieu!*" Louise blazed. "I came because I was told there were Frenchmen here who'd relish a delicacy or two to relieve their exile! Do you think I enjoyed several hours in the hot sun in a boat to be turned away when I get here?"

"Pardon, Madame. Er, if you'll follow me."

He led her towards the house but not before she said impatiently, "Come, Toto, hurry with those sweetmeats."

They were ushered into a room and a frowning officer soon arrived.

"Ah, M'sieur! At last! Your nice *commandant* suggested I bring you some of my famous delicacies to try. If you like them, I will see if I can arrange a special delivery each week."

Deftly she flicked the muslin from the top tray. "Do taste a jelly, M'sieur, and tell me what you think."

The officer reached out and helped himself to one. "*Grâce de Dieu,* but these are very fine, Madame!" he said, in open admiration. "And those are . . . ?"

"Coconut and pistachio, M'sieur. You have good taste. The other gentlemen of your establishment, do they enjoy fine food also?" she asked suggestively.

"We shall find out, Madame. Do come this way."

Dutifully Renzi scuttled behind, bobbing his head low as they came into a drawing room where a number of other officers were relaxing with brandy.

"*Tout le monde*—attention, if you please! Do try these *friandises* of Madame Vernou's. They are splendid indeed, and if we approve of them, she will arrange a regular supply."

"For a trifle only," Louise added firmly, "and paid in advance. Put the trays down, Toto. No, not there, you simpleton. On the big table."

Her porter hastened to obey, overwhelmed by the presence of so many fine gentlemen. "Now go to the kitchen and wait for me. This is no place for such as you," she said, in haughty tones. "And don't leave that old bag here either."

He hurried out and found the kitchen. He looked around furtively, nodding to a little scullerymaid, who introduced herself shyly, then darted away.

Nearly opposite there was a room, its door open. He saw tables with untidy piles of papers and journals, walls lined with file-shelves and maps: it could have only one purpose.

In an agony of frustration Renzi knew that all he wanted was just a few paces from him.

But there were three men in there still at work. What he would not give for one minute—no, twenty seconds—alone in that room!

Instead he had to stay where he was, waiting in a stew of frustration.

A burst of good-natured laughter broke out from the drawing room, with exclamations of surprise and gratification.

"*Merde!*" one of the men in the operations room swore. "What's going on in there?"

Renzi suspected that another tray of sweetmeats had been revealed for there were sudden gasps of wonderment and delight.

"Well, damn it, I'm finding out!" the man said, and left.

"And I'm not leaving it for those greedy bastards," retorted another, and stormed out, closely followed by the last.

Renzi teetered with indecision. He had been granted exactly what he wanted—if he took his life in his hands and stepped inside.

In a haze of unreality he found himself standing in the centre of the operations room.

Scrawled times and places on a blackboard, maps with red and blue crosses, documents with an official cast—it was all here. And he had seconds to decide what to do.

Copy them? No time, and that was not evidence. Discover some fact to prove he had been witness to the operation? Again, no time . . .

A burst of voices set his heart thumping but he couldn't leave. The journals—without thinking he picked up the thickest. Times, dates, places, ships—and deployments! Steal it! The bag—where the hell was it? He snatched at it and the journal thumped to the bottom. He added another for good measure.

"Toto! Toto! Come here, you lazy villain, and collect up these dishes!"

He bolted from the room and stood panting with reaction, willing his heart to slow and his body to droop. The three men pushed past him back to the operations room, brushing crumbs from their lips. How long before they discovered what was missing?

"Quickly, now!" Louise scolded, catching something of his tension.

He worked hurriedly, putting the empty dishes and trays into the bag and flashed a look of urgency at her.

"That's very fine, good sirs! More of the candied papaya and honey-cakes, too. *À bientôt, Messieurs!*"

Trying not to let their haste show, they headed for the landing stage. Louise had paid a boatman well to be there for them so they could leave quickly. While they pressed on, Renzi told her what he had done and of the incalculable prize under the dishes in his bag.

"No sacrifice is too great to get these into English hands," he said, trying not to sound theatrical, even if it was the truth.

When they arrived at the waterfront there was no boat. Stunned, Renzi tried to think. A quick survey of the small harbour showed no vessel waiting off, or another on its way.

"There's only one thing we can do," he muttered: they had to lie low until they could find a way off the island. He saw a road that led to an orchard up the slope, ironically not far from the fort. Trying not to look conspicuous they moved away quickly. At the end of the fruit trees a meandering path led further. They passed a returning field worker, who gaped, then shouted after them.

Without looking back they hurried on, finding that the track led to a makeshift pig-pen. Then the thud of a gun sounded from the fort, and a flag of some kind was hoisted rapidly.

There was no alternative but to go on. Renzi led the way past the startled animals and they came to a wall of thick tropical undergrowth. Louise froze, holding back. Renzi urged her to continue. "I—I c-cannot!" she blurted, her face a mask of fear. *"La Scolopendra!"*

Renzi knew the gun at the fort was probably a summons to the soldiery and then the hunt would be on in earnest—they had to make the interior by dark, where they could hide.

Louise burst into tears. "I'm h-holding you up, M'sieur Renzi. Go on, I beg!" With a sob it came out: a species of giant millipede a foot or more long with savage venom infested these forests, and a childhood terror had developed into a phobia.

"Louise, you must come with me! Be brave!" He held her hand and tried to pull her on but she resisted.

He took the bag, threw out the dishes, fashioned the drawstring into a bowline, and slipped it over his shoulder.

"Forgive me, Madame," he said, lifted her up and plunged into the wilderness of deep green whipping fronds and soaring palms. She cried out in terror, then shut her eyes and gripped tightly as Renzi pushed on.

After they had reached deep into the tropical forest she tapped his shoulder gently. Renzi stopped and let her slide to the ground.

"*Mon cher,* I am better now," she said, and tried to smile.

Renzi could see she was not, but accepted it for the act of courage it was. She seemed to sense his feeling and impulsively kissed him. "Shall we go on?"

When they'd first arrived, he'd taken a mental bearing of the centre of the small, round island and tried to stay with it as they pushed through. If this was the same kind of dense lowland rainforest as he had seen in other parts of the Caribbean the going would become difficult, but fortunately here the ground cover was more open, less intertwined, and they made progress.

An hour passed and the growth thinned. A bare upland area showed ahead. Cautiously Renzi ventured there and looked back where they'd come. Spread across his vision, and no more than a mile off, he saw a line of soldiers beating as they advanced.

"We have to get away," he said urgently. "Where should we go? What's to the north?"

"Well, only another three miles. It's where the old fort used to be," she panted. Her dress was soiled and she tried to smooth her dishevelled hair, somehow finding pins to put it up again.

"Then this is where we go," Renzi said, and they started off once more. Gullies and outcrops slowed them but this had deterred cultivation and settlement. Their passage remained unseen.

Renzi did not mention it to Louise but he knew that their trail through the vegetation was almost certainly being picked up—and if the French were smart they would land another line of soldiers on the coast ahead, and then they would be trapped between the two. Keeping his fears to himself, he forced a gruelling pace.

The forest ended and neat rows of sugar-cane reared up. Renzi and Louise hurried down between them; at least they were making good speed. Renzi could see they were crossing to where the field ended in a cliff of sorts, the sparkling blue sea stretching placidly in every direction.

The cliff turned out to be located where a substantial ridge crossed the island. "This is La Grande Barre," Louise told him. Looking down from the vantage point, Renzi could see the flat northern end seemed to be all marshes and mangroves.

He glanced at the sun. Still too long until darkness. In the open, among the reeds and flat marshland, they would be rapidly spotted. It had to be accepted that the end was not far off.

Then, in the distance, drawn up on the grass away from the water's edge, Renzi spotted a fisherman's boat. "This way!" he urged, and found a track down the ridge to the swampland below.

He splashed in, holding the precious bag aloft, scattering marsh birds, which cawed raucously. Heedless of the sucking mud he headed in the direction of the boat.

Louise followed gamely, her dress now in tatters.

Muscles burning, they carried on doggedly until they reached firm ground—and the boat.

Renzi's heart sank. The craft was old; there was rainwater in the bilge and it had lain there for some time. No oars, no sail. It was of the native type, which meant that at least it was light and simple, with a single outrigger and a small mast.

"Look!" Louise's sudden cry made him jerk around. "There!"

Along the ridge soldiers were beginning to appear. A musket popped—they had been seen.

"Help me get this in the water!" Renzi gasped, trying to swing the boat around.

She took one end and heaved with all her might. It hardly moved. Voices carried faintly from the ridge—they were looking for a way down.

It galvanised them and, with a superhuman effort, they had it off the grass and on the sand. "Hurry, two branches!" Renzi gasped, gesturing at the palms.

He shoved the boat out into the waves where it bobbed gloriously. "Get in!"

Clutching the wide-leaved branches Louise sat demurely while Renzi flung in the bag and launched the craft seawards. The branches were woefully poor oars but at least they made way against the waves.

Startled by a sudden slap and gout of water Renzi knew they were under fire but refused to look back. They laboured on desperately—and then what Renzi had forlornly hoped for came true. The simple shape of the island meant that when the current offshore met the rounded coastline it diverged to clear the northern end. The boat was now being carried gently seawards on its way around the last point.

The shoreline retreated, the land became an island—and they were free.

Exhausted, Renzi slumped back. They had got away—but did this mean they were safe? No doubt the soldiers would find a boat and come after them.

But the elements were kind. The current increased, whirling them ever away from the island—and a soft sunset promised concealing dark before long.

Reaction left Renzi weak and he lowered himself down into the narrow bottom of the boat, staring at the night sky. Louise lay down next to him, the constricted space pressing them into one another. It felt natural to remain together as they gazed up at the stars.

"How lovely they are!" she murmured. "I've never really stopped to admire them."

Her hand crept trustfully into his and together they drifted into an exhausted sleep.

"Easy now!" Kydd called to the seamen at the hoist. He looked down in great concern as first Louise and then Renzi were brought aboard. They were in a frightful state—muddy, clothing torn, almost incoherent.

Louise disappeared quickly to make herself presentable but Renzi could not be parted from a filthy bag he kept clutched to his chest insisting they talk that very instant.

In Kydd's great cabin he emptied its contents on the table.

"There!" he cried hoarsely. "It wasn't on Guadeloupe, but it was on Marie-Galante."

"Nicholas, old fellow, you're not making sense," Kydd said gently. "And if we hadn't been on our way back, the pair of you would b' now be heading out well into the Atlantic—I'd have given you three days at the most before—"

"Look at these," Renzi gasped, with feeling. "Tell me what you think!"

Kydd picked up the soiled journals and his eyes opened wide. "Good God! This is a dispatch book, lists down orders to intercept, times, places—and this other—Why, damn it, you were right! This is an orderly book for a fleet—I have to eat my words, m' friend. You were right!"

"So?"

"These go to the admiral as fast as *L'Aurore* can fly. I'll hear the story later."

Hannibal's bower anchor plunged into the green translucency of St John's Road in Antigua. Tension aboard had grown unbearable for there wasn't a man who didn't feel the ship teetering on the edge. In the next days there would be a climax—the only question being in what form.

Tyrell, clearly oblivious to all this, called away his gig and was off ashore at the earliest opportunity.

The time had come.

"Gentlemen, I'll remind you of your pledge," Griffith said heavily. "I'm away now to Admiral Cochrane to lay out our position. You'll not let me down now, will you?"

Bowden knew what he was saying. Without their support he was a first lieutenant going behind the back of his captain to foment his own cause, and his heart went out to the man doing what he felt was right and at such risk.

"We're with you, sir," he said stoutly.

They left the ship in the charge of Mason who, pale-faced, stood lonely on the quarterdeck, watching as the boat took *Hannibal*'s officers away.

✦ ✦ ✦

"Lieutenant Griffith," the flag-lieutenant announced, ushering him into the admiral's office.

"Well? What's so urgent, pray, that it cannot wait?" Cochrane said irritably, looking up from his work.

Griffith took a deep breath. "Sir. I have a document with me. It lays out in detail certain . . . deviations from character in our captain that in our opinion—"

"You're not making yourself plain," barked the admiral. "For if you're delating upon your superior, you, sir, stand in contempt for it."

"Sir, it bears upon the fitness of *Hannibal* to lie in the line-of-battle," the lieutenant said doggedly. "The readiness of the men to follow and—"

"You're bringing an action against your captain? Have a care, sir, have a care!" Cochrane interrupted, a dangerous edge to his voice.

Griffith blanched, but went on, "This document, sir, is signed by every officer in *Hannibal* without exception. It details—"

"Every officer?" The admiral went rigid. "Then this is another matter entirely! Tell me why I should not take it that you have provoked them into a mutinous conspiracy against their lawful captain and commander?"

"S-sir. These same officers are present and wait without. They beg to be heard on the matter."

Cochrane slowly rose from his desk, his face tight. "This stinks of contumacy and I won't have it! You have overstepped yourself, sir, and you shall hear of it from higher powers than myself."

"May they come in, sir?"

"You try my patience too far, Mr Griffith," he rapped.

The lieutenant remained standing, stiff-faced, but made no attempt to take back his words.

"Very well," the admiral said at length. "Tell 'em to enter."

He stood in a grim quarterdeck brace, waiting.

The officers of *Hannibal* filed in, taking position in a line before the admiral.

"Now, sir, *you* will tell me what this is about," Cochrane snapped, jabbing a finger at Bowden.

"Sir," Bowden began, his throat tight, "Lieutenant Griffith is of a mind with us all that Captain Tyrell is, er, has a condition of humours that we believe does tend to, um, have its effect on his judgement to the detriment of his authority."

"You're trying to tell me he's mad, is *that* it?" The pugnacious tone intimidated.

"Not for me to say, sir."

The admiral wheeled on Griffith. "Then what does your surgeon think? Hey?"

"He claims as how he's not qualified in this matter, sir."

"Then you're wanting me to send for a head-doctor from Bermuda? This is as good as condemning the man, and I won't do it, do you hear?"

"Sir, if—"

"Be silent, Lieutenant!"

Cochrane was clearly in a quandary. If he took measures against Tyrell it would bring down a storm of opposition from other captains, some senior and influential. If, on the other hand, he ignored the warnings and a cataclysm took place, it could easily rebound on his own head.

Bowden watched tensely while Cochrane paced up and down. It had gone too far: whatever was ultimately decided, it was inevitable that his career would be irretrievably affected.

"You're all guilty of contumacious association, you know that, don't you? I can put you under open arrest this instant—but I'm not. For the sake of appearances and the good of the Service, I'll allow you to retract this nonsense and return aboard to your duties, no stain to attach to your characters, and we'll hear no more of it."

Griffith did not look at the others but replied calmly, "Sir, for the sake of our conscience we cannot do this."

"Then you leave me no other alternative . . ."

Bowden waited for the blow to fall—but there were voices, a disturbance outside.

Cochrane looked up in irritation. There was a hurried knock and his flag-lieutenant appeared. "Sorry to disturb, sir, but there's news. Captain Kydd, *L'Aurore* frigate, begs for an immediate meeting."

Kydd did not return until well into the afternoon and immediately announced that the ship was under sailing orders. "You've started a pretty moil, Nicholas." He chuckled. "Our admiral is mounting an immediate assault on Marie-Galante."

"Ah. Delay would have been fatal, of course," Renzi said with relief. "When?"

"We sail tomorrow, land at first light the day after, and if this is to be anything like Curaçao, the island will be ours by midday."

"With what forces?"

"That we have at hand. Frigates in the main, being for the same reason that they can close with the shore. One ship-of-the-line to lie off."

"And who will be leading this armament, pray?" Renzi asked delicately.

"Well, er, the senior captain of our little band claims the honour and will not be denied. The captain of the battleship, that is."

"It's not . . ."

"Captain Tyrell will lead the expedition, yes."

"There's talk of unrest in *Hannibal.*"

"At the first whiff o' powder-smoke they'll be away like good 'uns, you mark my words," Kydd said positively. "We've other things to think on. The plantocracy hereabouts have word of something in the wind concerning a stroke against the French and want to honour us with a gathering tonight afore we go."

"Dear fellow, would you be offended overmuch if I declined? My greatest ambition in life at this time is to sleep for a week, and this hour does seem the perfect time to begin."

"It would do your soul good, old trout," Kydd teased, but Renzi would not be diverted.

The warm tropical dusk promised much. St John's society had gleefully turned out at very short notice to honour the sons of Neptune with the flimsy excuse that it was in fact in remembrance of the nearby Battle of the Saintes in 1782, even if the anniversary was some months ahead.

Kydd had indulged Tysoe's fuss and worry: full dress uniform was not to be hurried and he wanted to cut a figure before the daughter of the chairman of the Association of Planters. For one of Captain Kydd's eminence, a carriage was made available and he sat in solitary splendour as it moved off in a jingle of leather and expensive harness. At the door of the Great House, under the torch-flames, those come to welcome the heroes of the hour had assembled, among them Chairman Wrexham and his daughter.

Kydd allowed himself to be handed down from the carriage and returned Wrexham's courtly bow with an elegant leg, conscious of Amelia's barely concealed delight.

Pleasantries were exchanged, then the chairman murmured politely, "Sir, my daughter being in want of a gentleman escort, it would oblige me if you . . ."

They entered the brightly lit reception room together, Kydd aware of the light pressure of her gloved hand on his arm. Shyly she introduced the notables of Antigua, this planter, that commissioner, and unaccountably her aunt Jane, a knowing woman, who sized him up rapidly.

He caught the envy in a group of naval officers nearby and swelled with pride.

"You're finding your way in our little society then, Mr Kydd," Wrexham said, with a smile.

Kydd responded with a wordless bow while Amelia bobbed, her grip on his arm tightening.

The dinner was a splendid affair. The chairman, his wife, Kydd and Amelia sat at one end while at the other the commander-in-chief held court with the senior captains. Even the presence of a stiff-faced Tyrell several places down could not dampen Kydd's happiness.

The wine was French and of high quality. The chairman eased into a smile at Kydd's knowledgeable appreciation, a result of Renzi's patient tutelage. He felt a twinge of guilt. How Renzi would have enjoyed this evening—perhaps he should have pressed him further.

He was about to suggest a toast to absent friends when he happened to notice a flicked glance and slight frown on Wrexham's face. He looked down the table and saw Tyrell's glass empty yet again, and he was glaring about for a servant to refill it.

"Oh, Captain Tyrell. He's a Tartar right enough, but just the man to set before the Frenchies I'm persuaded," Kydd said firmly.

"I'm sure of it," Wrexham responded drily.

The evening proceeded in a delightful haze, thoughts of the morrow set aside in the warmth of the occasion.

"A capital night, sir!" Kydd beamed at a hard-faced planter a place or two down, lifting his glass in salute.

The man started, then came back warmly, "As it is our duty in these times to honour the warriors that defend us!"

He raised his glass and—

There was a sudden crash down the table.

Heads turned in alarm. It was Tyrell, who had slammed his glass down so hard it had shattered.

"I've got it! Be damned, I have it!" he bellowed into the silence.

All the guests gazed at him in astonishment. He continued, in fuddled triumph, "I never forget a face, an' there's many a rogue swung at the yardarm t' prove it!" His words were thick with drink but there was no denying their hypnotic power.

He turned slowly and pointed directly at Kydd, his red-rimmed stare ferocious and exulting. "You, sir! I know where I saw you before, damme!"

Kydd went cold.

"Hah! It was the old *Duke William* around the year 'ninety-four—or was it -three? No matter! How do I know? Because as a pawky Jack tar I had you stripped and flogged! Twelve lashes—contempt and mutinous behaviour, it was."

He sat back in satisfaction. "Told you I'd get it, hey!" He chortled, seeming not to notice the shock and consternation about him.

A wash of outrage flooded Kydd. He saw Amelia's face pale as she clutched at her father while further down a naval wife turned to stare at him, twitching at her husband's sleeve and whispering. Other captains swivelled to look at him in horrified fascination, their wives agog with the knowledge that they had been present at a scene they would talk about for a long time to come. Cochrane looked down the table at him, with an appalled expression, and from outside the room he heard the excited titter of servants.

Humiliation tore at Kydd. He shot to his feet and faced Tyrell, fists clenched, his chair crashing down behind him as he fought to keep control.

"Well? It's true, ain't it?" Tyrell grunted.

Kydd's mind scrabbled to hold on to reason. The captain of the ship had ordered the lashes, Tyrell only the first lieutenant, but in its essence it was quite correct. He had been found out—he had been a former common sailor and, not only that, evidently a bad one who had been convicted of criminal conduct and punished.

He tried to speak but it came out only as a hoarse croak. He knew if he stayed he was perilously near an act that would damn him for ever—he blindly swung about and stalked from the room, desperate for the clean night air.

Outside he stood unseeing, chest heaving with emotion.

He felt a hand on his arm. "Steady, old chap, it's not the end of the world." Lydiard had followed him out. "Shall we go somewhere?"

He felt himself urged away from the gaping onlookers and around the side of the house into the garden.

"Pay no mind to Tyrell. He's a disappointed man. Everyone knows it." He hesitated, then said, with deliberate concern, "Now, m' friend, you'll not be thinking of anything rash as you'll regret later, are you?"

The words penetrated: Lydiard was referring to a challenge to a duel.

Kydd's mind seized on the chance of a focus for his rage and wounded feelings. He would have choice of weapons, and it would be man-hacking cutlasses and—

An inner voice intervened. And it told him that in polite society under no circumstances could a gentleman ask for satisfaction if in fact the offending statement was true.

His shoulders slumped. "No," he said dully. "I can't."

"This is to mean, er, what was said was substantially, um, correct?" Lydiard said carefully.

"Yes," Kydd spat wretchedly. "An' may his soul roast in Hell!"

Lydiard looked around, then said softly, "They'll understand if you leave now. Might I offer you the hospitality of my cabin in *Anson?* I'm thinking a restorative brandy might answer, dear fellow."

"No! That is, I thank you kindly but I'll find my boat and get back aboard."

There was one he desperately needed to talk to now, and he was in *L'Aurore*.

✦ ✦ ✦

Renzi quietly told Tysoe to leave them and listened with the gravest attention to Kydd's account of the evening.

"May I know who was in attendance?"

"All the world!" Kydd hissed. "And Miss Amelia, God rot his bones!" He took a savage pull at his drink. "I'll—I'll slit his gizzard, the whoreson shicer!"

"That is not to be considered," Renzi said quickly. "More to the hour is what is to be concluded from the whole." He stood up and began pacing about the cabin. "We are obliged to say that your precipitate withdrawal was unfortunate. It tells the gathering that not only is the substance of what was said not to be denied, but that apparently you left before further damaging disclosures could be made."

"No! No! Be buggered to it, I'll not—"

"Dear fellow, do allow that it happened. The question now is rather what should be done about it."

"If that stinking scut crosses my hawse again—"

"Tom, do forgive if I lay it before you as no doubt it appears to those present."

"If you must."

"Er, by its nature the gentility is limited in size, not to say modest in numbers. It is not uncommon for them to observe persons with pretensions beyond their standing who do attempt to inveigle—"

"Good God!" exploded Kydd. "If you're—"

"—their way into company to which their quality does not entitle them. Their ready response is to close ranks against the interloper."

At Kydd's dangerous look, Renzi hurried on: "You see, they are not accustomed to the Navy's worthy practice of advancing in society such officers as do merit it, and cannot be blamed for confusion and dismay in your case."

"I'll not—"

"Therefore I can counsel only one course of action." He resumed his chair and waited.

"So—what am I to do?"

"You ride out the storm as it were. This is a matter for them to resolve. You can do nothing."

Kydd balled his fists.

"Dear Tom," Renzi continued softly, "you do have my utmost sensibility of your position, but I have to point out that it is past and to repine is futile. You will take a round turn and face the day with fortitude and composure, as is your calling as a gentleman."

It hit home. Kydd breathed deeply. "As always you have the right of it, Nicholas," he said raggedly. "I'm to go forward and damn any who point the finger."

A mirthless grin spread. "After all, am I not a post captain? They can't take that away."

"Stout fellow!" Renzi said, "It'll pass, you'll see."

"Nicholas."

"Yes, brother?"

"You're forgetting one thing."

"Oh? What's that?"

"Tomorrow I will see the bastard—and must take his orders. How is that to be borne, my friend?"

Chapter 12

It was a morning like any other. But before the day was out Kydd knew two things would have occurred: *L'Aurore* would have met the enemy in battle—and he would have come face to face with Tyrell.

Tense and uneasy, he left his cabin to make his way to the captains' conference in *Hannibal* for orders in the taking of Marie-Galante.

The watch was securing for sea but at Kydd's appearance on deck furtive glances and a sudden need to occupy themselves left no doubt as to what they were thinking. Kydd's face burned.

"My barge," he snapped at Curzon, whose studied blankness was just as revealing.

His boat's crew were paragons of behaviour but over his shoulder Kydd saw faces at *L'Aurore*'s gun-ports, others at the rails and more in the tops, watching.

He forced down his emotions. This was an operation against the enemy and he had to keep cool. His duty was to his men and no personal antagonisms must be allowed to deflect him.

Yet as they approached *Hannibal* his resolve wavered. Would Tyrell be waiting to greet each captain, and there in front of everybody expect him to shake his hand?

He couldn't do it, nor look him in the eye.

Telling the boat to hang back, he allowed Lydiard of *Anson* to board while he wrestled with his feelings. Then there was no more time.

The pipes pealed as he mounted the side and stepped aboard, but Tyrell was not on deck. Trying not to let his relief show, Kydd followed the first lieutenant to be introduced to the waiting captains, who stood together by the main-mast. But as he approached, the talking died away and they turned to face him warily.

"A good day, gentlemen," he said, with a brittle lightness.

There were muttered acknowledgements and then they turned back to their conversations. Kydd flushed with anger at the intolerable behaviour but then it dawned on him that they were probably hiding their embarrassment.

Out of the corner of his eye he saw Bowden standing some yards away; the young man smiled awkwardly at his old captain.

The first lieutenant cleared his throat. "Er, gentlemen? Captain Tyrell will welcome you in the great cabin now."

They began to file into the space, Kydd standing aside until they were all before him, then following. At the last minute he hesitated at the door and the marine sentry's eye swivelled to him in apprehension. There was no more delaying the moment so he stepped inside.

"Come in, then!" Tyrell was at the head of the table, getting his papers in order. He looked up sharply. "Sit down. We've no time to waste."

Kydd took the last chair, which was on Tyrell's right-hand side. He found himself so close he could feel the man's animal ferocity radiating, but Tyrell ignored him.

Kydd held rigid and forced himself to an icy cold.

"Right. The assault on Marie-Galante." Tyrell sat forward aggressively, glaring around the table. Apart from bloodshot eyes, he seemed untouched by the night before and had once more the tight, dangerous air of a ravening leopard.

"As senior, I'm in command. Therefore you'll obey my orders

without question. Is that clear?" he rapped.

He seemed oblivious to the hostile atmosphere building. "Now listen. My strategy is simple. If we secure the capital of this miserable island the rest will fall. That's Gron' Borg. It's defended by a fort that commands the harbour so we can't go in and take it from the front. But I have a plan."

He looked about him, as if inviting argument, then snapped, "And it's this. Red Party will land to the north of Gron' Borg, Blue Party to the south. And then?"

"They advance from both sides?" Lydiard drawled.

"No!" Tyrell barked triumphantly. "They head inland, both. When in the damned forest and out of sight, they turn inward, meet, and come in on the town and the fort from the land side. Clear?"

"While the fort is being engaged from seaward?" prompted a captain lower down the table.

"Of course!" Tyrell bristled.

"Who shall command the landing parties?" another asked. If there was to be any glory and distinction it would be for those facing the enemy. The rest would be mere spectators offshore.

"Why, the hero of Curaçao for one!" Tyrell turned and gave a beaming smile.

Kydd jerked back and stared. Was this a clumsy attempt to make up for his blunder of the night before?

"Um, thank you, Mr Tyrell." His voice sounded thick and unnatural.

"Mr Kydd will be leading the Blue Party and . . ."

He waited for their full attention. ". . . and I will lead the Red Party."

There were indrawn breaths but Tyrell went on remorselessly, his deep-set eyes restless. "We have seamen and marines in each party, but only as many as can be transported in our fit of boats. The Crapauds can be relied on to put up a fight, but we're more'n a match for any Frenchy trooper! Cold steel and a willing heart, that's how we'll win, and be damned to it, that's what we'll do or I'll know why."

Lydiard interjected quietly, "Rufus, I understood this operation to be something in the way of a strike to extirpate some kind of secret naval base, not a grand invasion."

"Yes, yes, that's being taken care of by Kydd's party. Your worry is to stop interference in the landings from Guadeloupe or similar. *Hannibal* will be off Point-a-Peter and after recovering boats the frigates cruise at the four corners of the island, three leagues to seaward. Shouldn't be too hard an assignment," he added sarcastically.

"It seems not," replied Lydiard, with the barest hint of irony.

"Good! I'll bid you all farewell. We sail in an hour. Mr Kydd to remain."

He watched them leave, then turned abruptly to his right. "You're taking the Blue Party," he growled. "You can do it?"

Kydd mumbled an acknowledgement.

"What's that?"

"I said, I can do it."

"You'll have to make up numbers from your own ship. We're short of volunteers."

"Yes."

"This damn-fool secret base—I take it you'll detach a flying column the same as failed in Curaçao?"

"I will," Kydd bit off.

Tyrell sat back and fiddled with a pencil.

Kydd waited. Was this going to be a grudging apology for his behaviour? Should he accept or . . .

"You wondered why I chose you for the Blue Party?"

"I did."

"'Cos you've a way with your men. Don't know why, and don't really care, but you seem to know 'em better than most."

Slowly it dawned on Kydd that Tyrell wasn't going to offer an apology because he didn't remember what he'd said in his drunken state. His burning anger began to cool. The man was a sot, lost to drink ashore—but his inexcusable behaviour was not driven by malice.

Tyrell's brow furrowed as though trying to recover a lost thought. "I'll confide to you now, Kydd, this is my first chance at distinction in a major action this war, and I'm going for it with all my heart. At the end we'll see the white ensign atop the biggest damn building in Gron' Borg and m' name will be right up there as conqueror of Marie-Galante."

Kydd, a Trafalgar veteran, had his views on what constituted a major action but he held his tongue.

He'd never forget what the man had done to him but for now there were bigger issues. "Right enough, Rufus. It'll be your name as will be talked of wherever men remember Marie-Galante."

That pleased Tyrell. "And pity help any who don't top it the tiger when bid!" he growled, his face like thunder.

Kydd stood up. "I'll get back aboard. Good fortune to you, Rufus." He did not hold out his hand, and Tyrell seemed not to notice. He turned on his heel and left.

Ignoring the nakedly curious looks on the upper deck, he signalled for his boat and told them to stretch out for *L'Aurore*. Oakley's pipe shrilled loudly and he came aboard to a set of faces agog.

"Get those men to work!" he roared, incensed. "The barky's like a pig-sty."

There was a great deal to do to complete for sea inside the hour. The naval system of divisions saw to it that each lieutenant had a fair share of every talent the ship possessed: topmen, midshipmen, gunners, those capable of bearing a musket or swinging a cutlass and even artificers. A landing party, however, had to be fit for purpose; this was a fight ashore and the Royal Marines would figure highly.

It had to be assumed that their assault on the fort from landward would not be protracted. Any sensible garrison commander, seeing himself surrounded, would not be inclined to hold out for long enough to warrant taking ladders and siege kit. Likewise, the artillery: with the countryside entirely in British hands, it would be foolish to await a formal battering before yielding.

For the flying column, it was a different matter. Thankfully, they had Renzi's detailed description, carefully sketched out, with his estimate of its defences. How it would be protected was any man's guess but if they moved fast and advanced on it from inland they had a good chance of surprise.

Renzi stood at his side as Kydd received his stream of reporting officers. "Nicholas, I'm giving you Mr Curzon and a midshipman, with Mr Clinton and eight of his marines, and a dozen armed seamen. Look after them, if you please."

"You'll be requiring Mr Gilbey to head the shore party?"

"Not on this occasion. Tyrell leads his party so it's to be expected I shall do likewise."

"Interesting. That Tyrell is taking a party himself, that is. Will it be his own men he leads? I wonder if they'll follow . . ."

Kydd raised an eyebrow. "We've both seen him in a tight corner before, against the revolutionaries in Brittany. There's many a man owes his life to his bloody-minded leadership."

"Umm. We shall see, I think."

On the hour a gun banged in *Hannibal* and her colours rose. They were on their way.

The assault was planned for dawn, allowing the expedition to pass in clear waters by Guadeloupe in the hours of darkness, to appear out of the mists of daybreak directly before the island of Marie-Galante.

As sunrise tinged the sea with pink and gold, the inhabitants of Marie-Galante and their defenders watched with disbelief then fear as a battleship and four frigates closed in to less than a mile offshore and boats, too many to count, started towards them, in each scarlet and gold, blue and white—and the glitter of steel.

From his own boat on its way to the end of the reef to the south, Kydd could see the Hannibals heading in a mile north towards Grande Anse. It was all going according to plan: they were both out of range of the fort above the town and could land unopposed.

The shoreline grew clearer. At Pointe des Basses the reef ended and he took in pale beaches and thick dark vegetation nearly down to the water's edge. Ideal for the landing.

"There, where the fallen tree touches the water," Kydd instructed Poulden, who obediently put over the tiller. The other craft were strung astern—it was going to be easy, just— But then he saw figures moving urgently among the thick growth and the first shots rang out in the still morning air, gunsmoke rising lazily. The four marines tasked in each boat got to work in the bows, firing at the origins of the smoke, methodically reloading in relays.

It was imperative to get men ashore, whatever the cost. Having the equivalent of five regiments' artillery afloat was a dead card, however—the ships would be firing on their own men.

As they drew nearer the shore the whip of bullets was more insistent.

"Pull, y' bastards! Lay out and pull for your lives!" Kydd bawled. The men heaved like demons and the boats flew; the firing fell off as they came in and the opposition melted away.

The boat hissed to a stop in the sand and the men scrambled out, following Kydd, army niceties, like forming up, lost in the urgency to gain a foothold. Fronds and branches whipped across his face as he led them on, nerves stretched to the extreme. He slashed at the vegetation with his sword until he came upon a semblance of a track that wound inland.

"Move yourselves!" he bellowed, and went along the path at a trot. He could hear the clink and jingle of the men panting behind him as they followed. Almost certainly the firing had been from a platoon hastily sent to delay them, but their expectation would be that the invaders would turn down the coast road to advance on Grand-Bourg, while of course they were heading inland.

After a couple of hundred yards Kydd slowed at a clearing and waited for his force to come up with him. "Well done, you men!" he acknowledged breathlessly. "We head into the country, then hook around until we're above the town. A mile or two at most. Where's Mr Renzi?"

His friend, solemnly flanked by both Curzon and Clinton, the Royal Marines lieutenant, was in plain but serviceable civilian dress with a wide hat set at a rakish angle.

Kydd gave him a tight smile. "Nicholas, you know where you want to go. Stay with us until you're ready to move on the base. March on!"

Almost without warning a rearing cliff, hundreds of feet high, loomed above the trees and palms. But they saw the path took a sideways loop following the contours and they made good speed, their altitude rising slightly and Grand-Bourg firmly in sight below.

Tyrell had been right: this route had taken the defenders completely by surprise and now they had only to meet in the heights above the capital, then together descend to victory.

The going got thicker as they neared the town. Sheltered depressions were covered with luxuriant growth, and at one of these Renzi decided to make his move. "The villa—it's down further, about a quarter-mile. I'll, er, leave you now, if I may."

Kydd watched Renzi and his party vanish downwards into the lush green, then ordered his men onwards.

The joining up would be very soon now.

Bowden was in the second boat behind Tyrell and could hear the man's roars as he urged on his rowers. It had been a fraught time in the lead-up to the landings; Tyrell seemed to have no idea of the knife-edge of feeling among the men. While the squadron was formed up there was no danger of a bloody mutiny, but there would be other times and places . . .

Tyrell's bulldog character, aroused by the coming battle, was transforming him. Petty spite and vindictiveness was replaced by a towering eagerness to fall on the enemy. The moods, the suspicions, the menace were gone, leaving a roaring, raging warrior.

Away to the right *L'Aurore*'s boats were nearly in, white puffs along the coastline showing where they were meeting with opposition. It seemed to have drawn the enemy's full attention for their own length of coast was quiet and the boats came to a rest in a sheltered sandy cove. Bowden remembered it was here that Columbus had landed to name the island.

There was an uncanny stillness but Tyrell stormed fearlessly inland and found a clearing. "To me!" he bellowed, raising his naked sword.

The men came on warily, sullen. Bowden formed them up in a rough file and moved them to Tyrell, who was waiting impatiently. They tramped forward into the thickening growth after him, but from none came the customary joking and easy talk to be expected of jack ashore.

Next to him marched Hinckley, an older captain in charge of the small detachment of the 69th Gloucestershires that made up a third of their force. "I mislike this quiet," he muttered. "I'd be happier were there scouts on our flank."

Bowden glanced at him. Hinckley had seen service around the world and was much respected by his men. "We'd be slowed, surely."

"We'd be slowed more should they press home an attack while your men are strung out like that." He had his own troops in a tight formation, muskets a-port, alert for anything.

As they trudged on inland, from out of sight ahead came the occasional bull roar of Tyrell's hectoring. Bowden fancied he could hear musket fire in the direction of the *L'Aurore* landing and, with a pang, wondered how they were faring—so like a dream had been his service in the frigate, utterly different from the sour moodiness in *Hannibal*.

But he had to accept that this was his duty . . . and with a turn of the stomach he remembered that after this action was over there had to be an accounting—a resolution to the dilemma the *Hannibal* officers faced.

Ragged firing broke out ahead. As one, the seamen dived for cover, wriggling into bushes and under broad-leafed ferns. The soldiers stayed in formation, nervously eyeing Hinckley.

"I'll go up and see what's afoot," Bowden said, loping forward in a crouch.

They were not far from the join-up position, the ridge above the town, but it quickly became clear that something had happened.

"God damn them for a parcel of old women!" choked Tyrell, hunkered down and gesturing angrily at the strewn articles of abandoned kit on the path and his men cowering in the vegetation. "As it's only a few Crapaud militia sent to delay us!"

There was desultory firing from positions off to the left and a stray bullet whipped through the branches and leaves above.

"Get up and move!" Tyrell roared in vexation. He stood up. "To the fore, advance, you mumping rogues—or I'll have every man jack o' you flogged to an inch o' your lives."

None came out from their hiding places.

"By God!" he yelled. "I'll have the hide off you for as cowardly a bunch of lubbers as ever I've heard on. We've an island to conquer—get on your feet *and go!*"

Still there was no movement and Tyrell's face turned red. "To hell and damnation with you for a scurvy crew who know no discipline! If I have to go alone I'll do it—d' you hear there?"

He hesitated for a few moments more. Then, with a roar of

frustration and with drawn sword, he raced forward across the seventy yards or so of clear ground ahead. There was no firing, and he made the ridge safely, flopping down at its crest. "Move, you chicken-hearted shabs!" he yelled, beckoning urgently back at them. "Forward, or fry in Hell for ever after I've hanged the lot o' you!"

There was a stirring but not one broke cover to join him.

Bowden's every instinct was to urge them on to go up with him but where did his real duty lie? His own men were still on their way and his place was with them.

He turned and raced back to call for Hinckley's soldiers.

This was the climax, Renzi told himself, as they pressed forward down the path. Not only for the process of clearing his reputation but for the elimination of the biggest threat that existed to the British holdings in the Caribbean, the largest source of revenue to a country locked in war against a world-toppling tyrant.

He led the way; Curzon hurried close behind. He'd taken care before to register that the villa lay in a particular fold in the hills slightly to the northeast, which they were now descending.

He stopped. The faded orange tiles of the roof were visible through the foliage below.

Now for the final act.

"I believe their attention will be on our fleet and the landings and they are not troubling to look behind them," he told Curzon and Clinton. "They'll be considering their position, whether to abandon now or wait until the situation is clearer. I do believe they'll remain for a while longer—to destroy such a successful operation unnecessarily would be a sad mistake for them."

Scouts returned with the welcome news that, but for watchers on the balcony, there seemed to be no sign of anything approaching a frenzied defence.

They had the luxury of time to prepare.

"Your suggestions, gentlemen?" Renzi invited.

Clinton began crisply, "A file of men to each side, out of sight. L'tenant Curzon with the remainder at the ready here. The two files meet and advance with me from the front. The instinct of the defenders is to break for the rear, where we will give them due welcome."

"Then I will be with you, Mr Clinton," Renzi said firmly.

"Oh—no, sir. We've brought you here now and Mr Kydd was most insistent that—"

"We cannot delay further, sir."

"Very well, Mr Renzi," Clinton said, with a lopsided grin. "Sar'nt Dodd—the right-hand side."

Stealthily they threaded down past the villa to the road. Clinton watched for Dodd's signal that his group was ready, then the two broke into a run, approaching each other and turning to take position. With shouts of dismay, the balcony cleared on an instant.

Renzi paused, letting first one then the other squad enter the garden, firing as they went. Three men burst out from the house but were dropped with musket fire before they had made a few yards. Dodd raced for the door and took position to one side. Musket butts smashed it inwards. Dodd and three others disappeared inside.

Unable to contain himself Renzi hurried to join them. In the disorder he heard shouts and a single shot, followed by running feet. Then came a smell of burning. He knew where it had to be and motioned to a marine to deal with the door to the operations room. It flew open and inside he saw a man bent over a small fire trying to burn papers. He jerked up in despair. Renzi knocked him aside and stamped on the flames.

Everything was in a chaos of disarray, documents and empty drawers, with office paraphernalia scattered about the floor.

"Secure the room!" Renzi ordered loudly.

He picked up a singed paper. With rising exultation he saw it was an order on a vessel to assume a specified position to take the

English trading ketch *Sunrise*. Another was a return on goods seized on a prize, signed by an illegible hand.

"Sah!" It was Dodd, fighting down a broad smile. "Mr Curzon's compliments an' could you attend on him, out the back, like."

"Very well. Nothing to be touched here, if you please."

Curzon was in the garden. Two lines of marines and seamen grinned triumphantly at a huddle in the centre of nearly a dozen individuals, some in uniform.

"Ah, Mr Renzi," he drawled. "I'd like to introduce the former owners of this villa who thought to run. None got away, o' course, so you have the entire gang here for your inspection."

Renzi gave a short bow. It was the end of a perfect day. From them he would learn just how the operation functioned: where the fleet was located, its system of communication, intelligence . . . So many things needed answers to draw a line under the whole incredible enterprise.

Kydd stopped and held up his hand. "Quiet!" he hissed. They heard shots from the general direction of the ridge selected for the joining up.

"Forward!" he growled. "And watch your front."

The path wound along the contour on the flank of the hill, but until they were fully around, whatever was happening was obscured.

A little further on, they came to a ravine and a small wooden bridge.

"Stop!" He heard popping on the other side of the hill where he guessed the ridge must begin. If that was so, Tyrell was in some kind of engagement—but this bridge would make a classic defensive position that could stop an army.

He debated whether to send men on to it to see if they drew fire, then took it upon himself. "Cover me," he muttered, and stood up to make his run.

The first shot knocked his cocked hat into the ravine, another plucked viciously at his sleeve. He dropped down again immediately.

"We've got to get to Cap'n Tyrell," he said, more to himself than anyone in particular. "Give me that," he told a seaman, and took his musket, slinging it at his back, before securing the belt pouch of ammunition.

"Sir, what are you—"

But Kydd had already moved out, slithering through the undergrowth until he found the bridge supports. He launched himself forward and up, grasping one of the timbers and using it to swing up and under the roadway. The musket was a clumsy and weighty hindrance.

The criss-cross of struts was child's play to a seasoned topman and he went rapidly from one to another, the floor of the ravine, with a gushing river far below, nothing for one at home a hundred feet up in wildly heaving rigging.

He reached the other side and unslung the musket, cautiously rising to face where he'd seen the enemy gunsmoke. Something moved and he fired at it.

Dismayed by the sudden appearance on their side of the ravine of an attacker they rose to fire down at him—but half a dozen muskets crashed out from the British seamen and two fell; others ran for their lives.

Kydd finished reloading and pulled himself up. Without waiting for the others, he plunged ahead, musket at the ready.

Within yards he found himself at the edge of a clearing. It was the ridge above the town, and there was Tyrell, lying full-length just below the crest.

"Captain Tyrell, ahoy!" he shouted, and went towards him.

Tyrell did not look around, lying oddly still. Uneasy, Kydd quickened his pace, then broke into a run.

"Rufus!" he called, but in his concentration on the scene he tripped on a tussock and fell. The musket went off into the ground with a muffled report. Shame-faced, he retrieved the still smoking weapon and went up to Tyrell.

Stunned, he saw that he was dead. Kydd stared down at the body of the one who had done so much to hurt him, now no more.

Suddenly a man was beside him—he hadn't heard him approach. Startled, he swung round. It was Hinckley, the army captain, who knelt beside Tyrell to examine the wound, then rose slowly, looking at Kydd with an odd expression.

"If you please, sir," he said formally, holding out his hands.

Puzzled, Kydd passed him the musket. Without taking his eyes off Kydd's he delicately smelt the muzzle, then lowered it.

"You have a difficulty, Captain?" Kydd asked with irritation. They had to complete the joining for the final push on Grand-Bourg without delay and there was no time for whatever army silliness this was.

"He was shot from behind."

"He . . . ?"

"Not from the front."

Then it dawned. "You—you think I killed him?" Kydd said, incredulous.

"That is not for me to say, sir."

Renzi asked that they step inside, to the biggest room of the villa. Taking a comfortable chair, he watched while they filed in and stood in line before him.

There were nervous clerks, stolid functionaries and military men, warily eyeing the Royal Marines who stood smartly at the doorway. Renzi went up to the dark-featured individual he'd first seen in Curaçao. "Duperré—this is you, sir?"

The man spread his hands. "No, sir, I am desolated to tell you I am not."

"M'sieur Duperré to step forward, if you please."

A blank-faced man of years inclined his head. "I am he."

Renzi gave a grim smile. This could not possibly be the head of the most insidious and successful naval operation of recent times.

"Er, I'll see Mme Bossu now, I believe."

"Bossu?"

"From the kitchens. Do fetch her for me."

It took some time to find the little scullery maid hiding under the stairs; Renzi had met her briefly when he had been disguised as Louise Vernou's porter.

"My dear. Be so kind as to point out M'sieur Duperré."

Trembling she indicated a sharp-faced officer, a *capitaine de frégate* in undress uniform.

So that was the man. "Excellent! My congratulations, sir, on a truly impressive operation." Something made him hesitate. How was it that only a relatively low-ranking officer was directing such an enterprise at fleet level?

He turned to the maid. "And who, pray, is in charge here? Who gives the orders?"

Boldly, she flung out an arm to a somewhat portly gentleman in the dress of a planter, who returned a wan smile.

"I see. Thank you, my dear, you've been most helpful."

Renzi beamed at the gathering and invited the planter to a nearby study. "Do sit, er . . . ?"

The man did not speak; neither did he take a seat.

"Oh, do not stand on ceremony. We have much to talk of, I believe."

The man sat slowly.

"Your naval operation has been truly a wonder and amazement to us—you have my condolences that it is now concluded."

No words were forthcoming, so Renzi went on, "As will stand to the eternal credit of the French Navy."

Suddenly the man's face broke into a rueful grin. "Well, be damned to it but you've landed us fair 'n' square!" He chuckled.

"You're American?" Renzi said, in astonishment.

"Right 'nough. Jonathan Miller's my handle."

"You give the orders?" Renzi said in disbelief.

"I do, an' I don't take kindly to this guff about the French Navy takin' all the credit."

"What do you mean?"

"Who'm I talkin' to?"

"Smith," Renzi said neutrally. "Nicholas Smith."

Miller gave a conspiratorial smile. "It'll do as well as mine, I guess."

"You were saying?" prompted Renzi.

"Well . . ."

"We have the operations room and all the papers," Renzi said, "largely unburned. It shouldn't take long to put it all together."

With a sigh Miller began, "It's quite a story, Mr Smith."

"I've got time."

"A splash o' wine would help."

Renzi called for some, then settled back to hear Miller's tale.

"I'm a businessman from Charleston, where I'm known as one savvy trader, I'll have you believe."

"Go on."

Miller took charge of the wine and poured a glass for them both, then drank deeply.

"It's like this. In business when you see an opportunity you go at it with both hands, you know what I mean?"

"Quite. Please continue."

"The French here, they have a problem. You. So I figure a way out for 'em."

"You did? This is a naval matter, I'll remind you."

"Ha! No, it's not—it's a business prospect."

"Er, I don't follow."

"They can't ship sugar to France on account o' your cruisers. No sugar, no trade, no revenue. I'm in the business to remedy just that."

"How?"

"Like I said, it's a business. We work together, partners like. I lay out the cash, supply the necessaries and take care o' the management and they . . . well, they stump up the letters of marque."

"I don't understand—those are for privateers."

"Just so! Yours truly has his own fleet of 'em, funded, run and managed by me, but under the French flag."

"A fleet of privateers?"

"Why not? Have 'em working together, send 'em where the meat is. That's why I've got the French Navy—they do all the operations stuff, signals and such. I concentrate on the money-making."

Renzi gave a half-smile. Privateering was a business like any other, with investors and suppliers, profits and losses. By opening up to large scale—a fleet—it would be possible to pool expenses, lay in supplies wholesale and oversee manning efficiencies. When combined with the expertise of a navy in fleet-level deployments, the effects would be—had been—devastating.

He sat back in admiration. By funding the operation Miller had provided the French with a powerful naval tool and at no expense. It had been a huge capital risk but had no doubt paid him back handsomely.

It was masterful—and it threw up as many questions as it answered.

"Do tell me, Mr Miller, how did you realise on your prizes? There are no French courts to condemn same that I know of in this part of the world."

"Ah, well, no harm to tell you now, seeing as it's all over."

He helped himself to another glass. "We take only ships we know about, and we plan smart. Make up papers as says she's an American, new-bought from the English who are too frightened to sail. Papers say as how we've been tradin' with French territory on our own account, as is legal for a neutral. She arrives in Charleston. We've a sympathetic Revenoo man who switches papers to show she's a US trader heading for France under our own dear flag. So—the French madames get their sugar, we split the proceeds and everyone's happy."

"Why are you telling me this? You know we'll take action."

"'Cos in them papers you'll not catch my name on a one. And on the other, I'd be a fool to think you British are going to take Boney's Decree without you do something like it yourselves. So there's only so long this'n is going to work—I've made my pile, time to get out."

"Well, while you're in the mood, pray tell me, if you will, how this business works, at all. I've a suspicion it's a very tight operation, well organised, brilliantly run."

There was no harm in showing his admiration for this American entrepreneur.

Miller settled and said expansively, "Right. Well, first we has a network. Of business intelligence. Every sugar port in the Caribbee has its wharf lumpers as knows when a ship's down to sail. They tips my man on the island the wink and we set to work. Our tricksy papers are made up and, with location instructions, sent out to the nearest deployed privateer."

"I don't see how you know where they'll be, and—"

"I'm gettin' to that. The sugar boat is taken, the prize crew has their papers and off they sail to Charleston. The privateer returns. Now, you were askin' about the privateer fleet. Well, we has above a dozen places o' rendezvous. Here we keep 'em supplied with victuals an' water such as they don't ever have to make a port, keeping right out of sight o' your frigates an' such. We therefore knows where they is, see?"

"How then do you keep in touch with your fleet? A navy has dispatch cutters, avisos, that sort of thing."

"Shark-meat fishermen. They'd cross the Caribbean for a dollar in hand."

Of course! Like a swarm of mosquitoes off some coasts, their movements would never be questioned. Carrying a pack of papers, instructions—it was brilliant.

"Tell me, Mr Miller, in all our naval patrols we've never once caught up with one of your privateers. Why is that, do you think?"

The American gave a boyish smile. "As we have our man in your admiral's office, o' course. Can't tell you his name, you'll understand, but he's been mighty obliging in the article of getting your patrol orders to us for a fair fee."

In a flash of insight Renzi knew who it must be, and said smoothly, "I own I was well flammed by the information about Curaçao. Was that your . . . ?"

"Aye, it was. You was getting too close to the real thing, so I arranged a little show as would discredit your idea."

Renzi sat back. It *was* Wilikins. The only one to know if he'd taken the bait in order for Miller to put it in train. "And it worked, I do confess."

"Um, do you tell me now, Mr Smith, how did you catch on to us at all?"

"I'll let you know if, first, you tell me something. What became of the crews of the prizes you captured?"

"Oh, well. Had to make it all pay, so had an arrangement with Emperor Dessalines in Haiti. Quite took to the idea of running white slaves."

"You . . . sold them into slavery?"

"Don't take on so. You'll get 'em back, should you make a ruckus. Can't be seen to have any kind o' slavery, his nation founded on the back of a slave revolt."

Renzi shook his head in disbelief and admiration. The whole thing could only have worked with meticulous attention to detail, immaculate management and business acumen on a heroic scale.

"Very well. This is how you were dished, Mr Miller."

There was no need to involve Louise but by the time he had finished there was admiration on both sides. With nothing in writing and everything hearsay, there was every likelihood that the man would get away with whatever he could salvage from the sudden demise of his business.

In a way, Renzi could only honour him for the achievement.

Chapter 13

Dodd entered the room diffidently. "Can I show you something, sir?" he asked, hovering.

"Oh, er, I think we've concluded our little talk," Renzi said. "Thank you, Mr Miller, for a very enlightening conversation."

He rose and left with the sergeant. There were more than enough men to safeguard their capture and the prisoners could await developments.

Dodd led him out of the front of the house. "There, sir," he said, pointing at the fort where a ridiculously large Union Flag flew proudly aloft.

Renzi beamed. They had done it! Now to savour the sweets of victory.

He handed over to Curzon and stepped out for the fort. He would hear details of the action first, then join Kydd in *L'Aurore* for a suitably rousing celebration.

At the gate two Royal Marine sentries from the ship recognised him and, with huge grins, elaborately presented arms. He doffed his hat to them and went inside.

It was a bedlam of noisy activity and Renzi quickly picked up that this had been selected as the provisional seat of government of the new military ruler of Marie-Galante.

"Er, where's the, er, governor?" he asked a distracted officer.

"Oh—in the end office," he said, and bustled off.

Renzi had a duty before anything else to report that the prime objective of the assault had been secured, so he went down the corridor to the large office at the end. He knocked at the open door.

At the commandant's desk sat Kydd, looking worried, an army adjutant politely waiting while he read a document.

"Ahoy there!" Renzi said lightly.

"Oh? Ah—it's you, Nicholas." He turned to the army officer. "Do spare me ten minutes, if you will."

"Certainly, sir," the man said, and left quietly.

Kydd, deep lines of tension in his face, motioned to Renzi to a seat. "Did you find your base?"

"Indeed. All's under hatches, including His Knobbs. It's the end for them."

"Glad to hear it," Kydd said, but his tone betrayed deep distraction.

"You're governor, then?"

"I'm senior naval officer in charge, if that's what you mean. I keep post until relieved by a civil appointee."

"Not Tyrell?"

"Captain Tyrell fell in the action."

"I should say I'm sorry to hear that."

"And I hope even sorrier to hear that I'll probably swing for it," Kydd said bitterly.

Renzi couldn't believe his ears. "I thought you said—"

"He was shot from behind. Captain Hinckley saw me standing over the body with a smoking gun."

"You—you didn't—"

"No," Kydd said coldly. "I did not. But I'm being blamed for it."

"How can this be so?"

Kydd explained the simple circumstances behind the situation, then went on sourly, "As there's none higher than me to have me arrested, I'm free as one of your summer clouds. I can do what I like—which is anything, as here everyone is under martial law and I'm the last authority."

It was bizarre—and deadly serious.

"So what will happen?"

"I can't blame Hinckley. He saw what he saw and has a duty to lay the information at the proper level—after we return." His face went bleak. "Until then I must do my duty."

"You'll see it through, brother, never fear."

"With every wardroom and mess-deck in the squadron alive with the gossip that I've taken my revenge? A hard thing to get by, Nicholas."

Renzi could think of nothing to say that was not feeble in the face of what Kydd had to endure now. At a stroke his elation had evaporated and he was left with a lowering sense of inevitability.

"Thus, old friend, you see I have to get on. I'll join you in *L'Aurore* when I can."

So close to Antigua, the news brought an instant response from St John's. An interim administrator was appointed and sent in the same vessel that brought Kydd's recall. He would go in *L'Aurore* as, in the sight of all, he remained her lawful captain.

When she picked up her moorings in St John's Road, Kydd's pennant still flew defiantly; it would take nothing less than a court-martial to decree its hauling down. Aware that every eye in the fleet was now on him, he boarded his barge in immaculate full dress uniform with all the dignity he could muster.

It was more than two miles, past every ship of the Leeward Islands Squadron, before he was able to arrive at the stone jetty. He could feel dozens of telescopes, hundreds of eyes, all feasting on the spectacle of the hour. He sat alone, looking neither left nor right,

Poulden giving his orders in a subdued manner, the men avoiding his eye as they pulled their oars.

And there was not a thing he could do—neither shout his innocence to the skies nor blaze his contempt on all who could believe him capable of the act of murder.

Instead he ignored the gaping onlookers and boarded his carriage with his head held high to be whisked away to the admiral's residence.

Half expecting the guard turned out and a provost with an arrest warrant waiting, he was relieved to be shown immediately into Cochrane's office.

"Get out, Flags," the admiral told his aide and waited impatiently until they were alone.

"Sit down," he told Kydd testily. "We all know what this is about."

He fixed his eyes in a piercing gaze on him. "Did you do it?"

Kydd gulped, as he held back the torrent of feeling that threatened to unman him. "No, sir."

"Hinckley saw only you, standing with a gun just fired over the body, no one else in sight. What do you say to that?"

"I—I can't account for it, sir. I saw Captain Tyrell, started up towards him and tripped. The gun went off. When I reached him I found he was already dead."

"Damn it all," blazed Cochrane, slamming his hand on the desk and rising in frustration. "You—the captain of a prime frigate—and you're saying you fell over! Tripped! For God's sake, give me *something* I can use to stop this going to trial." He began pacing the room, his expression grim. "You know you've robbed me of my victory," he said, with a twisted smile. "There's going to be nothing but this affair spoken of in London these six months."

Something of the sense of what he'd said penetrated and he tried to make amends. He sat in a chair opposite. "I'll grant he was a tyrant, a miserable dog who deserved his fate—but, Hell's bells, the world won't see it that way."

Kydd replied in a low voice, "One of my previous officers serving in *Hannibal* told me in confidence he thought the man was mad—he could be right."

"That's as may be. But the whole thing's monstrous! It has to stop—the first post captain this age to be tried for his life! Boney will make much of this and the Tory press will never let it drop."

He got up again and resumed pacing. "You know I'm unable to do anything for you, Kydd. I can't prevent this going forward, for then we'd all be in a pretty pickle."

Finally he stopped, went to his desk and regarded Kydd sorrowfully. "I now have to act, I'm sorry. Send for some lawyer coves as will put things all shipshape before the, um, trial begins."

Kydd's face was stony. There was nothing to say: his future was now irrevocably cast into a single track with only one ending.

Cochrane brightened. "I can do *something,* damn it! No open arrest for our victor of Marie-Galante. For you I offer the hospitality of the flag-officer's residence, quarters fit for a hero."

"Thank you, sir," Kydd said, almost in a whisper. That would be a mercy at least—a prison cell of luxury.

"Providing, um, that you give me your word of honour and so forth . . ."

It had happened too quickly. Within the space of hours only, Renzi had lost his closest friend to a bolt from the blue that had neatly snared him in as tight a grip as it was possible to get. And for all his learning and logic, he had found that he was totally helpless in the face of it.

He knew the ways of the Navy: unlike shore-side law there would be swift justice, a need to get a distasteful business out of the way as soon as possible and the ships back on station. In the Mediterranean he recalled the commander-in-chief convicting on the Saturday with executions on the Sunday—would this be Cochrane's way?

Renzi had had to try something. His forlorn hope had been to rifle through any legal work he could lay hands on for some stray loophole, but in the thickets of legalese he was getting nowhere.

Hearing the boatswain's mate piping aboard an officer he looked up from his reading. Strange, he'd heard that all *L'Aurore*'s officers who could had resolved to stay ashore in sympathy and support of their captain.

Shortly there was a knock at the door of the great cabin.

"Why, Mr Bowden," he said, sincerely pleased to see the young man. "How kind in you to visit."

"I'd rather it were in different circumstances, Mr Renzi, I really do," he said, looking around wistfully, before awkwardly taking Kydd's armchair.

"You've come to see what's to do, old fellow."

"In a word—yes."

Renzi sighed. "One thing we can be sure of . . ."

". . . that he did not kill Captain Tyrell."

"Just so.

"And another: that unless the real murderer is caught there's every prospect that . . . it will end badly."

Bowden bit his lip. "That is so true, Mr Renzi. And what gives me the most pain is that there's not a shadow of a doubt in my mind that the Hannibals did this thing. However, they gave their sworn and solemn testimony that it was none of them."

"So the world will say Captain Kydd it must be. With motive and good opportunity, together with the evidence of a just-fired musket, I think we must take it there's little chance he'll escape."

"It . . . it would appear that is so," Bowden said quietly, his face tight. "Am I right—that is to say, is it realistic to trust that the captain will be afforded a firing party rather than the noose?"

"Let's not think on these things, my friend," Renzi said, his head in his hands. "It may not come to pass."

"There must be something we can do!" burst out Bowden, "We can't just sit and wait for things to happen."

Renzi looked up wearily. "I'm no lawyer but in this little reading I've managed there's not the slightest hope. Whether the jury is of naval captains or men from the street, with the facts they have, they'll be obliged to convict."

"Then . . ."

"Then we cannot prevent events taking their dolorous course."

On the way back to *Hannibal* Bowden felt anger rising. That a man he admired above all others was to be brought down through none of his doing—there had to be a way out!

The irony of it was, of course, that Kydd was being unjustly condemned by the very men he had arisen from, those he understood so well, the kind with whom he had once been shipmates.

There were legends that, as a young officer, Kydd had set aside his uniform to take on at their level a common seaman in a bare-knuckle duel, and other tales of him directly appealing to his men, who had not let him down.

So Bowden would do the same. Follow Kydd's example and appeal to the Hannibals directly. It was the only course left open, the last remaining chance, and, by God, he would take it.

There was one terrible risk, however: in going to the men he was laying himself and Kydd open to the charge of interfering with witnesses, which would have the inevitable consequence of sealing his fate beyond retrieving.

It stopped him cold.

What would Kydd himself do? There could be no doubt: he would go ahead in faith.

✦ ✦ ✦

Hannibal was in a very different state. The dread presence in the after cabins was no longer there—it was as if a hellish portent always present had passed on. Men spoke in subdued tones, only half believing what had happened. The officers had gone ashore to be away from the sense of death and menace and Bowden had the wardroom to himself.

In a rising fever of resolution he considered his move.

How would Kydd go about this? The last thing he'd do was muster them by division. Instead he would doff his uniform. He would go down on the mess-deck to pass among them, feel their temper, show that he knew them and cared about them.

Bowden stood up, then self-consciously took off his coat and tucked his cocked hat under his arm as he had seen Kydd do when on informal visits to a forward part of the ship.

Then, quite deliberately, he left the cabin spaces and went to the after hatchway, hearing the accustomed noise and rough jollity of the men at their supper and grog. At the top of the ladder he teetered at the thought of what he was about to do—then descended.

The long-hallowed custom was that the men were left to themselves for their meal and grog, to talk freely and get off their chest any rankling matter without fear of being overheard by an officer. He had now broken that code.

Heads turned in astonishment at his appearance; as he walked slowly between the tables conversations stopped. Like a widening ripple, the sudden quiet spread out until the whole mess-deck was craning round to see what was happening.

Bowden reached the gratings over the main hatchway and stopped. The atmosphere was close. It stank of bodies and the smoke of the rush dips that lit each table in flickering gold, and which touched, too, the massive black iron of the guns between in a martial gleam.

He looked forward, then aft, until he was sure of their attention.

Then he spoke. "Hannibals. Shipmates. I think you know why I'm here."

There was a ripple of murmurs that quickly died away.

"In fact I'm sure you do. That's why I'll be brief. I do apologise for my intrusion into your time, which I would never contemplate in any other circumstances."

He saw interest turn to guarded resentment and realised, in a pang of despair, that while he could follow Kydd's lead in going among them he could never talk to them in their own cant, the sea-talk common to all seamen that revealed beyond doubt that the speaker was one of them.

"It's a plea. For common humanity to as noble an officer as it's been my honour to serve with."

There was a stillness that was absolute. "And for justice. Is it right that a man should be punished for the sins of another?"

Now the sea of faces showed nothing but a stolid blankness. He knew the signs: they were closing ranks to an officer.

"I appeal to you! On your manhood, *do not let this thing happen!*" The surge of passion caught him by surprise but he didn't care. This was Kydd's last chance.

"Let the truth come out—I beg of you . . ."

There was no whisper, no movement. Simply a glassy stare.

"I—I'm going now to the foredeck. There I'll be waiting—for any who cherishes justice and truth, who will save a great man for his country. And for the sake of his own conscience before God."

He could do no more.

Slowly he walked forward, past the mess-tables, the young seamen, old shellbacks. Ignorant waisters, long-service petty officers and the countless honest Jack tars who were the core of any ship's company.

Up the ladderway, slowly, dignified, and past the ship's bell to the furthest deck forward. He went to the centre, sat cross-legged, motionless, and waited.

Time passed. He had chosen this place deliberately. It was before-the-mast territory, a seaman's recreation space and sacred to the purpose, which any officer would not dream of trespassing upon in times of relaxation, as now.

This way they could approach him without fear, on their own ground. There might be before long a shame-faced confession, the men in a body coming forward with the truth.

He waited longer.

There was the sound of footsteps. A single person—who would it be that was—

But it was merely the watch on deck, a seaman sent to trim the riding light in the bows. He passed by with his lanthorn, his set face studiously ignoring Bowden. He performed his task, returning without a single glance at the extraordinary sight of an officer sitting on the foredeck, where by now there should have been companionable knots of sailors with clay pipes and leather pots of grog talking easily about their day, perhaps some with a violin or a tuneful voice.

Bowden realised he had to face up to the bitter fact: he had failed completely. None had come up to the foredeck. In a way it was not surprising: if some were inclined to break ranks and approach him they would be seen and marked down as informers. But he had been hoping for a collective resolve. And it had not happened.

"You realise you were taking a terrible risk, old chap."

"Interfering with witnesses, I know. But, by God, I had to try—and I truly believe they would not have informed upon me to the authorities."

Renzi felt for Bowden, his helplessness in the face of a pitiless Fate, but he carried its weight on his shoulders, too. He had come up with two schemes for rescuing Kydd by stealth but both foundered on the knowledge that he would certainly refuse, sturdily trusting in decency and common law.

He was hollow-eyed with worry, and Bowden looked much the same. They had run out of ideas and, with that, any options for the future.

Bowden wrung his hands over his failure with the Hannibals. "As I talked, I could see I'd lost them. There was no common ground, no way to communicate, speak their language . . ."

"Stop!" Renzi cried, as a flash of desperate inspiration came. "We've one last throw of the die. What if . . ."

The boat put off once more for *Hannibal.* It held only one passenger and hooked on at the fore-chains where no visiting boat would ever deign to go. *Hannibal*'s mate-of-the-watch sent the quartermaster hurrying forward to intercept the stranger, but by the time he reached the fore-mast a figure had swung over the bulwarks and was inboard.

"Hey, you—what d'ye think—"

"Out o' my way, cully! I got business wi' the Hannibals," the thick-set man growled, knocking him aside.

He slid down the fore-ladder, crossed purposefully to the hatchway and clattered down to the main-deck.

In an age-old routine men were clearing the tables to raise them up against the side of the ship; in the dog-watches the space had changed first from a gun-deck to a mess-deck, and now was transforming again into the open space where at the pipe "Down hammocks!" it would be their communal bedroom.

"Who are you, then?" the stranger was asked in astonishment.

Men crowded around to see what apparition out of the night had suddenly appeared in their midst.

The man said nothing, folding his arms and staring about him. More came up, and when the hubbub had died, he spoke.

"I'm Toby Stirk, gunner's mate o' Billy Roarer," he grated.

Puzzled looks passed between the men; the quartermaster hovered uncertainly.

He spoke louder. "An' I'm come aboard *Hannibal* to tip me daddle to the gullion what did for Cap'n Tyrell."

"Aye, well . . ."

"See, we goes back a long spell. I was gun captain in th' old *Duke William* in the last war, when Mantrap was first lootenant o' the barky."

Glances of fellow feeling and a dawning respect began to appear.

"A right bastard then as well, I'd reckon," one said.

"Worse'n that," Stirk spat, his eyes glowing.

There were growls of sympathy and a stir in his audience. "Come on, Jeb—show yerself!"

A tall, serious-looking seaman came reluctantly forward.

"Jeremiah Haywood."

"You did 'im?" Stirk said quietly.

"Aye, I did—but I'm not proud of it, I'll have thee know," the man said, in a troubled voice. "Shootin' in the back ain't right for any man."

There were encouraging shouts, and he went on, "Gives me two dozen f'r bein' slow in stays, an' another dozen afore the first was healed. When I saw him in front o' m' musket I just lost m' rag an' let fly, is all."

"Right. Well, let me go on an' finish m' yarn about *Duke William*. Could be interestin' to some."

He paused, letting all eyes find his. "See, I'm rememberin' a young able seaman, runs afoul o' the bugger. No fault o' his, and a prime sailorman as ever there was, but he's triced up and gets the lash as nearly sees 'im fish-meat. Didn't I tell you his name? Why, it was young Tom Kydd as was."

Realisation came slowly, but when it did there were sharp intakes of breath and uneasy looks.

"Yes, mates. One of us. Come aft the hard way, now he always takes care o' them as fights the ship for him. I've known him off 'n' on for years since, and *never* 'ave I seen 'im let down 'is shipmates. Never."

Haywood turned pale.

"Now he's in a right stew, no one t' look out for 'im, no bugger to speak up for 'im. An' all because us jolly tars won't see 'im right in the article of owning t' the crime."

He turned and faced Haywood, looking at him steadily. "I'm not the one t' peach on another, but if Tom Kydd gets his'n, on account another won't step forward, I'd let every ship, watch, every messdeck an' every shellback in the whole o' King George's Navy know the name o' the one who let him suffer. This I swear!"

In the shocked silence not a soul moved.

Then Haywood threw back his shoulders as though getting rid of a load. "No need for threats, mate. M' mind was made up beforetimes. I'll go. He'll not swing."

Stirk nodded slowly. "Cuffin. I'm still goin' to tell it like it is—that as brave a cove as I know did the right thing when he could've walked away from it all." He held out his hand. "I want to shake yer hand, Mr Haywood."

He did so, slowly and solemnly.

Turning quickly, Haywood pushed through the crowd, heading aft. "Where yer goin', Jeb?" someone called.

"I said I'd do it, an' I am—an' that's right now."

The others hurried after him, but he strode on.

Stirk forced his way through and grabbed him by the arm. "Jeb, mate. Let's see it's done right *by you*. Not a lot o' sense to give yourself over without you has someone t' speak for ye. Don't yez have L'tenant Bowden servin' in this hooker still?"

"Aye. An' he's aboard, in his cabin this hour."

"So let's see him."

The crowd had now swollen to more than a hundred and others swarmed up from the identical lower deck to join the throng. The young master's mate tried to stop them, but Stirk was having none of it. "Ask L'tenant Bowden if he's at liberty t' come an' talk."

Bowden appeared out of the cabin spaces, looking tired and bewildered. "Mr Stirk, what are you . . . What do all these men want?"

"They's askin' f'r a steer, like," he said to the young lieutenant, realising it must look like rank mutiny.

"Er, what do you mean?"

It was the work of brief minutes to explain.

Bowden looked incredulous for a moment, then found his tongue. "You did right, you men. And I'm to do my part."

To the master's mate, he snapped an order: "Away all boats!"

"B-but, sir, I can't—"

"Damn your eyes! I'm off to see the admiral. Do you question my order, sir?" As senior officer on board HMS *Hannibal* he had every right, of course.

Hundreds of sailors swarmed down the side and tumbled into the boats, shipping oars and setting out for the shore. They passed ship after ship of the squadron, dark and lifeless as they settled down for the night, then too late coming to their senses as the boats pulled by, fully loaded with excited men.

At the stone steps the seamen disembarked and immediately hoisted Haywood on to their shoulders, setting off with Bowden proud and determined at their head through a late-night St John's rudely awakened by the excitement.

It was exhilarating and fearful, shocking and exotic to be caught up in events that had changed things so fast and so completely. As they turned into the avenue leading to the admiral's residence, the enormity of what they were about to do must have penetrated for the excited shouts died away until there was now nothing but a silent body of hundreds of men tramping up to the torch-lit entrance of the Admiral's Pen.

From the lights within, Bowden guessed that a card party was in progress—Cochrane was known to be partial to his bridge. Bowden held up his hand, and when the men had shuffled to a stop, he went up to the door and knocked.

A footman answered and was shocked by what he saw out in the darkness silently waiting. "S-sir?"

"Admiral Cochrane. On a matter of extreme urgency," Bowden demanded.

"Er, yes, sir. Immediately, sir!"

There was a slight delay before an irritated Cochrane appeared.

"What the devil?" he spluttered, seeing the hundreds of men quietly before him.

"Sir," Bowden said quickly, "these men have come in support of their shipmate, who begs he might be allowed to admit to the death of Captain Tyrell."

"Am I hearing you right, Mr Bowden? He knows what he's about in so doing, I trust."

"He does, sir. And he's firm in his mind that it's the right thing to do in the circumstances."

Cochrane hesitated only for a moment, then threw to the footman inside, "Blue drawing room!"

"Well, Mr Bowden, do come in, and your men too."

The room was soon crowded beyond belief. The admiral stood before them, bemused but in firm charge.

"Now what's this about, Lieutenant?"

Bowden brought Haywood to the front and said, "This is the man, sir—Jeremiah Haywood, main topman."

The admiral brought his fierce gaze on to Haywood. "So you wish to admit to slaying Captain Tyrell."

"Yes, sir. It weren't Mr Kydd, no, sir." His voice quavered but he returned the gaze steadily.

"Then you'd better tell me about it—and be aware, it may well be put up as evidence later."

"Aye, sir. Well, it were like this. We was advancing up t' this ridge, like, an' because the Frogs was firin' at us we took cover under all this green stuff. I looks up an' sees Cap'n Tyrell flop down under the ridge, right ahead o' me. And, well, 'cos I'd taken two dozen in two days from him just afore, I saw red an' fired at him when—"

Quick as a flash, Cochrane intervened: "Ah, now I see what happened. Very clear, now I know."

He looked benignly at the topman. "It was very courageous of you, Haywood, to bring this to my attention and you have my heartiest approbation of your act."

He turned to Bowden. "Well, that clears that up. For the sake of Mr Kydd, just as well."

"Sir?" the lieutenant said uncertainly.

"Can't you see it, man? It was an accident, is all! Any fool can see that. Your man taking hasty cover in all those sticks and leaves, accidents with a loaded musket will happen, a twig caught in the trigger, that kind of thing . . ."

"No, sir, I did it, an' I own to it."

"Nonsense! You had an accident and didn't want to admit to it to your officer until you saw Captain Kydd unjustly accused. Quite understandable."

"Wha'? No, sir, I really—"

"Let's leave it at that, shall we? You men will want to get back to your ship before you're, er, missed."

Bowden, his mind in a flood of relief, could only stammer, "Th-thank you, sir. And on behalf of—"

But Cochrane had already returned to his guests. He smiled at his wife. "Ah, yes. I'd almost forgotten. My dear, do see if Captain Kydd is free to join us."

✦ ✦ ✦

Kydd stood on his quarterdeck once more, pink with pleasure at the honour the wardroom had done him in laying on this reception and dinner in *L'Aurore*.

"Welcome aboard, madam," he said, to yet another lady of station, delighted to be personally greeted by the captain. As his unjust detention had been quickly dismissed at the highest level, it would never do for it to be noticed by lesser mortals.

The deck was quickly filling with notables and friends but this was the reception—only special guests would move on to the dinner afterwards. One in particular, Louise Vernou, was received with the utmost warmth by *L'Aurore*'s captain as she approached on Renzi's arm.

Yet in the midst of all his happiness Kydd had to accept that the fortunate turn of events had not extended to remedy one recent adversity. He could not get out of his mind the shock—the horror—on the faces of the dinner guests when Tyrell had done his worst and he had been revealed as a base-born common sailor.

His happiness faded when he realised that while his naval colleagues' sentiments were genuine and deeply felt those of society were not. They were here for one reason and one only—to be seen with the victor of Marie-Galante. After this occasion, when the memory dimmed, he could not expect to be welcomed at events where the high-born disported.

"Why, Captain, you're thinking on other things?"

Kydd turned in surprise. It was Wrexham—and next to him Miss Amelia.

"Oh, er, just checking the lay of the downhaul," he managed.

"After such a stroke, you should be proud of yourself, sir!" the planter said warmly. "I've above a dozen ships that can now sail without fear, my credit restored and, dare I say it, my competition removed. The whole of the Leeward Islands owes you much, sir, now the vermin are put down and trade is resumed."

"I thank you for your kind words, sir, but do make notice that I'm one only of many who achieved this victory."

"None the less, I'd be honoured to shake your hand, sir."

Shyly coming forward, Amelia dropped him a curtsy and confided, "And I should offer you my sincerest congratulations on your recent conquest, sir."

"Accepted with pleasure," Kydd said, his spirits returning. "Shall I be seeing you below at dinner?"

A fife and fiddle started by the main-mast and people began to drift across to witness the singular display of a barefoot sailor executing a hornpipe.

One more boat was on its way—and it had the duty mate-of-the-watch hurrying to Kydd in consternation. "Sir! Admiral Cochrane to board!"

The side-party was hastily mustered and Cochrane mounted the side with all due gravity.

But as the ceremonials concluded the admiral took Kydd aside. "I'm sorry to take this occasion to break it to you, Mr Kydd, but I have grave news."

He looked around, then continued sadly, "There are duties of an admiral that may never be termed pleasant, and this is one of them."

Tensing, Kydd waited.

"Captain, I have to tell you that my request to the Admiralty to take you into my command has been denied. You are to quit my station and return to England forthwith."

Stunned, Kydd mumbled something, at the same time realising that Cochrane had had no need to inform him in this way: he had done so in order that the evening might now be seen as the ship's last event in the Caribbean.

"I'll not tarry. You'll have many you'll want to see this night."

He saw Cochrane over the side, his thoughts in a whirl. To leave the warmth and beauty of the Caribbean was a wrench but he suspected it had something to do with the forthcoming court-martial of Popham, the leader of the doomed Buenos Aires expedition. But, on the other hand, it meant they were going home.

He hugged the news to himself when they went below for dinner, graciously accepting the chair of honour at the head of the table.

Amelia and her father, of course, were not two places down. "So happy you were able to come," he said politely to Wrexham.

"Why should we not?" the man replied, with surprise.

"Oh, er . . ."

Kydd recoiled once more at the vision of the shocking scene the last time they had dined together, and emboldened by *L'Aurore*'s splendid Caribbean punch he admitted as much. "I feared you would not wish to be seen with a . . . a common fore-mast hand."

Wrexham gave a start. "Sir! I do believe you have misconstrued the entire affair! We were shocked, it is true, even appalled, and that is no exaggeration. But this, sir, was not at any aspersions on yourself, rather at the behaviour of one claiming the character of gentleman. I do not wish to speak ill of the dead, but Captain Tyrell's want of conduct in the open discussion of your past is beyond belief."

"So, you're saying . . . ?"

"Your antecedents are of no account to us. There are many, if not the majority, of society in these islands with humble beginnings, and if we were to exclude such from our fellowship then it would make for a strange situation indeed."

Kydd was infused with a rising lightness and a flood of release.

"Then I pray you will find it in you to attend at our society gatherings in the future with every sense of our respect and admiration, Captain."

"I thank you, sir," Kydd replied, trying not to look at Amelia.

But it couldn't be put off for much longer.

He found a spoon and, looking down the table, tapped it sharply against a glass. The gathering fell quiet.

"Fellow officers, new friends and old, I have to tell you that Admiral Cochrane came aboard to give me news. And it is this: in a very short while *L'Aurore* will put to sea. She will sail—for England."

There were gasps of surprise.

"Our secondment to the Leeward Islands Squadron has been revoked by the Admiralty and we must return forthwith."

"*Mes chers amis—je suis désolé.* I will miss you all so dreadfully!" Louise drew out a handkerchief and Renzi reached to console her.

"Damn it! We'll catch the season if we're quick!" Curzon chortled, his face brightening.

"To England?" Buckle was anything but ecstatic, his face lengthening in what appeared to be dejection at the thought.

"Cheer up, Mr Buckle. England's not so bad you must despair of it!" his captain offered.

"Sir!"

The word was spoken so fiercely, so intensely, that it caught Kydd by surprise. "Yes, Mr Bowden?"

"Is it possible—that is to say, should the parties be willing, um . . ."

"You're hard to catch, young fellow."

"I'm understanding what he's saying, sir," Buckle said, with an equal passion. "And this party is willing indeed!"

"Wha'?"

"Sir, I formally request an exchange with Lieutenant Buckle into this ship, he to stay in the Caribbean."

"And ain't that the truth?" Buckle blurted.

What could he say? To have Bowden back in *L'Aurore*'s ship's company in whatever adventures lay ahead . . .

With a broad grin Kydd snatched up his glass and, in a ringing voice, proclaimed, "We're to be quit o' the fair Caribbee, but God rest ye, merry gentlemen, we'll be home for Christmas!"

Author's Note

In the Georgian age the Caribbean was one of the most truly beautiful—and deadly—places on earth where, as if counterbalancing Nature's gifts, fever claimed countless lives.

Even now, the majority of the thousands of far-scattered islands are much as they were in Kydd's day, hardly touched by the centuries, albeit with the more accessible destinations well visited by tourists. For me, there can be little to beat the view from high in the Blue Mountains of Jamaica (where Kathy and I stayed on location research) down to the sinuous length of the Palisades to the legendary Port Royal and the fleet anchorage within. The town itself is in a sad state of decay but I spent many happy hours in the small archives and even unearthed some brown and curling correspondence from a certain Captain Nelson written while on station, complete with a flourishing pre-amputation signature.

The most atmospheric of all Caribbean sites was Antigua—not the cruise-ship St John's in the north, but English Harbour in the south, where a perfectly preserved eighteenth-century naval dockyard could at a pinch even now set about a storm-racked frigate there under the guns of Shirley Heights. In Spanish Town there are parts still existing that Kydd would recognise, such as the memorial to Rodney's great action at the Saintes, with its robust portrayal of ships-of-the-line and the stricken French fleet, ironically refurbished with the aid of an EU grant sponsored by the French. Guadeloupe is as Gallic as the Riviera and as pretty still as Renzi found it. Grand-Bourg on Marie-Galante is somewhat spoiled by development, but the rest of the island has enchanting parts and enjoys a reputation for its peach-fed iguana.

The Caymans are doing well, due in no small part to the generosity of King George III who, in response to the islanders' bravery in coming to the aid of ten ships wrecked one night in a tempest, bestowed a tax-free status that is in force to this day. Cayman Brac is a wonderful spot for scuba and, apart from scattered settlement, presents the same seaward aspect as Kydd encountered. Curaçao is still appealingly Dutch; her multi-coloured houses in neat rows much as they were then. The interior waters of the Schottegat, however, are now home to oil-tankers rather than privateers, and pretty little marinas nestle under the once formidable forts.

Looked at through modern eyes it's hard to conceive of the colossal importance of the West Indies to Britain during Kydd's time. At the start of the Napoleonic wars, four-fifths of all overseas Exchequer receipts came from these parts, mainly sugar and sugar products. More than two million gallons of rum a year made its way over the Atlantic, and Renzi's brother was not exaggerating in the slightest the voracious appetite of sweet-toothed Britain for his crop. Consequently the islands were fought over bitterly, the record held by St Lucia, which changed hands no fewer than fourteen times in the period of the wars.

Without an effective naval strategy France found it impossible to defend her own islands and secure her own imports and consequently suffered. Napoleon's decree, the Continental System, was a clever move, for it closed off Europe not only to Britain's sugar but also to its increasingly important manufactured goods, threatening bankruptcy and revolution. It also contained the seed of his own destruction. The continent, with a well-developed sugar habit and unwilling to forgo the baubles and ironmongery produced so cheaply by the industrial revolution, fell victim to widespread smuggling and it failed in its object, again for want of an effective military sea arm to compel it. When Napoleon turned on his ally Russia in 1812, for not enforcing it vigorously enough, the end was in sight for him and his system. At the peace of 1815 most of the islands were returned to their previous owners, Danish, Dutch and even Swedish; each still retains its distinctiveness, but all were involved in the ever-vital sugar trade.

America, however, did handsomely out of the war as neutral, freighting for both sides, but when months later the British responded with their own decree Cousin Jonathan found his business opportunities sharply declining, his fast-growing merchant fleet now idle. This, no doubt, contributed to the frustration that boiled over into the war of 1812, the first conducted with an economic objective openly at its heart.

And in another important historical development less than one year following the end of this book, Kydd's valet Tysoe would see the slave trade not only stopped by Britain but actively opposed by this nation, which nobly employed its naval supremacy in the cause of its suppression. Acting under a legal framework that regarded slave-trading in the same light as piracy, the Royal Navy chased and seized ships under any flag that carried on the odious trade, but it was not until 1834 that slavery itself was abolished. The irony is that by this time industrial methods of extraction from sugar-beet in Europe had been found and the Caribbean had lost its importance.

Readers who have followed the series will note that this is the second book set in the Caribbean. I am not sure yet when the two friends will return to this sultry clime but I can promise an important personal milestone for Renzi in the near future.

It is the writer's name that is on the cover but many people contribute directly and indirectly to any literary endeavour. To everyone who assisted in some way in the research for this book, I am deeply grateful. I am also appreciative of the electronic charts produced by the Hydrographic Office of the Admiralty at Taunton, which have replaced the paper ones I used when I first began writing the series, and which have made navigational computations just a matter of a few clicks of the mouse. And I would like to pay special tribute to my publisher Hodder & Stoughton—editors Oliver Johnson and Anne Perry, publicist Poppy North, copy editor Hazel Orme, and all the other consummate professionals at 338 Euston Road, London.

As ever, my heartfelt appreciation goes to my wife and literary partner, Kathy, and my agent Carole Blake, who this year celebrates a luminous career in the book trade spanning fifty years. As the Georgians would say, I drink her health in a bumper!

Glossary

a-caper	Dutch; abroad on a warlike mischief
a-taunto	all standing proudly on end, as masts
a-tupping	as on a farm with a ram among the ewes
Abolitionists	the political movement in England that ended with the abolition of slavery
Admiral's Pen	the admiral's residence, after Jamaican term for a holding
aloes	a medicinal plant whose leaf gel relieves skin ailments
avast	stop immediately
belaying pin	a wooden pin set for convenience into a holed rail to which ropes coming from aloft are tied
binnacle	the protective casing around the compass
bonehead	a useless seaman
bower	the most favoured anchor
broadside	the entire side of a ship; in gunnery, all the guns on that side
buckra	term for white man, from Ibo, *mbakara*
bugaboo	variant of "bogey"

calipash, calipee	the upper and lower shells of a turtle
catblash	nonsense, no content, as in a cat loudly vomiting only a fur-ball
cathead	beam set into the bow of a ship such that when an anchor is heaved in clear of the water a tackle might be attached to swing it in to the ship's side for stowing
clerk of the cheque	a senior dockyard official who comes aboard to muster the crew before disbursing pay entitlements
cobbs	Spanish dollars, from Gibraltar garrison
cruiser	a lone man-o'-war, usually a frigate, tasked to range the seas looking for prey
Dansker	a Danish national
dit	sea term for a polished story, informally told
fore-bitter	naval song performed by seamen in leisure time forward around the fore-bitts
fried milk	a sweet milk pudding with crunchy top
gunroom	in a large ship, the gunners' abode; in frigates, the officers' dining and mess room
gunwale	sides of a ship where strengthened to take gun-port piercing
gyre	a spiral motion or vortex as in a large-scale ocean current or air mass
hugger-mugger	clandestine
invest	to lay siege to
jalousie	louvred window that can be opened to allow air-flow but restrict rain entry
jerk	spiced meat dried over a wood fire

keckling	improvised padding around an anchor cable to prevent chafing or damage from sharp coral
kedge	an anchor light enough to be taken to a distance by a boat to allow the ship to haul itself up to it
kooner-man	Creole for King's sailor
lasking	sailing easily downwind
letter of marque	legal document proving the vessel is duly authorised by a state to engage in privateering
lubber	a man hopeless in his nauticals
lubber's hole	an aperture in the tops that allows a sailor climbing the shrouds to take the easy way through and on up
mauby beer	tree-bark based beer, widely known in the Caribbean, variously spiced and sweetened
mole	long pier usually of stone, set out in a harbour to break the force of the waves
mumchance	to stand tongue-tied
prame	shallow draft but fully ship-rigged French invasion frigate
prigger	thief
privateer	private man-o'-war; licensed by the state to capture enemy ships
quarters	after the ship is cleared for action the men close up at quarters for battle
quips & quillets	idiosyncrasies, from classical "quodlibet," a polite disputation on nice points
reefer	midshipman, from their part-of-ship for handing sail on the yards

reprisal	legal device to justify a privateer to take action against a state for the purpose of obtaining pecuniary redress
roadstead	the approaches to a harbour where ships may safely anchor
scow	derogatory term for vessel, after flat barge in ports used to discharge waste from anchored ships
scran	food at sea, from northern English for broken victuals, scraps
shab	eighteenth-century term for ill-dressed person, from shabbaroon
shaddock	large round fruit with a coarse-grained pulp, after the popularising seventeenth-century Captain Shaddock
soursop	Caribbean fruit with a creamy sour flavour
Spithead	area off Portsmouth where the fleet anchors when in port
stingo	the stronger brews of English beer
tack	in order to gain ground against the wind a square-rigged vessel must first take the wind closely on one side then the other
Tuileries	the royal palace of the doomed King Louis, later taken for his own by Emperor Bonaparte
volunteer	opposite of pressed man; also rate of youngster before being made midshipman
yaw	to slew either side of the true course, intentionally or otherwise
younker	affectionate term for youngster
zephyr	a barely perceptible breeze